# PIECES

## *of the*

# HEART

KAREN WHITE

D0029595

FICTION FOR THE WAY WE LIVE

NAL Accent
Published by New American Library, a division of
Penguin Group (USA) Inc., 375 Hudson Street,
New York, New York 10014, USA
Penguin Group (Canada), 90 Eglinton Avenue East, Suite 700, Toronto,
Ontario M4P 2Y3, Canada (a division of Pearson Penguin Canada Inc.)
Penguin Books Ltd., 80 Strand, London WC2R 0RL, England
Penguin Ireland, 25 St. Stephen's Green, Dublin 2,
Ireland (a division of Penguin Books Ltd.)
Penguin Group (Australia), 250 Camberwell Road, Camberwell, Victoria 3124,
Australia (a division of Pearson Australia Group Pty. Ltd.)
Penguin Books India Pvt. Ltd., 11 Community Centre, Panchsheel Park,
New Delhi - 110 017, India
Penguin Group (NZ), 67 Apollo Drive, Mairangi Bay,
Auckland 1311, New Zealand (a division of Pearson New Zealand Ltd.)
Penguin Books (South Africa) (Pty.) Ltd., 24 Sturdee Avenue,
Rosebank, Johannesburg 2196, South Africa

Penguin Books Ltd., Registered Offices:
80 Strand, London WC2R 0RL, England

First published by NAL Accent, an imprint of New American Library,
a division of Penguin Group (USA) Inc.

First Printing, April 2006
10

REGISTERED TRADEMARK—MARCA REGISTRADA

LIBRARY OF CONGRESS CATALOGING-IN-PUBLICATION DATA:

White, Karen (Karen S.)
Pieces of the heart/Karen White.
p. cm.
ISBN 0-451-21767-5 (pbk.)
1. Mothers and daughters—Fiction.   2. North Carolina—Fiction.
3. Domestic Fiction.   I. Title.
PS3623.H5776P54 2006
813'.6—dc22          2005027372

Set in Adobe Garamond
Designed by Ginger Legato

Printed in the United States of America

PUBLISHER'S NOTE

This is a work of fiction. Names, characters, places, and incidents either are the product of the author's imagination or are used fictitiously, and any resemblance to actual persons, living or dead, business establishments, events, or locales is entirely coincidental.

The publisher does not have any control over and does not assume any responsibility for author or third-party Web sites or their content.

Praise for
*The Color of Light*

"[White's] prose is lyrical, and she weaves in elements of mysticism and romance without being heavy-handed. This is an accomplished novel about loss and renewal, and readers will be taken with the people and stories of Pawleys Island."                                        —*Booklist*

"The reader will hear the ocean roar and the seagulls scream as the past reluctantly gives up its ghosts in this beautiful, enticing, and engrossing novel."                              —*RT Bookclub Magazine* (4½ stars)

"A story as rich as a coastal summer . . . dark secrets, heartache, a magnificent South Carolina setting, and a great love story."
                         —*New York Times* bestselling author Deborah Smith

"An engaging read with a delicious taste of the mysterious."
                         —*New York Times* bestselling author Haywood Smith

"Karen White's novel is as lush as the Lowcountry, where the characters' wounded souls come home to mend in unexpected and magical ways."
                    —Patti Callahan Henry, award-winning author of *Losing the Moon*

*continued . . .*

Written by today's freshest new talents and selected by New American Library, NAL Accent novels touch on subjects close to a woman's heart, from friendship to family to finding our place in the world. The Conversation Guides included in each book are intended to enrich the individual reading experience, as well as encourage us to explore these topics together—because books, and life, are meant for sharing.

Visit us online at www.penguin.com

# Praise for the novels
## of Karen White

"The fresh voice of Karen White intrigues and delights."
—Sandra Chastain, contributor to *Blessings at Mossy Creek*

"Warmly Southern and deeply moving."
—Deborah Smith, author of *Charming Grace*

"Karen White writes with passion and poignancy."
—Deb Stover, award-winning author of *Mulligan Magic*

"[A] sweet book . . . highly recommended."          —*Booklist*

"Karen White is one author you won't forget. . . . This is a masterpiece in the study of relationships. Brava!"          —Reader to Readers Reviews

"This is not only romance at its best—this is a fully realized view of life at its fullest."          —Readers & Writers Ink Reviews

"*After the Rain* is an elegantly enchanting Southern novel. . . . Fans will recognize the beauty of White's evocative prose."          —WordWeaving

"In the tradition of Catherine Anderson and Deborah Smith, Karen White's *After the Rain* is an incredibly poignant contemporary bursting with southern charm."
—Patricia Rouse, Rouse's Romance Readers Groups

"Don't miss this book!"          —*Rendezvous*

"Character-driven and strongly written . . . *After the Rain* . . . marks Karen White as a rising star and an author to watch."
—*Romantic Times Book Club Magazine*

With love to my wonderful Connor
because he says he deserves it,
and because he does.

# ACKNOWLEDGMENTS

A book populated by people who quilt and written by somebody who has never quilted in her life required lots of help. So thank you, Martha Murphy, for answering my sophomoric questions, and also to Lisa McGuire, who showed me my first memory quilt.

I would also like to acknowledge Dr. Leonard C. Viril, for his help regarding organ donations and the particulars of living with a heart transplant.

As always, thanks to Tim, Meghan and Connor, who still endure living with me despite the fact that they know what going through deadline dementia is like. I couldn't do this without their love and support.

And thanks to Susan Crandall, Wendy Wax, Jenni Grizzle and Sandra Chastain—wonderful writers all, as well as fantastic readers who help me write the best book that I can.

# CHAPTER I

CAROLINE SAT AND WATCHED THE SMALL ROCK DROP FROM HER hand and into the dark, still water of Lake Ophelia, breaking the surface with a small plop. The ripples eddied out in tiny circles, gradually spreading into great gaping spheres of silent water, reaching out toward the depths of the lake until she couldn't see them anymore. Not for the first time, it reminded her of how a single event in life could reach out forever, drowning you in a circle of memories that never let go.

Two children, a boy and a girl, ran out onto a dock two houses down on the same side of the lake, the girl's shrieks echoing in the late-afternoon air as her brother maneuvered to push her in. Their mother stood behind them, saying something and shaking her head, but they ignored her until they both landed in the water, creating small waves that bumped into Caroline's dock.

The mother spotted Caroline and waved before picking up discarded socks and sneakers. Caroline hesitated at first, then waved back. Out of habit, her hand fell to her chest to pull the neck of her T-shirt higher, and she felt the ridge of the old incision beneath her shirt.

She rested her cheek against drawn-up knees and stared at the fading waves as a chorus of cicadas erupted into sound, then quieted just as suddenly. She closed her eyes, seeing the lake against her dark eyelids. *I've missed the water.* She let a toe dip into the surface, smelling her own sweat and the green scent that hovered over the lake in late summer. *I've been gone too long from the water. And you, too, Jude. Always you.*

The tap of her mother's heels against the wooden dock announced her presence. Caroline didn't turn around, but remained staring out at the lake toward Hart's Peak in the near distance. The sky was clear enough that she could make out the face of the fabled Ophelia on the side of the mountain, a woman supposedly cursed and turned to stone centuries before.

"There're a lot more houses than I remember—and a lot fewer trees. It's hardly the same place anymore." Caroline sighed and watched a black-and-white loon settle on a dock piling in front of one of the enormous cookie-cutter houses across the lake and wondered if her brother, Jude, would even recognize any of it. He had always loved this place, the pungent smell of the lake and the warmth of the people who lived around it. Only the cold stone face of Ophelia herself seemed not to have changed.

Caroline could hear her pulse beating in her head, recognizing it as a warning sign from her doctor. Closing her eyes, she took long, slow breaths, focusing on the smell of the water and the sound of the lake nudging the dock under her, and waited for her pulse to slow. With her eyes still closed, she said, "At least we can be thankful for the ban on waverunners."

As if on cue, an engine started up across the lake and a teenage boy shot off from a dock on a sapphire-blue waverunner, the solitary loon and other birds rising in a panic all along the edge of the lake.

Her mother sounded apologetic. "Some of the new people are on the town council. They voted down the ban eight to one."

"Damn," Caroline said, forgetting that her mother didn't like her to swear. "Who was the holdout?"

"Rainy Martin. She's always been such an environmentalist."

Caroline looked up at her mother, the ash-blond hair a shade darker than her own. "What about you, Mom?"

Margaret Collier crossed her arms and met Caroline's gaze. "They're my neighbors and I didn't want there to be any bad will between us. Besides, it's not so bad. You can hardly hear the noise from inside the house."

Caroline shook her head slowly. "Good ol' Rainy. This world would be a much better place with more people like her in it." Even saying the name filled Caroline with warmth. Rainy was the one connection to Jude she clung to, the only person who knew what she'd lost.

"Dad would have voted with Rainy."

Her mother's back stiffened. "Yes, well, your father has made his life in California for the last twelve years, so any speculation as to what he would or would not do is pointless."

The waverunner came closer, drowning out Caroline's thoughts and making her pulse thrum louder in her head. She took another deep breath.

When the noise had faded enough to be heard, Margaret said, "Dinner's almost ready. I'm having a steak but I'm making you a skinless chicken breast." She paused, the air heavy with all the unsaid words that had grown between them in a lifetime.

Caroline looked up at her mother again. "I was hoping we could stop by Roberta's Bar-B-Que Shack for dinner. I remember going there every Saturday when we were at the lake."

"Oh."

Her tone made Caroline snap to attention. It was the same tone Margaret used to tell her daughter news like all the cookies were gone or nobody had called to ask her to the high school dance. She normally delivered the bad news faster, as if somehow Caroline would miss the details and not be as upset. It usually just made Caroline's stomach turn over and set her teeth on edge.

"Roberta's changed ownership about a year ago. I'm sure I mentioned it to you at some point. She was bought out by one of those big chains. I've been there a couple of times—it's not bad. I could put the meat in the fridge if you'd prefer to go there."

Caroline swallowed her disappointment, wondering why she suddenly wanted to cry. "No, that's all right." She forced a polite smile. "I can eat at a chain restaurant every night in Atlanta. Chicken breast is fine." She had a brief flash of memory of her and Jude in Roberta's kitchen, sitting on tall stools and helping her make her famous barbecue sauce, and she felt the urge to cry again.

Margaret cleared her throat. "I saw you hadn't unpacked yet, so I put away your things in your old room. I noticed you didn't pack a bathing suit."

Caroline closed her eyes and took three deep breaths, forcing her irritation to flow out of her body from her nose and ears and mouth, as Dr. Northcutt had suggested. She imagined a small puff emanating from her left nostril but that was it. The irritation was definitely still there.

She stood and faced her mother, plastering her well-worn polite smile on her face again. "I haven't worn a bathing suit since I was eighteen. Surely you've noticed that in the last thirteen years."

Her mother's head pulled back slightly in the way she had of hiding her hurt. But Caroline knew better than to feel guilt, because Margaret Ryan Collier could give as good as she got. Like an offended porcupine with sharpened quills, her mother raised an eyebrow.

"Now, Caroline—not that I don't think a woman your age shouldn't be figure-conscious; I just don't think it's necessary with only the two of us around. You know that you could wear a potato sack and I'd still think you were beautiful."

Caroline stared at her mother, once again thinking she should have her DNA checked. She took three more deep breaths, and imagined a larger puff of irritation floating out of her right ear. She was *not* going to argue with her mother. She had been forced into a leave of absence to rusticate at the lake to get away from stress, after all. Although more than once during the two-hour drive from Atlanta in her mother's Cadillac she'd wondered if giving her mother a quick shove out of the moving vehicle would alleviate most of the stress from her life.

Caroline smiled again, her face stiff. "My figure has nothing to do with my not wearing a bathing suit." She thought of the scar on her chest again and how it still hurt her to know that her mother never seemed to remember it. "I'm hungry. Let's go eat." She stood and walked toward the house, the familiar feeling of needing to put as much space between them overriding everything else. "I need to wash up first."

Her mother's voice called out to her. "Your chicken is almost ready, and I made a salad. You wouldn't be hurting my feelings, though, if you just had the salad. I have low-fat dressing, too."

Caroline's smile fell as she counted to ten again, but she didn't turn around to respond. She kept walking toward the house, its weathered gray boards familiar yet strange to her at the same time.

*Damn,* she thought, wearily pulling open the back screen door. It had taken only three and a half hours in her mother's presence to elevate her blood pressure and make her cuss. "Damn," she said out loud, letting the screen door bang shut behind her.

# CHAPTER 2

CAROLINE STUMBLED THROUGH THE MUDROOM AND INTO THE great room with its high-beamed ceiling, memories of the old house guiding her toward the small bedroom in the back. Her mind registered the changes her mother had made in the thirteen years since Caroline had been there.

As she passed through the back of the house, she saw that the pale pink walls were now painted a neutral cream, and the thin metal blinds had been replaced with wooden plantation shutters. After her parents' divorce and her father's move to the West Coast, Margaret's career as an interior designer had progressed by astonishing degrees. She'd even had a living room featured in *Atlanta Home* magazine. Unfortunately, during the remodeling of her childhood vacation home, Caroline had been forced to listen to the things that were being removed from the lake house and of the new, seemingly improved items that were taking their places. It had been like a debridement of an infected wound to speed healing. Yet it had always seemed to Caroline to be more like putting a Band-Aid on a bleeding artery. She hadn't returned to see the wreckage.

Caroline looked with some surprise at her old room. It was unchanged—even down to the rose-colored chenille bedspread and the big yellow dog Jude had won for her at a long-ago Harvest Moon festival. It still had the smear on the faded yellow of its cheek where ketchup had dripped from her brother's hot dog as he'd tried to show her how he could shove it into his mouth in one bite.

She absently stroked the dog's head as she glanced around at the old unpainted pine furniture with pink drawer pulls and the plastic beaded ropes that hung in front of her closet door. Caroline had thought them cool and magical but her mother considered them tacky and not appropriate for their Atlanta home. But they'd been a Christmas gift from Jude, so they were allowed to hang in her closet at the lake house, where it wasn't possible for anyone who mattered to know that Margaret Collier allowed hippie beads into her home.

Caroline heard her mother gently open and shut the screened door before the tapping of her heels across the pine floors marked her passage to the kitchen. Silverware clinked on the wood surface of the kitchen table, followed by the sound of the oven door screeching open. *She's baking the steaks with the chicken breast.* Caroline stifled a grin at her mother's ineptitude with the outdoor grill and lifted the hippie beads, listening to them clack against the pale white closet door frame.

"Dinner's ready," her mother called out.

She wanted to say she wasn't hungry, but her stomach grumbled as she stuck her head out the door. Glancing back into her room, she spotted her now-empty suitcase sitting against the wall near the dresser and remembered how there had once been two twin beds in the room. The second bed had been moved to the adjacent bedroom at her own insistence when she was twelve and much too old to be sharing a room with a brother who was eleven months younger than her.

"Coming," she said, taking a deep breath and counting slowly to ten before heading for the kitchen. She'd stick to safe topics like the weather and the cost of milk. The soft notes of a Chopin prelude drifted through the great room from tiny Bose speakers poised inconspicuously behind a large fern and a framed child's pastel drawing, the telltale scrawl of Jude's signature blasted across the bottom in blue crayon. She scanned the walls quickly for the Andrew Wyeth print she'd given her mother for Christmas the previous year and felt the familiar stab of disappointment when she didn't see it. She let her fingers slide over the closed top of the piano, and wondered briefly why her mother still kept it.

Walking toward the kitchen, she heard the first drops of rain against the skylights. Rainstorms in the mountains always caught you by surprise, like jumping into cold water on a hot day. She watched her mother toss the salad, studying her in her high heels and apron for a moment before she became aware of Caroline's presence.

Margaret Collier had one of those faces that seemed to get better with age. Instead of filling out and sagging, her skin had tightened over beautiful bones, sharpening her nose and her chin. It was as if life had shrunk her somehow, made her more compact and better able to duck the sharp winds life had a habit of blowing at you.

Her mother turned her head and smiled, her makeup fresh and perfect. Caroline couldn't think of a time she'd seen her without makeup. Even Christmas morning her mother never appeared downstairs without at least powder, eyeliner, and her signature red lipstick. Jude used to say that he wasn't sure if he'd recognize her without it.

"Have a seat, dear. I'll be done in just a minute."

"I don't mind helping. Why don't I finish the salad?"

Her mother waved her toward the table. "Don't be silly. You're here on doctor's orders to relax. Take a seat and I'll have this on the table in just a second."

"Smells good." Caroline pulled out a chair and sat down, noticing the linen napkins and silver napkin rings. Their starched whiteness and perfect creases were as formal as the strange, polite dance she and her mother seemed to be performing.

"You've done a lot with the house."

Margaret smiled. "Yes, I suppose I have. It's been a sort of experimental work in progress. Do you like it?"

Caroline watched her mother take out a pitcher of sweet tea and set it on the table, and avoided meeting her eyes. "It's . . . different." It was all she could allow. How could she explain that it wasn't about liking it or not? It was more like staring at the stump of a severed limb. It was about missing something that was no longer there.

To change the subject she asked, "Where's that Wyeth print I gave you last year?" and then immediately wished she hadn't said it. Her comment went beyond white starchiness and crisp creases. It bordered on real emotions and deep hurt, of things not spoken aloud by implicit agreement.

Her mother sat down, an uncomfortable flush rising in her

cheeks. "I haven't hung it yet. Guess I'm still looking for the perfect spot." She raised her eyes to her daughter's. "Actually, I thought you'd let me hang it in your apartment. You don't have a thing on the walls—or on the windows for that matter. I wish you'd let me do the whole thing—pro bono, of course."

Slowly Caroline pulled her napkin from the shiny sterling ring and placed it on her lap, listening to the pelting of rain on the roof. "I don't like living around a lot of fuss. Besides, I'm rarely there. My job keeps me at the office."

She watched her mother mirror her own movements with the napkin. "Maybe you'd feel more of a desire to leave your office if you had a nice place to come home to. I hope you've been listening to Dr. Northcutt. You've got to stop working so hard. You've been lucky with just a stress attack as a warning. It could be worse next time— much worse."

Caroline absently rubbed the part of her shirt that lay over the slight ridge of the old scar. "I like my work. That was just . . . a bad day." She began scooping salad onto her plate. "I thought you had choir tonight."

Margaret took a sip of tea. "I do, but I thought I'd stay with you because it's your first night here since . . ." Her voice trailed away.

Caroline tried not to sound overeager. "No, you should go. I don't mind being by myself. Really. Besides, I'm kind of in the mood for a good movie. Maybe I'll go down to the movie theater and see what's playing."

Her mother was silent for a moment and busied herself with brushing imaginary crumbs from her place mat. "They've closed. I think it's been some eight or nine years. Couldn't afford to repair the damage from that horrible winter storm so they just closed up shop."

Caroline could almost smell the popcorn and feel the chill of the air-conditioning on bare shoulders in the old theater as she sat between Jude and Shelby Martin watching afternoon matinees. She felt chilled all of a sudden, as the ghosts of old memories stood up and left her, leaving her cold and alone.

She felt agitated and uncertain, and the silent counting in her head wasn't working anymore. She hadn't wanted to be here anyway, so why did it matter so much that nothing was the way she had re-membered? *Because it's like I'm burying Jude again.* She focused on the linen napkin in her lap.

"It's just us, Mom. No need to get all fancy with cloth napkins."

Margaret stood and retrieved the breadbasket from the counter before reseating herself. "I'm not being fancy. Paper napkins belong in preschools and truck stops. This is neither." She smiled and slid the bowl across the table.

Caroline picked up the pitcher and poured tea into her glass. "It just seems like a lot of trouble and expense for the two of us."

"Not at all. I bought a set of twelve napkins on sale at Steinmart for less than it would have cost for an entire package of paper nap-kins." She handed the breadbasket to Caroline before taking a piece herself. "But I suppose being a career woman making your own money, you wouldn't have to worry about things like that."

Caroline dug into her salad, studiously avoiding looking at the dried-out chicken breast in the middle of her plate. *God, why am I here?* She tried counting to ten again but failed to push back the call for battle that always seemed to raise its flag whenever she was in a conversation with her mother.

"I'm an accountant, Mom. I'm more aware than most people of how much things cost and how much money I spend. Linen versus paper napkins has absolutely nothing to do with money. It's about convenience. I mean, who wants to wash their napkins, then iron and fold them after every meal? Only those people with way too much leisure time on their hands use linen napkins."

Her mother blinked, then delicately began cutting into her steak. After putting a minuscule bite in her mouth, she chewed thoughtfully before finally replying. "Actually, Caroline, it has noth-ing to do with convenience and everything to do with civilization. Using paper napkins is no worse than eschewing silverware and re-verting back to our caveman days and eating with our hands."

Rain hit against the windows in a steady rhythm, Caroline's heartbeat racing to catch up. *This is it,* she thought. She was either going to die of a heart attack right then and there or she was going to kill her mother.

She forced the polite smile back on her face. "You know, Mom—I really don't want you to miss choir practice on my account. You go on ahead. I haven't seen Rainy Martin in a long time, and I'd like to stop by and say hello before it gets dark." She pushed back from the table, making the tea in the glasses shake. "And don't worry about the dishes—I'll do them when I get back."

Margaret's fork hovered uncertainly in the air. "But it's raining."

"As you always used to say, I'm not sweet enough to melt."

Her mother gave her a crooked grin. "I'd forgotten that." Her shoulders slouched against the back of her chair, and for the first time in Caroline's memory, Margaret Collier looked old. "All right, then. But at least wear your raincoat so you don't catch a chill. And put some lipstick on—it'll brighten your complexion. You never know who you might run into."

Something about her mother's defeated stance made Caroline push back the call to battle. Besides, she didn't even own a lipstick, so the point was moot, anyway. Margaret looked up at her daughter for a moment, the fine lines around her eyes and mouth visible under the harsh light from the overhead fixture. It made her look vulnerable, fragile almost. Caroline felt a stab of panic, a feeling of time lost, passing too quickly. She kissed her mother's cheek and Margaret looked up, surprised. "Have fun at choir," Caroline said, hiding her embarrassment by turning away and leaving the room.

She found her hooded rain jacket hanging neatly in her closet. The few clothes on the rod had been hung by type so that all the pants were together and so were her blouses and skirts. She was on the verge of smiling when she noticed there was no sign of the four pairs of old sweats she had brought for her three-month stay, and she found herself practicing deep breathing again.

Despite the darkening gloom and splattering rain, Caroline felt her spirits lift. In the years since she had last been to Hart's Peak, when she had given up everything in her life that marked the "before" and delved into her life that had become the "after," Rainy Martin had remained her only constant. Caroline suspected it was because Rainy was the only one she knew who hadn't insisted that she cry.

She walked past her mother's dark blue Cadillac in the garage and slid into the driver's seat of the dusty old Buick. In the same way people reserved old shoes for rainy days, Margaret Collier had a respectable car that was used only on days when ruinous salt lay thick on mountain roads.

Moving out of the driveway, she headed out toward the rain-slicked road, listening to the *thump-thump* of the intermittent windshield wipers. Static-filled elevator music from her mother's favorite station crackled as she wound her way down the familiar road, hardly wider than a single car, pausing at each curve to check for oncoming traffic and passing no one.

The rain had slowed to a drizzle, soaking everything in a fine mist and adding to her restlessness. Flipping off the radio, she lowered her window and took a deep breath. She loved the smell of rain, of wet leaves and damp earth, and the slap of feet against soggy pavement. It reminded her of Jude and how he would open his bedroom window during rainstorms and how she'd use her bath towel to help him dry the rain off the windowsill before their mother found out.

She made her way onto the main highway that led into Hart's Valley, crossing the old railroad tracks that marked the outskirts of the town. Feeling the need to walk the remaining mile, she parallel-parked the car on the nearly deserted road. She trudged along Main Street, passing the Laundromat that now apparently doubled as a Thai food takeout, and pausing in front of the old post office that had been converted into a real estate office with hideous green awnings. There was something wrong here, something akin to changing the colors of the national flag or wearing sandals in winter. She felt the restlessness creep up on her again and she continued on, walking faster and faster, eager to feel the comfort that only Rainy could seem to give her.

Tucking her head into the hood of her jacket, she made her way through the steady drizzle to the crossroads of Main Street and Highland Avenue, staring through the mist at the battered sign above the door: RAINY DAYS. It was an old house that had been converted into a store while keeping the kitchen and the upstairs intact. She glanced at her watch. It was past six o'clock and the CLOSED sign sat in the window, but Caroline knew that Rainy Martin's store was never closed to her.

As she waited at the crosswalk for the light to change, her gaze skidded over the bare-wood storefront and focused on the sign in the window: FOR SALE. She blinked, hoping it would go away and feeling the thrum of her heartbeat in her ears. The yellow-and-red sign stayed where it was, a final nail in the coffin of how things used to be and would never be again.

Maybe it was because she knew it was the lull in the tourist season—most of the summer people had fled back to suburbia, and it was too early for the fall-foliage folks—or maybe it was the confusion and anger that warped her senses. Either way, she assumed the road would be deserted and didn't look first before stepping off the curb and into the street.

At the same moment, a brand-spanking-new black pickup truck whizzed by her, close enough that she could see the buttons on the bright plaid shirt of the male driver as he stared straight ahead, oblivious to the woman he was in the process of almost killing.

Caroline jumped back onto the curb just in time to catch the bulk of a puddle sent spraying by the truck's tires. She could taste the mud and gravel on her upper lip as the sound of the truck faded around the next corner. Numbly, she stared down at her jacket, wondering if her face looked as bad. If some days you were the bug and other days the windshield, today she was definitely a windshield. She felt the absurd need to cry and tried to uplift her mood with the thought that the day was almost over and there wasn't time for it to get any worse.

She spat out a piece of grit that had found its way past her lips and onto her tongue as she turned in the direction of the disappearing truck. *Damn tourists.* The new truck was a dead giveaway as to the owner's tourist status. Nobody in Hart's Valley drove new cars. Except for the damned tourists.

Feeling the water squelching inside her shoes with every step, Caroline slogged her way across the street and up the front porch steps of Rainy Days. She hadn't even raised her hand to knock when the door was flung open, the bells above the door clanging in greeting.

Rainy Martin stood on the threshold, her hair hidden beneath a leopard-print bandanna, her face devoid of makeup, and her bare toes peeping out from baggy overalls. It had been thirteen years since Caroline had last seen her, but it felt like thirteen minutes. Rainy was as familiar as her own skin.

The older woman opened her arms wide. "Good Lord, child. Looks like you've been pulled backward through a mud hole. Come in, come in, and let's get you cleaned up."

Maybe it was the remembered scents of potpourri and pipe tobacco inside the cluttered store, or maybe it was the memory of how soft Rainy's crocheted sweater felt against her cheek, but Caroline realized she was crying and being enveloped in strong, warm arms that seemed thinner than she remembered. There was something almost frail in the feel of the bone through knitted wool, but there was strength, too, like the taut strands of a hammock's rope. "Hush, girl. It's going to be all right."

And Caroline was ten years old again, and she knew that without a doubt Rainy would make everything all right for her. She always had.

She drew back her head and gave a loud sniffle. "I'm sorry. I don't know why I'm crying like this. It's just that everything seems to have changed and then some. . . . Moron nearly ran me over and my mother said . . ."

Rainy raised her hand. "Say no more. If you've been speaking with your mother, I understand." She placed both of her hands, covered in silver and turquoise rings, on Caroline's shoulders, and pushed her toward the back of the shop. "Go wash up in the restroom and I'll put some of my tea on to boil. Then we can have a long talk about Margaret and hypothesize about why she wears so much makeup."

Caroline smiled and hiccupped at the same time. It was the eighth wonder of the world—the lifelong friendship between Margaret Collier and Rainy Martin. She'd long ago given up trying to understand it, but she hadn't completely given up on her theory that she had been switched at birth and given to the wrong mother.

Wiping her nose on the sleeve of the jacket, something she would never have dared to do in her mother's presence, she found her way to the bathroom and flicked on the light. Like the rest of the shop, the room was small and cluttered but done with such a free and artistic hand, it was hard to remember you were in a bathroom. The walls were covered with the artwork of local artists, and a short set of wall shelves carried an entire army of small clay people with eyes made of bulging blue beads and wearing clothes of quilting scraps. A hand-sewn quilt had been tacked to the ceiling, but even it had a price tag dangling from a corner.

As her focus rested on the mirror above the sink, her recovered good mood took a nosedive. She did look like she'd been pulled through something backward—and then beaten and dragged for several miles. With angry strokes, she splashed soap and water on her face and at her hairline where mud was starting to congeal. Keeping her eyes shut, she patted around the basin looking for a towel but succeeded only in grabbing a roll of toilet paper.

After tearing off a large wad big enough to dry her face, she missed the edge of the counter when she moved to put the roll back. Dabbing at her eyes with the wad of toilet tissue, she bent to retrieve the errant roll, only to knock her head on one of the shelves on her way up. She winced as she heard each and every clay person take a suicide dive to the linoleum floor. *Shit!* She cursed through clenched teeth, but she was sure it was loud enough to be heard outside the door. "Don't worry—I'll pay for any damage," she called out.

She sopped up the rest of the water on her face, then dropped the tissue into the garbage pail. It wasn't until she was facing the door that she saw the sign. EVERYTHING MUST GO! The needling restlessness now boiled out from inside her, making room for the panic, grief, and anger that she'd been pushing below the surface ever since the waverunner had poked a hole in her bubble of imagined serenity.

Her hand shook as she pushed open the bathroom door. "You can't sell this place, Rainy. . . ." She stopped talking when she realized that Rainy wasn't alone and that the last words the visitor had spoken were just now registering, something about a title transfer and remaining inventory. A man—a very large one, judging by the way he towered over the five-foot-nine Rainy—was leaning against the life-size carved bear that had guarded the cash register since the beginning of time.

"I'm sorry; I didn't realize you had company." She was about to give him a polite smile when she saw that the man was holding her teacup—the New Orleans mug with the chip at the top—and he was wearing a bright plaid shirt with white buttons running down the front. She stopped in front of him. "Excuse me, but do you drive a black Nissan pickup?"

He straightened, making him the same height as the bear, and smiled at Caroline. "Yes, I do, but she's not for sale."

She felt the blood rush to her head at about the same time all of her doctor's warnings took refuge somewhere outside conscious thought. A tinge of conscience brushed her brain as she realized that this man was a total stranger and probably had no clue that he had nearly killed her. Then she remembered what he and Rainy had been talking about, and how the closing of Rainy Days would be like another death to her, and that was the last thing she would ever give up.

She jabbed her index finger at him like an angry wasp. "You have a lot of nerve. You almost ran me over with your stupid truck, dumped mud and muck and God knows what else all over me, and then you have the audacity to even *think* you could possibly buy this store and pretend you belong here just so you can yuk it up with your buddies from whatever city you crawled out of."

She didn't even pause for breath or consider that she was essentially just a visitor from Atlanta, even when she noticed that Rainy was trying not to smile and the stranger had a similar expression. "I wish all you damned tourists would just go home. You come up here with your fancy cars and funny clothes and do nothing but pollute our air and crowd our roads. It's too late in the season, buddy. Why don't you just go on home to Charlotte or Atlanta or wherever you're from and shoot each other so there's less of you all to bother us."

Neither Rainy nor the stranger had moved during her entire tirade, and he continued staring at her with that strange half smile. Caroline remained where she was, taking deep breaths and waiting for a reaction. Finally she turned to Rainy. "I'm sorry; I'm not in the mood to chat anymore. I'll stop by another time so we can catch up in *privacy*."

She kissed Rainy on the cheek and headed for the door, feeling completely righteous.

"Excuse me, ma'am."

Caroline turned to face the stranger, tossing around in her head whether she should accept his apology or not. "Yes?"

"You might want to remove that patch of toilet paper sticking to your cheek before you leave. It looks kinda funny."

Rainy had the good sense to keep quiet as Caroline, with as much dignity as she could summon, pulled open the door and left the shop.

# CHAPTER 3

JEWEL REED PAUSED FOR A MOMENT WITH HER BACK AGAINST THE bedroom door, listening for the sound of the buzz saw coming from her father's workroom. The reassuring whine of the tool started up again, drowning out even the waverunner on the lake and giving Jewel a chance to sneak into the unused bedroom, snapping the door shut behind her.

The blinds were closed, blocking out the morning sun. Small arms of escaped sunbeams reached toward the stack of cardboard boxes, the packing tape still sealed along the seams. One year wasn't a long time to have lived in a new place, but it was sure long enough to have unpacked all the moving boxes already.

She listened furtively again for the sound of the saw before turning back to the boxes. It wasn't as if her father had actually *said* she wasn't supposed to be messing with her mother's things, so what she was doing wasn't *technically* wrong. Besides, if she was real careful, he'd never find out.

She headed to the trunk pushed up against the wall between the windows with three boxes stacked on it. Jewel grunted as she tried to lift the one on top. Inch by inch, she shifted it closer and closer to the edge of the box beneath, then stumbled backward to catch it as it pitched forward. Unable to grab the smooth surface, she watched the box slide to the hardwood floor, landing with a loud thump.

Jewel froze, holding her breath and listening for her dad to call up to her. She heard the sound of the buzz saw instead and she sighed with relief before turning her attention to the box that had conveniently landed on its bottom. With nails nearly chewed to the quick, she managed to pick at the packing tape until she could pry it up and pull it off with a satisfying rip.

Crumpled white packing paper lay on top, and Jewel placed her hands on it, ready to toss it aside, but paused. These were her mother's things—things she had owned, touched, and used during her brief life and were deemed too personal to be given away by her father. She felt her first twinge of guilt and glanced back at the closed door. It was almost like prying into her parents' personal love story, the quieted words between them now contained inside the cardboard boxes and trunk in front of her.

She squeezed her eyes shut. Thinking about her mother always made her want to cry, but she had promised herself that she wouldn't. Ever since her mom had died almost three years ago, her dad had been looking at her funny, as if wondering why she wouldn't cry. She couldn't tell him. She didn't really know him, after all. It had always been mostly her and her mother because her dad was always working. But if he had asked, she would have told him that crying for her mother would have been like a permanent good-bye. It was what people did when they said good-bye to people they wouldn't see for a while, or when something precious was broken. Or at a funeral. It was acknowledging that something was gone from your life for good.

Lifting the first wad of paper, she threw it to the floor. Her mom wasn't gone from her life. Jewel couldn't see her, but she was there. She felt her. And she saw her mother every time she looked in a mirror—just the thirteen-year-old version of herself with the same long red curly hair.

As she grabbed the next wad of paper, she had the reassuring thought that maybe her mom was making her do this. Her dad seemed to be frozen when it came to grieving for her mom. Sure, he had packed them up and moved them from Charleston to Hicksville, quit his job as a lawyer and started making furniture. He said it was a new beginning for both of them. He had even started trying to have conversations with her.

As if that wasn't retarded enough, he'd left her mom's things in boxes in the extra room, like monuments to dead people you saw in old cemeteries. But her mother hadn't wanted a monument. Her ashes had been scattered into the Atlantic Ocean, flooding the wind with the spirit of the wonderful person who had been her mother. Jewel remembered how the sky had darkened for a moment, then brightened with sharp bands of sunlight electrifying it. But only she and her Grandma Rainy had noticed, probably because everybody else had been busy crying. Crying over things you couldn't bring back made you miss out on the really cool things life seemed to throw at you when you least expected it.

She bent inside the box and lifted wrapped items that felt a lot like the metal and glass holders for her mom's yoga candles and placed them on the floor beside the box. She leaned in again, her hands grabbing hold of a soft, cotton gauze skirt, and she knew before looking at it what it would be. It was the red-and-gold sari her mother had brought back from her parents' honeymoon to India. Every time her mother wore it, she'd say how she and Jewel's father were going to go back again someday when he wasn't so busy at work. But they never did.

Jewel lifted the sari and several more items of clothing out of the box, raising them to her face and sniffing deeply, smelling her mother's scent of floral soap and earth. *I miss you, Mom. I miss you so much.* She swallowed thickly as she put the clothing on the floor next to the candleholders, wondering if her dad had kept her mother's nightgown to help him go to sleep at night. Jewel didn't hear him stumbling about the darkened house in the middle of the night anymore, so maybe he'd found something of her mother's to help him get through the long nights.

She peered in the half-empty box again and saw what looked like a folded quilt—something she'd never seen before. Wrinkling her brow, she pulled it out, catching the scent of mothballs as she did. The fabrics were dark blue and maroon, colors she didn't associate with her mom. In fact, she didn't associate quilts with her mom at all. She looked closer at the panel covering the top fold and read the quilted lettering: HPHS 1992. *Hart's Peak High School?* Below it was a brown fabric football, the hand-stitching around the edges tiny and perfect. Nineteen-ninety had been her mother's graduation year, but what was the football all about? To her knowledge, her mother had never willingly watched a football game in her entire life. Or quilted.

But this quilt was different from other quilts she'd seen. It looked like it had been pieced together from a scrapbook—with silk-screened photos and pieces of material that looked like they were from baby blankets or favorite shirts.

As she moved toward the window to get a better look at it, something fell from inside the folds of the quilt and hit her on the foot. Crying out in pain, she dropped the quilt and bent down to see what had fallen.

The large floral journal had landed on its side and was now propped up against the wall, the stiff front cover opened and lying flat on the floor, the pages waving at her as they flipped through to the end.

Picking it up, she placed it in her lap and studied the inside cover. In a young girl's hand, doodles and circles chased flowers and bees along the border, and sketched in large, cloudlike letters were the words, *This diary belongs to Shelby Ann Martin. Keep Out. Private Property.*

*Mom,* Jewel thought, brushing her fingers over the lettering in the same way her mother had brushed her fingers over her face when she was a child.

She stared at it for several minutes, listening to the intermittent sound of the buzz saw coming from her father's workroom. Her mother's girlhood diary. Some small part of her told her to put it away. But a greater part wanted to read it, to read about her mother and the girl she had once been. Jewel hugged it to her chest. Maybe this was her mom's way of sharing her past. Sort of a compensation for there being no more years to share.

With confidence now, she opened the front cover, pausing for a moment to stare at the first page covered in various incarnations of her mother's signature. The last was close to her adult signature, recognized by its similarity to the one she'd used on Jewel's report cards and permission slips for swim team.

She sat back against the wall and began to read.

*August 22, 1984*

> *I had another big headache today. It was one of the headaches I get where I see stars and faces and other things that aren't really there. I thought I saw a little red-haired girl that looked familiar to me, and I tried to paint her in art class with the new middle school art teacher, Miss Mikrut. She took away my paintbrush because we were supposed to be using pastel chalk to draw a dumb vase of flowers. Miss Mikrut is stupid and dumb and I hate her. She made my headache worse so my mama had to come get me and bring me home. Jude was in the fourth-grade language arts room and saw me go to the nurse's office. He pretended he was sick, too, so Mama brought him home with me and we watched* The Wizard of Oz *with the sound off and ate chicken soup until Mrs. Collier came and got him. I heard her tell Jude that he had no business playing with a girl who was two years older and already in middle school. He didn't say anything because I knew he couldn't explain. Nobody but Caroline really understands how we're like shadows of each other. Later I tried to draw the red-haired girl but I had already forgotten what she looked like.*

Jewel lifted her gaze from the small, rounded cursive lettering and stared at the closed door, realizing that the buzz saw sounds had stopped. She stood and placed everything except the diary back into the box, stuffing the quilt on top. She had to leave the top open because the packing tape was all gone but she shoved the quilt in far enough so that it didn't stick out over the edges of the box.

She picked up the journal and quickly left the room, closing the door softly behind her.

Drew flicked off the power switch on his buzz saw and stopped, listening. The house was perfectly quiet: no loud music from Jewel's room, or TV blaring from the living room. And no shrieking on the phone to her girlfriends. He had no idea if they actually said any-thing to one another, but there was certainly a lot of shrieking. He'd hoped that in the year since they'd moved to Lake Ophelia his daughter would have chosen to spend time talking with him instead of listening to loud noises that seemed to obliterate the emptiness that moved around the two of them still. They had not yet found a way to get through it and find a way into each other's lives.

He looked down at the table he had made, at the rich patina of the cherrywood, at the smooth, graceful lines of the legs, the irregu-lar sides of the tabletop. He was creating something new here, some-thing his years as a lawyer had never prepared him for, but something Shelby had always told him he had within him. It had taken her death to give him the courage to reach inside and pull out the yearning that his father had succeeded for years in suppressing.

If only he could make Jewel understand this. Instead she looked at him with hostile eyes, silently accusing him of running from his grief and ruining her life in the process.

He moved to the door of his workroom and opened it, surprised again at the silence.

"Jewel?"

A muffled response answered him. "What?"

"Why is everything so quiet?"

There was a short pause. "I'm reading."

That alone was enough to cause worry. He was about to say something else to her when he heard the sound of two female voices outside on the lake side of the house. They were raised in argument.

He walked to the large glass door and peered out toward his dock that sat adjacent to his neighbors', the Colliers. He spotted Margaret and another woman who sat on the dock in a lawn chair, her back to him, her hair scraped back in a long blond ponytail. She and Margaret seemed to be fighting over some handheld device and were playing a bizarre game of tug-of-war with it. The other woman stood and Drew put his hand on the door as he watched Margaret pull the device into her hand and raise it high over her head. From the younger woman's stance, Drew had no doubt that she wouldn't stop at shoving Margaret into the lake to get back whatever it was.

Margaret seemed to have the same thought as she drew back her arm and threw it pretty far out into the lake.

Sliding open the door, he rushed outside, forcing a smile as he approached the two women. He saw the recognition in the younger woman's eyes at the same time he registered where he'd seen her before.

"Oh, God. Not you. Please."

He smiled in her direction, feeling oddly smug at her embarrassment, hoping she was remembering the toilet paper on her face. Rainy had told him who she was the night before but hadn't had a chance to tell him more before she'd received a telephone call. "It's nice to see you again, too. Is there anything I can help with? Carry a chair, dive into the lake to retrieve something?"

"You could go sniff the bottom of the lake."

Margaret moved between them. "Hello, Drew. Please don't mind Caroline. She's . . . delicate."

"I am *not* delicate, and I wish you'd stop telling that to people. What I *am* is pissed off. You just threw my BlackBerry into the lake. Now what in the hell am I supposed to do? How do you expect me to keep tabs on what's going on at the office?"

Mother and daughter faced each other, and Drew almost smiled at how alike they were.

Margaret put her hands on her hips. "You're not supposed to be keeping tabs on the office because you've taken a leave of absence. They'll survive—but you won't if you don't start taking care of yourself."

Margaret turned to Drew with an apologetic smile. "Please forgive us. I don't mean to argue in public, but sometimes Caroline forgets herself and will pick a fight anywhere."

Outraged, Caroline put her hands on her hips, accentuating her strong resemblance to her mother. Drew pulled on his self-preservation instincts and did not point this out. Caroline's voice practically quavered. "*I'm* not the one tossing expensive equipment into the lake—equipment that doesn't even belong to you."

Ignoring her, Margaret continued to address herself to Drew. "Her doctor has ordered her to get completely away from stress—

mostly caused by her job. Dr. Northcutt said that she's so stressed that not only is it bad for her heart but she's also started to have digestive problems that he normally doesn't see in patients under sixty."

"Mother!" Caroline dropped back into the lawn chair and put her hand over her eyes.

Margaret nodded in her daughter's direction. "I'm just trying to explain to our new neighbor, Mr. Reed, how delicate your heart is and how everyone, including our neighbors, needs to work together to keep stress out of your life."

Caroline shook her head, her hands now pressing against either side of her face like a vise. "Living with you and next door to him will probably kill me within days without intervention. A job as an air-traffic controller would be less stressful." She jerked to a stand and faced Margaret, her face a mottled red. "Mom, I know that you're going to say that you're doing this because you love me, and deep, deep down inside me somewhere I might even believe that's true. But if you open your mouth to say one word to me right now, I can't be responsible for what I might do. So I'm going inside to lie down and practice breathing and maybe tie my hands behind my back so I won't hurt myself or anyone else. Do not follow me. Please."

She turned her back on them without another word and stalked toward the house. For the second time in as many days, Drew had the pleasure of watching her retreating backside and had the thought that somebody's boot could do a lot of good planted on her rear end.

When Margaret looked up at him again he expected to see anger or at least embarrassment. He saw neither. Instead it looked like she was about to cry.

"Are you all right?"

She clenched her lips together and nodded. "I'll be fine. I'm used to it." She sent him a weak smile. "She's not really like that, you know. She's just . . . hurt. And she's been hurting for a very long time. I just don't know how to make it better. I thought that . . ." Margaret looked back at him, as if remembering she wasn't alone. "I'm sorry. I don't mean to burden you with all our family's woes. I just didn't want you to think I'd raised a monster."

He smiled back at her. "I wouldn't think that at all, Mrs. Collier. Besides, Rainy seems to have a particular fondness for your daughter, which says a lot." Although in this particular instance, he might doubt his mother-in-law's judgment.

Margaret clutched his arm. "Yes, well. I guess I'd better go in. But I'm glad I saw you. I wanted to invite you and your daughter over for supper Saturday night."

"That's nice of you, Mrs. Collier, but I don't think your daughter likes me very much. . . ."

"Drew—first, call me Margaret. Second, Caroline doesn't seem to like anything very much unless it's a column of numbers. Just give her time, and maybe you'll see what I used to see when she was a young girl." She patted his arm. "I'll see you and Jewel at six then."

It wasn't a question and he realized he wasn't expected to answer, either. She said good night and he watched her go back to the house, noticing how she stopped at the back door and squared her shoulders before entering in the exact same way her daughter had done minutes before.

# CHAPTER 4

✣

CAROLINE HEARD THE CALL OF THE LOON IN THE DARK OF HER dream and she stirred, picturing the long, sleek body of the water bird sluicing into the deepest parts of the lake, down to the invisible places that lived only in her memories and pushed insistently at the placid surface of her life.

Opening her eyes, she crossed to her window and stared out across the lake where Hart's Peak sat shadowed under a full moon and heard the loon again, its call something between a cry and a laugh. She remembered the times she and Jude had slipped their canoe into the black water in search of the elusive bird, always disappointed but gratified, too, knowing that this was a secret adventure they shared while their parents slept: a quest to look for something they couldn't see. Their loon—they called it that even though they were never sure if it was the same one—returned to the lake each summer, even though it wasn't supposed to. Loons, Jude explained, summered in Canada and the northern states, not the mountains of North Carolina. But each summer the loon called, and she and Jude went out to find it.

Straining her eyes, Caroline tried to make out the profile of Ophelia, of the smooth stone forehead that remained unlined over the centuries as she stood sentinel over the lake that bore her name—never aging, never dreaming, never living; just being. Thinking of the mystical woman made her sad, and the restless feeling of the past weeks fell on her again. Silently she slipped on her fuzzy slippers and ancient terry cloth robe and moved through the house to the back porch and down to the dock.

The loon called again, and Caroline watched as its dark shape moved across the surface of the lake, hearing the *flap-flap-flap* of its feet against the water as it gained momentum to drag its ungainly body into the air. During Caroline's awkward adolescent years, her mother had likened her to the loon: ungainly and clumsy on land, but sleek and powerful in the water. She hadn't been all that upset, because even back then she had recognized the truth in it. Caroline's swimming had been her refuge from being an awkward teenager, and she had the trophies to prove it. She didn't know where those trophies were anymore. They had been forgotten and left behind somewhere in her haste to grow up and get beyond the horrible summer of her seventeenth year.

The loon dove under the surface, leaving the lake silent again. Caroline sat and pulled her knees into her chest, turning her head toward her neighbor's house. She was surprised to see a light on in the small addition stuck onto the back of the house. It was probably that annoying man Drew Something-or-other. *God.* Just thinking his name made her skin crawl with irritation. She was pretty sure it had nothing to do with the humiliating toilet-paper incident, either. It was more to do with his being a bump on what she had thought would be an uncluttered road to recovery. She'd envisioned lying on the sofa or the dock for three months, keeping in touch with the office through her BlackBerry, and not having to do anything except tolerate her mother and catch up with Rainy.

She thought of her BlackBerry at the bottom of the lake and swore under her breath just as the loon crashed through the surface and flew away, its late-night snack clutched in its beak. It made her miss the water again and the way it made her feel: strong, sleek. Beautiful.

She stood and stared at the black water, her body itching to feel the cold wetness, her hands cupping on their own as if remembering moving water with deft strokes. *I've been too long from the water.*

Turning her back, she faced her mother's house again just in time to see the light go off in her neighbor's house. *Probably up late plotting the transformation of Rainy's shop into a burger franchise.* She felt her heart pound. Until now she'd forgotten about the FOR SALE sign in the shop's window. She'd go see Rainy tomorrow and demand to know what that was all about. No way could she be allowed to sell it to that . . . tourist. Soon there would be nothing left to remember Jude's presence. Only old memories held by people who were getting older every day.

She felt weepy again. *Damn! What is wrong with me?* Plopping herself into the chaise longue on the back patio, she sucked in the night air one large lungful at a time. She lay back and closed her eyes, just to rest for a moment before going back to bed. But there was something about the night air, something about the smell of the lake that brought Jude back to her. She could almost feel him beside her in the canoe, paddling silently. Absently she moved her fingers over the old chest scar and fell asleep with her hand pressed against her heart, dreaming of slipping farther and farther out onto the dark lake with only the call of the loon to guide her.

Caroline awoke to the smell of coffee, the loon's cry still fresh in her mind. She sat up, disoriented for a moment, with a terrible stiffness in her neck where it had been pressed into an unnatural position against the back of the chaise. Her mother stood before her, completely dressed in a crisply ironed linen pantsuit and a freshly made-up face. She held a wooden breakfast tray with a plate of wheat toast, turkey bacon, and scrambled faux eggs, and a steaming cup of coffee. Tucked neatly under the china plate lay a snowy-white linen napkin. Caroline could be on her deathbed and her mother would still be trying to make her point about napkins. The woman never gave up.

Caroline tried to sit up straighter and felt every bone in her body protest as she moved them out of cramped positions and allowed her mother to place the breakfast tray on her lap.

"Honey, if your bed isn't comfortable, I'll give you mine. I don't know how good the night air is on your health."

Caroline pasted what she hoped was a pleasant smile on her face. "Fresh air's good for me." She picked up the mug and took a sip of coffee. "Thanks for breakfast."

"You're welcome. It's all low-fat and low-calorie. I have some low-sugar jam for your toast if you'd like some."

Caroline looked down at the butterless toast and tried to be thankful. "No, thanks. This is fine."

Her mother wiped off the seat of a green lawn chair with the palm of her hand, then sat on the edge, facing Caroline. "What would you like to do today?"

Caught by surprise, Caroline stammered, "I, uh, I thought I'd go see Rainy. But you don't need to come with me. I'm sure you've got your own plans."

"Nonsense. I need to go see Rainy anyway. She just got back from Atlanta from her last round with chemo and I should go see how she's doing."

Caroline's mouth went dry around a forkful of eggs. "What? What chemo?"

Margaret frowned, deep furrows creasing her forehead, reminding Caroline again of how quickly she seemed to be aging. Or maybe this was the first time in a long while she had really looked at her mother.

"Oh, I thought Rainy would have told you by now." She straightened her back. "She's got ovarian cancer, but she's responding real well to treatment. Not that a stubborn old coot like Rainy would ever allow cancer to get the better of her. I always knew it didn't stand a chance."

"Mom! How can you talk like that? She's your best friend and she's got cancer." Completely losing her appetite, Caroline moved the breakfast tray off her lap and sat up. "I've got to go see her. I can't believe nobody told me." Angry now, she turned on her mother. "How could you not tell me?"

Margaret stood and stared her daughter in the eye. "It's hard to tell you things when the only communication I have with you is by e-mail or by leaving you a message on your voice mail." She paused. "Then you had your stress attack and she and I decided you didn't need anything else to upset you."

A small ball of guilt found its way into Caroline's throat. Her contact with her mother for years had been strictly superficial, easily compartmentalized into snippets of information that could be imparted without being discussed. She always thought she liked it that way. Caroline took a deep breath. "I need to see her."

A loud buzzing sounded from the laundry room. Margaret turned and said, "I'm going to go fold towels. Let me know when you're ready to go and I'll drive you."

Resigned, Caroline watched her mother march off to the laundry room as if she were walking on a fashion runway; then she carried the breakfast tray back to the kitchen, shuffling in her fuzzy slippers.

She had almost made it to her room to get dressed when the doorbell rang. She looked toward the laundry room to see if her mom had heard over the noise of the washing machine. When Margaret didn't appear, Caroline moved toward the front door, then yanked it open.

Drew What's-his-name stood on the covered front porch, a large dark wood cabinet with glass doors sitting on the floor next to him. He didn't even have the manners to smile and look her in the eye and pretend she looked normal. Instead his eyes roamed over her bulky robe, fluffy slippers, and bare pale legs, then up to the chair creases on her face before resting on her hair. "Rough night?"

She stared at him for a long moment, trying not to look as embarrassed as she felt. "Are you lost? I can draw you a map to show you the way home, if you like. No charge."

He was still staring at her hair. "How do you get it to stay up like that?"

She started to close the door on him, but he stuck his hand out to stop it from shutting completely. "Is your mother in? She's expecting me."

Margaret appeared from the laundry room, a look of horror crossing her face as she took in Caroline's appearance and the man at the door. While greeting Drew, she reached into the hall table drawer, pulled out a tube of lipstick, and handed it to Caroline. Caroline stared at it, thinking that putting lipstick on her face at this point would be a bit like hanging ornaments on a dead tree. She slipped the tube into the pocket of her robe and crossed her arms, prepared for battle. Except no one was paying any attention to her.

Drew lifted up the piece of furniture in two parts and brought them in from the porch at her mother's direction, declining her offer of help and making two trips. The furniture came to rest against the blank wall below Jude's drawing and next to the closed-up piano. Curious, Caroline followed them into the great room.

Both Drew and Margaret were looking at her with expectant expressions. Her mother spoke first. "Well, what do you think?"

Curious, Caroline stepped forward, looking closely at the piece of furniture for the first time. It had short, squat legs that had been carved to resemble crescent moons. The top and sides were made of a dark-colored wood, with an inlaid checkerboard pattern marching around the perimeter. But the pediment intrigued her the most. Across the top were what appeared to be ocean waves in different sizes, like the surf rolling forcefully to shore. It was nothing a machine could ever have made. She knelt before it, awed, and slid her hands across the smooth wood. It made something inside of her spin, as if the connection between artist and viewer had been firmly made. She used to get the same feeling when listening to Jude play the piano. "It's beautiful."

And then she wished she hadn't uttered a word, because it sounded so inadequate. She'd worked in the furniture manufacturing business her entire career and knew what to look for in a quality piece of furniture. This was simply art.

"It's exquisite," she said as she stood.

"Thank you." Drew bent down and retrieved a shelf that he'd brought in from the porch and placed it inside.

Caroline looked at him in confusion. "Where did you buy it?"

"I didn't." He picked up another shelf and put it in place.

She rolled her eyes. "Okay, so where did you steal it?"

Her mother laid a hand on her arm. "Caroline, don't be silly. He made it—that's what he does. He makes furniture. It's for all your swimming trophies."

Caroline wasn't sure which bit of news stunned her more—the fact that Drew What's-his-name had the carpentry skills of a master craftsman or that her mother even remembered that she had won any swimming trophies.

Margaret continued. "I've been keeping your trophies all these years, hoping to find someplace wonderful to put them. I thought they'd look great here, in this house, since this is where you learned to swim. When Drew showed me some of the pieces he was work-ing on, I knew immediately that he'd be the one who could make something special." She smiled broadly. "I'm glad you agree."

Caroline couldn't say anything, so she reached out and smoothed her hand over the top of the cabinet again, smelling fresh-cut wood and stain. Awe, surprise, and anger seemed to swirl around in her head, making her heart beat faster. She concentrated on tak-ing deep breaths while she stared at the waves racing across the top of the cabinet. *I've missed the water,* she thought again, remembering the loon and the way her body had ached as she'd looked out onto the lake.

Drew was no longer staring at her hair and was now looking into her eyes. He had nice eyes, dark blue and clear with few creases around them, as if he didn't spend a lot of time laughing. "My daughter, Jewel, wants to try out for the swim team—but I'm mak-ing her sit out this year and work on her confidence. She's a good swimmer, but she needs to build some strength and stamina. I think it would be too dangerous just to put her in the water before she's ready. Maybe you can coach her and give her some pointers."

She dropped her hand. "I don't swim anymore. I haven't for a long time, so I don't think I'd be able to help." She drew her robe closer around her body and pulled her lips away from her teeth to resemble a smile. "I need to go get dressed now." She hurried from the room, eager to get away before anybody could see her cry.

*May 16, 1985*

> *Jude is moving to Atlanta. He says his dad's been offered a job at a big Atlanta hospital and that they'll still keep their house for vacations and weekends. But it won't be the same. I have bad headaches now when I see Jude saying good-bye to me and I'm thinking that I'm seeing him move away. These headaches are so bad I can taste them, and they taste like black asphalt after a summer rainstorm. It's burned and smoky and I*

*wonder if it's the dream I'm smelling or something real that hasn't happened yet. That happens to me sometimes, and it's scary. Mama knows something's up with that because she's looking at me weird. She doesn't even have to ask if my head hurts—she just knows and makes me one of her hot drinks. But the dreams always stay after the headache goes away. It's like when a camera flash goes off but you still see the light for a long time. I think life's like that: Each moment is so quick, but you remember them forever.*

Jewel heard the front door shut and immediately slammed the diary closed, then stuck it under her mattress.

Her father called from downstairs, "Jewel?"

She stayed on her bed where she'd been reading and shouted, "I'm here!"

Her father paused for a moment and then she heard his footsteps on the stairs. He hated shouting—he said it reminded him too much of growing up with Grandpa—and preferred to speak softly face-to-face. Which was fine with her as long as it didn't require her to move from her comfortable perch.

There was a brief tapping on her door and she did a quick check to make sure the diary was out of sight before telling him to come in.

"I have to deliver some chairs to Grandma Rainy's store—do you want to come with me?"

Jewel leaped from the bed before remembering that wasn't her style. She sat back down on the bed and shrugged. "Whatever."

Her dad stared at her for a long moment without saying anything. "Okay—go hop in the truck. I'm ready to go."

She waited until she heard her dad reach the bottom of the steps before grabbing her backpack and racing to follow him.

Her dad had already started the truck and had it in gear by the time she climbed into the passenger seat. In her opinion, the whole switch from city lawyer to country woodcarver had been weird. But buying the pickup truck had sent her over the edge. She could even stand the new plaid shirts and jeans more than she could stand having to climb up to get inside the truck.

The windows were rolled down and she stared out at the scenery as her dad wound the truck down the mountain. They passed an ice-cream shop and she almost asked him to stop before she remembered that she wasn't speaking to him.

As if reading her mind, he said, "I've been thinking. I'll arrange for private swimming lessons for you, if you like. That way when you try out next year, you'll be more confident and more ready to be on the team."

She shifted her head to look at him, keeping her face expressionless. She should cut him a break. After all, her mother had died while swimming, although technically it wasn't the water that had killed her. Her mother had just happened to have had a massive brain aneurysm while swimming off the shore of Sullivan's Island, where Jewel and her mom had been vacationing. As usual, her dad had stayed behind in Charleston to work and hadn't been there. Yeah, she should cut him a break. Except he was being completely unreasonable about the swim-team thing.

"I'm a good swimmer, Dad. I can handle it."

He didn't say anything for a while but concentrated on navigating the winding road. Finally he said, "I think it's best that you wait."

She turned her head back to the window and kept her eyes straight ahead, making all the scenery go by in a blur.

Her dad missed the point entirely that she didn't want to talk. He cleared his throat and said, "Have you had any headaches lately?"

"Not really—not any bad ones, anyway."

"Good. You're scheduled to see Dr. Oifer next week for a checkup. He'll probably schedule you for another MRI to make sure everything's okay."

"That's totally not necessary. I've already had three and there's been nothing there. I'm just one of those people unlucky enough to have migraines. That's it."

She felt her dad tense beside her and she knew they were both thinking of her mother and how she had died. But Jewel couldn't think of anything to say that might make it better, so she remained silent, staring out the window.

Her dad had barely put the truck in front of her grandmother's store before Jewel hopped out and crossed the parking lot, noticing the new Cadillac parked next to them. As she looked at the Georgia plates, she felt the first prickling behind her eyes—always a sign of a headache. She stopped for a moment and closed her eyes and could see in the darkness behind her lids the kaleidoscope circle of light that stayed there. There wasn't any pain yet, but it was only a matter of time.

She took the steps in one leap and threw open the door. "Grandma!" she yelled, feeling the first stab of pain at the base of her skull. Jewel spotted two ladies standing near a quilt rack holding a quilt of deep blue and red. The older one Jewel recognized as her neighbor, Mrs. Collier, but she was sure she'd never seen the slim blonde who stood behind with her lips tightly pressed into a single line. But there was something familiar about her, something about the eyes and the way they stared out at the world that made her think she'd seen her before.

Grandma Rainy came through the kitchen door and spotted Jewel immediately. Grandma came toward her with a knowing look and pressed Jewel's head against her bosom. "It's the start of a bad one, isn't it? Come on back to the kitchen and I'll get you some tea right away."

Rainy nodded to the two ladies as she led Jewel away, and Jewel glanced back to see the young woman again. The blonde was staring back at her, her skin even paler than before, as if she, too, recognized something in Jewel.

Jewel closed her eyes again, succumbing to the dark pain that now engulfed her and to the warm embrace of her grandmother's arms.

# CHAPTER 5

D REW WATCHED RAINY PULL HIS DAUGHTER OUT OF THE ROOM and took a step toward them, but Rainy waved a hand in his direction, making him stop. "She'll be fine—it's just a headache. I'm going to get her something to drink and she'll be better in no time."

He watched as the door that led to the kitchen swung shut in his face, leaving him staring at the solid expanse of wood. He thought for a moment of staying there with his nose pressed against the door rather than forcing a conversation with the other two occupants in the room.

"Well, hello, there, Drew. It's good to see you again so soon, isn't it, Caroline?" Without giving her daughter a chance to answer, Margaret Collier continued, "Was that Jewel? I haven't seen her since I was here in April. I'd swear she's grown six inches since then! She looks more like a sixteen-year-old than a thirteen-year-old, that's for sure. And she's looking more and more like Shelby, isn't she?"

Drew smiled, unexpectedly pleased to see that somebody besides him had noticed the resemblance between Jewel and her mother. As a toddler, the similarities had been subtle, except for the color of her hair, but as Jewel approached adolescence, her mother's stamp was becoming more apparent. It was almost as if the decision as to whom Jewel would look like had been temporarily suspended, leaving her to choose.

"Yes, she is." He watched as comprehension dawned on Caroline's face.

"She's Shelby's daughter? So you're . . . Well, I knew she'd married; I just didn't realize . . ." Blushing, Caroline let her voice trail away as if realizing what she had been about to say out loud.

"Yes, Shelby was my wife. After she died, I decided it was best for Jewel to move up here from Charleston to live full-time."

Caroline's face softened. "I'm sorry. Shelby and my brother—Jude—were best friends. We hung out a lot growing up."

The tentative way she said her brother's name, as if the consonants and vowels were rusty on her lips, reminded him of the way he said his dead wife's name, and knew they were both living with the presence of ghosts.

She looked down at her unpolished, blunt fingernails. "Shelby was probably the nicest person I've ever known. She always knew the right thing to say." She focused again on Drew's face and her smile faded as if remembering who he was and that she didn't like him very much. "I'm sorry for your loss."

"Thank you," he said, nodding in acknowledgment as she turned away from him and began running her fingers reverently over a quilt thrown over a stand. Drew studied her for a moment, noting the complete lack of jewelry and makeup. Her hair was pulled back with a rubber band in a sleek blond ponytail and she wore a white T-shirt and jeans. If he hadn't already known that she was an accountant, it would have been his first guess. She was clearly a person who didn't allow a lot of garnishes into her life that might interfere with her appraisal of cold, hard numbers.

Caroline smiled again just as he was about to look away and he stopped, unable to make himself not stare. She was gently rubbing her fingers over a quilted patch and smiling to herself at a silent thought. The smile transformed her, softened her face and eyes, and turned her into a woman he could almost believe he wanted to get to know. But then she turned toward him, and the cold mask slipped over her face again. She dropped the quilt and lifted her hands to press against her heart in an automatic gesture before she turned away from him again and walked toward the kitchen door where Rainy and Jewel had disappeared minutes before.

Drew stared at the closed door for a long time, then headed back to his truck to unload furniture.

Caroline pushed through the kitchen door, relieved to be away from Drew's appraising stare. He had unnerved her. He had been staring at her as if he could read her private thoughts, and it had scared the crap out of her. She had been thinking about the time she,

Jude, and Shelby had skipped school to go fishing. They had fallen asleep in the boat and gotten so sunburned they blistered, making it impossible to disguise their truancy. She had been about to laugh out loud at the memory when she felt Drew's gaze on her, and it was as if he had shared the memory with her. She'd turned her back on him, unable to breathe for a moment. Her memories were her own now, and the girl she had been was gone forever, just like Shelby and Jude. They were all dead now, in a way.

Jewel sat at the old pine table with her feet propped up on a chair and her forehead covered with a damp dishcloth. Rainy had just set down a mug of steaming tea in front of her.

"Here now, sweetie. Take slow sips so you don't burn your tongue and you'll feel better in a few minutes."

The girl gave a weak nod and held the cloth to her forehead with one hand as she reached for the mug with the other.

Rainy smiled in Caroline's direction. "She gets these headaches sometimes. Why don't you sit down and I'll get you something, too. You're looking pasty."

Caroline did as she was told and pulled out a chair, being careful not to jostle the young girl across from her. She looked at Rainy, remembering how frail she had seemed when she'd hugged her, and noticed how baggy the overalls were and how the flesh seemed to hang from her thin forearms. When Rainy turned around with a mug, Caroline saw with a start that the long braids that had always been a fixture on Rainy's head were gone, replaced by wispy gray strands that were partially covered by an ugly tie-dyed scarf.

"Why didn't you tell me you were sick, Rainy?"

Rainy regarded her steadily for a long moment. "Would it have made any difference to you? You had problems of your own, as I recall. Besides, I knew it wasn't anything I couldn't handle. And there was nothing you could have done anyway."

Stabbing guilt hit Caroline like a physical punch. Would it have made a difference? Would she have run out of her quiet, ordered life to be with her? She looked down into the dark tea, seeing the reflection of the old glass fixture above the table that had been there ever since she could remember. She knew the answer and it wasn't the one she wanted to hear. It had taken a near-death experience to bring her back here. She doubted anything else would have.

Caroline felt a warm hand on her own and looked up into Rainy's face, which showed her years of living undisguised by makeup. "It's okay. I understand."

Caroline looked down again to blink away the sting in her eyes. She nodded, knowing that Rainy really did understand. She always had.

"Is that why you're selling the store?"

Rainy shrugged. "Partly. But I guess it's time. My Bill, before he passed on, tried to get me to retire so we could travel some together. See the Grand Canyon and Old Faithful and the Golden Gate Bridge. I've never been farther than Charlotte, you know." She leaned heavily on the sink while she tugged the dishwasher door open. "So I suppose I should see what's on the other side of the mountain before Jesus calls me home."

The kitchen door opened again and Margaret breezed in, impeccable as always, without a strand of hair out of place despite the drizzle outside. She spotted Rainy and walked over to her. "There you are, you old coot. I've been gone for three months and now that I'm back you don't even bother to call or say hello when I stop by to see you."

Her mother enveloped Rainy in a tight embrace, reflecting their decades-long friendship, then held her at arm's length, her eyes misty. "Your color's back. I think you're beating this thing." She squeezed Rainy's shoulders. "I knew you could do it."

Rainy's eyes looked suspiciously bright. "Oh, stop. I'm not on my deathbed yet." She blinked her eyes and stared closely at Margaret's face. "Your mustache needs bleaching."

Margaret dropped her hands and dabbed at her eyes with a knuckle. "It's good to see you, too. And your chin hairs could stand to become better acquainted with a tweezer, dear."

Jewel had lifted the cloth from her forehead and was staring at the older women in confusion. Caroline took a sip from her mug. "Don't pay any attention to them, and don't even try to understand them. I've been around them for thirty years and I still don't get it."

Jewel smiled and sat up, taking the cloth off her forehead and bunching it in her hands. "You live next door to us on the lake, don't you?"

Caroline nodded. "Yes. I knew your mom. She was a really great person. I'm sorry she's gone." She gave her a slight smile. "You look a lot like her."

Jewel glanced down at her hands and the wadded cloth, and for a moment Caroline thought it was Shelby sitting in front of her. The flaming red hair was the same, as was the slim, muscular body. But the shape of the face was different: Its high cheekbones and dimpled chin were definitely a legacy of some other limb off the family tree. As she lifted her eyes back to Caroline's face, she was all Shelby again. Not in the color, but in the way they were shaped and in the light that seemed to shine behind them. Jewel's dark green eyes, the color of the lake at sunset, were calm and warm and seemed to hold facets of deep knowledge unavailable to most humans.

"Thank you." Jewel smiled and took a sip from her mug. "You're the swimmer, right? I saw my dad making the trophy case for you."

Caroline slid her chair back, scraping the old linoleum checkerboard floor, and watched her mother and Rainy empty the dishwasher. Their entire conversation consisted of Margaret trying to get Rainy to sit down and rest and Rainy trying to snatch dishes and glasses out of Margaret's hands so she could put them away herself.

She turned back to Jewel. "No, actually I'm a former swimmer. I haven't been in the water for years."

"How come?"

*Because I can't.* "Um, no time for it. My job keeps me pretty busy." She drained her mug, hoping to signal an end to the conversation.

Jewel leaned forward on her elbows, glancing over to the arguing women as if to make sure nobody overheard. "I want to try out for the swim team, but my dad says I need to be a stronger swimmer before he'll allow it. Maybe you can coach me—in secret." She held out a hand to stop Caroline's protest, misinterpreting her objection. "Not because he won't allow it—he suggested it, actually. But because he'll be jumping in the water with us, telling me what I can and cannot do and generally making my life miserable if he knows about it."

Caroline almost smiled. There was something so likable about this girl. Something so familiar. But she couldn't help her. She couldn't. "I'm sorry, Jewel. I'd like to help but I just can't."

The young girl stared at her with those eyes that seemed a lot older than the face they were a part of. "Okay. Whatever."

Rainy came to stand by Jewel's chair and put an arm loosely around her shoulders. "How's the headache?"

"Much better. I just have those little weird spots in the corner of my eyes, but the pain's gone."

Rainy nodded. "Good. We got that one in time. You need to remember to treat your headache the minute you know it's coming. It's a lot easier to get rid of that way." She brushed hair off of Jewel's forehead, and the young girl closed her eyes and let her head rest against Rainy's side.

Margaret approached the table and placed two well-manicured hands on the back of a chair. "Did you tell Caroline about Shelby's memory quilt you're making for Jewel?"

Rainy kissed the top of Jewel's head before stepping away. "No, I didn't. I was waiting until she'd been here for a while before showing it to her."

Margaret's brows creased. "Whatever for? It's a beautiful quilt, Rainy. And Caroline loves quilting. Remember all those beautiful memory quilts she did back in high school? I'm sure she'd love to see Shelby's."

Caroline felt a sinking in the pit of her stomach. Shelby and Jude had been so close that any memory quilt of Shelby's was bound to have a reference to Jude. Rainy was right: She definitely wasn't ready. She looked at her mother with a flash of anger. How could it be that Rainy Martin knew exactly how Caroline would feel, yet her own mother hadn't a clue?

Jewel stood and tugged on Caroline's shoulder. "Come on. I'll show you."

Seeing no way out, Caroline forced a smile and stood. "Thanks. I'd love to see it."

She followed the young girl into what had once been the dining room in the old house and was now Rainy's workroom, trying not to drag her feet.

Margaret paused in the doorway and turned back to Rainy. "Are you sure we're not tiring you out? Maybe you should stay in the kitchen and sit down. Jewel can show us the quilt."

"I am just fine, Margaret. Maybe you should stay behind and rest. You're starting to show your age."

"I am not! And just so you know, dressing like a twelve-year-old in baggy overalls does *not* make you look any younger."

Caroline rolled her eyes and followed Jewel into the room.

Jewel stood in front of the large worktable in the middle of the room. The old dining room was her favorite, the dark oak paneling and fancy molding around the ceiling still decorating the room long after its final use as a family eating place. Sometimes, when she was alone in this room, she could see the Ryan family—a mother, father, grandmother, and two girls, seated at a large plank table holding hands with their heads bowed. The Ryans had left Hart's Valley forty years before, but they'd left an impression on their house. Jewel wondered if maybe other people could see them, too, if only they'd open their minds wide enough.

She looked down at the bright scraps of fabrics that littered the table and the double row of squares that had already been stitched together. These first squares were made from her mother's baby blankets and sleepers, the yellow and pink bunnies and floral patterns completely at odds with the memory of a mother who had favored bright geometric shapes of her own designs.

But, she supposed, that was what a memory quilt was for. It showed a life from the beginning to the end, mapping out the changes of a person in the course of a lifetime, the stitches tying the squares together like days tying together years.

Jewel looked up and saw that Caroline was standing apart, as if afraid to come closer. Her grandmother and Mrs. Collier had finished arguing and were picking up various scraps of fabric and talking excitedly to each other.

Mrs. Collier held up a light-blue-and-white-checked gingham dress. "Oh, I remember this! Was it kindergarten or first grade? For Halloween, Shelby was Dorothy, Caroline was the Wicked Witch, and Jude went as Scarecrow—remember?" She fingered the light cotton fabric in silence for a moment. "I'm surprised this isn't worn out. Caroline wore hers every day for a month."

Caroline looked at her mother. "Jude was in second grade, I was in third, and Shelby in fourth. And I was Glenda the Good Witch and Jude was the Lion. He wanted to be Scarecrow, but you had already made the lion costume. The kids made fun of him at school."

Mrs. Collier put down the gingham dress, her face pinched like she was sucking on a sourball. "I don't remember that."

Caroline came closer to the table and lightly touched the pleated skirt of a cheerleading uniform. "You wouldn't. Jude never told you because he didn't want to hurt your feelings."

"I never knew," Mrs. Collier said softly as she laid her hand gently on the gingham fabric again.

Caroline looked as if she wanted to say something else and even lifted a hand as if to touch her mother, but quickly dropped it and with a jerk of her chin went back to examining the items on the table.

Jewel watched as the three women circled the table as if waltzing with memories. She felt a little zing in her head again as the tension in the room became almost touchable. If Caroline and her mother accidentally bumped into each other, Jewel figured there'd probably be lightning.

Caroline leaned closer to get a better look at a class photograph, the one that showed Jewel's mom in fourth grade holding hands in a playground with a boy who came up to her shoulders. Suddenly Jewel realized who that boy was. A deep blue aura seemed to grow around Caroline and crept into Jewel's head again, giving her blind spots on the edges of her vision.

Grandma Rainy put a hand on Caroline's arm. "You made such beautiful memory quilts when you were in high school. I would love for you to help me and Jewel make Shelby's."

Caroline's aura deepened almost to purple. If grief and old sadness had a color, it would be that one. Her dad had it sometimes, too.

Caroline backed away from the table, shaking her head. "I . . . can't. I haven't quilted in years. I wouldn't even know how to begin."

Jewel watched as her grandmother and Mrs. Collier exchanged glances, and the sharp, stabbing pains in her head nearly obliterated her sight. The door opened and she felt her dad walk into the room, and the tension in the room came crashing down on her head. Whatever was between Caroline and her mother was even worse when it came to Caroline and her dad.

Her father turned to Grandma Rainy. "I've put all the chairs in the back room. I'll bring the table next time." He glanced around at the solemn faces. "Everything okay in here?" He gave a pointed glance at Caroline. "Anybody throwing things?"

She felt her grandmother put an arm around her shoulders. "Everything's fine. I'm going to get Jewel another cup of tea; then you can take her home." She threw a look over her shoulder at Caroline. "And think about helping us out with the quilt. You really have a gift, and I could sure use the help."

Jewel stared back at Caroline through the pain swallowing her head and saw a lost girl who seemed to be drowning on solid ground and didn't know how to come up for air. She closed her eyes again and let her grandmother lead her from the room.

# CHAPTER 6

❧

*July 3, 1986*

> *The Colliers have come back to their house for the summer. Jude has grown about four inches and is taller than Caroline now. I think that really pisses her off. I think she always thought of her height as something she could point out to people— especially her mom—as if to say that at least in one area of her life she was bigger than Jude.*
>
> *We all went swimming in the lake yesterday. The water is still freezing, so after a quick jump I was back on the dock. Jude didn't want me to be lonely so he tucked us up in a big towel and we sat together and watched Caroline swim. She's so beautiful in the water. She wraps the water around her body like it's a part of her, and nobody can move faster. She's got a closetful of trophies to prove it.*
>
> *Jude says that Caroline only feels beautiful when she's in the water. Which is silly, really. Caroline could be really pretty if she made any effort. But maybe that's what happens to a person whose trophies are hidden away in a closet.*

Caroline rapped on the neighbors' door, hoping that Jewel was home. She'd seen Drew drive away in his truck but hadn't seen anybody in the passenger seat. Knowing this might be her only chance, she'd fled from her house and run next door.

It took a few minutes for anyone to answer, and Caroline was halfway down the back steps before Jewel opened the door, a surprised look on her face.

"Sorry I took so long. I was . . . reading."

Caroline tried hard to hide her surprise at how much Jewel resembled her mother, Shelby. It would take a while of being around her to get over the shock. But right now it was a little like seeing a ghost. She smiled. "That's all right. I'm sorry to disturb you."

Jewel shrugged. "It'll still be there when I get back to it." She looked at Caroline expectantly.

Caroline glanced back over her shoulder, making sure she didn't see her mother marching across the yard toward her. "Um, can I come in? I have a favor to ask."

"My dad's not here, but he should be back in a couple of hours."

"Actually, I wanted to talk with you."

Jewel moved back and Caroline entered the house, quickly closing the door behind her and effectively hiding her from her mother's sight. She felt all of thirteen years old again, sneaking out to the lake in the middle of the night with Jude.

The young girl motioned for her to follow. "Want a Coke or something?"

"Yes. Thanks." She tried not to be nosy as she followed Jewel's bouncing ponytail into the kitchen, but Caroline couldn't help but notice the incredible furniture that seemed to be crammed against every available wall. The pieces all reflected good lines and artistry, much like her trophy cabinet, and she wondered if they had all been made by the same man.

Caroline slid onto a black-painted bar stool, its four legs twisted like corkscrews. She resisted the urge to squat down next to the chair and examine it more closely and instead focused her attention on Jewel as the girl placed a Coke can in front of her and then, as if on second thought, pulled a glass from the cabinet and placed it on the counter.

Jewel sat down across from her on a matching stool and rested her chin in her hands. "So, what did you want to talk about?"

Those eyes were so disconcerting, Caroline faltered in her resolve as she stared into old eyes set in such a young face. To pull herself together, she took her time pouring her drink into the glass before taking a fortifying sip. She smiled. "I was wondering if I could use your phone."

Jewel looked at her for a moment in confusion. "Is yours out? I'll have to check, because ours is probably out, too. . . ."

"No, there's nothing wrong with our phones. I just needed to use one . . . in privacy." She smiled again. "My cell phone doesn't work out here, and my BlackBerry's at the bottom of the lake. I need to call my office in Atlanta, but my mother . . . Well, it's complicated. To avoid a conflict, I just thought I could pop over here on a semiregular basis to use your phone. I have a phone card, so there'd be no long-distance charges, and we could just sort of keep this between the two of us."

Caroline waited expectantly for a simple "fine" or "great," but instead Jewel sat across from her with a frown on her face and began gnawing at her bottom lip as if she were really contemplating a more complicated answer than "yes."

"I don't know. . . ."

"Well, I guess you could tell your dad if you'd prefer not to keep anything from him. Just as long as he knows not to mention it to my mother. I know Rainy would let me use her phone, except then I'd have to get in a car and drive instead of just walking next door."

Jewel continued to stare at her as she worried her lip. Then she smiled. "I think we can work something out."

"Work something out?"

"Yeah—like a bargain or trade or something."

Caroline narrowed her eyes. "What do you mean, 'a bargain or trade or something'? It won't cost you anything. All I'm trying to do is make some phone calls in peace."

"Oh, I understand that. I'm just seeing if I can somehow work this to my advantage."

Caroline almost smiled. "I see," she said, nodding her head slowly. "Sort of like, 'I'll scratch your back, and you'll scratch mine'?"

"Exactly." Jewel smiled broadly. "Except it would be more along the lines of you get to use my phone, and I get coaching."

For a long moment Caroline felt as if her head were being held underwater and she couldn't fill her lungs with air. "No," she finally managed.

"I'm a good swimmer. I know my dad doesn't think so, but I am. I just need a coach to help me be a more competitive swimmer so I can make the swim team. And I'd be a quick learner. . . ."

Caroline shook her head. "No. It's not that. It's just that . . . I can't. I haven't been in the water in almost thirteen years."

Jewel regarded her silently, her eyes probing where Caroline didn't want to go. "Why?"

*Why?* How could she explain something she didn't really understand herself? *Because I have a horrible scar that will show in a bathing suit? Because it reminds me of my dead brother?* "Because I haven't had time. I don't think I could even float now, so I couldn't possibly be the right person. . . ."

Jewel leaned forward. "I've seen your trophies. I think you're the perfect person to coach me." She smiled angelically. "Especially if you need to use the phone in peace."

Caroline stood abruptly, knocking over her empty Coke can. "I'll have to think about it."

Jewel stood too. "My mom died while swimming, you know. But I don't think she'd want me to stay away from the water. She'd have been the first person to kick my butt and push me into the lake and tell me to get over it."

A corner of Caroline's mouth turned up. "Yeah. That sounds like Shelby." And then she thought of the water again, of the cool weight of it against her bare skin. She could feel her heart beating heavily in her chest, the feeling of restlessness falling on her again. She needed to get outside. She needed to breathe. "I need to go. Thanks for the Coke." Taking deep breaths, she made her way to the back door without waiting for Jewel.

Jewel called out to her, "I'll see you Saturday."

Caroline turned back, a questioning look on her face.

"At dinner. Your mom invited me and my dad."

Caroline nodded slowly, then continued walking. Maybe if she walked fast enough she'd be back in Atlanta before anybody noticed.

Drew ran his hand over the smooth wood of the rocking chair, feeling the power of creation under his fingertips. He leaned forward and blew off a small scattering of sawdust, then straightened to get an overall perspective.

He'd have to wait and see what Mrs. Collier thought, but in his own mind it was perfection. The curves of the spindles and arms were soft and round, like a woman's body, the seat of the chair like the shape of feminine hips. He wasn't sure where the inspiration had come from; maybe it was the thoughts of Shelby that followed him while he worked. Maybe the outline of a woman's body embracing empty space was really what his life had become.

Drew propped the back door open, then hoisted the chair and carried it next door. As he approached the back steps he heard the halting notes of a piano. He set the chair down on the porch and paused a moment to listen.

He recognized the Chopin nocturne from one of Shelby's cassette tapes he kept in the glove box of his truck because he hadn't had the heart to give them away. The notes from the piano were choppy and unpracticed, but the depth of emotion erased all imperfections. The notes became music, and the music touched that part of him that he'd been able to reach only through woodcarving tools and sandpaper since Shelby's death. It refreshed him and unnerved him at the same time as he realized he had a fifty-fifty chance of figuring out who the pianist was.

He knocked on the door and the music immediately ceased as if turned off by a switch. There was a long pause and then the sound of footsteps walking across wood floors to the door. He forced a smile when Caroline answered.

She was barefoot and wore jean shorts and a high-necked T-shirt. Her hair was swept back in a ponytail and her face was bare of even a trace of makeup. Her skin was pale, as if it had been kept away from the sun for a very long time. A corner of his mouth quirked up. It would be like her, he thought, to shun the warmth and brightness of the sun, and he wondered again what had made her be like that.

"Was that you playing?"

Caroline turned her head over her shoulder as if seeking another person to answer. Drew followed her gaze to the upright piano set against the wall in the great room. The lid had been closed over the keys as if to hide the evidence. "Yes."

"Have you been playing for a long time?"

"No."

"That was Chopin, wasn't it?"

She sighed, as if the effort of issuing monosyllabic responses were too much for her. "Yes."

"Is your mother home?"

"No."

He shoved his hands in his pockets and looked away for a moment, trying not to grin. She reminded him so much of Jewel's prepubescent attitude it was hard to believe that Caroline wasn't thirteen. And then he remembered the smile that had radiated from her face when she'd been examining the quilt in Rainy Days, and he looked back at Caroline, trying to fathom where that woman was and why she was kept hidden.

Drew nodded toward the rocking chair on the porch floor beside him. "I've brought a chair over for your mother on approval. If she likes it, I can make three more for her."

Caroline glanced over at the chair as if noticing it for the first time. She left her position as guardian of the back door and placed both hands on the arms of the chair. Slowly she slid her hands around the curved headrest and down the rest of the chair until she reached the rockers at the bottom. It was like watching a woman caress a new lover for the first time, and Drew had to look away for a moment.

Finally she said, "It's very feminine, isn't it? It reminds me of a pregnant woman almost. Sort of lush and round and ripe. I've never seen anything like it."

Drew stared at her in surprise. *Lush and round and ripe.* Those were the same words that had bounced around his head as he'd been making the chair. He shifted the chair over so that the seat of it was facing Caroline. "Do you want to take it for a trial spin?"

She gave him a tentative smile before sitting down, placing her hands on the armrests, closing her eyes, and leaning her head back. She was swallowed by the chair like a child in her mother's arms, and for the second time since he'd known her he saw the wariness leave her face. Once again he was intrigued by this woman and the masks she wore and wondered if getting beneath them would be worth the bruises he'd have to endure.

She pushed her feet against the porch floor and rocked back and forth a few times before opening her eyes again, and for a moment Drew was broadsided by their gray-green intensity. Until she spoke. "You could make a fortune mass-producing your furniture. I've seen only two pieces up close, but if there's more where this stuff came from, the sky's the limit."

Something deflated inside of him. He'd thought for a moment that she understood that what she was sitting in wasn't just a piece of furniture. He should have realized that he'd known her long enough to have known better.

He leaned over her. "Get up. Please," he added.

She stood, obviously annoyed. "It's just silly for you to be selling your furniture piece by piece at Rainy's when you could be making a lot of money. Trust me—I know a lot about it. I've worked for a furniture manufacturer for over ten years. Kobylt Brothers Furniture— maybe you've heard of them?"

Drew lifted the chair and moved it to safety at the other side of the porch. "I'm not interested."

"Why not? Your pieces are so unique. I could see an entire line coming from just a few of your designs. It could even be called the Drew . . ." She paused, and he could see she was having trouble coming up with his last name. He didn't enlighten her.

Caroline waved her hand through the air. "Well, whatever. It could be a big deal for you."

"I don't want or need a big deal. I'm happy the way things are." Despite his words, he felt the old spark ignite inside of him. *It's been so long.* Pushing the thought away, he moved toward the porch steps. "Just tell your mother I was here and to let me know if she wants more of these chairs."

She followed him with a determined gait. "Can I come see your workroom and check out more of your stuff? I'd love to tell my boss—"

"No." He cut her off and kept walking.

She had the decency to stay on the bottom step instead of following him home like a lost puppy. "I just want to come and see what else—"

He turned abruptly, keeping his anger tightly in check. If there was one thing he had learned from his father it was that the only thing anger ever guaranteed was an awkward apology later. "What part of 'no' didn't you understand? Maybe in Atlanta it's different, but up here in the mountains it means 'absolutely, positively no, not ever.' " He turned back around and continued walking.

"Don't just walk away from me! I'm trying to help you, and you won't even give me the time of day to listen to a possibly lucrative business arrange—"

He heard something scrape against wood and then shatter, and for a moment he thought she'd thrown something at him. But when he turned around to look he saw a pot and its bright red geranium splattered on the cement walkway at the bottom of the porch steps, and Caroline was slumped next to it on the bottom step, where she'd apparently fallen and knocked over the pot. One pale arm clung to the railing, preventing her body from joining the unfortunate plant.

He reached her in several long strides and was alarmed at how blanched the skin on her face appeared. He placed the back of his hand to her cheek, then drew it back, the feel of it reminding him of Shelby after they had pulled her from the water.

"Where can I find your mother?"

She had managed to fold herself in half and had her forehead resting on her knees. She didn't look at him, but her voice was full of alarm. "No! I'll be all right. I just got a little light-headed, that's all. I'll be fine in a minute."

He looked at her doubtfully. "Can I at least bring you inside? Call a doctor?"

She shook her head in response, her forehead still pressed into her knees.

"Go jump in the lake?" The side of her cheek wrinkled and he knew she was smiling.

"Now there's a thought."

Relieved that she seemed like herself, he straightened. "I'm going to get you a glass of water and some damp washcloths. I'll be right back."

Surprisingly she didn't argue, so he went inside and quickly found what he was looking for, as well as a cordless phone, and he picked it up, too. When he returned he saw that she hadn't moved from her turtle-in-a-shell position, her face pressed neatly against the tops of her knees.

He squatted next to her. "Do you want to move to the lounge chair? You might be more comfortable, and the view is better."

She sent him a sharp look, and he was sure now that she was on the road to recovery. She didn't brush away his hands when he bent to help her up, so he knew she wasn't totally herself yet. He settled her into the lounge chair and handed her the glass of water. She took brief little sips, as if she were suspicious of too much of a good thing.

She leaned her head back, and Drew placed one of the washcloths on her forehead. He moved forward to pull the neck of her T-shirt down so it wouldn't get wet from the second washcloth, but she pushed his hand away, a look of panic crossing her face, then pulled at the neck of her shirt to raise it higher.

"I'm fine. I don't need another one."

"But if you put this on your neck, it will cool you off quicker."

"I don't want it." She paused for a moment. "But thank you."

He sat down on the edge of an adjacent Adirondack chair and placed the unused washcloth next to him. "Are you going to be okay? I still think I should call your mother or at least a doctor."

Caroline shook her head. "No. Really. I'll be fine."

He rested his elbows on his thighs and steepled his fingers. "Does this happen often?"

She didn't answer right away. "It didn't used to. It's happened a couple of times at work—which is why I'm here now. I'm supposed to be staying calm and getting better." She opened one eye and looked at him meaningfully. "But that doesn't seem to be happening."

She closed her eyes again, and he stared down at her pale, fragile skin and saw the blue veins on her hands and arms. Whether or not it was what she'd intended to do, the guilt hit him hard and deep. His father had done a pretty good job of teaching him all about guilt, and Drew had been an avid learner.

Drew was pretty sure he wasn't the one who'd been arguing before Caroline had collapsed on the porch steps. But when he saw her with her eyes closed and her physical frailty more evident, the guilt almost overwhelmed him. And when he thought of the way she'd looked the one time he'd seen her smile, and he'd seen the woman beneath the mask, he knew it was more than guilt that made him open his mouth.

"Are you supposed to be doing anything while you're here besides relaxing? Like exercising or something?"

She seemed to answer reluctantly. "Yeah—I'm supposed be doing light cardio. But unless I missed it, there doesn't seem to be a gym in Hart's Valley."

He couldn't help himself and laughed out loud. "You don't need a gym to exercise, you know. There are miles and miles of forest trails here on Hart's Peak."

"I know that. But it rains a lot and sometimes it's too hot or cold to be outside. It's a lot easier in a gym."

He snorted and she opened her eyes. "And here I was thinking you were the resident and I was the visitor." He smirked. "Tourist."

She threw the washcloth from her forehead at him but he caught it before it made contact. "I know a lot more about this mountain and valley than you'll ever know. My family has owned this house for almost forty-five years, and I've been coming here since I was in diapers. You can't call *me* the tourist." She looked away for a moment, and she seemed to be grappling for the right words and the right attitude to say them with. Lifting her chin, she said, "And I don't want to be caught out on a trail somewhere and have . . . an episode . . . without help nearby."

He had a good idea what it must have taken for her to admit to that chink in her armor. Despite the lift of her chin, he had seen her vulnerability. It had reminded him suddenly of Shelby, of the way she had always faced the world as a strong, independent woman, but whose eyes held depths of loss and secrets he had never felt privy to.

Drew sat back. "I'm not suggesting you go alone. I'd like to learn more about the back hills and places only the locals know about. You could be my tour guide, and you'd be getting good exercise, too."

She frowned and he added, "And I promise not to talk to you at all."

Her head fell back against the lounge chair again and she crossed her arms over her chest. She smirked. "There's a trail at the top of the mountain where people fall off all the time. I'd be happy to show you that one."

His desire to help her diminished somewhat, but unfortunately the guilt did not. "Thanks for the offer, but I'm sure there're trails closer to the valley and lake that might be more fun for both of us. I'd learn about my new home and you'd get your exercise and pass the time more quickly so you can return to Atlanta and whatever it is you do there."

"I'm an accountant."

"And I never would have guessed that."

She narrowed her eyes at him again in an expression that was beginning to be very familiar.

"So . . . what do you say? I think it would be a nice, easy trade."

She snorted. "You're a lot like Jewel, you know? God forbid either one of you ever does something just to be nice."

"To you?" Now it was his turn to snort. "You're not really the type to inspire the warm fuzzies, are you? People need to have some kind of reciprocal guarantee in their dealings with you to make sure they're not turned to stone or something."

She began to sit up but he held her shoulders firmly back against the chair. "Now don't go getting upset again or I *will* call your mother." She relaxed but glared at him as he stood to leave. "Just think about it and let me know." He moved the phone closer to her so she could reach it, then wrote his phone number down on the cover of a magazine that was lying next to it. "I'll be home if you need anything."

"Like a gun?" She smiled sweetly at him and he couldn't resist smiling back.

"Don't give me any ideas." He started to turn away before he re-membered something she'd said earlier. "What did you mean about Jewel and me being just alike?"

She waved her hand in the air. "Nothing important—just that she drives a hard bargain."

"Yeah, that sounds like Jewel. I'll take that as a compliment."

Caroline raised an eyebrow but didn't say anything. She lay back once more on the chair and watched him as he turned around again, and for a moment she looked like a tiny, helpless kitten . . . with very, very sharp claws.

He was almost to his back door when he heard her call out, "Thank you." He turned around to look and saw that she'd already turned her head away.

"You're welcome," he called back, then let himself into the house.

# CHAPTER 7

❧

JEWEL LEANED HER BIKE AGAINST THE WINDOW WITH THE FOR SALE sign in it, then climbed the steps to her grandmother's shop. It was still early in the morning, and Jewel was glad to see there were no customers parked in front of Rainy Days. She opened the unlocked door, not even bothering to test it first. It was one of things she enjoyed most about living in Hart's Valley. In Charleston you locked everything, and her dad would never have allowed her to ride her bike anywhere except the driveway behind locked gates. She enjoyed the freedom and the way she could watch the sky fade from blue to purple at the end of the day without city lights and lots of buildings to block the way. Not that she would ever admit any of it to her dad.

The bells chimed as she got a whiff of rose potpourri and bolts of new fabric and something else that she called magic. She wouldn't describe it to anyone that way, but the smell of Rainy Days was very much magic. Maybe it was because it was there she felt her mother the most. Sometimes she even imagined that she saw her over near the cash register where Rainy kept the jars of candy and gumballs. Being here made her feel not so alone in the world anymore.

"Back here!" her grandmother shouted, and Jewel followed the voice to the back room, where quilting scraps were now littering the table and floor as if a tree full of them had been shaken and the fabric leaves allowed to land wherever they would.

Rainy was poised at the sewing machine table in the corner, threading the bobbin, and looked up over the tops of her bifocals. "Hi, sweetie. Your dad called and said you were on your way over."

Jewel rolled her eyes. "Why don't you call him back and say that a rabid deer attacked me, then carried me off to his evil lair to pelt me with fern fronds."

Rainy took off her glasses and stood so she could hug Jewel. "Now, now—he's your father, and it's his job to worry about you and make sure you're safe. Besides, we don't have ferns here, so he'd know I was lying."

They smiled at each other before Rainy pulled away and began looking at the fabric scraps strewn across the table. "I'm looking for some yellow satin with appliquéd daisies—it's from a formal dress your mother wore in high school. I know it was here yesterday, but I can't seem to find it anywhere now that I need it."

Jewel bent over the table and began looking, her fingers outstretched as she sifted through colors and patterns and memories. She stole a glance at her grandmother. "Was Mom a big football fan?"

Rainy shook her head, concentrating on the bright colors beneath her hands. "Not really. Well, not until Jude started playing. He'd made the football team here at the high school before his dad moved them all to Atlanta. He was a real star—the youngest quarterback we'd had for a long time." Rainy's head was bent forward, but Jewel could see the creases in her cheek as she smiled. "He sure loved that game. I don't know if he ever played again once they moved, which was a real shame."

"So he didn't graduate from Hart's Peak High School?"

Rainy paused, her hands still. "No, sweetie. Jude never graduated. He died his senior year. But I know he always had plans to join his graduating class here at Hart's Peak, at least for the ceremony. I don't think he really ever called Atlanta home."

Jewel was about to ask another question when the bell above the door chimed, followed quickly by the sound of the door slamming.

Rainy shouted, "Back here, Caroline."

Jewel looked at her with raised eyebrows, and Rainy looked back with the same expression.

"Her mother called right after your dad did to let me know Caroline was on her way."

Jewel almost laughed as they both turned to see Caroline enter.

Caroline didn't see Jewel at first as she walked into the cluttered room. But when she spotted her with her red hair tied back in a ponytail she thought for a moment she was seeing Shelby's ghost. It wasn't a frightening feeling at all. Instead Caroline almost felt relief, as if asking for forgiveness were still within reach.

She continued walking toward Rainy and held up a bag from Rich's department store. "I hope you don't mind my just popping in. My mother asked me to bring this to you."

Rainy took the small brown bag and opened it. She pulled out a sample-size jar with a screw-on lid and read the label out loud. "I can't read the French words, but I can read this part in English: 'For the mature skin.'" She frowned. "Can't think why your mother would be sending this to me." She dropped the jar back into the bag and placed it under her sewing table. "Think I'll put some on my butt and make sure I tell her how soft it is next time I see her."

Jewel laughed out loud, and Caroline grinned in her direction before turning back to Rainy. "Maybe we should trade, then. She gave me some hemorrhoid cream to shrink the pores on my nose and cheeks."

Rainy snorted. "Remind me before you leave to go hunt down a can of WD-40 for you to give to your mother. You can tell her it's for her creaky joints."

Jewel laughed again. "I've gotta run. I've got things to do, and I need to be fast or my dad will report me missing." She sent Caroline a meaningful glance. "And I'll see you tonight."

Caroline raised her hand in farewell. She hadn't even thought about the deal Jewel had suggested in the few days since they had spoken about it. It was ridiculous, really. She wasn't going to let a thirteen-year-old force her into going back into the water; she'd avoided that for over a decade. Besides, she had alternatives.

"Do you mind if I use your phone?"

Rainy looked up over her bifocals. "Not if you're using it to call your office in Atlanta. Margaret gave me strict orders not to allow you to sneak behind her back and get yourself all stressed-out again. She said your boss has made arrangements for your absence and there's no need to check in. You're here to rest, remember."

Caroline felt somehow betrayed. It had always been her and Rainy against the world. And for a while her dad had been on her side, too. "If I don't keep tabs on things while I'm away, it will be even more stressful when I return. I don't plan on getting worked up just by talking for a few minutes on the phone."

Rainy sat back down behind the sewing machine and began replacing the bobbin. "Drew told me what happened yesterday on your front porch. Be thankful I haven't told Margaret about it. She'd have you strapped down in a chair where you couldn't escape."

Heat flooded Caroline's face as she recalled how she'd almost fainted and how Drew had been the one to witness it. She supposed she should be thankful that he hadn't mentioned it to her mother.

"I just forgot to breathe deeply, that's all. I got a little light-headed—nothing serious and certainly nothing my mother needs to know."

Rainy raised her eyebrows again. "She loves you, you know."

Caroline picked up a portion of faded yellow satin with appliquéd daisies hanging on by single threads. "Yeah. Like a Venus fly-trap loves a fly. Sometimes I wonder if I should have gone to live with my dad."

Rainy gave her full attention to Caroline. "No, you don't. And don't ever say that in Margaret's hearing or you'll answer to me. There are things you don't understand that your mother had to deal with after . . . after Jude died. Just believe me when I tell you that the best thing for you was to remain with your mama. I know you two have always had difficulty seeing eye-to-eye, but that's only because you're so much alike."

"We're nothing alike. That's why I miss my dad. We used to be able to talk about anything."

Rainy took off her glasses and began rubbing the lenses with the hem of her shirt. "When's the last time he called you just to talk?"

"I . . . He's a doctor, Rainy—you know that. He doesn't have a lot of time." Caroline felt flustered. Rainy always had a way of peeling off all the layers and leaving the stinking onion. Except she was wrong about Margaret. "And my mom and I are completely different. We have nothing in common."

Rainy just snorted.

Unsettled, Caroline looked down at the shimmery yellow fabric she'd been holding and stared at the desperately clinging flowers, faded and with curled corners, but somehow still attached to the bright satin. She felt an odd sort of kinship with them.

The unsettled feeling hit her again, and with a flick of her wrist she tossed the scrap onto the table. Rainy looked up. "Hey, let me see that. I've been looking for that piece of material all morning."

Caroline picked it up again and held it out to Rainy. "And why are you using a sewing machine? You'd be banned for life from any quilting circles if that got around, you know."

Rainy smirked. "Yes, well, we'll keep this between you and me, okay? Besides, I'm just using the machine to do some mending and hemming of the fabric squares. My arthritis is getting so bad that it's hard to do the small handwork." She gave a heavy sigh and took the fabric.

Caroline noticed how thin her arm was, and how the once strong and capable hand seemed almost transparent, like a brittle oak leaf left on the ground too long. She knelt by the sewing table and looked up into Rainy's face. "How are you doing? Really. Mom said you'd finished your last chemo treatment, but that doesn't tell me anything. I want the truth. I'm not delicate, regardless of what she's been saying."

Rainy touched Caroline's cheek, her finger callused from years of quilting, of pushing needles in and out of fabric, stitching pieces together. That was how Caroline had always thought of her: the solid presence that always held the loose scraps of her life together. Caroline felt the panic grab hold.

The older woman smiled. "I'm not done with this world yet, hon, so don't be fretting." She sighed and dropped her finger. "I do get more tired than I used to, and I sure do wish I had more help with this quilt for Jewel."

Caroline knew that had been aimed directly at her, and her eyes dropped from Rainy's face. She'd once loved the feel of pushing a needle through fabric, the ability to lose herself for hours creating lively, colorful quilts for other people. It had been her way of getting inside people's lives in a way her innate shyness otherwise prevented. It had made her popular and sought after, and for the first time existing in the same social circles Jude had become accustomed to since birth.

She recalled the memory quilt she'd started making for Jude before he'd died, that had somehow disappeared in the lost months following his funeral, months she couldn't recall even now. Oddly, all she could remember from that time were colors—of wet leaves, gray skies, and the stark white walls of a hospital room. And when she'd finally returned home, Jude's quilt was gone.

Caroline looked at the fabric Rainy still held in her hand. "What's this one from?"

"A dress Shelby wore at the junior prom. She asked Jude to come up from Atlanta for it. She didn't care that he was an underclassman— she wouldn't go with anybody else. They were like that, you know. Inseparable."

"I remember." The old grief rose to the surface, and Caroline stood. "I can't help you, you know. I'd like to, but I can't. Anything that reminds me of him . . . I just . . . can't."

Rainy took off her glasses. "Do you think I don't understand that? Don't you think I grieved when Shelby died?" She leaned forward, her eyes narrowing. "But I wasn't the one who died. I still have a life to live, and I try my best every day to live it to the fullest. Shelby wouldn't have wanted it any other way."

Caroline was silent for a moment, unable to find the words to make Rainy understand. "How did it happen? Shelby, I mean."

"She was on vacation on Sullivan's Island. She was swimming and had a brain aneurysm and drowned before anyone could bring her in to shore." She drew a deep breath. "Jewel was with her. She tried as hard as she could to swim back carrying her mother, and she's a good swimmer, but she was only ten. Her little muscles just weren't strong enough, and she would have drowned, too, if help hadn't arrived when it did."

Caroline let that sink in for a moment as she thought of the calm and cool Jewel struggling with the body of her mother and trying to bring her to shore. "Where was Drew?"

Rainy's fingers plucked at the yellow fabric on the sewing table as if trying to bring it back to life. "He'd had every intention of being there, but he had to stay in Charleston for an extra day to get some work done before joining Shelby and Jewel." She looked squarely up at Caroline. "Sometimes punishing ourselves for bad choices in our past isn't the best way to live our future."

Caroline rubbed her eyes. "No, probably not." She wondered for a moment if she should share with Rainy what she'd never told anybody before—about the dreams she'd had after Jude's death. But then she looked up at the fragile woman, at the scarf that covered a nearly bald head, and knew she couldn't burden her with one more thing.

Caroline walked back to the table and swept her hand through the sea of fabric, her fingers briefly clutching at memories before letting them go. "Jewel's headaches—does she get them often?"

Rainy nodded. "Too often. We've taken her to doctors and had all sorts of tests, and the only thing they've been able to do for her is tell her what not to eat and give her strong pills to make the pain easier to take." She snorted.

"I was just wondering, you know, with Shelby having a brain aneurysm . . ."

"Her daddy and I were concerned about that, too. That's why we took her to a specialist in California last summer. He said that there's nothing wrong with Jewel, and what happened to her mama was a one-of-a-kind event and not something Jewel could have inherited."

"That's good." She drew a deep breath to finally broach the subject she'd come to discuss, but her next words were drowned out by the ringing of the telephone.

Rainy picked up the cordless by her feet on the third ring.

"Yes, she's here. Yes, I got the package. No, don't know if I'll use it—not on my face, anyway." There was silence for a few minutes, then, "Yes, I'll do that."

Rainy hung up the phone, then looked at Caroline. "That was your mother. She wanted to make sure that you'd gotten here safely. And she wants me to let her know when you leave so she'll know when to expect you."

Caroline rolled her eyes. "This is insane. I am not twelve years old." She held up her hand to deflect anything Rainy might say in defense of Margaret. "I don't want to get into this now—that's not what I came here for. I actually wanted to talk to you about selling Rainy Days."

Rainy pushed back her chair from the sewing table and stretched out her legs as if she were preparing to watch a show. Caroline leaned against the table, her arms crossed over her chest, and cleared her throat. "I don't think you should sell it—not to Drew, at least."

Rainy raised an eyebrow.

"He doesn't know the first thing about marketing. I mean, he's creating one-of-a-kind pieces that could make him a sheer fortune if he'd allow them to be mass-produced, but he doesn't want to do that. Imagine what he'd do to your store with an attitude like that—'if it's popular don't sell it.' He'd run it into the ground within a year."

Warm brown eyes contemplated Caroline for a long moment. "Have you had much of a chance to get to know Drew?"

"No—thankfully. No offense, of course, to Shelby, but the man seems a little . . . slow." Grudgingly, she added, "Although he makes the most beautiful pieces of furniture I think I have ever seen."

Rainy's mouth quirked a bit. "Um-hmm. Well, it's too late now. It's a done deal. I'm planning on sticking around until the end of the year, and then he'll take over. We're having the contracts drawn up now."

Caroline straightened. "But . . . but the 'for sale' sign is still in the window. Surely this is still negotiable."

Rainy stood and made her way through the kitchen to the front of the store with Caroline following close behind. "I'd forgotten I had that there. I'll take care of that right now." She reached into the window display and plucked out the sign. "There. Done."

Caroline felt the unmistakable urge to cry. "But, Rainy, this can't be the end of it."

Rainy put her arm around Caroline's shoulders and started leading her back toward the kitchen. "Honey, every ending is just really a beginning of something different. I know Drew's heart isn't into owning a country store up in the middle of nowhere. But I also know he'll do his best by it until he figures out what he really should be doing."

Caroline stopped walking and looked up at Rainy. "And what would that be?"

Rainy just shook her head and continued to propel Caroline toward the back of the old house. "Hell if I know. But we all have to figure out what we want to be when we grow up—no matter how old we are. It just takes some people longer than others to find out what that is." She looked pointedly at Caroline, making her squirm.

"But Drew needs this right now. He has a lot of guilt—thinking he should have been there with Shelby, that maybe she wouldn't have died if he had been. Things had been . . . well, difficult in their marriage for a few years. I guess he felt for whatever reason that he needed to work constantly to prove himself to his father, even if it meant taking time away from Shelby and Jewel. And something . . . changed in him after Jewel was born."

She shook her head slightly at the confused look Caroline wore. "No, it wasn't like that—he adored his daughter. And loved Shelby. I've just never been able to figure it out." She walked toward the kitchen. "Anyway, this is something he needs right now—for him and Jewel both. He'll work through it and move on, which will be the best thing for everyone involved. A person can't move forward if he keeps his feet glued to the ground."

She sent another pointed look at Caroline, but before Caroline could respond, Rainy said, "Come on into the kitchen with me and I'll make us some tea. Then you can help me oil the hinges on my back door with that stuff your mama sent."

Caroline pushed back the need to defend herself and allowed a reluctant smile to tug at her lips as she followed Rainy through the kitchen door.

*December 26, 1986*

*Jude has come back. He talked his family into spending Christmas up in the mountains even though it's tradition for them to spend it at their grandmother's in Savannah. But*

*Mama says Jude could talk the blue down from the sky, and I think she's right.*

*Jude, Caroline, and I went hiking today all the way up to poor old Ophelia. Legend says that a long, long time ago she was a real woman who was cursed and turned to stone. We had our picnic lunch right on the ledge under her nose and Jude made us laugh until our sides hurt with all these booger jokes.*

*We spent a lot of time talking about Ophelia and what she must have done that was so bad. I said I couldn't imagine anything worse than being turned to stone—to be forced to watch other people's lives and not be a part of it. Jude said the only thing worse would be to be alone without friends and family. That made a lot of sense to me because Jude always seems to be in the middle of a crowd. But the weird thing was that Caroline said nothing at all.*

# CHAPTER 8

PIANO MUSIC FLOATED FROM INSIDE THE HOUSE INTO THE COOL, damp air as Drew stood uncomfortably on the Colliers' front porch. But this time it was a lively scherzo with none of the minor chords he'd heard Caroline play before that made him think of the deep end of the ocean.

Jewel slouched against the railing behind him, trying to look bored. She'd brushed her hair and pulled it back in a thick ponytail, showing off bright silver earrings in the shape of crescent moons. With a start, he realized that they had been Shelby's.

The door opened and Margaret Collier smiled broadly as she stood there wearing a flowing silk caftan, something Elizabeth Taylor might have worn in her heyday. "I thought I heard someone knocking—I didn't realize the music was on so loud." She opened the door wider for her guests to come inside.

Drew motioned for Jewel to precede him into the house as they followed Mrs. Collier inside. He looked around for Caroline. "I didn't realize it was the stereo. I thought it might have been Caroline on the piano."

Margaret closed the door and began herding them into the great room. "Oh, no. Caroline doesn't know how to play a note. Her brother was quite gifted, but I could never convince Caroline to give it a try."

Jewel paused by a large framed picture on the far wall as Drew followed Margaret, feeling confused. "But I heard her play—and she was pretty good, if I recall correctly."

He felt Caroline's presence behind him before she spoke. "When I'm bored I sometimes sit at the piano and play random keys. I guess to the untrained ear it could sound like Chopin."

Drew turned to look at Caroline to see if she was joking, but she met his gaze with a half smile that would have fooled him if he hadn't seen the flash of desperation in her eyes.

Margaret indicated a spot on the sofa for him to sit before she turned her attention to her daughter. "We're going to have a drink first so you'll have time to change for dinner."

"I did change." She indicated her T-shirt and jeans.

Her mother's perfectly lined eyebrows rose. "But you're wearing jeans."

Caroline's expression matched her mother's like a mirror image, and Drew suppressed a laugh.

"And you're wearing a nightgown."

Margaret's lips tightened in a smile. "Why don't you take drink orders, dear. I have a papaya-and-spinach smoothie in the refrigerator for you."

Drew felt as if he should be keeping score, but the barbs were flying so fast he was afraid he'd lose track. Jewel came up to stand beside him and he realized she was also wearing jeans. He felt as if he'd made some huge social gaffe, but Margaret appeared not to have noticed. It seemed almost as if everyone was off her radar screen except her daughter.

Jewel tugged on Caroline's arm. "Come on; I'll help."

Drew looked at the retreating form of his daughter, seeing Shelby in every step she took. It wasn't just the red hair or the tilt of her head—it had more to do with the human awareness that had always appeared to guide Shelby's actions. It had never bothered him that Jewel seemed not to have inherited a single thing from him. She had received the best from Shelby, and that was enough.

When they took their seats at the dining table, Caroline pulled her linen napkin out of its ring and looked pointedly at her mother, and Margaret answered with a matching expression. Caroline wordlessly put the napkin in her lap. Drew wasn't exactly sure what that had been about, but he could at least see who'd won that round. *Score one for Margaret.* He smiled, then quickly coughed into his napkin.

Margaret looked up at her daughter. "Where's your medicine?"

A slight flush appeared on Caroline's pale cheeks. "I'll take it later."

Margaret folded her napkin and put it next to her plate as she stood. "You know your stomach tolerates the pills better if you take them with a meal. I'll go get them."

Caroline looked down in her lap, her cheeks now flaming red and a small tic visible in her jaw, as if she were clenching her teeth very tightly. Her chest was moving in and out very rapidly, and he could hear the breath whistle out of her mouth. She reminded him of Shelby in childbirth, practicing the breathing techniques she had learned in her Lamaze classes when she was pregnant, and he had the absurd urge to laugh.

Margaret appeared with a green slushy concoction—presumably the papaya-and-spinach smoothie—and placed it next to the glass of iced tea Caroline had poured for herself. Then Margaret placed four pills of varying colors and sizes next to the glass before seating herself again.

"Could you please pass the bread?" Drew asked, trying to switch everybody's attention from Caroline, whose chin now seemed to be firmly pressed into her chest in an apparent attempt to disappear.

"What are those pills for?" Jewel asked at the same time.

Unfortunately, Jewel was sitting on the far end of the table from him, so he couldn't pinch her. Along with all the good traits she'd inherited from Shelby, she'd also received an uncanny forthrightness that took no prisoners.

Caroline finally lifted her head from her chest, meeting Jewel's eyes. "They're organ transplant antirejection drugs. I have to take them every day of my life." She took the breadbasket and handed it to Drew as if she had just made a comment about the weather.

Jewel's eyes widened. "Wow," she said, and Drew did a quick mental calculation to see if his leg was long enough to reach under the table and kick her gently in the shins. It wasn't. "What sort of organ transplant did you have?"

Without blinking, Caroline faced Jewel again. "Heart. I had a heart transplant."

Drew saw Jewel lean forward, as if prepared to play Twenty

Questions. Without thinking, he picked up the breadbasket and knocked it into the glass of thick green liquid, sending its contents spilling out onto the white linen tablecloth and Caroline's pale pink T-shirt.

They all sat in appalled silence for a brief moment, watching the spread of green form abstract elementary artwork. At the same moment, all four of them stood and began mopping up smoothie and moving plates and silverware out of the way. Caroline mumbled a quick, "Excuse me, I need to go change," then turned from the table and walked away without another word.

Caroline sat on the edge of her bed and stared at her reflection in the mirror, not really seeing the pink shirt with the growing green stain across the chest. Instead she saw the white walls and white ceilings of a hospital room, could almost feel the tubes in her arms and smell the sickly clean aroma that had clung to her skin and hair.

She closed her eyes, not wanting the memories to take her to the places that had led up to the hospital room. She rubbed her arms hard, turning the skin pink and waiting for the burning sensation to bring her back into the present. Standing, she slid the soiled shirt over her head and tossed it in her bathroom sink to soak. Her serviceable white cotton bra was tinged green on the left cup, and it soon joined the shirt in the sink.

Pulling open the lingerie drawer, she dug past all the lacy confections her mother had sent her from Victoria's Secret that still had the tags on, and pulled out a plain beige racer-back bra whose straps had begun to fray. After yanking a T-shirt from another drawer, she turned her back on her reflection, unwilling to look at the puckered pink scar that bisected her chest like a line of demarcation outlining the before and after of her life.

The neck of the shirt snagged on her ponytail as a soft knock sounded on the door. Resigned to another confrontation with her mother, Caroline faced the door with her head and arms still stuck in the top of the shirt. "Come in."

"It's me."

Caroline recognized Jewel's voice and gave a huge tug on her shirt, yanking so hard on her ponytail it made her eyes water. Jewel's face peered at her through a crack in the door, a wide smile on her face. "Room service." She bumped the door open wider with her rear end, then leaned over to pick something up before entering the room. She carried the breadbasket that had been spared the green deluge, and Caroline's untouched glass of iced tea. "You didn't come back right away, and I thought you might be hungry."

Without being asked, Jewel sat on the bed next to Caroline and held out the bread. Unable to deny the hunger pangs that had been hitting her at regular intervals for over an hour, Caroline took a wheat roll and bit into it. "Did you bring any butter?"

Jewel shook her head. "There wasn't any on the table—I guess your mom doesn't believe in it or something."

Caroline rolled her eyes and took another bite. "Thanks anyway."

"I also brought these. I figure they must be important." Jewel opened her hand to display the four pills Caroline's mother had put on the table. "I've never met anyone who's had a transplant before."

Caroline stared at the pills suspiciously. "Did my mother send you in here?"

Jewel shook her head. "They're busy cleaning up. The smell of that smoothie was going to make me puke, so I figured I'd come see you instead." She picked up her own bread roll with her free hand and took a bite.

Caroline grabbed the pills and started popping them one by one, followed by a gulp of iced tea, until they were gone.

Jewel looked at her with somber eyes. "What are those for?"

Caroline leaned back on outstretched arms. "So my body doesn't treat the heart as a foreign object and reject it. The other pills are to counteract the side effects of the antirejection drugs." There was something about the girl that made her easy to talk to. Caroline thought it might have been her eyes, and the way they reminded her so much of Shelby. Or maybe it was the open attitude Jewel had about her that made her seem so nonjudgmental. Or maybe it was because it was easy to talk to someone who didn't know the whole truth and couldn't be appalled by it.

They sat for a few minutes on the bed, quietly chewing their bread rolls and listening to the clink of china and silverware from the other side of the door. Jewel finally broke the silence.

"So, are you going to coach me?"

Caroline gave a deep sigh. She wasn't prepared for this conversation at all. "I haven't decided."

Jewel turned to look at her again with those eyes that seemed so much older than her face. "Does your not wanting to do it have anything to do with that scar on your chest?"

The air seemed to thin, and Caroline was left gasping for breath. How could she know? Her hand clutched at the part of her shirt that covered the scar, and she was unable to answer.

Jewel continued: "It's probably not the scar itself but something else—something that it reminds you of?"

Caroline narrowed her eyes and stared at Jewel. "I don't want to talk about this."

"I don't want to talk about it, either. I just want you to coach me to be a better competitive swimmer." She leaned back on her arms, imitating the way Caroline had been sitting just a few minutes before. "My mom loved this lady called Eleanor Roosevelt. She was a president's wife, you know? And my mom had this book of quotes where she'd cut out her favorite ones and hang them on our refrigerator, or tack them on my bulletin board in my room if she thought I needed it." She sent Caroline a half smile. "Anyway, her favorite quote was one from Eleanor that said something like, 'Find the one thing that scares you the most and do it.'"

Goose bumps filtered down Caroline's spine, as if somebody had blown a breath on the back of her neck. It was the same thing Shelby had told her on the day that Caroline had finally found the strength to get up out of her hospital bed and begin her life again.

Caroline cleared her throat, unable to meet Jewel's eyes. "So what's that got to do with me?"

Jewel leaned toward Caroline, their foreheads almost touching, and spoke softly. "I'm afraid of the water. And that's why I have to make the swim team."

Caroline closed her eyes, seeing the ten-year-old Jewel struggling to bring her mother's body in to shore. She opened her eyes, gasping for breath as if she had drowned but had somehow found the strength to break above the surface at the last moment. Caroline looked at Jewel and felt the oddest impulse to hug this strange, brave girl. There was something about the set of her shoulders and the firm jut of her jaw that seemed to give Caroline strength, too. *Find the one thing that scares you the most and do it.*

Caroline wiped her hands over her face and took a deep breath. "Okay. I'll coach you. But I'm not getting in the water. I can do a good enough job on the sidelines."

A look of triumph passed over Jewel's face. "All right! Can we start Tuesday? School starts on Monday, but I figure I can just start getting up early to get my swimming done before the school bus comes at eight thirty. My dad usually leaves for Rainy Days at seven thirty every weekday—he's learning the business from Rainy, so he's there most mornings. I figure we can start at seven thirty-five."

Caroline stared at Jewel's eager expression, trying to remember the last time she had felt like that. But all she could recall was the cold numbness that had taken over her body thirteen years before. She smiled wearily. "How about seven forty, just to make sure. And I'll talk to my mother about keeping it under wraps from your dad."

Jewel nearly bounced off the bed. "I can't wait!" She picked up the breadbasket and the empty water glass. "I'll bring the gelatin powder—I heard somewhere that it's what swimmers use to give them an extra boost of energy."

Tucking her knees under her chin, Caroline smiled. "I like cherry flavored, by the way."

Jewel opened the door and paused for a moment. "Are you not allowed to go in the water because of your heart?"

Caroline paused a moment before answering. "Not exactly. I'm a little more susceptible to infection than most people, so my doctors would want me to swim in a chlorinated pool instead of a lake.

But I'm supposed to be as active as the next person. I just choose not to swim anymore."

Jewel stared at her for a long moment with Shelby's eyes. "Okay, then. Tuesday morning at seven forty on the dock. There's a community center with a pool in Truro we can use when the weather gets nasty and when I'm ready to be timed. I figured we can use the lake at first to work on my strokes."

"Sounds like a plan." Caroline waved her hand. "Tell my mom I'll be out in a minute."

Jewel nodded, then closed the door behind her. Caroline remained where she was, with her forehead pressed against her knees, and wondered what she had just gotten herself into. Ever since she had returned to Hart's Valley, people had been trying to make her do the things she had long since relegated to the secret place in her heart she had thought sealed forever.

She stood and walked to the bathroom, where she began filling the sink. The water turned a light green as it reached the shirt, and Caroline had a flash of memory of Drew pushing the breadbasket into the glass, almost as if he'd done it on purpose.

Caroline reached her hands under the tepid water, watching her outstretched fingers warp and bend under the ripples caused by the running faucet, until she no longer recognized them as her own.

*March 29, 1987*

> *My mom and I are in Atlanta visiting with the Colliers now. We were invited to come for Jude's piano recital. He's really amazing. When he sits at the piano and begins playing such beautiful sounds, it's hard to remember that this is the same boy who was the star quarterback on his football team, is the instigator for the best practical jokes, and loves fast cars. Maybe that's why everyone loves him—because there're so many different parts of him to love. That's what Caroline says, anyway. Sometimes I think she must be jealous of all the attention he re-*

*ceives, but I know she loves him as much as everybody else does. She seems happy enough to walk in his shadow, but I can't help wonder if sometimes she wishes she could share the spotlight with him, or even stand in it on her own. Her swimming puts her in the spotlight—but not with their mother. It's not that Mrs. Collier isn't proud of Caroline and all her trophies; it's just that she doesn't understand it. But Caroline's mother is a musician, and she shares the love of the piano and music with Jude, and that's what's made all the difference. Caroline says it doesn't matter, but I wonder if it's a lot like having a bruise that you can usually forget about but then it hurts like heck when somebody presses on it.*

Jewel heard the sound of a car door slamming next door and jumped up from the bed where she'd been reading. Looking out her bedroom window on the side of the house, she spotted her grandmother's truck pulled up in the Colliers' driveway. Quickly stowing the diary under her mattress, she raced from her room and down the stairs, calling out a quick, "I'll be next door," to her father's closed workroom door as she raced outside.

She'd just caught up with her grandmother on the front porch when Mrs. Collier opened the door. Her eyes widened when she caught sight of Grandma Rainy. "I can't wait for you to see this—it's going to be such a surprise!"

"Oh, boy," said Rainy. "Can't imagine what this could be. Last time I saw you this excited you'd just discovered that fast-acting laxative."

"Oh, hush," Mrs. Collier said, eyeing Jewel standing behind her grandmother. "I'm sure I don't know what you're referring to."

Rainy snorted and followed Mrs. Collier into the house, Jewel tagging along close behind. Mrs. Collier kept talking as they walked. "Drew helped me with this. He started before Caroline came from Atlanta, and just waited for her to leave the house to put on the finishing touches."

"Where is Caroline?" Jewel addressed the back of Mrs. Collier's perfectly curled and sprayed hair that looked as if it would take a hurricane to loosen a strand.

"I sent her to the grocery store for some soy milk. I wanted your grandmother here when Caroline got back so we could surprise her together."

They wound their way through the kitchen to the laundry room and the connecting storeroom that Mrs. Collier explained had once held old furniture and other stuff from before the house's most recent redecorating. Jewel hadn't seen the house before, but she thought it now looked a lot like those pictures she saw in the magazines at the doctor's office. It was pretty, but she couldn't imagine putting her feet up on any of the sofa cushions to watch a movie.

As they entered the laundry room, Jewel smelled fresh lumber and paint, reminding her of her dad. Mrs. Collier paused by the closed door to the storeroom and put her hand on the door handle. "Are you ready?"

Both Jewel and her grandmother waited with raised eyebrows, wondering what could be so wonderful about an old storeroom that had just received a new coat of paint. Rainy smirked. "Glad I remembered to take my medication this morning so I won't have a heart attack from the excitement."

Ignoring her, Mrs. Collier turned the door handle and pushed it open. "Ta-da!"

Jewel and her grandmother stood looking past Margaret into a room that resembled a small craft shop. Cedar shelves had been built against the longest wall and were now stocked with rolls of brightly colored fabric and batting material. Clear plastic bins lined the lower shelves, all clearly labeled by thread color and needle size to indicate their contents.

Jewel looked up at her grandmother, surprised to see her frowning. Rainy turned to Mrs. Collier. "What's all this for?"

"For Caroline, of course! Remember how much she loved quilting? I think this is just the thing she needs to get started again."

Grandma Rainy was still frowning. "Do you think she's ready?"

"Of course she's ready—she's just always too busy with her job to quilt, but now that she's here for a few months, it's the perfect time to get back into it." Mrs. Collier's expression faltered as she stared at Rainy's frown.

Rainy continued. "That's not what I meant. Remember when my Bill was sick in the hospital, right before he passed on? I used to love to knit, always had a knitting project and my needles in a bag at my feet wherever I went. I was knitting a blanket for Shelby and nearly finished it, too, sitting by Bill's hospital bed. But when he died, I couldn't stand the thought of knitting. It reminded me too much of a bad time in my life, no matter how much I had used to love it." Grandma Rainy took one of Mrs. Collier's hands, as if to soften her words. "I think quilting for Caroline is that way. It makes her think of . . . a tough time. And I don't think she's ready to go back there yet."

Mrs. Collier pulled away, her back to them, and nobody said anything for a long moment. Then her shoulders seemed to droop, reminding Jewel of a flower that had been left in a vase without water too long. "How could I not know this? How can I continue to do the wrong things where Caroline is concerned?"

Grandma Rainy surprised Jewel by leaning forward and hugging her friend. "Just keep loving her. And keep trying. Eventually you'll both figure it out." She gave Mrs. Collier a smacking kiss on the cheek. "Assuming you live that long, seeing how long in the tooth you are already."

Mrs. Collier's cheek trembled into a small smile, and Jewel saw her grandmother squeeze her friend's hand again. Feeling the need to say something, Jewel said, "I think it's pretty cool. I wish I could quilt. Then I could use all this stuff."

The two older women looked at her with identical gleams in their eyes, but before they could say anything, they heard the front door slam shut and Caroline call out, "I'm back. You can call off the search party."

Before the three of them could decide on a plan, Caroline had stuck her head through the laundry room doorway. They remained where they were, like three Goldilocks caught by Baby Bear.

Caroline walked toward them, clutching a paper grocery sack in her arms. "What are y'all up to?" As much as they tried to cluster and hide the open doorway behind them, Caroline apparently had no trouble seeing what was there. Jewel saw the light in her eyes fade.

Jewel was the first to speak. "Your mom and my grandma are going to teach me how to make a memory quilt so I can help with my mom's." *Why did I say that?* There was nothing so lame in the world as quilting, and if the kids at school ever found out, they'd never let her hear the end of it.

Caroline looked suspiciously from Mrs. Collier's face to Rainy's. "Oh. That's nice." She peeked inside the room again, and Jewel could tell from the way she held her body forward that she wanted to go in and look closer. But when she caught Mrs. Collier's hopeful expression, Caroline backed away. "Well, have fun. I've got to go put the milk in the fridge."

They all watched Caroline's retreating back until Mrs. Collier said, "Well, that went better than I expected."

Jewel felt her grandmother's hand on her back, pushing her forward. "Yep, and it looks like we'd better set up a sewing circle in your living room, Margaret, so we can start Jewel's quilting lessons."

Jewel didn't try to hold back her groan as Grandma Rainy propelled her out the door.

# CHAPTER 9

❧

CAROLINE TURNED OVER IN HER BED AGAIN, SEARCHING FOR A comfortable spot, and stared at the sliver of moonlight on the wall. She'd had the dream again, the same one she'd been having since she'd returned to Hart's Valley. She'd had it the first time the night she'd come home from the hospital after Jude had died. In the dream, she'd been walking down a dark path where she couldn't see anything except for the path in front of her. She wasn't scared, because she knew there had been somebody walking with her. She couldn't see, but she was sure it was Jude.

She glanced at the glow of numbers on her alarm clock. It was still the middle of the night, and a long way until dawn.

She flopped over again and closed her eyes, but still she could see shelves of fabric and quilting supplies, could smell the fresh lumber and paint. She had wanted to go into that back room and explore, feel the cotton beneath her fingers and lay the patterns out in her mind. Sitting up, she pressed her backbone against the headboard and forced her mind to stay in her dark bedroom and out of the back storeroom where her heart and mind were not allowed to go.

The loon called from the lake, its cry strident against the solid wall of night that surrounded Caroline in her bed. Pushing the covers back, she slid her feet into her slippers and shuffled out to the back door, surprised to find it already open. She paused with her hands on the latch of the screen door as she caught the sound of a sigh coming from one of the chairs on the porch. Pressing her forehead against the screen, she spotted her mother.

Margaret sat unmoving in the rocking chair, her body poised on the edge of the seat as if she, too, had been listening to the call of the loon. Her mother still wore her outfit from the dinner party, and her helmet of hair reflected the moonlight like a solid sheet of steel.

Caroline started to open the door but stopped when she heard a sob and noticed for the first time that her mother's shoulders were bent forward, like the stem of a flower weighed down by rain.

The crying melded with the loon's, and Caroline looked toward the lake trying to seek guidance as to what to do next. But the loon lapsed into silence, the night broken only by the soft sobs of her mother.

Quietly Caroline pushed the door open. She stared for a long moment, seeing only a stranger. Her mother didn't sob, and her shoulders never slouched. Even when she had come to the hospital to tell Caroline that Jude had been buried, Margaret had stood stoically erect, a delicate lace handkerchief occasionally dabbed at her eyes. She remembered her mother looking at her own dry eyes, and how Caroline couldn't explain to her how mere tears could never express the endless wells of grief that echoed through her body and in the new heart beating there.

She watched her mother turn her face up toward the night sky, her elegant features outlined by the forgiving strokes of moonlight. Caroline froze, her mother's expression mesmerizing in its awfulness. It startled her, made her want to turn back inside and not look anymore, but she stared hard, and the knowledge of what she saw grabbed her heart and squeezed. For the first time in almost fourteen years, Caroline saw the face of a mother whose child had died. In all those years, Caroline had always known herself to be the girl who'd lost her brother, but she had never—not once—seemed to recall that her mother had also lost a son.

She wanted to go to Margaret, to offer words of comfort, but she remained where she was, unsure of what she would say. They had never spoken the same language, their words always seeming to get lost in translation. And Caroline would always, always be the child who had lived instead of the beautiful boy who hadn't. She thought she could see that every time she looked in her mother's eyes.

A small cluster of fireflies rose out of the grass and onto the porch, encircling Margaret. They bobbed up and down around her head, like little pats of a mother whispering *hush* to a crying child. Her mother bowed her head, her sobs now intermittent and her shoulders still. The loon called out to the restless moon, its voice closer and more insistent.

Gently Caroline let the screen door close, then backed away, leaving her mother to her own grief and the cries of a lonely loon.

Jewel watched her father's truck back out of the driveway before throwing on her bathing suit, grabbing a towel and goggles, then racing out the door toward the dock. She was in time to see Caroline staggering from her own house, a can of Coke clutched in her hand. Dark circles ringed her eyes, and her pale lips blended into her face, making her look like she didn't have a mouth.

Jewel slid out of her flip-flops. "I've got some concealer and lipstick if you want to borrow some."

Caroline regarded her with half-open eyes. "No, thanks. I like the zombie look." She looked pointedly to where Jewel's flip-flops and towel lay on the dock. "Did you bring your cordless phone?"

"Nope. I figured we'd have time to go inside my house after the lesson and before the school bus comes. Don't know if the signal would go this far." She smiled at Caroline's disbelieving smirk. "Promise. I won't go back on our deal."

Caroline plopped herself down on the dock and took a big swig of Coke. "All right. But first things first." Her gaze slid up and down Jewel's bikini—the same bikini that Jewel had twisted her dad's arm to get him to buy for her. "If you show up for tryouts in that bathing suit, you'll be laughed out of the pool. Don't you have a one-piece or at least something that is guaranteed to stay on your body when you dive in?"

"You mean I can't work on my tan and swim at the same time?"

Caroline took another swig of Coke and stared at her with raised eyebrows. "You've got a lot to learn. Go change."

With an exaggerated sigh, Jewel jogged toward the house.

"Could you bring me another Coke? I need all the caffeine I can get."

Jewel stopped and faced Caroline. "Is all that caffeine okay for you to drink—I mean, with your heart and all?"

Caroline sounded annoyed. "Yes, it's fine. Unless you want me keeling over in a dead sleep."

"All right, all right." Jewel turned and began her trek back to the house, but couldn't resist calling over her shoulder, "I guess the worst all that caffeine could do would be to curl your hair, which might be an improvement." She heard the empty Coke can hit the grass behind her, and she laughed as she ran up the steps to the back door.

Five minutes later, wearing a boring but acceptable one-piece bathing suit, she found Caroline sitting on the edge of the dock, her chin resting on her pulled-up knees. She was staring at the water like a person would look at somebody she used to know but couldn't remember their name.

Jewel took a long look at the water, too, before closing her eyes and searching for her mother's face. She could see it sometimes against the light-tinged blackness of her eyelids, and she looked for her whenever she needed a swift shove from behind. *Find the one thing that scares you the most and do it.* With a deep breath Jewel broke into a run, dashing past Caroline. "Cannonball!" she yelled before hitting the surface of the lake and creating a huge wall of water that went crashing toward the dock.

Surfacing, she laughed at a drenched Caroline, who was trying to rework the wet strands of her hair into another ponytail.

"No—leave it down." Jewel was about to add, *It looks better that way,* but decided that would be the best way to get Caroline to scrape her hair back again. Instead she said, "It'll dry faster."

"Gee, thanks for the advice." Jewel could tell that Caroline was trying very hard not to smile. "New swimming rule. Ten push-ups for every splash."

"No fair! I guess some people just can't take a joke." She stayed where she was, not yet willing to swim farther away from the dock. "Hey, I can touch the bottom."

"Yeah—so remember, no diving." Caroline's forehead wrinkled. "Haven't you been in the lake before?"

Jewel shook her head. "My dad doesn't let me swim where there aren't any lifeguards. He always takes me to the pool in Truro."

Caroline nodded. "Well, just watch out for the sharks."

"What?" Jewel jumped forward and swam toward the dock.

Caroline threw back her head and laughed out loud. "It's a lake, silly. There aren't any sharks in there." Then she stopped laughing as if somebody had flipped a switch. "I'm sorry. I shouldn't have said that. I forgot that you were afraid of the water."

Jewel shrugged. "That's all right—it was pretty funny." She took a deep breath, just now feeling the chilliness of the water, and looked up into Caroline's face. "You look pretty when you laugh. You should do it more often."

She wished she hadn't said that, because Caroline's eyes seemed to close while remaining completely open.

"Yeah, well, I'm an accountant. Accountants aren't supposed to laugh." Caroline leaned forward as if she were about to stick her hand in the water to test the temperature, then pulled back. "Your teeth are chattering—let's get you moving. Why don't you show me your freestyle stroke?"

Jewel looked apprehensively behind her. "Can I swim right in front of the dock or do you want me to go deeper?"

"You can just swim parallel to the dock. That way your feet can touch bottom when you need to rest."

Jewel nodded, looking down at the greenish-brown water. She could see her hands beneath the surface, but they were distorted and blurred, like dream hands. She felt the muddy silt beneath her toes, and something small bumped into her calf, making her want to leap back onto the dock. Instead she looked up at Caroline. "Will you stay right there, and not go anywhere else while I'm in here?"

"Yeah. I'll stay right here. Promise."

She swished her arms in the water, feeling the cool push of it against her skin. "I'll try not to do something stupid like drown, since I know how much you hate getting in the water."

Caroline looked surprised for a moment, then gave her a half smile. "Thanks. I appreciate that. Now start swimming so I can see how much work we have to do."

Jewel swam for half an hour, showing each stroke to Caroline and then working on part of each one until her muscles burned under her skin. She focused on the light of the sun and the woman sitting on the dock as she swam back and forth, and tried not to think too hard about the unseen things beneath her. Her mother had taught her how to do that, how it was important to pay attention to the things in life that offered light and hope, and not to worry about the things you couldn't see.

She stopped for a moment while working on her butterfly kick, needing to catch her breath. Standing near the dock, she slid her goggles down to her neck and saw Mrs. Collier coming from the house and walking toward them. Caroline didn't turn around to look, but Jewel could tell she knew by the way her shoulders straightened and her whole expression changed, looking like a person getting ready to slap a mosquito.

Mrs. Collier stopped next to Caroline. "I brought some sunscreen. You know how easily you burn." She squirted lotion on her fingers and bent toward Caroline.

Caroline lifted her hand, blocking her mother's fingertips. "Mom, I'm perfectly capable of doing it myself." She took the lotion from her mother and began applying it to her own face.

Mrs. Collier's lips tightened as she studied Caroline. "Make sure you get the tips of your ears and the back of your neck."

Caroline paused in the middle of slathering the back of her neck. "This isn't rocket science, Mom. I know how to apply sunscreen."

Mrs. Collier brushed at the skirt of her dress. "Well, how was I to know you were so smart? You're the one sitting out here without any sunscreen on."

Jewel wanted to laugh at the identical expressions the two women had on their faces. It reminded her of a cat she used to have that would stare at herself in the mirror, never realizing she was seeing her own reflection.

They both looked at Jewel, then rolled their eyes, and this time Jewel did laugh, hiding the sound by quickly ducking under the water, watching the bubbles rise to the surface toward the sun.

Caroline's eyes fluttered open and she had a brief moment of panic, wondering where she was. But then her gaze settled on the pale pink walls and the yellow stuffed dog in the corner and she closed her eyes again, hopelessly wishing she were back in her white apartment in Atlanta.

She'd had the dream again, the one where she was walking along a dark path with an unseen companion beside her. It didn't frighten her; instead she was left with a feeling of knowing where she was but still feeling lost. She closed her eyes again, hoping to reclaim sleep.

Her eyes popped open as she registered the note taped to the inside of her door. She shuffled to the door and read on her mother's embossed stationery, *I had to run a few errands but I'll be back by lunchtime. I made oatmeal for you—it's already in the microwave, so all you have to do is push the start button.*

Caroline wrinkled her nose at the thought of the dry, organic oatmeal her mother made for her each morning. If she hurried, she could make a batch of pancakes and coat them with butter and syrup before Margaret got back—assuming her mother even kept those contraband items in the house.

She caught a glimpse of herself in the dresser mirror as she opened her bedroom door and almost laughed at the reflection of the girl in the Mickey Mouse T-shirt and the hair that looked like she'd had a nasty encounter with a light socket. She didn't care. Nobody was there to see her, and besides, she had pancakes to make.

Racing around the kitchen, she found all the ingredients she needed, including real eggs and butter, and felt a flash of irritation at her mother that she'd been holding out on her.

After making the batter, Caroline reached under the cabinet where all the seldom-used appliances were kept and held back a groan. The pancake griddle, about twenty years old but still shining like new, was the same one she and Jude had used as kids—the one on which heat never went higher than low. That would add at least ten minutes to her cooking time. Glancing at the clock over the stove, she estimated how much time she had left and shoved the plug into the electrical socket on the wall. She'd eat her pancakes in a locked bathroom if she had to.

Unable just to stand and watch the slow progress of her pancakes, she wandered into the great room, her gaze alighting on the piano and drawing her toward it. She stared at it for a long time before sitting down on the bench and lifting the cover off the keys. Striking the first note, she held it down with the pedal, closing her eyes and listening to the sound as it faded.

When she was a young girl, she would lie under the grand piano in her mother's living room, listening to Jude play. The sound would overtake her, rolling her under like a wave in the ocean, until she could no longer tell the difference between music and water. But the piano was her brother's domain, and no prompting by their mother had ever convinced Caroline to learn to play. She could never compete with the beauty of Jude's talent, and she was happy simply to listen, then leave the room when her mother would join Jude on the piano bench for a duet.

Her hands sat on the keyboard, her fingers stroking keys from a memory she didn't remember having, playing the melody of a song she'd heard long ago. This newly discovered ability surprised and frightened her. It was a bit like finding out the truth about Santa Claus when she was eight; she'd been shocked to find her letters to Santa in her mother's desk drawer, then had not been able to sleep for days figuring out the Easter Bunny and Tooth Fairy and wondering what else her parents had lied to her about.

She pressed her fingers against the keys with more confidence, marveling at the sounds she created, hearing the melody in her head and then transferring it to the keyboard. She pressed the pedal down with her right foot, instinctively knowing when to sustain a note and when to release it. It was like diving into the cool depths of the lake, surrounding herself with something that made sense in her heart.

Something thumped behind her. She jumped off the piano bench and whirled around. Drew Reed stood there wearing a tool belt, with sawdust in his hair. Jewel stood next to him carrying what looked like a table leaf. Drew smiled. "Sorry, didn't mean to surprise you, but you didn't hear us knocking."

Caroline reached behind her and closed the keyboard lid with a thump. "That's all right. I was just making breakfast."

He was staring at her hair and she could tell he was trying not to smile. "How *do* you make your hair go like that?"

Pushing past him with as much dignity as somebody who was wearing a long Mickey Mouse T-shirt and floppy slippers could muster, she walked into the kitchen to rescue her pancakes from the griddle, smelling the acrid scent of burned batter.

Drew followed her into the kitchen, Jewel tagging along behind him. He leaned against a counter. "So you do play piano, then."

Caroline was careful not to look at him. "No, I really don't. I play a little by ear, that's all."

"That's interesting. Your mother made it sound like you were tone-deaf."

With a heavy sigh, Caroline scraped her blackened pancakes into the food disposal, making sure to wash away all evidence. "Well, that's because I didn't really try to play until now. I guess being bored to death makes a person desperate." She poured dish soap and water into the sink to wash the mixing bowl and griddle.

Caroline looked over her shoulder and saw both Drew and Jewel studying her. "Pardon me for asking, but why are you in my house?"

Drew straightened, adjusting his tool belt. "Your mom asked me to make a worktable and benches for the living room. Jewel's been helping me carry them over. They're out on the porch, ready to bring inside, if that's all right with you."

Caroline's stomach grumbled as she rinsed the last of the pancake batter down the drain. "Don't let me stop you."

After she finished washing, drying, and putting away the dishes, she walked into the living room, noticing that all the existing furniture had been pushed against the walls and an enormous pine table now stood in the middle of the room. As she had expected, it was a marvelous piece of work. A month ago she would have bet a large sum of money that she would never call a pine worktable art, but now, staring at Drew Reed's handiwork, she was speechless.

All four legs of the table were different, she noticed as she knelt in front of the first one. The foot of each leg was a human foot, and the table leg was made up of short puffs of ocean waves, breaking into froth on the underside of the table. As Drew and Jewel brought the benches in, Caroline examined another leg. This one had the foot of a young girl, and the leg was a patchwork of different patterns like a wooden quilt.

She faced Drew as he arranged a bench under the table. "Please—let me just take a picture of this table and send it to my boss. I believe you'd be pleasantly surprised at what I think we can offer you."

He glanced up at her face and something flickered in his eyes. After a pause that anybody else would have missed, he said, "No, thanks. And please don't ask me again."

Caroline opened her mouth to do just that when Jewel plopped herself on the bench and caught Caroline's attention. "I read somewhere that sometimes people with organ transplants suddenly get a talent that they never had before and they find out that the person whose organ they have once had that talent. Isn't that neat? Maybe the person whose heart you have was really musical or something. Could you find out?"

The coldness started at the top of Caroline's head and stole down her body until she felt as if she'd fallen under ice and couldn't find the hole to come up for air.

The front door opened and Margaret walked in, sparing Caroline from searching for an answer. Margaret greeted everyone, raising an eyebrow at Caroline's appearance as she moved toward the table. "It's beautiful, Drew—just like I knew it would be. Thank you so much for the rush order."

"It was my pleasure." He leaned down to allow Margaret to place a kiss on his cheek.

Margaret smiled. "Why don't you two sit down and I'll get you something cool to drink and Caroline can go get some clothes on."

Everybody's voices seemed to be coming from far away, as if muffled by the ice that seemed to surround her. She found her own voice. "Yes. I'll go do that."

As she walked toward her bedroom, she heard Margaret call out, "Did something burn? I definitely smell something burning." And then, as Caroline reached the sanctuary of her room, Margaret said, "Caroline! Why is your oatmeal still in the microwave?"

Caroline's response was the sound of her door snapping closed.

# CHAPTER 10

❧

*June 21, 1987*

*Mama let me pick where I wanted to go on summer vaca-
tion, so we're on Sullivan's Island again. Next to Hart's Valley,
it's my favorite place in the world. Maybe it's because I've always lived near the water. But with a lake you can see the beginning and end of it, unlike the ocean that seems to go on
forever. Sailing from one end of the lake to the other is nice, but
you always know where you're going. I'd like to sail to the other
side of the ocean, just to see what's there. Jude says it's because
that's the way I look at life—it's so much more exciting when
you don't know what's on the other side of the day you're in. You
just expect the best, deal with the bumps, and pray that your
boat doesn't fall apart under the big waves.*

*Jude's with us this week. We invited Caroline, too, but she
couldn't go. Mrs. Collier has her going to this charm school in
Atlanta to learn how to walk and dress. I'm glad I wasn't there
when Mrs. Collier told her about it—I'm sure the walls are
showing scorch marks! You'd think Mrs. Collier would understand that the more she pushes Caroline to go one way, the
more Caroline will push just as hard to go the other direction.
I feel sorry for them both. It's like they're communicating with
walkie-talkies that are set on different channels. They're both
saying the same thing, but the other one always hears something else.*

*Yesterday Jude pulled a small piece of driftwood out of the
ocean. I think it's very old and I like to imagine it bumping
along the bottom of the ocean while explorers sailed above it. It's*

*got deep grooves and pits and lines that go from one end to the other and then lines that go nowhere at all. But taken all together, it's so beautiful. I told Jude I'm putting it on my bookshelf at home. It will remind me of him and life in general. Because if you think about it, every day is full of wrong turns and roads that take us nowhere. But when you stand back and look at it, you can see how beautiful it all turned out and that you're standing where you're supposed to be.*

Jewel closed her mother's diary and slid off her bed. Opening her door, she stuck her head out into the hallway and listened for sounds from her dad's workroom. When the buzz saw started she knew the coast was clear, and she crept into the closed-off room that her dad never talked about.

The air always seemed different in here. It was almost like walking into an empty church before services, the silence itself holding its breath, the anticipation pushing at your back, making you move forward. Like all the people who had been there before were sitting there, invisible, waiting for someone to come in and breathe the life back into them.

She knelt by the trunk on the floor and opened the lid slowly, not sure what to expect from this trunk that smelled like her mother. Taking out the quilt on top, she draped it over the bed, then began to take everything out and spread it on the floor. The previous week she'd taken the quilt out of the box it had been in, and placed it in the trunk. It was easier to put it back that way, without struggling with retaping the box.

She found the piece of driftwood near the bottom, wrapped in a football jersey with the number 02 stamped on the front. She touched the dried wood, letting her fingers run along the lines and ridges, feeling her mother's hand guiding her own as her short, clipped nails dipped in and out of the wooden crevasses. Gently she set it aside, then placed everything else back, but paused as she lifted the quilt, noticing again how the bottom half of it lay empty and unfinished. Who did it belong to and why was it stored in her mother's trunk? She felt the urge to put it away, that somehow it wasn't ready to be taken out. Maybe it was her mother talking to her again, the way she sometimes did in dreams.

Jewel picked up everything she'd put on the floor, then refolded the quilt and carefully placed it on top inside the trunk before closing the lid. Then she crept back to her room with the piece of driftwood, thinking of the best place to put it and hoping her dad wouldn't notice.

Drew pulled up in front of Rainy's store and turned off the truck's engine. He supposed he should start calling it his own store, seeing as how the papers had already been signed and his name would soon be on the deed. He waited for a rush of satisfaction, or at least a sense of completion, but all he could feel as he stared through the windshield at the weathered boards and broad display window was bewilderment.

*How did I get here?* He slowly got out of the truck and leaned on the door for a moment and thought of Shelby. She had always encouraged him to find his dream, to go where his heart led. It had taken him a while to understand why it was so important to her, and when he'd figured it out, the end result had to been to chase him further and further into his work existence as a lawyer, and away from her and the life he thought they'd had.

But now Shelby was gone, and he had Jewel to raise all by himself. He'd hoped that moving to Hart's Valley would be the perfect solution—he could follow his dream of creating beautiful furniture, and he'd have more time for Jewel. Except he and Jewel seemed to avoid each other, and while he loved creating the furniture pieces he'd been making, there was still something else, another piece of the puzzle, waiting to be fitted into place. If only he could figure out what it was.

Leaving the truck, he was halfway up the wooden steps of the store when he heard a car pulling up behind him. Turning, he smiled his best jury-clinching smile as he faced Caroline Collier. It had been her idea to meet in Rainy's parking lot so her mother wouldn't have to panic over their hiking trip.

"Good morning," he said, still smiling.

"Yeah, whatever," she said, climbing out of her mother's Cadillac.

"It's so nice to meet another chirpy early bird like me. Don't you just love mornings?"

Caroline only grunted, then reached inside the car and pulled out an enormous travel coffee mug and took a big gulp.

Drew's gaze took in Caroline's outfit, from the tank top and cutoff jeans shorts to her thin white legs with short ankle socks and . . . Keds?

His smile faltered a bit. "We're going hiking, remember? Not taking a leisurely stroll around the lake."

She looked at him with half-closed eyes and took another sip of her coffee. "This is all I have. Guess we can't go. I'll just go home and crawl back into bed."

"Good try." He motioned toward the front door of the store. "Let's go in and have a chat with Rainy until the stores in Truro open. There's a great sportsman's warehouse there that should have what you need."

She looked at him as if she hadn't heard a word. "Do you have a cell phone I can use?"

"Nope. Don't need one; don't want one."

"Great." Gulping more coffee, she preceded him into the store.

They found Rainy in the back dining room. All the quilting supplies had already been carted over to the Colliers' for Jewel's quilting lessons—not that he believed that for a second. Jewel's desire to quilt was about as believable as Caroline whooping for joy and doing cartwheels across the parking lot. He grinned at the thought, then grinned even more when he caught Caroline looking at him.

Rainy smiled up at them. Her lime-green headscarf matched the T-shirt she wore under her overalls. Rainy Martin was the only person he knew—besides Shelby—who had the ability to keep smiling even during the worst of times. He recalled the days following Shelby's death when Rainy had come to stay with him and Jewel. He had been like a cracked piece of glass, and Rainy's strong, capable hands had held him together so the pieces couldn't fall out.

He kissed her cheek, noticing for the first time that the dining room table was now covered with pictures and articles torn from magazines and newspapers, all of them depicting a foreign locale or travel destination. "What are these for?"

"Oh, just ideas for my trip. I figure that the word *retirement* won't sound so final if I have something to look forward to. Else I might as well have you start making my pine box." She winked at him before picking up a postcard of the Sydney Opera House and fanning herself with it. "It always amazes me to see people retire from life long before their bodies are ready for it."

Rainy looked at Caroline, who lingered in the doorway, appearing pinched and wary as she nursed her coffee. "Your mother called. She saw that you left looking like you were headed outdoors, so she wanted to make sure you remembered your sunscreen."

Caroline opened her mouth to say something but Rainy cut her off. "And, no, you can't use my phone."

Caroline stuck her jaw out. "That's okay. I have other sources."

Rainy looked down at the table and began to rearrange the pictures. "Fine. Just as long as it's not my phone. I don't want your mother knocking me into next week. And she'd do it, too. She might look small, but she's a bruiser."

Drew almost laughed out loud at the mental picture of demure Margaret Collier using any sort of physical violence, but the impulse stopped when he caught sight of Caroline's face as she approached the table.

Her fingertips wandered across a yellowed travel brochure with Big Ben on the front before he picked it up and opened it. "I remember these." A small smile brushed across her face, illuminating it for a brief moment. Drew continued to watch her, fascinated at the change.

Rainy laughed out loud. "Well, you should. They were the source of the biggest whupping you ever got."

Caroline actually laughed. "Yeah, they were, weren't they?"

Drew wanted to ask what they were talking about, but he was too busy watching Caroline and the way an old memory made her face shine like it was lit from within. He hardly recognized her as the taciturn woman next door.

"When Caroline was in high school," Rainy explained, "she and Jude and Shelby collected all these travel brochures for me. Even back then I was planning on taking a big trip sometime when Bill and me could get away. Anyway, Caroline got it in her head that it would be a good idea if the three of them took a trip, too, even though me and Margaret had already said no. So what does Caroline do? She sneaks her mother's credit card out of her wallet and books the reservations over the phone." She slapped her denim-covered knee and snorted. "Can you believe that? And Caroline planned that all on her own—and took the punishment all on her own, too."

Caroline sat down at the table and began leafing through all the brochures. With a smirk, she said, "Actually, it was my idea to go first-class. The rest was all Jude's doing—but I had to make the actual phone calls, since I could imitate mom's voice." She smiled to herself, her eyes almost closed, as if seeing old friends long since gone. "I even called the school so we would be excused for the week we were planning to be in Europe."

Drew stared at the pale, serious woman in front of him, wondering what had happened to the mischievous girl she had once been. He sat down next to her. "How did you get caught?"

"My mom found our itinerary. She saw it under my bed when she was snooping."

Rainy cleared her throat. "Now, Caroline—you know that's not what happened. She was hiding your birthday present under your bed because it was the one place you never looked. Your itinerary was lying there clear as day, and Margaret couldn't help but see it."

Caroline flipped over a pamphlet from the Louvre and laughed softly. "I almost had her believing it was for your trip when the mail arrived and in it was the American Express bill." She leaned back in her chair and laughed out loud, a surprisingly rich, throaty laugh. It was the laugh of a person who laughed often and from the heart. "I'd never seen her so mad—I thought her head would pop off like a cork from a champagne bottle."

Drew found her laughter contagious and couldn't help but laugh, too, at the image of Margaret Collier's head propelling off her shoulders. He could see the whole thing from Caroline's young eyes and wondered again what had happened to her in the years since that had taken the laughter from her. If he had the inclination to get to know her better, which he didn't, he'd look forward to the challenge of finding out what it was and bringing the laughter back to her eyes.

She caught him staring at her, and the laughter faded from her voice. Her face dimmed again, as if a cloud had passed over the sun, stealing away all color. Softly she said, "I never made the trip either." With a deep sigh she added, "And, as it turned out, it was probably a good thing my mom stopped it when she did. We couldn't have gotten on the plane without passports—something I'd forgotten about completely—not to mention the criminal charges for unauthorized use of a credit card." She glanced at her watch, signaling that the conversation was over. "Come on, city boy—looks like the stores should be open by now. Then I'll show you what a squirrel looks like and you can play bodyguard in case I decide to pass out and fall off a cliff or something."

"You sure know how to make an ordinary day sound exciting."

Caroline stood and threw her backpack purse over her shoulder. Kissing Rainy's cheek, she said, "If my mother calls, tell her I'm in the back room taking a nap."

Rainy just shook her head slowly.

After telling Rainy good-bye, Drew followed Caroline out of the store, watching the swing of her ponytail. Even though he told himself every day that he didn't miss the corporate world, he could at least admit that he missed the daily challenges of accomplishing the impossible. He'd always thought that was what had made him a successful attorney—and a lousy husband and father. A little challenge like Caroline Collier could be just what he needed. He didn't need to get personal—just make her laugh.

Drew smiled broadly and held the door open for her. "After you, ma'am."

"Beauty before age," she said as she walked past him.

He followed her toward his truck, the thrill of a challenge lightening his step.

Caroline settled herself in the passenger seat of Drew's pickup

truck, wondering again why she had agreed to this. The man bothered her. He couldn't take a hint when it was time to back off. Every
time she caught him looking at her it seemed he was planning something—something to change her. It made her feel like a spider
trapped under a magnifying glass on a hot day. She wondered how
long it would be before she felt the burn.

They had barely left the parking lot before Drew leaned over
and popped open the glove box. "There's some sunscreen in there."

"*Et tu, Brute?*"

His smirk matched hers. "Your mother is just being a parent.
She's only showing you that she loves you."

Caroline took the tube of sunscreen out of the glove box and
opened it. "But she doesn't have to treat me like a five-year-old."

"Then maybe you should stop acting like one."

She was still thinking of a comeback when Drew let out a loud
curse and slammed on the brakes before running the truck up on the
grass on the side of the road. A large tractor-trailer rumbled past
them, rattling the truck. For a moment she thought she was going
to throw up. The sound of the squealing brakes and then the wheels
going up over the grass had sent her arms over her face as she waited
for the truck to flip. It was only after Drew had slammed his door
that she opened her eyes and began practicing breathing again.

Caroline stuck her head out the window and looked behind
her and spotted Jewel on a bicycle struggling to make it up the hill
on the side of the narrow, two-lane mountain road they had just
come up.

Drew marched behind the truck to where Jewel had given up
and dismounted from the bike. Making sure she could be steady on
her feet, Caroline followed in case she needed to be a referee.

"What in the hell do you think you're doing?"

Jewel looked up at her father with a smile that Caroline could
see wasn't as confident as she was trying to make it. "I'm riding my
bike. You said I could."

"When I said you could ride your bike, I assumed you meant up
and down our street—not on the highway!"

"But you didn't say I couldn't."

Drew opened his mouth but no words came out, though his face had turned a dangerous shade of red. Caroline wondered why Jewel hadn't stepped back. After a deep breath Drew pointed to the truck. "Not another word. Get in the truck. I'm putting your bike into the back, and don't expect to see it for at least a month. And it's going to be at least that long before you're allowed outside without me accompanying you."

"That's not fair! I was only—"

"I said not another word. Get in the truck. You're going shopping with us, and I don't want to hear a peep out of you until we get home."

Caroline sent her a warning glance and motioned for Jewel to get in the middle of the front seat before following her inside, and she found that her hands were still shaking.

Drew climbed in behind the wheel and started the engine. They rode in an uncomfortable silence for about ten minutes. Then, under her breath, Jewel said, "He is *so* clueless about being a dad."

Caroline hesitated before putting an arm around the young girl. "He's just trying to be a parent, Jewel. If he didn't love you, he wouldn't be so hard on you."

Jewel sniffed and a tear dropped on her forearm. "Well, he doesn't have to treat me like a little kid."

After a long pause, Caroline said, "No, probably not. But my guess would be that his reaction came completely from his concern for you and not any real wish to embarrass you."

Silence fell inside the truck again while Caroline studiously avoided looking at Drew and seeing his "I told you so" look. Then fat pellets of rain began to hit the windshield, and the fear and panic that she'd managed to hold at bay rushed to the surface of her skin, pushing at her like tiny needles.

Drew leaned forward to peer up at the sky, then looked at Jewel, who continued to stare straight ahead. "Maybe we can go to the Y for a swim after we finish our shopping. Caroline's welcome to come, too."

Caroline answered too quickly, "No. But thank you. I'll need to get home, if you wouldn't mind."

"No, I wouldn't mind. Just thought you might like a swim. It's great exercise, you know."

"I know." Finally her eyes met his and she saw him dip his gaze to where her hand had clutched at her tank top over her chest. She released her grip, then turned away and stared out the window, where the drops were now hitting the glass in earnest. She watched as rain dripped from trees and puddled like swollen tears on the road. She gripped the door handle tightly, feeling the old fear again, and closed her eyes. The truck slowed and her eyes fluttered open as she glanced at Drew. She caught his look of concern before he turned back to watch the road, keeping his speed to below the speed limit, regardless of the line of cars behind him. She supposed she should be grateful for his concern, but it bothered her too much that he could read her so well.

Embarrassed, Caroline released her grip on the door handle and concentrated on her breathing, trying to ignore the sound of the wheels against wet pavement. She was fine when she was the one behind the wheel, but once she became a passenger without control, the fear consumed her. A warm hand crept into hers and squeezed. Surprised, Caroline turned to see Jewel looking up at her.

"It's okay. Dad's a good driver." Jewel blinked her eyes a couple of times. "Dad, could you take me to Rainy's? I feel a bad headache coming on."

"Will do," he said, patting her on the leg as he pulled into a side road to turn around. "Caroline and I can run our errands another time."

"Thank you," Caroline whispered, then closed her eyes and tried to concentrate on the warm hand in hers and the soft hum of the engine so she wouldn't have to listen to the rain.

# CHAPTER 11

❧

CAROLINE TIPTOED PAST HER MOTHER'S OPEN BEDROOM DOOR, hoping to sneak by unnoticed. She might be almost thirty years old now, but she still remembered from childhood the floorboards to avoid and had almost made it to her own room when she heard her mother call out. Her mom had always claimed to have six ears and eyes in the back of her head, and Caroline was inclined to believe it. She paused for a moment before answering, surprised to remember that her mother didn't say that anymore. Her mother had stopped claiming extrasensory powers when Jude died, as if her sixth sense had somehow failed her forever on that rainy night in November.

"Yes?" Caroline lingered in the doorway.

Her mother lay in bed propped against a large pillow with a magazine on her lap. She patted the mattress next to her. "Come sit."

Caroline sat on the edge of the mattress, smelling the aroma of Youth Dew body cream, another childhood memory. A thick cloth headband held her mother's hair back from her face so that it wouldn't stick to the gooey white mask spread over her forehead, nose, and cheeks. "You look great, Mom. Going out?"

"No, I'm saving all this splendor just for you." She reached for the jar of cream on her bedside table and unscrewed the lid.

Caroline shrank back. "Don't even think about it."

"Humor me this once, all right? I think you'll enjoy it. Not only does it tighten the pores and lift your skin, but it's also scented with vanilla and chamomile to help you relax." She gave Caroline a pointed look. "I know you haven't been sleeping well—I hear you up all hours of the night. This might help."

Their eyes met, but all Caroline could see was her mother crying on the back porch while the loon called from the lake. Her mother waited, as if expecting her to argue. Instead Caroline moved forward and tilted her face, as if giving in to this one small thing might somehow bridge the distance between them that words always seemed to mangle.

The cream felt cold as Margaret's gentle fingers spread it over her skin, and she smiled at her mother's facial gyrations as she motioned for Caroline to flatten a cheek or lift her jaw.

"So, what was the best thing that happened to you today?" her mother asked.

The words brought back memories of the nightly ritual when she and Jude would sit on their mother's bed and talk about their day. She had once looked forward to it, but now she pulled back, the rawness around her heart still fresh after all these years. "I took a nap."

Margaret didn't say anything for a few minutes as she wiped her hands on a tissue and screwed the lid back on the jar. "And what was the worst thing that happened to you today?"

"I woke up."

"I see." She leaned back on her pillow and regarded Caroline for a long moment. "You don't have to meet at Rainy's before you go hiking with Drew, you know. I think it's a good idea."

Caroline threw her hands up. "How do you know these things? I didn't tell anybody."

Her mom shrugged. "It's something a mother gains when her first child is born. There's not a lot that goes on around you that I miss." She smiled, making the face mask crack over her laugh lines. "Plus, I'm nosy. When I saw you sneaking out of here this morning, I made a few phone calls. It's a small town—nobody misses much around here."

"Well, I'm an adult now. You don't have to follow my every move, you know. I can take care of myself."

"I know." She put her hand on Caroline's. "But I'll always be your mother—that will never change."

Caroline pulled her hand away and stood, remembering the swim meets when her mother hadn't been there, and the Halloween they had stayed inside because Jude had been too scared to go out. But she felt her heart beginning to beat faster, so she pushed back the memories and took deep breaths filled with chamomile and vanilla.

"I'm tired. I think I'll go to bed now."

"Let the mask sit for fifteen minutes before you wash it off."

Caroline nodded, wanting to explain, to say more. There was so much unsaid between them, but thinking of it exhausted her. It was too much, and all in the past. No good could ever come from dredging up old hurts. Instead, all she said was, "Good night." She paused at the doorway. "Can I use your phone to call Dad? I haven't spoken to him in a couple of weeks."

"You don't need my permission to call your dad, you know. But he's in Hawaii this week with his new girlfriend. He won't be back until Sunday."

The disappointment settled on Caroline like a dense fog, and she felt an odd compulsion to talk to her mother about it. But the old resentments pushed at her, propelling her out of the room. "Good night," she said again.

"Sweet dreams." It was what her mother had always said when she'd tucked Caroline and Jude into bed when they were children.

Caroline didn't answer. She'd long since forgotten what a sweet dream was. She moved down the silent hallway, then quietly responded, "Don't let the bedbugs bite." She let herself into her darkened bedroom, and listened for the loon out on the lake.

*August 8, 1987*

> *Jude and Caroline go back to Atlanta tomorrow. They've been at the lake house for a month but it hardly seems long at all. Especially because I've been in bed with one of my horrible headaches for the last two days. Nothing seems to be helping. At least I was able to have my fifteenth birthday before the headache came. It started as my mom and me were driving*

*back after getting my driver's permit in Truro. Jude came with us and was begging for my mom to let him drive when the headache started. Everything went black all of a sudden and Mom had to grab the wheel and steer us to the side of the road. I don't know what it means, because I can't see anything except this horrible blackness. Whatever it is, I don't think it's good.*

*Caroline came over yesterday to keep me company. She brought a quilt she's working on for an end-of-year team present for her swim coach. Her quilts are more than just patches and different stitches—they're works of art. She has this amazing eye for color and placement, and for story, too. Her quilts tell stories so that even if you don't know the person it belongs to, you can read the story of their life. She sat quietly by my bed and hand-stitched until I fell asleep. And when I woke up, she was still there. That's the great thing about Caroline that I'm not sure if anybody else notices. She's always there for you. She doesn't talk much but she takes everything in and doesn't miss a thing. And she has the greatest laugh—it could make a whole room of grumpy people smile. Jude says she's shy, but I think she's just busy taking everything in. In psychology class we talk about people who internalize other people's feelings—and I think that's what Caroline does. She takes in everybody's happiness or sadness and makes it her own. It's strange, but sometimes I think I'm the only one who notices this about her. I think that's how she wants it, though. She's the big swimming star, in a place where she can hide behind medals and ribbons and statistics. It's how she protects herself, I think. I wonder how long it will take before her family sees it, too.*

Jewel sat on the bench at the round craft table in Mrs. Collier's living room. She picked a seat that faced the television just in case she was allowed to relieve the boredom. Glancing at the clock, she saw that she had exactly two hours and twenty-three minutes before she could make her escape. Making sure she wasn't being observed by

Grandma Rainy or Mrs. Collier, she set the alarm on her watch. She
had to be home in time for Lauren's phone call. If she wasn't there,
her dad would answer and might mention Jewel was quilting. Her
best friend would never let her hear the end of it.

Grandma Rainy approached the table with a wadded quilt in
her hands. Lifting it high, she opened it in a quick move, creating a
halo of color above them before it settled on the table's surface.

Jewel crossed her legs and shook her ankle impatiently. "How
long is it going to take to do all this?"

Rainy put her forefinger to her mouth. "Shh. Don't let Caroline
hear. You're doing this because you want to, remember?"

"Whatever." Jewel examined the quilt in front of her with a crit-
ical eye, unconsciously comparing it to the quilt in her mother's
trunk. This one, too, was unfinished, but there was something else
not quite right about it—something Jewel couldn't identify. There
was no border yet, and only the first row and a half of fabric squares
had been attached, leaving the rest a blank canvas. It reminded her
of a piece of furniture that her father had sanded only once. He
called it his rough draft, saying it was no better than a tree in the forest. You could see the beauty of the wood already, but it wouldn't be
until the third or fourth sanding that you could finally understand
what her father meant.

It struck her then that this was her mother's life in front of her,
and that the women around the quilting table would be filling in her
mother's life square by square until each important event had been
recorded with thread and needle by the loving hands of people who
had known her. It seemed to her that she should be a part of it, that
maybe somehow her mother would want this and approve. She remembered what she had read in her mother's diary and realized that
Caroline should be involved, too, to put the final sandings on the
quilt.

Not that she'd enjoy any of it, of course, but if she had to do it,
she might as well do it right.

As if reading her mind, Rainy asked, "Where's Caroline?"

Mrs. Collier placed a large pincushion on the edge of the table
and spoke in a loud whisper. "She's in the kitchen getting snacks to-

gether and brewing sweet tea. I thought if I kept her around here we could somehow get her interested enough to join us."

Grandma Rainy nodded her head while her gaze strayed to the curved wooden benches. "Is this where we're going to sit?"

"Well, yes, Rainy. You could go sit on the dock but it would be a far jog to change thread."

"That's not what I meant. I was just hoping that maybe there would be cushions or something. Recovering cancer patients can be delicate."

Mrs. Collier pursed her lips like Jewel had seen her mother do after telling her she was too sick to go to school when she felt perfectly fine. Mrs. Collier gave a delicate snort, if there could be such a thing, and said, "Maybe it's that your rear end has gotten so big that it needs a large cushion to support it." Without skipping a beat, she turned to Jewel. "Honey, could you go out to the back porch and grab the cushions off the patio furniture? We don't want your grandma to have a sore fanny, do we?"

Jewel jumped up as Rainy said, "My rear end isn't nearly as big as your ears. Did you know that your ears and nose continue to grow even after your dead?"

"Thanks for sharing that, Rainy. I'll make sure that you've got an extra-deep coffin to accommodate your nose."

"Fine. And I'll make sure you have one wide enough for those skin flaps on the side of your head that you call ears."

Jewel had reached the kitchen, where she nearly ran into Caroline taking an iced-tea pitcher from the refrigerator. Their eyes met and they started laughing.

Caroline placed the pitcher on the counter. "I can't believe they're best friends—it defies logic."

"I've said that for years." Jewel leaned back on the counter and crossed her arms, forgetting her errand for a moment. "Were you like that with my mom?"

Caroline turned her back and began taking glasses from the cabinet. "Not really—it was more that way between her and my brother, Jude. They could talk about anything together. And sometimes they didn't even need to talk—it was like they could guess what the other was thinking."

Jewel watched Caroline put ice cubes into each glass, an equal number put precisely one by one in stacks of three. Maybe that was how accountants did it, but it seemed like a waste of time to her. Or maybe Caroline did things like that to keep her mind busy so she wouldn't have to think about the hard stuff.

"Do you still think about him every day?"

Caroline dropped the ice bucket on the counter, making the glasses bounce. "Yes. I do."

"I think about my mom every day, too. Except you think about your brother in a different way."

Slowly Caroline turned to face her. "What do you mean?"

Instead of answering right away, Jewel pushed off from the counter. "Come help me with these cushions. Hold the door and I'll hand some to you." She waited until Caroline came to the back door before she answered. "Well, when I think about Mom, I feel good inside. It's not that I don't miss her—I do—but I know she loved me and that she had a great life and that she's in a good place now. I don't think she'd want me to have a bad attitude about life just because she's not here."

"I don't have a bad atti—"

Jewel handed her three large cushions, covering Caroline's face and making her stagger against the door.

She continued. "But when you think about your brother, you wish he were here with you, and when you realize that's never going to happen, you get angry and everything else doesn't matter because you don't have that one thing." Jewel grabbed more cushions and moved toward the back door. "My mom would say that crying for the moon is a lot like sitting in a rocking chair: It keeps you busy but it won't get you anywhere."

Caroline turned her face sideways so she could speak. "Has anyone ever told you that you talk way too much?"

"Yep. My dad tells me every day." She motioned for Caroline to move ahead, then followed her into the kitchen. "Come on, let's give the old ladies their butt pads."

"Wait. You can't just say something like that and then walk away."

"Sure I can. My mom always told me it was the best way to get people to open up and talk about things they don't want to but probably need to. If you're annoying enough about it, it will make the person you're talking to argue with you."

She plopped the cushions down on the floor at the feet of Mrs. Collier, who'd just sat down at a card table near the benches. On top of the table she'd piled about ten shoe boxes full of photographs still in their white sleeves from the developer's.

Caroline dropped her cushions, too, and stared at her mother. "What are those for?"

Mrs. Collier smiled innocently. "Well, I know you're not interested in helping us with the quilt, but I thought you might want to go through these old pictures and pull out ones with Shelby in them that might silk-screen well onto a quilting square."

Jewel smiled to herself. Mrs. Collier might look like a sweet old lady who used linen napkins and knew where to hang a picture, but she could probably run a company, solve the world's problems, and hire a hit man all at the same time. She was a lot like Grandma Rainy. Maybe that was why they were such good friends.

Mrs. Collier got up from the chair. "You can sit here. I'll go get the iced tea while Jewel and Rainy start discussing color schemes for the quilt. You can listen with half an ear and give them advice while you're looking through those pictures."

Without waiting for Caroline's response, Mrs. Collier turned toward the kitchen, and Jewel didn't miss the triumphant smile on her face. It was almost as good as the look Caroline wore—of a person who'd just been hit by an unexpected wave. Her shoulders slumped in a defeated gesture as if she were realizing that it was probably as useless to argue with her mother as it was to fight the incoming tide. Jewel stared at Mrs. Collier's retreating back and once again wondered how such a thin old woman could be so relentlessly strong.

# CHAPTER 12

CAROLINE WAS UP EARLY, EAGER TO BE OUT OF THE HOUSE BEFORE her mother awoke and fussed over her or, worse, decided to come with her. There wasn't enough caffeine in the world to help her navigate a long conversation with her mom over the jagged rocks of the past.

She stood on the back porch and stretched, feeling the resistance of muscles that hadn't been used to capacity in years. Sometime in the middle of the night the idea had come to her. Maybe it had come from staring at Shelby's empty quilt the day before. There were boxes and boxes of potential scraps and mementos from a short life well lived. It would be a challenge to decide what would go on it and what wouldn't fit in the confines of a quilt. She imagined it would be a lot like being asked to evacuate your home and be allowed to take only one small bag.

And then she thought of the possibility of her own quilt. She had never started one for herself, and in her mind's eye it was yard after yard of empty fabric. When she tried to think of what would go on it she realized there might be one box of mementos, and all of them would be from her first eighteen years of life. The rest would be empty, like Shelby's, but not because she hadn't been there to live them.

The thought had saddened and frightened her and had pulled her to the back porch to wait out the rest of the night. It was then that the idea had come to her that she needed to do *something*. Something that would breathe life back into her lungs. Something that would be worthy of filling the empty squares on her imaginary quilt.

Caroline touched her toes, the pain from her tight hamstrings unfamiliar and excruciating. It was hard to remember when she'd been in top swimmer's form, with all of her muscles supple and strong. That had been a very long time ago, and she wasn't even sure if that would be her goal. Right now all she wanted to do was take a walk around the lake to see if she could do it. If she got short of breath she would sit down, or call out to one of the nearby houses. However she did it, she just needed to *do* it. And if she hurried, she'd be back in plenty of time for Jewel's swimming lesson.

She started on the narrow dirt path that circled the lake and bisected the backyards and docks of the houses. Her arms pumped steadily at her sides, but she kept a moderate pace, paying attention to her heart rate. She slowed down if her heart raced too wildly and stopped twice to sit on a dock chair and rest. But her legs tingled and her breath deepened as she gulped in the lake breeze that stirred the water. It felt good to move again.

She was nearly three-quarters of the way around when a movement from a tall stand of grass by the water's edge caught her attention. Thinking it might be a nesting bird, she cautiously approached, making sure she didn't make any noise. Peering over the tall grass, she found herself staring down into the frightened red eyes of an injured loon.

She'd seen the loon only from a distance before, outlined against the night sky, and it startled her to realize just how big it was. It jerked its gray-brown-capped head as if to clear its vision and then stared at her again with its red eyes set in a black-and-white face. Only one of its legs was visible, set way back on its body as designed by Mother Nature for superior swimming ability, but it seemed to lie on the ground at an odd angle. It was hurt, and for a moment she felt a prickling of tears in her own eyes. She needed to help it, but had no idea how.

Moving closer, she noticed that one wing appeared to be bent in the wrong direction. It gave her another panicked look and she stopped, doing the only thing she could think of to reassure it: She started singing. Unfortunately the first song that came to mind was a jingle from a fast-food commercial. She wasn't quite sure who was more startled by the sound—her or the bird.

"If you keep singing like that, you might kill it."

She hadn't heard Drew approach. He wore running shorts and a T-shirt, and his face and body were soaked in sweat. Leaning forward, he had his hands on his knees, breathing deeply.

"I'm trying to soothe it. Let me know if you have any better ideas." She looked back at the loon and felt an embarrassing rush of tears. What was it about this bird that was affecting her so? "He's really hurt, and he'll die if I don't do something."

Drew's voice was gentle when he spoke again. "You're right. We can't just leave him here." He looked around the grass and then across the lake to where the distant hum of an engine sounded. "Damned waverunners. That's probably what happened to our little friend here." He lifted his shirt, showing off an admirable torso, and wiped his face with the hem. "Why don't I run back home? I've got a box big enough to put him in and some heavy work gloves in case he decides to bite. Once we get him in the box, we can take him to get help. Any idea where the nearest vet is?"

"No—but Rainy's probably as good as any vet. She's been patching up pets ever since I've known her."

Drew nodded. "All right. Stay here and I'll be back as fast as I can." He took a step and then said, "Just don't sing to him, okay? He's suffered enough."

She looked for something substantial to throw at him but had to settle for grabbing a handful of grass and dirt and throwing it in his direction. "Hurry up," she said, hiding her smile until she was sure he wasn't looking.

They found Rainy behind a counter in the store, doing an inventory of hand-knitted sweaters. Drew felt a moment of guilt. He'd said he would do the inventory, but he kept on finding excuses to avoid the store. Maybe it was because Rainy was more than happy to stay where she was until she could finalize the plans for her trip. Or maybe it was because he had no idea what he would do if he found out that he'd made a mistake.

Caroline rushed over to Rainy. "We found a loon. It looks like it might have a damaged leg and a broken wing."

Drew set the box on the floor, aware that no sound came from the box. He had padded it well with lake grass, but the bird had stopped struggling after it had been put inside. Drew wondered if it was preparing for a fight or had just given up. He was almost afraid to glance inside. If the loon were dead, he didn't think he could stand the look on Caroline's face. She had sat in the back of the truck with her arm around the box the whole way to Rainy's store, and he had to keep stealing looks in the rearview mirror to double-check that this was the same Caroline Collier he knew.

"Let me take a look." Rainy knelt by the box and carefully opened the top. The bird, with its long flat beak and red eyes, stared up at Rainy, then made a strange cawing sound, as if it had seen something to recognize in Rainy. She ignored the offered gloves Drew held out to her and instead reached inside to gently stroke the back on the short, black-and-white neck. She cooed and spoke gibberish to the loon, seeming to calm it a lot more than Caroline's singing had.

"What happened to you, sweetie?" Rainy asked as she gingerly stroked the wounded leg, feeling for a broken bone. "Looks like something got you good." Her hands reached the wing, and the bird reacted by trying to tuck both wings against its side and stand upright on its one good foot.

Caroline reached into the box, settling her hand gently on the back of the loon. "No, no—don't do that."

"What's he trying to do?" Drew asked.

Without looking at anybody in particular, Caroline explained, "When a loon is disturbed, he does this kind of penguin dance to scare away his enemies. It takes a lot of energy, and sometimes, if the danger doesn't go away, the loon will keep dancing until he dies from exhaustion."

Drew peered inside the box. "Is that why they call loons crazy?"

Rainy indicated a blanket thrown over a display chest and he went to retrieve it.

"Actually, that's a myth," Caroline said. "The Chippewa called him 'the most handsome of birds,' and said the loon had magical powers." She sat back on her heels and watched as Rainy lifted the bird from the box and settled it on her blanket-covered lap. "They also said that—" She cut off her words abruptly, making clear it wasn't something she wanted to share. Rainy gave her an encouraging look, but Caroline looked away and remained silent.

Rainy sat with the bird on her lap and kept stroking the head, the loon subdued and relaxed under her hands.

Caroline sat nearby, watching the bird closely, and began speaking to no one in particular. "Don't really know why we have loons on Lake Ophelia—they're not supposed to be here. They breed and live in Canada and some of the northern states, then migrate down here to the southern coast for the winter. Guess a family made a pit stop here and decided to stay and come back every year."

Rainy eased her legs out in front of her to better see the bird's injuries. "Looks like we've got a lot of work to do before you fly to the coast for the winter, hmmm?"

The loon nodded as if agreeing, then settled back down.

"I think I'll stay here today with the loon. Mom wanted me to help her organize something in the quilting room, but I think that can wait," Caroline said.

"Don't be silly," Rainy said. "I'll be fine. There's not much I don't know about fixing broken animals."

Caroline looked at the bird as if unsure. "I don't mind staying. . . ."

"I'll be fine—really. Nothing to worry about." She smiled down at the bird nestled into her lap. "See? We're old friends already."

Standing, Caroline brushed dust off her knees. "All right then. But if my mother calls, please don't tell her that I touched the bird. She'll have the rabies shots ready before I get back."

Drew frowned as he looked at the uncounted inventory. "Do you want me to stay and finish this? You'll be busy with the bird."

"I'll be fine—really. I'd rather do it myself, anyway—harder to mess up. Plus, I don't really expect a horde of customers, what with it being the off-season. So you two go on and do whatever it is you need, and when you get back I'll still be here."

They said their good-byes, then Caroline reluctantly followed him out to the truck.

They traveled silently for a few miles before she asked if she could turn on the radio.

"You're not going to sing, are you?"

She couldn't hold back her smile. "No. Promise."

They rode the rest of the way listening to a country music station, and he watched from the corner of his eye as her fingers seemed to accompany the music on an invisible piano. She caught him looking at her and followed his gaze as if she had been unaware of her actions, then clasped both hands together in a ball on her lap.

"How do you know so much about loons?" he asked.

She looked down at her hands and clasped them tighter. "My brother, Jude. He loved them, so he checked out every book he could find in the library and learned just about everything about a loon it's possible to know without actually being one." She smiled at the memory, and her hands loosened their grip.

"What was that other thing about loons you were going to say back there at Rainy's? You started, and then you stopped and you left me curious."

Her hands closed into a tight ball again. "I don't remember. Something to do with the loon's call and what it meant to the Indians."

He was silent for a moment. "I wish I had known him. Shelby talked about him all the time. He must have been a great guy."

She looked at him, her face relaxed for the first time since he'd met her. It was a pretty face, and definitely one that he would have pursued if he didn't know better.

"He was. Everybody loved Jude. He was one of those people who got along with everybody, and was good at everything he did." She looked like she was going to say something else, but stopped and glanced down at her hands again.

"What? Say it."

Her smile deepened and she ran her hand nervously through her ponytail. "Oh, it's just that I always thought Shelby and Jude would get married. They were like two halves of the same person. She was two years older, but you never would have guessed it."

"But then he died."

She turned toward her window and nodded.

"Seventeen's pretty young to die." He didn't know why he kept prodding her. At first he thought it was because it was such a challenge to get her to open up. But after he saw her smile, it became something else entirely.

He watched as her hand clutched at her heart, gripping the fabric of her shirt without her even seeming to notice it.

"Yeah. Way too young."

"I remember the year. I was a senior at UNC and Shelby was a sophomore. I think I'd been in love with her since I first saw her in art history class her freshman year. I would have pursued her then, but she made it very clear that there was no room for anybody else but Jude. So we just became very good friends."

Caroline's brows drew together. "She certainly didn't waste any time marrying you after Jude died. It was within a year. I think that's why I lost contact with her. I don't think I ever forgave her for that."

He stared hard out of the windshield. Finally he said, "She never stopped loving him."

She turned her head to look at him but didn't say anything.

"I knew it when I married her, too." He shrugged, trying to slide the heaviness off his shoulders. "She loved me, in a way. But I know she never really got over losing Jude."

"Didn't that bother you—knowing you weren't her first choice?"

He stretched his fingers on the steering wheel, noticing the new calluses and chipped nails. "No. It's hard to be jealous of a dead man. And I loved her. I always felt that having a little bit of her heart was better than nothing at all."

Glancing over at her, he saw that her knuckles were white where she clutched at her shirt and she was practicing her breathing exercises again. It was time to back down. He let a lightness he didn't feel into his voice. "Is that why you don't like me—because Shelby married me?"

She relaxed against the car seat and dropped her hands to her lap. "No, that's certainly a reason, but there're plenty of others."

He threw back his head and laughed. He could see her trying to hide her answering smile by turning her head toward the window, but he saw the creases in her cheek. "Good one. You know, I suspect there's a lot more of that in you. I'd be lying if I said I wasn't looking forward to letting some of that out."

"That's assuming I tolerate your presence long enough for you to try."

He laughed again as they headed up the mountain, glad to have finally caught a glimpse of the girl who had once planned a trip around the world using her mother's credit card.

*October 2, 1987*

*Me and Mama have to check the bird feeder out back every day now and refill it. All those birds from the cold up north are stopping down here on their way to the Georgia coast or Florida. I like to think that it's the same birds each year, hoping to catch a glimpse of me. It makes it easier to watch them leave, knowing that I'll see them again.*

*Lake Ophelia is full of the cries of loons at night. It's odd to hear so many at one time. Jude says that they're solitary birds, with usually just a single family at a lake. I don't think it's because they don't like company, though. I think it's because a single cry is so incredibly beautiful. Sort of like people, really. They sometimes have to be by themselves to be able to work on the thing that makes their world more beautiful. When I see Jude practicing the piano or Caroline quilting, I think of the solitary loon out on the lake on a summer night, crying out to the moon.*

*We do have a pair of loons that come back every summer and nest. They're not supposed to be here, because they like the colder lakes up north, but this pair seems to have a fondness for our lake. Jude joked that it's because he asked them to. I didn't tell him, but I think he's right. He can pretty much get anything he wants just by asking.*

*Last summer, we were fishing at twilight out in the middle of the lake and we saw a loon run across the water in the funny way they have of taking flight. I heard its call straight overhead and I'd never heard it so close before. It made my skin tingle, and my scalp tightened like it does when I get one of my headaches. Jude was watching it, too, and he was frowning and his eyes were sad. He grabbed my hand and I felt a spark that made me feel funny in ways I'd never thought about with him before. We sat holding hands for almost an hour, not talking, just feeling. And then he rowed the boat back to the dock and helped me out. He didn't have to say that he had felt the same thing I had.*

*It wasn't until later that he told me that the Chippewa Indians had considered the cry of the loon to be an omen of death. He smiled when he told me, so I can only hope that he just said it to scare me.*

Jewel closed the diary and went back to the room where her mother's things were kept. She pulled out the quilt and spread it on the bed in the same way Rainy had spread her mother's quilt out on the craft table. As she had been reading her mother's diary, a niggling thought had kept bothering her, and she'd come to find out if she'd remembered correctly.

Closely examining each completed square, she tried to remember where she'd spotted what she was looking for. When she exhausted her search, she began at the top again, and worked her way through each square more slowly this time. She was about to give up and fold it back into the trunk when she had another thought. Picking up the top corner, she looked at the stitching in the border. There, in pale gold thread, was hand-stitched the outline of a bird shaped like a duck but with a long, flat beak and legs that were oddly set way back on its body.

A tingling at the back of her scalp warned her that a headache was on its way. But she sat on the bed with the quilt on her lap for several minutes, hearing a silent voice inside her head telling her that the quilt wasn't ready to be taken out of the trunk. Her fingers toyed with the stitching of the bird as she sat and thought about what it all meant.

Eventually she got up and folded the quilt back, where it would wait until it was ready to be seen.

# CHAPTER 13

CAROLINE WAITED UNTIL SHE HEARD DREW'S TRUCK PULL AWAY before she walked across the yard and knocked on Jewel's back door. She was surprised to see Jewel already in her swimming suit.

"Hi. I know I'm early, but I wanted to make a quick phone call to my boss in Atlanta before our lesson this morning."

Jewel opened the door wider. "Sure. You know where the phone is."

Passing through the rear of the house, Caroline once again noted the incredible furniture in the rooms they passed. She paused at the dining room, empty except for a table and two chairs.

Jewel moved into the room ahead of her. "My dad's not finished with this room yet. He's planning on making more chairs and a buffet table to store my mom's pottery."

Caroline squatted to look at the large breakfront and ran her hand over the carvings, her fingers outlining the dips and creases of the wood, almost sensing the passion of the man as he created something beautiful from a solid block of wood. She jerked her hand away, as if she could feel the connection between herself and the craftsman.

"I think he means for this furniture to be all about my mom." Jewel pointed to the top of the cabinet. "See—here's an unfinished canvas of a painting she was working on when she died. If you look around the edges of the chest, you'll find her paintbrushes and things she kept around her workroom that helped her paint."

Caroline stood and walked around the table slowly, taking everything in and wondering anew at the artistry of the work and still not being able to associate it with the artist. "What did your dad do before he came here?"

"He was a partner in a big law firm. He always worked a lot."

Caroline's eyes widened. "You're kidding."

"No. Seriously. Why do you think I'm kidding?"

"Oh, nothing. I'm just . . . surprised. I mean, he really has a talent for furniture making. I just can't see the same guy who makes this furniture as a lawyer, that's all."

Jewel sat down in one of the chairs and ran her hand over the smooth surface of the table. "Yeah, my mom used to say the same thing. They argued a lot about it. He said that he was as good a lawyer as he was a furniture maker. I think my mom understood that—but she hated that he spent all of his time as a lawyer. That pretty much didn't leave any time for anything else."

"Does he miss it? Being a lawyer, I mean."

"Yeah, I think he does. He loves making furniture, but I think he misses being a lawyer; not that legal things got him so excited, but more like he misses mixing with other people, and arguing to get his way, and basically using his brain. After Mom died, he had this stupid idea that we needed to change our lives completely, so we sold everything and moved up here. He even bought a pickup truck. He looks *so* ridiculous in it."

Caroline didn't agree at all, but she kept the thought to herself. "So you don't like it here in Hart's Valley?"

The girl shrugged. "It's not that bad—not that I'll tell my dad that, of course. But I don't think my dad's any happier than he was before. He bought Grandma Rainy's shop, but he doesn't seem real excited about it. As much as he loves making his furniture, I think he needs to have his brain challenged in a different way, too, you know?"

"Tell me about it. I think I'm going to die of brain atrophy if I don't start using mine again. Speaking of which, I'm going to go use your phone now. Why don't you go outside and start your stretches? I'll be there in just a minute."

Jewel rose from her chair slowly. "What about you? You said you were an accountant. Didn't you ever miss the quilting you used to do?"

Caroline stilled, amazed again at this young girl who always seemed to see things much more clearly than most adults she knew. "I kept myself too busy to think about it."

Jewel stared at her with those eyes that made Caroline want to squirm under their scrutiny. "My mom used to tell me that it's always the things you avoid that are the things you should do first. The more you avoid them, the harder they seem to chase you."

"What's that supposed to mean?"

"Well, maybe you should get back into quilting again. I mean, what else are you going to do while you're up here?"

Caroline pushed a chair under the table a little too hard, making it knock into the wood. "I don't think so. I'm so out of practice, and I have no patience for it anymore."

Jewel just stared at her, not saying anything.

"I mean, where would I start?"

"Well, there's my mother's quilt. You'd have your mom and my grandma to help you get started. Plus, you knew my mom. You'd be able to add stuff that would make it special."

"I don't know. . . ."

"Oh, come on. If you don't like it, you can quit. Just give it a try."

Caroline felt herself wavering, could almost feel the cotton fabric under her fingers and the tug and pull of a needle guiding thread. "Well, maybe just once, to get everybody started . . ."

"Great! We're meeting at your house tonight at seven o'clock. I'll tell Grandma Rainy that you're coming. See you outside."

Caroline stared at Jewel's retreating back, wondering what had just happened.

Jewel turned around in the doorway. "Do you remember if my mom ever started a quilt for somebody?"

"No, definitely not. She hated to sew and wouldn't have anything to do with it. Her thing was painting."

Jewel looked as if she wanted to say something else but then closed her mouth. Then she took off again and called out, "See you outside," before Caroline heard the sound of the back screen door slamming shut.

Caroline sat in her dad's old director's chair, one of the few of her father's possessions her mother hadn't yet thrown out. The bottom sagged and the navy-blue color had long since faded to a washed denim, but she loved it. It was one of the only things at the lake house that hadn't changed.

She took a long sip of coffee, the last of the caffeinated coffee she had brought with her before her exile from Atlanta. Anything that might stir her heart had been efficiently banned from the house by her mother. She took another sip, feeling a familiar heaviness in her chest and thinking that she'd been relatively successful doing pretty much the same thing for the last thirteen years.

"Nothing like a quiet night on the lake, is there?"

Caroline turned to see Drew approaching, his hands tucked deep into the pockets of his khaki pants, his button-down shirt untucked at the waist and sprinkled liberally with sawdust.

"When it's quiet, anyway." She turned back to the lake.

"If I didn't have utter confidence in my suave style and easygoing nature, I would think that you were trying to give me the brush-off."

She looked at him and raised an eyebrow.

"Well, thank you. I think I will sit for a while." He sat down on the deck beside her, stretching out his long legs and crossing them at the ankles.

"Did you come down here just to harass me?"

"No, actually. I came for my cordless phone." He held out his hand. "Can I have it back, please?"

Caroline tried her best to look affronted. "What makes you think I've got it?"

It was his turn to raise an eyebrow. "I went to use it and saw it wasn't there, and it took me less than one second to figure out where it might be. Did you get any reception down here?"

With a heavy sigh, she reached under her cardigan and pulled out the phone. "No. Not that it would matter, anyway. When I do speak with my boss or my coworkers they all tell me not to worry about anything, to take it easy and they'll take care of everything."

"Hard to imagine that the world turns without you, isn't it?"

"It's not that at all. I love my job and I want to make sure it's still there when I get back."

"It's a good thing to love your job. There're too many people out there who are tied to their desks doing something they dread getting up for every morning. But the one thing about a job is that it can't love you back."

His words stung, especially since her mother had spoken almost the identical words when she'd come to the hospital after Caroline's first panic attack. How could she ever explain to them that it was more than just loving her job? It was more like loving the way it filled that huge empty void inside her so she wouldn't have to think about anything else.

She stood and began folding up her chair. "You don't know the first thing about me, and you certainly don't have the right to be making judgment calls about me."

He stood, too, and reached to take the chair she was trying to fold while balancing her coffee mug in the other hand. "You're right. I'm sorry. And I wasn't really talking about you at all. I was making an observation about my own life."

"Oh." She felt her anger deflate a little. "I'm . . . sorry."

"But if you heard some truth, then maybe it's a good thing I said it."

She reached for her chair to yank it out of his grasp, but when he lifted it, she saw a long, angry cut bisecting his forearm. A small beige Band-Aid inadequately stretched across the middle of it. "What happened? Did you irritate somebody so much that they bit you?"

"No, actually. It was our loon. Rainy made it an inside pen in her kitchen, and I went to move the darned thing and it attacked me."

The chair clattered to the dock as she let go of it to look at his cut. Something had softened inside her when he'd said *our loon*. "Weren't you wearing your gloves?"

"Well, it was acting so docile in Rainy's lap that I thought it was used to us humans, so I just reached in without any protection."

"Score one for the loon," she said under her breath as she studied the cut. His skin felt warm under her fingers, surprising her somehow. She jerked her head up and realized they were standing very close, unnerving her. He was smiling at her, completely comfortable being that near.

She dropped his hand, feeling hot and flushed all of a sudden. "Come on up to the house. My mom has an arsenal of emergency first-aid supplies, so I know we'll have something to fix you up better than that little Band-Aid."

She began walking, sensing him following close behind her.

"Are you going to use Merthiolate?"

Caroline stopped in surprise, then laughed out loud, recalling the time she, Jude, and Shelby had taken a ride on Caroline's bicycle banana seat and had hit a curb, mangling the bike and tearing skin off of arms and legs. Caroline's mother had panicked and had rushed out of the house with a large bottle of Merthiolate, the red-staining, germ-killing, scream-out-loud-painful antiseptic. She kept telling them that the more it hurt, the more germs it was killing. Her mother had made Caroline go first, and she remembered holding in her own screams so Jude wouldn't be scared. Their skin had been streaked red from the medicine so that when Rainy came to pick up Shelby, it appeared that they had been thrown into a combine, and she had nearly fainted. It had been an experience they had never forgotten, and one that had made them laugh every time they thought about it.

"Did Shelby tell you about the Merthiolate?"

She heard the smile in his voice. "Yeah, she did. Can't say I've ever been treated by it, but I think I'd rather my arm fall off. Less painful that way."

She sent him a sidelong glance. "Maybe my mother still has some hanging around inside a medicine cabinet. If not, we'll use the boring old pain-free stuff."

As they reached the porch steps, Drew put a hand on her arm and gently pulled her to face him. "You should laugh more often, you know. It's good for you."

Her lighthearted mood faded, his words bringing her back to the present and reminding her of the reason she didn't laugh anymore. She pulled away from him and reached for the doorknob.

He stood right behind her. "You can't run away forever, you

know. Eventually everything you've been running from will find you. It'll be like an oncoming wave, and if you're not looking for it, it can drown you."

She struggled to keep her breathing even. "You don't know. You can't possibly know."

"You're right. I can't. But I can speak from my own experience. Maybe your being here with your mother is your second chance. And that's something most of us never get."

What was it about this man who refused to tiptoe around her feelings like everybody else? She felt an alarming urge either to push him hard or hold him close. She did neither. Instead, she turned away and opened the door. "Let's go see if we can find some of that Merthiolate."

She heard him chuckle behind her as he followed her inside.

Rainy, Margaret, and Jewel were already sitting around the table with a quilt spread between them.

Rainy stood and came toward them. "This is girl time, Drew. What are you doing here?"

He held out his arm. "Caroline doesn't think my doctoring is good enough. She's come to make sure my arm doesn't putrify."

Rainy smiled widely at Caroline. "Too bad they don't make Merthiolate anymore, huh?"

Caroline laughed again, a sound he realized he had begun listening for, waiting for it in the same way he imagined the desert waited for rain.

He turned to see if Margaret was laughing, too, but she only looked at them in confusion as if she had no idea what they were talking about.

Caroline seemed to notice, too, and she quickly sobered. "I'll get him fixed up and have him out of here as soon as possible, if not sooner."

"And then you can come join us," Rainy said. "Jewel told us that you agreed to help get us started. We're trying to decide how the whole thing is going to be laid out."

Caroline pursed her lips, as if regretting a rash promise. "I'm pretty tired. . . ."

Margaret Collier piped up. "It's still early, dear. I'll make us some of that low-salt, butter-free popcorn that you love so much, all right? All that crunching should wake you up."

Drew waggled his eyebrows at her. "Or you could come over to my house and watch TV with me."

"I'll be right there, Mom. Save me a spot." She headed toward the back hallway, not waiting to see if he followed.

They walked through what he figured was Margaret Collier's bedroom on the way to her bathroom. A large four-poster bed dominated the room, but what really caught his attention were the numerous framed photographs liberally sprinkled on the bedside tables, dresser, and walls. A large photo near the bed caught his attention, and he picked it up to examine it more closely.

Caroline popped her head out of the bathroom. "Did you get lost?"

"No, just taking a break."

She moved to stand next to him. "From what?"

"You."

She tried to take the picture from him. "Come on, I haven't got all night."

He held firmly to the frame. "Is this Jude?"

Caroline nodded, her hands dropping to her sides as they both looked at the picture of a boy in a football uniform, kneeling on one knee with his helmet tucked under an arm.

"He looks a lot like you." The boy in the picture was blond, with gray-green eyes. His wide, engaging smile captured Drew's attention. There were hints in it of Caroline, and he wondered if she had ever smiled like that, without any hint of the sadness that now haunted her eyes.

"Yeah. People used to think we were twins. I was just a little over a year older than him, but we were about the same height for a long time before he outgrew me. He would get such a kick out of it, too.

He never even had to get a fake ID because he'd never get carded—just me. It was embarrassing."

Carefully, Drew put the picture back on the table and glanced around the room. "Where are all your swimming pictures?"

"Good question. You'll have to ask my mother. It's actually kind of hard to find a picture of me—there aren't that many. Tons of Jude, though."

She said it blithely, like it didn't bother her.

"Maybe I'll ask her," he said as he followed Caroline to the bathroom and waited for her to pull out antiseptic and bandages.

Her fingers were cool on his skin, and he could tell she didn't like being this near to him. It made him stand even closer.

"What have you got against quilting?"

She looked up from where she was dabbing at his wound with a cotton ball, and he could tell she was startled to find his face so close to hers. It was a technique that had always worked in the courtroom.

"Nothing." She went back to applying antiseptic, and he thought for a minute that she wasn't going to say anything else. Instead she said, "Was there anything that you used to love doing but it reminded you so much of Shelby that it hurt every time you did it?"

He thought for a moment. "Not really. Not anymore. That's why I moved here. She was always the one encouraging me to make furniture."

"It's . . . different for me. I was . . . I was with Jude when . . . when he died. That's the only thing I see when I pick up a needle." She reached for the box of bandages and knocked it over, spilling most of them onto the floor. "Damn. Why do you always seem to make me talk about things I don't want to? Can't you just leave me alone?"

She grabbed a handful of bandages that had stayed on the edge of the counter and began peeling the wrappers.

He made his voice gentle. "Maybe that's what's wrong with you. Nobody makes you face what's hurting you."

Caroline began sticking three large Band-Aids on his forearm, a few more than necessary in his opinion, but certainly enough to pull off most of the hair on his arm.

"Nothing's wrong with me. Before I was forced to come here, I was perfectly fine."

"Fine—but not happy, I would suspect, or you would have used that word."

She stared at him, and he was surprised to see tears in her eyes. "Stop trying to analyze me. I've had plenty of that over the years, and none of it helped. I learned to help myself and have earned the quiet, uneventful, and—yes—boring life that I have. It's the only peace I've found after thirteen years, and I don't need you digging up old stuff that doesn't matter anymore."

Caroline ran out of the bathroom, and he followed, watching her hesitate at her own bedroom door as if that were where she really wanted to be. Instead she turned back toward the great room, where Jewel and the two older women waited. She straightened her shoulders and took a deep breath, then walked in.

He heard the smile in her voice. "Okay, I'm here. I'm going to sit here and sort through these pictures and allow you to pick my brain. But don't ask me to sew anything. That's just for beginners and old ladies. I'm merely the consultant on this project."

Drew watched as she took a seat near the craft table, understanding a little more about what it had cost her to enter that room, and feeling a flicker of admiration for that false bravado that lurked inside of her, occasionally forced to the surface when she was at her most vulnerable.

He said his good-byes, then left the women to their quilt and their memories.

# CHAPTER 14

Caroline sat at the folding table and stared at the boxes of photographs in front of her. She schooled herself to think like an accountant, in straight black-and-white columns. She would organize the pictures by subject and date and try not to notice the familiar faces that stared at her from the past.

She had just picked up the oldest packet—the ones of Shelby's infancy and early childhood—when Jewel called out in a strident voice from the craft table, "Caroline! We need your help!"

"Oh, come on. You haven't even had a chance to get started. How could you possibly need my help already?"

All three faces turned toward her, managing to look as lost and pathetic as she thought possible.

"All right." She stood and walked toward them, steeling herself to look over their shoulders at the quilt. "What seems to be the problem?"

Rainy flattened her hands against the quilt, her gold wedding band loose on her shriveled finger. "I started the first row without any real plan, which might have been a big mistake. You've always been a master at mixing colors and patterns so that it looks like it all belongs. I don't think we need to redo the first row, but I'd like your help in planning the next one."

Jewel popped off the bench as if she had been eagerly waiting a chance to escape. "I'm going to find something good on the stereo. I'll be right back."

Caroline walked slowly around the table, examining the piles of scraps and the bucket of fabrics Rainy had brought with her. She reached inside and pulled out a multicolored remnant containing every shade of blue. The colors were wrapped around one another like ribbons, each part separate but melding together at the edges to become whole. Blue had been Shelby's favorite color.

She held it up to Rainy. "You'll need to get more of this. I think it would be perfect for the border, to tie it all in together."

"Actually Margaret picked that out. She said it reminded her of Shelby and should be used in the quilt."

Caroline looked at her mother with surprise. Her mother had known Shelby all her life, but she never would have suspected that Margaret could look at that same piece of fabric and see what she saw. "Good choice, Mom. Can you get more?"

Her mother nodded, looking almost shy at the compliment. "They had a whole roll of it at the fabric store. Shouldn't be any problem."

"Great." Caroline continued her inspection, pulling out different scraps and fabrics and piecing them together, then taking them apart. She felt her heart slow to a steady rhythm, and her breathing quickened as she recognized the old excitement of creating something new and beautiful out of old scraps and memories. The pain was there, too, but it was pushed aside by the thoughts of Shelby and how much she would love it, and by the new purpose Caroline felt. It was almost as if she'd gone too long without water and it was finally beginning to rain.

"I think we should keep going with the idea you started with— soft pastels and baby hues and then each row growing more and more bright and vibrant."

Rainy took a hold of Caroline's hand and squeezed it. "Perfect. That's exactly how I remember her."

The loud bass of an Avril Lavigne song pounded from the stereo as Jewel joined them again and picked up a scrap of magenta fabric. "Wow—speaking of bright! You practically need sunglasses to look at this one." She waved it in front of Caroline's face. "Where will this one go? The year she married my dad?"

The old pain returned, extinguishing the excitement the way a strong breath would blow out a candle. She took the pink fabric from Jewel. "No, I think we'll use the magenta for when you were born."

Jewel wrinkled her brow. "Why not when she got married—isn't that more important on the quilt because it came first?"

Caroline took the cloth and focused on breathing the pain away. "Getting married was a high point in her year for her, I'm sure. But it was also a difficult year, too. She lost a good friend."

Jewel nodded slowly. "But wouldn't it be more realistic if on that row we showed a couple of really bright squares alongside some pale ones? My mom wasn't one of those people who would let sadness take over everything."

Once again, Jewel's ability to get to the heart of something without really appearing to try caught Caroline unaware. As she had felt with Jewel's father earlier, she wasn't sure if she should hug her or start defending her own actions. She caught her mother's gaze, and before she could read the "I told you so" look she was sure would appear, she set the fabric square back on the table and stepped away.

"That's a great idea—why don't we go with that one? But I think you all have enough to get started right now, so I guess I can leave. I'll be in my room if you need anything else."

She'd made it across the room before Jewel called her back. "One more thing—I forgot to tell you earlier. The athletic club at my school is having a booth at the Harvest Moon festival at the end of next month. We're using the money to buy new uniforms for some of the teams—including Windbreakers for the swim team." She raised her eyebrows as if to indicate to Caroline that was the main reason she was mentioning it. "We're looking for more vendors—those are the people who sell things—and I remember Grandma Rainy saying that you used to make these cute quilted place mats when you were in high school and that they always seemed to sell like cheap nail polish."

She was about to give her automatic response of no, when Shelby's words floated through her mind. *Find the one thing that scares you the most and do it.* She looked at the eager face of the young girl and remembered how hard she swam each morning and how she still looked at the water with revulsion but dove in anyway. "Yeah, I can make a few place mats. Just tell me how many you want and what else I'll need to do."

Feeling as if she'd done her good deed for the day, Caroline turned toward her room, but her mother called her back. With a sinking feeling, she faced the room again.

"Remember how they used to auction off one of your memory quilts? The winner would get to pick out the colors and give you all her memorabilia and you'd make one for them. It was always *the* highest moneymaker for your swim team, remember?"

She groaned inwardly. Having a conversation with her mother felt a lot like being tied to a sinking boat. She didn't want to be where she was, but she didn't have any choice about it, either. "Yes, Mom. I remember."

"Wouldn't it be great for you to do it again? And since you have so much time now, you could auction off two quilts. Think of all the money you'd bring in for the athletic association!"

Rainy stood, placing her hand on Margaret's arm. "Now, Margaret—give the girl a chance to breathe. She's supposed to be here to rest, not spend all of her time and energy making memory quilts for strangers."

Caroline sent a look of gratitude to Rainy. But when she saw the disappointment on her mother's face, she had to add, "I'll think about it," before saying good night to everyone again and turning toward her bedroom.

Jewel's voice followed her down the hallway. "Besides—she's going to help with Mama's quilt, and that's going to take a lot of time. And why would she want to help the swim team out, anyway? I'm not allowed to be on the team, and she won't even think about getting in the water anymore."

She almost turned back and marched into the room to defend herself. But what Jewel had said was true and there wasn't anything she could say that would change a thing.

As an afterthought, she turned toward the garage instead of her room, taking her purse off a hook in the back hallway as she passed through it. Staring at Shelby's quilt, she had realized what needed to be added to the border. But she wanted to see the loon again to study the shape of the bill and the curve of the head to make sure she got it right. Besides, she'd been thinking of the injured bird all day and how she hadn't heard its call the night before. The lake at night was as lonesome as the stone Ophelia without the loon to cry out to the still water. She wondered if the loon missed the water as much as the water missed the loon.

*January 5, 1990*

*Caroline is going to make a quilt for Jude. He's always asked her for one, but she keeps telling him that he's into so many different things that the quilt would have to be a mile long and a mile high to fit everything on it. But then yesterday while we were ice-skating Jude did something that I think made her change her mind. Gayla Sperron (who thinks she's so great because she's a cheerleader and her dad owns the Mercedes dealership in Truro) was making fun of Caroline by saying she was going to be an old maid because she made quilts and she was never going to get married because her skin would be so wrinkled from all that swimming and she would be blind from all that close needlework. Jude dumped an entire Coke on her head and took Caroline home.*

*I think Gayla is just jealous of Caroline because she sees what Caroline is really like behind the glasses and the face without makeup—and even Gayla knows that when that mask comes off there will be no competition! I just hope that I'll be around when that happens.*

*Anyway, Caroline said she was ready to do a quilt for Jude. She doesn't know how long it will take her—especially since she says she'll only work on it while they're here for holidays (like now). She's started working on it at my mom's store but has asked me if I could keep it in my hope chest when she goes back to Atlanta. She said Jude is just like a little kid before Christmas—always searching for hidden presents. I guess that's just another reason why everybody loves him—he's always expecting something great in every dark corner. Caroline said she wished she could be more like him. She laughed and said that every time she looked in a closet or under a bed, the only thing she expected to see was her mother's face telling her to stop. It's funny how the biggest truths always seem to be hidden in humor.*

*Unfortunately, I think she's right. But not for the reasons Caroline thinks. As much of a jock as Jude is, he needs mothering. You know that expression "Still waters run deep"? That's Jude. Deep inside he's shy and insecure, and his mother knows this. He needs that extra attention from her, and she gives it to him so he can be the boy he wants to be. She protects him from unpleasant things because she knows how hard he'll take it. It's because of her that he always sees the sun behind every shadow.*

*It's different with Caroline, though. Mrs. Collier once told me that when Caroline was small she wouldn't let anybody show her how to tie her shoelaces—she wanted to do it all on her own. She stayed outside on the porch one whole day until she could figure it out and never once allowed her mother to help. I think Mrs. Collier has just learned to stay out of her way but make sure she's there to stop her before she gets hurt. I wouldn't want that job at all. It would be too much like holding up your hand to stop a speeding train.*

When Drew pulled up in the parking lot of Rainy Days, he saw Margaret Collier's Cadillac parked outside. Since he knew that the quilting bee was still happening at her house, he figured it had to be Caroline inside.

He looked for the key on his key ring and then remembered he hadn't put it there yet. He wasn't sure what he was waiting for. He didn't officially take charge of the store until November first, but Rainy had made it very clear that she already considered him to be the new owner. Testing the doorknob and finding it unlocked, he entered the store.

A soft humming came from the kitchen, and he walked through the darkened store toward it. The door was half-open and he stood for a moment looking in.

A circular pen made up of chicken wire and rushes took up most of the space in front of the bay window. The loon sat at the edge of the pen, one leg and one arm sporting bright white bandages, allowing itself to be stroked on the back by Caroline, who sat cross-legged on the other side of the chicken wire.

She was humming, but she had an expression on her face that made it clear her thoughts were far away from the kitchen in the back of Rainy's store. A slight smile curved her lips, as if she were privy to a joke, and it made her eyes sparkle.

"Thinking happy thoughts of me driving out of town and back to South Carolina?"

The sparkle in her eyes left when she spotted him.

"No, of course not." She bit her lip as if trying to keep from smiling. "I'm thinking of you flying out of town in a plane. That way you'd go faster."

"That's sweet of you. Thank you." He came closer to the pen. "How's our loon doing?"

"*Our* loon?"

"Yes, *our* loon. I don't remember you getting your arm all scratched up to get him here. He's as much mine as he is yours."

She stopped petting the bird and let her hands fall to her lap. "Yeah. I guess you're right. And if I forgot to say it, thank you for helping me save him."

Drew nodded and moved to sit next to her. They both stared into the pen at the broken bird as she spoke.

"Do you really want to know what I was thinking about when you came in?"

"As long as it won't make me blush."

She looked at him, startled, and her cheeks flushed.

"Sorry," he said. "I was only joking."

She began examining her hands in her lap as he'd seen her do before. It was almost as if she needed to be reminded that it was really her speaking. "I was thinking about the time Jude wanted to catch a loon in the middle of the night. He could always talk anybody into doing anything. He got me out of bed, then went and threw rocks at Shelby's window until she came out, too. Then he got a huge butterfly net out of the shed and piled all three of us in a two-person canoe. We followed the cry of the loon until we got to its nest next to the shore. We sat really still for almost an hour, waiting for it to take off. Jude should have known better—since he knows so much about loons—because we were right in the middle of its path. See, a loon is a really graceful swimmer, but it's the clumsiest thing on land and when it's trying to get airborne. It almost needs a runway to paddle its legs and flap its wings before it can rise in the air."

Drew rubbed his hands over his face. "I don't think I want to hear the rest of this."

"Yeah, well, that's pretty much what my mother said, too, when she heard us come inside at five in the morning soaking wet and the canoe missing."

"You were lucky nobody got hurt."

She rubbed her hands over her arms as if still feeling the chilly water of the lake. "Yes, we were. But even after all that, I would probably say it was still one of the best nights of my life."

He studied her for a moment, the pale skin over the fine bones, and found himself wishing that he had known her then, when she had laughed freely and had once felt the excitement of sitting on a darkened lake waiting to catch a wild bird.

"Did he ever catch one?"

She shook her head. "No. He said it was a good thing. That there should always be something out of reach to wish for."

"Like crying for the moon."

She looked at him oddly. "No, not really. Having a real goal is worthwhile. Wanting something you'll never have is a different thing entirely."

Drew was silent for a moment. " 'Crying for the moon' was Shelby's favorite expression. She could never understand why so many people spent so much of their energy wishing for something they couldn't have that they ignored what they did have."

Caroline turned away toward the loon, her face still and lovely in the soft evening light. He watched her swallow before she spoke.

"He's doing fine. He looks ridiculous with those bandages on him, but Rainy swears she knows what she's doing. She's always been one to put things back together."

"Did she help you—after your brother died?"

He didn't think she would answer at first. But it was as if the loon had somehow become a mediator, a conduit to translate their words while deleting anything the other might take offense to. Somehow the injured bird and the story she had told him had placed them on neutral ground—for now, anyway.

She nodded. "Rainy was there for me. She's always been there for me."

He felt his lawyerly instincts surface. He didn't want to spoil the rare noncombative mood, but he couldn't stop himself. "What about your mother? Did she help?"

He knew he'd made a mistake when he saw her straighten her back and lift her shoulders. "I couldn't cry, and all she could do was tell me there was something wrong with me because I wasn't crying. It was only because of Rainy's intervention that my mother didn't send me to a psychiatrist."

"What about your dad—were they divorced then?"

Her voice had changed. It wasn't the soft, dreamy voice she'd used to recount the story about Jude and the loon. This was the accountant's voice, and it had as much emotion in it as if she were calling out the bottom line in a profit/loss statement. "No. We were all one big, happy family before Jude died. And then my mom made it worse by chasing my dad away, too. She wouldn't even let me go live with him in California after the divorce."

She stood and brushed off the seat of her jeans with sharp slaps. "I've got to go. I wish you would stop dredging up the past. It serves absolutely no purpose but to bring back bad memories."

He resisted the urge to remind her that she was the one who'd started it. He'd enjoyed it too much to make her mad. "Not all of them were bad."

She finally met his eyes. "I think you need to leave now."

"It's my store."

"Not yet it's not. And I was here first."

He could see her concentrating on deep breathing again, so he backed down. Standing, he said, "Okay. I'll go now. Don't forget our shopping expedition in the morning."

She kept her gaze focused on the loon. "Don't let the door hit you in the butt on the way out."

He almost smiled. Instead he said, "By the way, did you know you've got a scrap of toilet paper in your hair?"

Her hands went up to her head.

"Just kidding. Figured you needed to lighten up before you stressed yourself out again."

He had the good sense to quickly leave the kitchen in time to hear the solid sound of a shoe hitting the closed kitchen door.

# CHAPTER 15

J EWEL CLOSED THE LID OF HER MOTHER'S TRUNK, CATCHING PART
of the quilt in the latch. As she bent to lift the lid and clear the
material, the door of the bedroom opened and her father stood
there, his eyes widened in surprise. In fact, it was more than surprise.
He looked as if he'd seen a ghost.

"Oh, it's you," he said after a brief moment. "I didn't expect you
to be here."

She quickly faced him, her back to the trunk with the piece of
quilt still hanging out of it. "Likewise."

Slowly he stepped into the room. "For a moment I thought . . ."
His words trailed away as if he were just realizing who he was speaking to.

"You thought I was Mama?"

He nodded. "Yeah. I guess I never really realized just how much
you look like her until just a minute ago." He laughed nervously and
walked over to the windows, where the stack of unopened boxes still
sat.

"What were you doing in here?"

She shrugged, trying to look casual. "Just hanging out. I'm still
missing some of my books and was wondering if maybe they might
be in one of these unopened boxes."

She watched as his gaze strayed to the boxes with the still-intact
packing tape stretched across the tops.

"Did you find anything?"

"What?" Her breath stuck in her throat.

"Your books. Did you find any of your books?"

"Oh. No." Without turning around, she tried to pinch the quilt
corner into the crease between the lid and the trunk. "Well, I gotta

go." She started moving toward the door but the guilt overtook her before her hand reached the knob. Mama had always told her that a lie was a lot like a hot dog in a microwave: If left alone, it just got bigger and bigger until it burst and made a real mess.

Jewel turned around and faced her dad again. "Sorry."

He looked at her sharply. "For what?"

"For being in here. I came because I wanted to see what was in here and go through Mama's things. I know you keep the door closed to keep me out, and I'm sorry that I trespassed."

He sat down on the bare mattress on the bed frame and let out a heavy sigh and even tried a smile. "Actually, I kept it closed because I didn't want you to be upset by seeing your mother's things." He looked down at his hands before looking up at her again. "I read you wrong a lot, don't I?"

Jewel spotted the flash of white still dangling out of the trunk and quickly moved to it, putting herself between the quilt and her dad. "You could have asked, you know. And I would have told you that being with Mama's things makes her a part of me again." She thought for a moment, trying to think of words that would make him understand without hurting his feelings. "See, I thought you kept the door closed because you didn't want to be reminded of her."

He stared at her for a long moment as if seeing her for the first time. "You amaze me. You really amaze me. How did you get to be so smart?"

She grinned. "I inherited it from my mother."

Her dad smiled, too, as he stood. "So I guess that means that we can start keeping this door open."

Jewel nodded, but kept her back against the trunk.

Her dad stopped in front of her and indicated the trunk. "Did you find anything interesting in there?"

She shrugged. "No—not really. Just some old stuff. Junk, actually." She added quickly, "But I'd still like to keep it."

He reached up and patted her on the head, and she realized it had been a long time since she'd allowed him close enough to touch her.

"I promise that I'll never take anything out of this room without talking to you first, okay?"

"It's a deal." She stuck out her hand as if to shake. He took it, then pulled her closer for a hug. She wanted to pull back at first, before she realized just how good it felt to be hugged by somebody who loved you—even if that person didn't seem to have the first clue about who you really were. She had always loved being hugged by her father, but after her mom died they had fallen out of the habit. It was as if they needed to draw up new rules now that there were only two players.

"I miss her too, you know. And . . . and I know I wasn't around a lot before and that you used to always go to your mother with your problems. But, well, if there's anything you need to talk about, I'm here, okay? No matter what I'm doing, if I'm in my workroom or whatever, I want you to come to me and I'll give you my undivided attention. Promise."

He ruffled her hair as if she were six again and set her away from him. His eyes looked suspiciously bright, so she looked away, not wanting to embarrass him.

"Well, except for me not being allowed to try out for the swim team, everything is fine in my world right now. But I'll keep you posted."

He wrinkled his forehead as he studied her. "Let's not argue over this right now. I've already told you that I need you to build up your confidence, all right? It hasn't been such a long time since . . . since your mother died."

She looked out the window, trying not to feel angry. "What if I could show you what a confident and strong swimmer I am now?"

"But how can you be? You hardly ever come with me to the Y to practice. And you won't let me hire you a coach."

"Right. So you can show up every day to tell us what I should and shouldn't be doing and what wasn't safe."

His face looked pinched, as if she'd just stepped on his bare foot with her wooden clog. "Whatever would make you think I'd do that?"

She stared back at him with raised eyebrows and her arms crossed over her chest. "Hello? Remember the first—and last—session I had with a coach at the Y? Instead of reading the newspaper like all the other normal dads, you put on your bathing suit and jumped in the pool and started telling the coach how much I was afraid of the water."

Now he looked like she'd stepped on his foot with both clogs. "It was just . . . well, it's hard to forget about your mother . . . and how you were with her when she died. I didn't want you to panic in the water around people who didn't understand what you'd been through. I just wanted to be there."

Jewel turned around and fiddled with the scrap of fabric that had been stuck in the latch so her dad couldn't see her face. She had a feeling her eyes were suspiciously bright, too. "Yeah, well, maybe we can go to the Y this weekend. I bet you'll be surprised."

He laughed, and it felt good to hear the sound. There hadn't been much of that in their house lately. "Okay, it's a deal. And I promise I'll sit by the side of the pool and pretend to read my newspaper." He studied her silently for a moment. "And have I already mentioned how smart I think you are?"

"Yeah, a couple times. But don't let that stop you."

He squeezed her shoulders, then ruffled her hair again. "Hey, I'm supposed to take Caroline shopping today for some good walking shoes. Do you want to come with us? If she bares her fangs, I might need your help to fend her off."

She elbowed him in the ribs. "Yeah, sure. Whatever. I don't have anything going on today anyway."

"All right. Just be ready to leave at eleven. Which means you should start now, because that gives you only two hours to get dressed."

"Oh, please. It only takes me so long to get ready before school because I like to crawl back into bed after you wake me up." She grinned up at him as he raised his eyebrow. "I can be ready in twenty minutes—just watch."

He looked at his wristwatch. "Okay. You're down to nineteen minutes and fifty-nine seconds, so you'd better hurry."

"I'm going, I'm going," she said. Then she stopped abruptly. "Does that mean you're going to let me try out for the swim team in the spring?"

"No. I still think you're too young and you won't be ready."

She felt the familiar flash of irritation but didn't want an argument to disturb the new truce she and her dad had somehow managed.

"Forty-five seconds," he said, looking at his watch again.

"All right," she said as she scurried out of the room, thinking that she had just shared more words with her dad in the last twenty minutes than she had in the last year. And that maybe it was a very good thing.

Caroline was surprised to see Jewel with Drew when he pulled into the driveway. He got out of the truck, then moved to her side to open her door. "I hope you don't mind if Jewel comes with us. She needed some sneakers for PE, so I thought I'd kill two birds with one stone."

"Glad to be considered a bird, I guess." She looked pointedly at the door he was holding open for her. "And I'm not feeble either. I'm quite capable of opening my own car door."

He smiled that sickeningly sweet smile that showed off his white teeth and annoying dimple. "I never said you weren't. But I wouldn't be able to call myself a Southern gentleman if I didn't open a door for a lady."

She rolled her eyes as she slid into the front seat and greeted Jewel. "Is he always this annoying or does he save it up just for me?"

Jewel nodded her head emphatically. "Oh, he's definitely like that with everyone. Although I will say he always opened doors for Mama. She never thought it was annoying."

"No, I guess she wouldn't have." She leaned her head back against the seat, remembering Shelby and how, at five-foot-three, she'd inspired the protectiveness of anyone who towered over her—which was just about everybody.

Drew started the engine and pulled out onto the road. "I was trying to make a list this morning of everything we might need besides your footgear." His gaze traveled down her legs to her Keds-clad feet. She crossed them at her ankles, tucking her feet away from his view. "And I wondered if we should pick up some energy bars or something to help with your stamina. But I didn't know if there were any ingredients you had to avoid because of your antirejection medication, so I figured you could pick out whatever you'll need while we're there."

He gripped the wheel tighter, as if trying to figure the right words. "And you'll probably want a fanny pack or small backpack to bring your medications and water bottles to swallow the pills."

She managed to repress a groan. She knew he was only being considerate, but she wished, just this once, that everybody didn't know about her condition so they wouldn't have to treat her differently. More than the scar, she hated that the most. "I've arranged to take my pills when I'm at home, so I won't need to be taking them with me on a little walk."

"I'm sorry, I didn't—"

"I had a heart transplant, not a brain transplant. And it hasn't made me feeble, either."

"I didn't mean to—"

"So what do you have to do differently?" Jewel asked with a sweet smile on her face.

"Nothing, really. My doctors have always told me that I can lead a relatively normal life. I don't need special treatment." She hated the way she sounded. She was just tired of giving the same explanation over and over again.

"Passing out in the middle of an argument doesn't seem normal to me." Drew sent her a pointed look.

"That was something completely different." She took a deep breath to explain, once again, what was wrong with her physically. She had found that as long as she kept her explanations to the physical scars, she wouldn't have to touch the other scars that nobody could see. "I haven't been taking care of myself. I have a stressful job, I don't eat right, and I never exercise. I have high cholesterol and even higher blood pressure. And a few months ago I had my first panic attack. The words alone sent my mother into her own panic attack, which is why I'm here. Okay, everybody? Now can we just drive to the store and get this over with?"

Everybody was quiet for a while and she considered the subject dropped. They stopped at a red light. It wasn't until they were rolling through the green light that Jewel spoke.

"It seems to me that your mom realizes how lucky you are to have that heart. Did you know that only a small percentage of the population checks the donor box on their driver's licenses? She probably feels as if you're taking a really incredible gift and throwing it away."

Spots erupted in front of her eyes, and she wondered for a moment if she'd stopped breathing completely, because no oxygen seemed to be entering her head. She always did that when the pain hit her too hard. It was a self-preserving mechanism, like the smoke alarms that turned on in the kitchen when her mother burned something on the stove.

She felt a warm hand on her forearm and thought it was Jewel until she opened her eyes and saw Drew's worried expression.

"Are you all right?"

She nodded. "I'll be fine. I . . . just . . . need to breathe."

Jewel grabbed her hand and squeezed. "We're almost there. I vote that we stop for lunch at Sidney's. They have the best chocolate shakes in the world."

Caroline managed a smile and nodded. "That's a great idea." Then she closed her eyes again and concentrated on the rise and fall of her chest until the truck stopped.

They pulled into a spot in front of Sidney's Deli and Drugs and then were seated at a small booth in the corner of the restaurant. An involuntary smile crossed her face as she remembered trips here with her mom and Jude. They had always ordered the same thing—grilled cheese, coleslaw, and chocolate shakes. Her mom had once claimed that one of Sidney's shakes could cure a person of anything. Caroline's smile faltered, knowing that however divine they were, there was nothing so easy that could take away the scars that never seemed to heal.

Sidney himself came to the table to take their order. He looked the same except he was grayer and rounder, as if his extra years on earth had somehow leached the color from him.

Caroline found herself speaking. "I'll have the grilled cheese special with coleslaw and the large extra-thick chocolate milk shake, extra cherries on the side in a bowl."

She caught Drew's gaze. "Don't say a word. It's comfort food. I figure I need that more than I need to watch my salt and cholesterol at the moment."

"I wasn't going to say a word."

"Sure you weren't."

"Really. I wasn't."

She studied him for a moment and could almost believe that he was telling her the truth. Maybe it was his lawyer eyes that made him so convincing. Or maybe it was the way he had touched her arm in the car that made her believe what he told her.

Jewel ordered the same thing. Caroline smiled and said, "Good choice."

"Grandma Rainy says the shakes are better than sex."

Drew's face turned an interesting shade of pink. "Jewel! That is not how young ladies are supposed to talk. You should know better."

Jewel stared at her father indignantly. "But Grandma R—"

Drew cut her off. "I don't care if the pope said it. That's not how you were raised."

"How would you know?"

Caroline wasn't sure whose face looked more horrified—Drew's or Jewel's. They both sat back on their respective benches and stared at each other in sullen silence. She watched them and felt guilty. It was good not being the center of attention for once, and to revert back to the girl she'd been before the accident. Back then she'd sat on the outside of her brother's social circle, invisible, but with eyes and ears that never missed a thing.

She looked now at father and daughter, at their similar poses and how each examined their fingernails as if they held great interest. A bystander wouldn't even think they were related, so dissimilar were their features. But anybody who studied them long enough could tell they were related at least by shared memories and by the things that were never said. Their lips moved silently, as if both were preparing to apologize, their faces mirroring the same grim image of something fragile and new ripped down the middle.

Sidney came out with their drinks and even managed to break a smile when he placed the overflowing shakes in front of her and Jewel. Caroline leaned over and sucked on the straw, almost overcome with the icy chocolate sweetness of it. It had been a long time since she could remember actually tasting what she put in her mouth. She imagined it felt a lot like getting a color television after living with black and white.

Closing her eyes, she said, "Rainy was right." Her eyes popped open. "Oh, my gosh—did I really just say that?" She clenched her hands over her mouth as if to prevent anything else from spilling out.

Jewel started laughing, and though Caroline could see he was trying to resist, Drew soon joined in.

With her mouth full of chocolate milk shake, Jewel said, "How would you know? You're not even married!"

Jewel continued laughing, but Caroline and Drew sobered quickly. Jewel spoke around her full mouth before swallowing. "Sorry. I meant that to be funny, but it didn't come out that way."

"Yeah, I figured. That's okay."

Jewel turned her full attention on Caroline. "So, why aren't you married?"

"Jewel!" Drew's face had turned to a mottled pink again.

Caroline held up her hand. "That's all right. I can answer that one." She forced a smile to show a lightness she didn't feel. "My work keeps me pretty busy, and the guys at the office are all either married or definitely not the kind you'd want to marry."

Caroline took another sip from her straw, trying not to notice that Jewel was wearing her contemplative face again, the one that reminded her of Shelby.

"Is it because of your heart? I mean, do you feel that since it started out as somebody else's that it's really not yours to give?"

The chocolate shake suddenly tasted like water. *Yes, yes, yes,* she wanted to shout. Nobody else had ever put into words the secret fears that had lived inside her for so many years. But they lived inside for a good reason, and she didn't think she'd ever be ready to expose them to the light of day.

Caroline took a long sip from her straw. When she thought she could speak again, she said, "No. It's just that . . . well, I'm not the marrying kind. My mother says I'm married to my work. Maybe she's right." She almost sighed out loud in relief when she spotted Sidney carrying their lunch order to the table.

She ate quickly, not pausing between bites to make room for words. She couldn't taste anything and she kept her head down, not wanting to see the identical expressions in two completely different pairs of eyes. And both expressions were telling her that neither one had believed a word.

# CHAPTER 16

J EWEL SAT IN TRURO'S GREAT OUTDOORS SHOP AND WATCHED AS
her dad and Caroline played tug-of-war without saying a word or
touching anything. Her mom used to tell her that her dad had a real
gift for making people talk—no matter how much they didn't want
to. That was why he'd been such a great lawyer. It was so obvious
Caroline Collier wanted to be left alone, and the more she retreated
to a corner, the more Jewel's dad would hover like a bee over honey.
If she didn't know better, Jewel would have thought that the two of
them were enjoying themselves.

Caroline slid the curtains across the rod in the dressing room for
about the fifth time and stomped out wearing hiking boots, socks,
and really short shorts, and barely resembling the woman who normally disguised herself in baggy T-shirts and jeans. Jewel's dad sat up
in his chair as they both watched Caroline tug at the hem of the
shorts.

"You look totally hot," Jewel said.

"What?"

Her dad cleared his throat. "I think she means that you should
get those. All those pockets and belt loops are perfect for hiking."

"Really? They're not too short?"

"Absolutely not." He cleared his throat again. "Did you find any
shirts? You'll want something to layer for cold mornings. And make
sure you have a bathing suit top to wear underneath for when it gets
warmer or you want to take a swim."

She went still, and Jewel wondered if her dad had said that on
purpose. She remembered seeing the scar on Caroline's chest the
night of the dinner party and knew Caroline would never let anybody see that scar if she could help it. But it seemed to her that the

actual scar wasn't what Caroline was hiding from other people. She had a distant hope that her dad wouldn't figure that out. As her mom had once said after watching her dad win a case, he could question somebody until they felt like they were lying naked under a microscope. Jewel couldn't help but think that would be the one thing Caroline Collier wouldn't be able to handle.

"I'll take the shorts and the boots—that's all I need." She turned back to the dressing room and slid the curtain back.

A few minutes later they stood together at the cash register as Jewel and her dad watched Caroline pull the money from her wallet. Every bill was flattened and facing the same direction, the denominations organized from lowest to highest.

Her dad leaned down and whispered loudly in her ear, "She's an accountant."

Caroline glared at him.

He responded by plucking a fuchsia sun visor off a nearby rack. "You might want one of these, too, in case you forget your sunscreen."

She looked at him for a long moment with a straight face before taking the visor and tossing it on the counter.

She paid for her items; then they left the store together. "So I guess this means we're all set for tomorrow, right?" At Caroline's nod, he continued. "I'd love to hike all the way up to Ophelia, if that's not too far for you. I stare at her every day, and I'm feeling that it's long past time I introduced myself."

Jewel's dad placed the clothes bag in the back of the truck before they all climbed in, Jewel in the middle. Caroline said, "It's been a long time since I climbed all the way up, but I'm pretty sure I still remember how to get there. It's an easy climb, with well-marked wide paths."

Her dad grinned in a way Jewel hadn't seen since her mother died. "Is it anywhere near that cliff you were telling me about where people fall off all the time?" He turned the key and started the engine with a loud hum.

"No. But I can certainly take you that way."

Jewel noticed Caroline's lips lifting before she turned away.

Her dad edged the truck out into the road. "No, that's all right. Another time, maybe."

Jewel sat back in her seat, enjoying the soothing rumble of the engine. She stared at the ceiling, spotting patterns on the neutral material that nobody else would. She could almost make out the profile of a woman staring out into a sea of beige car ceiling. "Who was Ophelia?"

Caroline shifted in her seat and shrugged. "Nobody knows for sure if she was even a real person. But, if she lived, it would have been about two hundred years ago."

"But what did she do that was so bad to have her cursed?"

Her dad looked at her with a frown, as if wondering where she'd heard of the legend. She almost told him about the diary, but held back. It was as if the same voice that told her to keep the quilt folded in the trunk were also telling her that it wasn't time for the diary to be known about, either.

She turned her head away from her father and pressed her cheek against the seat back, staring up at Caroline. Her hair had fallen out of its ponytail holder at the clothing store from slipping shirts on and off over her head, and Jewel had picked it off the floor and stuck it in her pocket. Caroline had great hair, and it was stupid to always keep it back in a ponytail.

Caroline began speaking as she fiddled with the strap of her seat belt. "I don't remember the story."

For the second time that morning, Jewel shared a look with her dad that pretty much said that they both thought what they were hearing could fertilize a cornfield. It was kind of fun realizing how much she and her dad seemed to see through Caroline—but not as much fun as watching her dad circling his prey. Her mom had always said that being around her dad kept people honest. She sneaked a look at Caroline and saw that she had turned her body to look out the window so that her back was practically facing them. Even she could read that body language. Whatever it was that Caroline Collier was trying to keep to herself, it didn't have a chance around her dad. And maybe that wouldn't be such a bad thing. From what Jewel could see, Caroline had more issues than *National Geographic*.

Her dad cleared his throat. "Well, as luck would have it, Shelby told me the story, and I seem to remember it pretty well. Seems that a young woman named Ophelia fell in love with a married man." He raised his eyebrows at her and Caroline as if to make sure he had an audience before continuing. "She was crazy in love and made up her mind that he was the only man she would ever want, even though it was clear that she could never have him. See, they didn't have divorces back then unless there were severe and extenuating circumstances. But Ophelia was an only daughter and had been spoiled by her parents since birth. She didn't know the meaning of the word *no* because she'd never been taught. Once she had her heart set on something, that's the way it would have to be.

"Anyway, the man must have loved her, too, because he petitioned the preacher and the judge for a divorce, saying his wife was a witch and that he wanted to marry a God-fearing woman like Ophelia.

"Now, two hundred years ago, you didn't take calling somebody a witch too lightly. They hauled the wife into jail, and when she didn't convince them otherwise, they burned her at the stake. But while she was up there being burned alive, she cursed Ophelia. She said that she was doomed never to have the one thing she wanted and that she would be turned to stone so that she would spend eternity wishing for something she could never have."

Jewel swallowed. "Wow. That's awesome. So what happened?"

Her dad continued. "The legend goes that the woman's husband took ill that day from a fever and died less than a week later. And then Ophelia disappeared, never to be seen again. Some say she killed herself and the animals got to her body so that it was never found. But then a storm came, wiping away all the vegetation on Hart's Peak. Soon after, people started noticing what looked like a face etched out on the stone, and everybody agreed that it must be Ophelia, turned to stone for all eternity, destined always to want what she could never have."

Caroline had relaxed into her seat and turned to face Jewel and her dad. Softly she said, "Jude could never stand a story without a happy ending. He used to tell people that just before the man's wife died on the stake, she caught a glimpse of the gates of hell. Afraid for her soul, she declared that through great pain and suffering Ophelia could reverse the curse and live again." She paused. "But she must give up the one thing she wanted."

Caroline shrugged, trying to appear relaxed, but Jewel could see her hands clenched into fists. "Doesn't look like she ever did, because her face is still up there." Smiling softly, she said, "Jude and I used to go look for her grave in the cemetery to see if a real person by that name ever existed. We never did."

Jewel leaned forward and flipped on the radio, figuring they had all heard enough about scorned women and old legends. She hummed along with half-closed eyes, watching Caroline's fingers accompanying the music on an invisible piano, playing notes that only she could hear.

*March 21, 1990*

*Jude has come up for a spring visit by himself. Mrs. Collier is letting Caroline go to a swimming camp this year that's run by the University of Georgia. It's really hard to get in, and Caroline said that anybody hoping to get a swimming scholarship needs to go to this camp during spring break. Mrs. Collier surprised everybody by saying yes without a fight. Caroline says it's because her mother wants to get rid of her for a week. Which is ridiculous, really. But maybe I was the only one who saw Mrs. Collier wipe her eyes when she told us last Christmas that Caroline had gotten into the camp. I think she's damned proud of her. We all are, but for a mom I guess it's different.*

*Instead of staying at his parents' empty house, Jude's staying here until his mom and dad come up in the next day or two. On the first night he brought his sleeping bag into my room like he always does and laid it on the floor, but my mother made him take it to the guest room. She said that now we are older, sleepovers in the same room aren't appropriate anymore. I know*

*Jude was as embarrassed as I was. Even after that time last summer when he held my hand while we were on the lake, I still tried not to think of Jude as a boy and me as a girl. We're best friends, and I don't want any of that to change.*

*But things are different. I guess things change whether you want them to or not. Like summer turning into fall. You'd have a hell of a time trying to put all the leaves back on the trees, so you might as well enjoy watching them fall before you make a huge pile to jump in. You still love the leaves, but in a different way. I suppose that's how I look at how I feel about Jude. When I was a little girl, I loved him like I loved my teddy bear and my favorite shoes and my collection of shells I'd found on my trips to the beach. But now that I'm older, he has become so much more to me. I need him in my life like the ocean needs the moon to shift her tides.*

*Last night we went for a long walk around the lake. We started right after supper when it was still light out, but by the time we'd made it halfway around, the sun seemed to melt into the most beautiful pink sky. That's when Jude kissed me. He surprised me at first because we hadn't even been holding hands. But when his lips touched mine, the pink of the sky seemed to sparkle in my mind, and I knew what all those romance novels my mom reads mean by fireworks exploding. He made me forever his at that moment, and I don't think I'll ever look at the cotton-candy color of a sky on fire without thinking of him.*

Caroline came home to find her mother sitting out on the deck drinking hot tea. The late-afternoon sun slanted across the backyard, lighting on her mother's hair and turning it from blond to gray. Caroline paused by the quilting table overlooking the picture window, the solitude of her bedroom pulling at her. But something in the slope of her mother's shoulders and the way her hands looked so frail against the china teacup made her move to the back door.

Margaret tipped her head. "I was wondering if you'd come join me." She smiled before reaching for her sweater draped around the back of the chair. It slipped to the ground and Caroline stooped to pick it up, staring into her mother's face as she did. The wrinkles appeared deeper out here, showing a woman who'd lived her sixty-six years.

She settled the sweater around her mother's shoulders; she felt how thin and vulnerable they felt and wondered how such an old lady could be her mother. Unexpectedly, Margaret set her hand on Caroline's. "I'm glad you came out."

Caroline dropped into a nearby seat, letting her shopping bag slide to the ground.

"What's all this?" Her mother eyed the bag with speculation.

"Oh, I did a little shopping in town today with Jewel and bought a few things."

"With Jewel, hmm? And who drove?"

Caroline dug into the shopping bag to hide her face, feeling the heat steal into her cheeks. She wasn't quite sure why, but she did know that she didn't want her mother drawing the wrong conclusions. "Drew did. I didn't argue because I'm trying to be nice to him—as tough as that is. He's probably the most annoying person I've ever met. But my company could make a fortune licensing his furniture designs."

"So how did it go?"

"How did what go?"

"Being nice to him."

"Oh. That. Well, it's a lot harder than I thought it would be. I'll try again tomorrow."

She thought she saw her mother smile as she dipped her head to take a sip from her tea. "I wouldn't think it would be that hard to be nice to a guy who looks like that."

"You think he's good-looking? I hadn't noticed." She took out the pair of shorts. "I got these and a pair of hiking boots."

"They're pretty short. Good for you. I always said you had a great pair of legs. Don't know why you always insist on hiding them."

Caroline stared at her mother. "You never said that—at least not to me, anyway."

Her mom tilted her head again, as if studying a puzzle she'd put all the pieces in but didn't recognize the picture. "No, maybe I didn't. I probably figured that if I told you, you'd hide them in long skirts or baggy pants." She smiled softly and stared out toward the setting sun drifting over the lake. "Do you remember the time you were in that horrible bike accident with Jude and Shelby? I was so afraid you'd scarred your legs that I grabbed a bottle of that terrible red stuff—what was it called?"

"Merthiolate," Caroline answered, unable to resist smiling back. "Yeah, I remember."

"Back then you practically lived in your swimsuit. You with those long, perfect legs—you were gorgeous in and out of the water. And I couldn't bear to think of you being embarrassed because of scarring." She took another sip of her tea and turned to Caroline. "You tried so hard to be brave and not scream, but I know how that must have hurt. I was so proud of you—even though you didn't speak to me for a week."

Caroline sat in the silence, feeling a bit like she'd just caught the Tooth Fairy putting a dollar under her pillow. The money was nice to have, but she wasn't sure she wanted to know who the Tooth Fairy really was.

"I never would have suspected. I always thought you did it so we wouldn't die of infection."

Her mother waved a dismissive hand through the air. "Nonsense. You three were so healthy, you could have fought off anything. As it was, I felt obligated to coat Jude with that vile stuff just so he wouldn't feel left out." She looked down into her teacup as if expecting it to give her an answer to something she hadn't yet asked.

Caroline leaned forward until her mother met her eyes. "I always thought you'd done it to punish me for hurting Jude."

Her mother's eyes widened and glistened with unshed tears. "I could never have picked a favorite, Caroline. I thought . . . well, when you became an only child, I thought things might be different."

Caroline stood and faced the lake. "I guess I had too much evidence to the contrary to make me feel any different. Nothing really changed after Jude died—except for Daddy leaving."

She didn't hear her mother stand, but she knew it was her hand that rested gently on her shoulder. "You're wrong, you know. It seemed to me that it became you and me against the world. Even if you didn't need me, I needed you."

The old hurt and disappointments kept Caroline from turning around. *What do you mean, I didn't need you?* She felt herself stiffen, unbending like a giant oak in a storm. If it bent just a little, it made it easier to fall over. "I wanted us to be a family again—with a brother and father. But you sent Daddy away and I knew that nothing would ever be the way I wanted it."

Her mother dropped her hand. "No, you're right. Nothing could be. Jude was gone forever. But that didn't mean that there wasn't something else for us out there—something to help us make a new start. I still think there is." Her voice trailed off into the late-afternoon sky.

Caroline looked up and saw the pale outline of the moon, waiting its turn behind the sun. Something in its frail loveliness made her want to cry. But she didn't. She hadn't cried in front of her mother since before Jude's death and she knew it was too late now.

The sound of Margaret's heels walking away made her turn around.

"I like the place mats you did—you left them out on the craft table and I couldn't resist looking at them. You have such a gift for color and pattern. I think they'll sell well."

Caroline nodded, feeling oddly pleased. "Yeah, I like the way they turned out." She stared long and hard at her mother. *Even if you didn't need me.* The words tugged at her like an insistent child, and she tried to make sense of them. She wondered what it had cost her mother to admit to that, and felt an urge to try to meet her halfway.

"I'm thinking about doing a quilt for auction. I mean, what else do I have to do while I'm here?" She shrugged, feeling the heaviness of her shoulders.

Margaret smiled, turning her into the young mother of Caroline's memory, and a flash of her mother picking her up after she'd fallen down when she was a child illuminated her mind. She had reached her arms up to place around her mother's neck and remembered her tears soaking into the cool linen of Margaret's dress. She hadn't been afraid to cry then.

"Wonderful. Well, I guess I'd better get dinner started. Would you like brown rice or couscous with your baked chicken?"

Caroline looked up at the moon again. "Why don't we go out for pizza instead?"

There was a slight pause. "All right. Pizza it is. Let me go change."

"Can I use the phone while you're getting dressed?"

Her mother had already opened the back door. "Don't push your luck, Caroline." She gave Caroline her stern-mother look but ruined it with a lift of her lips. "Give me five minutes and I'll meet you at the car."

Caroline quietly laughed and followed her mother inside.

# CHAPTER 17

CAROLINE SLID ON HER NEW HIKING SHORTS AND STOLE A glimpse in the tall mirror standing in the corner of her bedroom. She'd never call herself hot, but she didn't think she looked too bad, either. For no reason other than that the sun was shining and nobody was bothering her, she rolled the cuffs of her shorts up an inch, showing more thigh than she had since she'd last worn a bathing suit.

She searched for the ponytail holder she wore every day, then remembered she'd lost it in the store the day before when she'd been trying on clothes. A search through her dresser drawers didn't yield another, so she satisfied herself with tucking her hair behind her ears. She paused at the mirror, hardly recognizing the woman who stared back at her. This woman had soft hair that floated around a face that had a pinch of color to it and eyes that didn't seem so hollow. Maybe coming to the mountains had been the right thing. Or maybe that woman had always been there in the mirror and Caroline had never taken the time to really look at her. Perhaps it was a bit of both.

She grabbed her new hat, water bottle, sunscreen, and a sack lunch, then attempted to let herself out of the house without waking her mother. Drew had suggested meeting at Rainy's again, but after yesterday's conversation with her mother, she didn't think it would be so bad if her mother knew about her hikes. Her mother's words hit her again, warming her as they'd done when she'd first heard them. *Even if you didn't need me, I needed you.* The words had surprised her, and made her wonder what other secrets her mother had never shared with her. And how could she have never guessed that at one time in her mother's self-sufficient, independent life, she had actually needed her? Caroline shook her head as she fumbled with the back-door latch. She was almost thirty years old. Old enough to let some of the things hidden inside out in the open and see what the sun and light did to them.

"Take an apple with you!" her mother's voice called from the front of the house.

Caroline stuck her head back inside the door. "I got one already. And a power bar, too. I'll be with Drew, so you don't need to worry, okay?"

"I know—Rainy told me. You have fun. And don't forget your sunscreen."

Rolling her eyes, Caroline stepped out into the morning sunshine.

Drew was leaning against the passenger-side door of his truck when Caroline spotted him. So maybe her mother was right about him being good-looking—if you liked the annoying lawyerly carpenter type. She felt a momentary flash of power as his gaze swept her from head to toe then back again.

"I like those shorts."

"I believe you mentioned that yesterday." She allowed him to open the door, and as she climbed in, she said, "You might want to keep those eyes inside your head or else you might lose them."

He laughed, then made his way to the driver's side and behind the wheel. "Please promise me that you'll never be completely nice to me. It's too much fun this way."

Snapping her seat belt into place, she said, "I don't think that's going to be a problem. If you find me straying too close to nice, let me know and I'll happily adjust my attitude."

"I'll make sure to do that." He cranked the engine. "So, which way? I'm at your command."

"Now, that's tempting. There're lots of crevasses around here where a body would never be found. But I digress. How about Hart's Peak? You mentioned it yesterday, so I thought today we could go see Ophelia up close and then eat our lunches under her large nostrils."

"Wow—sounds like a Kodak moment."

"So would a picture of a lawyer being tossed off the edge, but

I've only got two hands and I need at least one to hold the camera. Take a left up here."

Caroline sat back in her seat for the rest of the drive, actually enjoying herself for the first time in a very long while. She didn't ruin the feeling by trying to think of why it had been so long. She directed Drew up the winding roads, pointing out different paths they could take later, and even sharing a few of the adventures she had shared with Jude and Shelby along those same paths. She wasn't sure why she felt compelled to share them with Drew, only that it seemed to easy to say Jude's name in his presence. It was almost as if by having loved and lost Shelby, he could somehow share a measure of her own grief. And, like Rainy, he didn't seem to expect her to cry.

He parked the truck on the side of a narrow road, edging it as close as he could to the outcropping of rock just on the off chance that a car would need to get by. Brightly colored leaves covered most of the nonpaved areas, reminding her that fall wasn't far off. It came earlier in the mountains, but always signaled an end to summer. It saddened her, the way the screen credits rolling at the end of a movie saddened her; the end had been announced, but nobody had bothered to tell her what happened next.

Feeling the early-morning chill to the air, she zipped up her sweatshirt, then reached inside the truck to get the rest of her stuff. The floor mat where she'd dumped everything was empty except for her water bottle. She looked up at Drew, who was in the process of strapping on a large backpack.

"Don't worry—I got it all. I figured you didn't need the extra weight of carrying a pack, so I just brought one that would fit everything."

She narrowed her eyes. "You're not trying to be nice to me, are you?"

"Absolutely not. I just wanted an excuse to make you go ahead of me so that there wouldn't be any sudden pushing from behind."

"Smart man." She pointed up a narrow leaf-strewn path. "Let's go this way. It'll take longer, but it's not as steep. Until I'm in shape, I think we should stick to the gentler slopes."

"Will do." He motioned for her to go ahead of him and she began climbing the path, feeling the gratifying pull on her muscles.

"Of course, being behind you also gives me a wonderful vantage point of your rear view and legs. I might have to stop and rest a little more frequently than usual."

She wanted to laugh out loud. Was he flirting with her? It had been so long since she'd taken her mind off of rows of numbers and bottom lines that she thought she'd become immune to the yin and yang of relationships. She kept her gaze focused forward and tried to keep the smile out of her voice. "If you say something like that one more time, I will push you and I will not help with the recovery of your body."

He laughed softly behind her. "Tough lady. Just the way I like them."

She gave him a warning look over her shoulder, then kept walking, feeling the steady thump of her heart, the tapping inside her chest a welcome reminder that it still beat there. Placing her hand on the scar, she increased her pace and led the way up the winding path.

They walked slowly and mostly in silence, as if by mutual agreement. Caroline stopped to rest several times, and he tried not to be obvious as he checked out her color and paid attention to her breathing.

While they walked, Drew followed behind Caroline, enjoying the view much more than he should have. He should go back to that store and buy those shorts in her size in every color. And not so much for the way they made her look, but because of the way they made her move. She wasn't the timid accountant with the acerbic tongue. Instead, the shorts seemed to transform her into a confident woman who strode forward without looking back. Even her hair, unbound from the military-style ponytail she normally wore, seemed to agree as it swayed and bounced with every step. He only wished that Caroline could see herself from this vantage point. He was pretty sure she'd see what he saw—a woman who embraced the past, not a woman who seemed to be buried in it.

He heard the sound of water before he saw the clear bubbling stream racing around rocks on its journey down the mountain. Caroline stopped and he moved closer, watching as the stream was guided into a dammed lake that lay on the other side of two large gray boulders, a small waterfall gushing between them and spilling into the lake. They appeared like sentinels guarding a private lake, allowing in only a privileged few.

"We used to come here to swim."

He watched her blond hair blow across her face, grasping at the small smile on her lips as if to keep it there. Squatting, he scooped his hand in the water. Its iciness stung him and he quickly shook it dry. "That's pretty cold. Can't imagine what it's like in the winter."

She stepped closer, a mysterious smile on her lips. "It's pretty damned cold, from what I remember."

"You speak from experience."

Caroline sat on a large rock, her feet near enough to the splashing water that dark moisture spots appeared at the toes of her shoes from the spray. "Jude used to dare us to swim across and back. The last one had to go again until there was nobody else left in the water. I always won."

He sat down next to her feeling the oddest compulsion to tuck her stray hair behind an ear. She looked so young sitting there on a rock with her knees pulled up and her fair hair blowing around her face; almost like the young woman she would have been if life hadn't interfered. "Did you pack your bathing suit?"

She drew back, shaking her head vigorously. "I don't swim, remember?"

"Well, I remember you *telling* me that, but I don't seem to remember why."

"That would be because I never gave you a reason because I don't have to give you one. In other words, it's really none of your business."

He took a deep breath, smelling the wet leaves and damp earth, and it reminded him of Shelby for a minute, of her earthiness and her scent after she'd been working in her garden. "You're wrong, you know. I think I know you well enough now that I can claim the right to stick my nose in your business. It's because of Jude and Shelby, I think. Their relationship makes us practically related."

She shook her head, then rested her chin on her knees. "I can say his name around you without . . . reliving certain thoughts. Maybe it's because you were married to Shelby and I used to be able to tell her anything." She looked at him, her gray-green eyes piercing. "But I certainly don't feel like we're related."

He didn't look away. "So why don't you swim anymore?"

Her expression hardened, but he could see she was trying to remain calm. "So why won't you let me sell your furniture ideas?"

He watched her for a long moment, unwilling to drop his gaze. "Touché," he said.

Caroline stood abruptly, the color bright in her cheeks. "I thought we were just going to have a little nature hike, and here you are trying to play shrink with me again. Either stop it right now or take me home. I keep telling you that I'm *fine*, but you won't seem to listen."

He stood, too. "I'm sorry, but I'm hard of hearing. That's what made me such a good lawyer."

"But did it make you a good husband?"

"Ouch." He tried to keep his tone light, but the words had stung much more than he wanted her to know.

She looked stricken, as if she'd been the one slapped. "I'm sorry. I shouldn't have said that."

She took a step backward, her foot slipping on the rock she'd been sitting on, and he grabbed her arms to steady her. "No, probably not. But you're right. It did make me a lousy husband—and father. I wasn't at first. And then I realized that Shelby . . . Well, it doesn't matter anymore. What matters now is why we moved here. I wanted to concentrate on Jewel, hoping to take the place of her wonderful mother and relearn how to be a father at the same time." He pulled her closer, trying to make his point. "The guilt nearly killed me when Shelby died—but I figured it would be more productive to continue living. What a waste that would be—living as if you were already dead."

She tried to push away from him, but he held firm to keep her from falling backward.

"You don't know the first thing about guilt!" She slapped at his chest, but he wouldn't let go.

"And you do? What is it, Caroline? What is it that has changed you from the loving and creative girl you used to be and into this prickly shadow of a woman I see every day?"

Her face turned a mottled red, and seeing her so wounded from his words was like a kick to the gut. He wasn't in a courtroom any longer. If only he could remember that where Caroline was concerned. But every time she told him a story from her childhood, he became more and more determined to find that girl again.

Slowly he released his grip. At the same time she pushed against him, the force sending her backward, her arms flying and her feet trying to find purchase on wet leaves and rocks. He reached for her, and their fingertips touched for a brief moment before she slipped over the edge and landed in the cold water of the lake below.

Drew quickly scrambled down the embankment, somehow managing to keep his balance. She'd disappeared under the water, and he had already thrown the backpack to the ground and was preparing to dive in when she surfaced, treading water and gulping for air. Before he could call out to her, she began a freestyle crawl toward the edge. He watched in awe, trying to think of what she reminded him of. On land she was frail and fragile, but in the water she was strong and confident, graceful and filled with subtle beauty. He felt as if he had finally caught a glimpse of the Caroline she had once been, and he knew then that he couldn't give up on her. She was there inside the hard shell she'd built around herself. He would find her; he had all the time in the world.

When she reached the edge she staggered from the water, and Drew was alarmed to see that her lips were a pale shade of blue. She stood shivering and glaring at him, like some water goddess that had gotten up on the wrong side of the bed, and he had the absurd urge to laugh. Instead he reached into the backpack and pulled out a pair of sweats.

He handed them to her, and she grabbed them without a word, slogging her way out of the water.

"Are you going to be all right? Your mom gave me her cell phone, and I can call for help if you need it."

She shook her head vigorously, spraying icy water on him. Instead of pressing the point, he turned his back to her. "Go ahead and change—I promise I won't look."

After a minute he felt her sodden shorts hit his back, quickly followed by her shirt and sweatshirt. He moved out of range before the boots could follow. He heard them land close by, and he smiled to himself, admiring her aim.

When he stopped hearing her grunting and swearing and the rustling of clothes and leaves, he turned around. "I have a pair of thick hiking socks, too, if you . . ." His words trailed off, lost somehow as he looked at her. She was the frail woman again, appearing even smaller in his oversize sweats, her wet hair hanging limply around her face. The neckline of the sweatshirt hung low over her chest, exposing the top of her bra and most of a long purple scar.

She seemed to know what he was staring at, and she quickly yanked the neckline up, her hands shaking, but he didn't think it was just the cold. As he moved toward her, he heard her teeth chattering, sending a startled alarm to his brain.

"We've got to get you warmed up."

Anticipating her resistance, he scooped her up in his arms before she could protest, and sat down on a dry patch of grass against a tree and away from the water, holding her close. Her body shivered under his fingers, each bone trembling like a fallen leaf in a strong wind. She surprised him by huddling into his chest, her hands folded against her face, shoulders rounded as if in defeat. That, more than anything, tugged at his conscience.

"I'm sorry," he said into her bowed head. "I didn't mean for that to happen."

Her body tensed for a moment, but the trembling soon took over. "I'm too c-c-c-cold to f-f-fight with you, so don't t-t-t-talk to me."

He pulled her closer, trying to transfer his body heat to her. "That's way too tempting for me to ignore." Being careful not to uproot her position, he struggled to untie the sweatshirt he'd knotted around his waist. He slipped the neck hole over her head, then pulled the rest of it over her body, leaving her arms clenched in front of her. Bending his face to the back of her neck, he breathed his warm breath onto her damp hair. "Your scar doesn't make you ugly, you know. There's no reason to be embarrassed about it."

He instinctively tightened his hold on her, anticipating her resistance. But instead he felt her shoulders begin shaking violently, and this time he knew it wasn't from the cold. *Why are you doing this, Drew? Why can't you leave her alone?* He wasn't sure of the answer. He knew only that she needed somebody desperately and that he was there. Being there was what Shelby told him had made her fall in love with him. And it was the first thing he'd stopped doing when he had finally acknowledged that he would never be Shelby's first choice.

Caroline's warm tears soaked through his shirt, and he pulled her closer.

"I d-d-d-don't c-c-c-cry. I n-n-never c-c-c-cry."

He cradled her head as something snapped inside him, like a bubble bursting from bright sunlight. He saw things with a clarity he usually experienced only while crafting out of a block of wood something he could see in his head. It wasn't about the scar. It had never been about the scar.

Lifting her face, he pressed his cheek against hers, remembering the words somebody else had once whispered in his own ear on the day he'd buried his father. "I wish I could show you, when you are lonely or in darkness, the astonishing light of your own being."

She pulled her head back slightly so she could look in his eyes. "Shelby . . . right?"

He nodded. "One of her favorites. She said it once to me, and I thought it was appropriate for you right now."

She dropped her eyes, staring at the middle of his chest where her tears had made a dark spot on his shirt. "It's not because of the scar that I don't swim."

"I know."

Her tear-soaked eyes flicked up, an unasked question lurking inside.

Drew spoke softly. "How did Jude die, Caroline? Does it have anything to do with your scar?"

Her brows puckered, and she nodded, her eyes studying his shirt again. Her trembling had subsided, but he kept his arms held tightly around her.

He waited until she looked up again and started to speak. "It was a car accident. Jude was killed in a car accident, and my heart was damaged so badly that I needed a new one."

He let the words sink in. "Were you driving?"

She looked away toward the lake and shook her head. "No. He was. I was in the passenger seat."

"Then why do you feel so responsible for his death?"

Her eyes were dry as she continued to stare out over the water. "Because I promised my mother that I wouldn't let him drive. He was being punished because he had just gotten another speeding ticket. But he was Jude, you see." A brittle smile lifted her lips, and just as quickly it died. "Nobody could ever tell him no. He told me Mom would never find out. So I switched seats and let him drive."

His grip tightened. "It was an accident, Caroline. You couldn't have stopped it."

"But he wasn't supposed to be driving. It had been raining, and when the car slipped on some wet leaves, he didn't know what to do."

He couldn't take looking at her empty face and dry eyes. Gently he pulled her head to his chest. "You can't keep blaming yourself. It was an accident."

"You don't understand. Jude wasn't supposed to die. Everybody loved him, and people like that just don't die." Her voice dropped to almost a whisper. "And every time my mother looks at me, I know that she can't help but think that the wrong child died."

*Oh, God.* He couldn't speak. All the words in the world could not heal the wounded woman he held in his arms. But then he remembered the woman who cared enough to save an injured bird and who had once planned to travel around the world, and he knew that he would have to at least try.

She kept her head on his chest until she slept, dry eyed. He kissed her lightly on the top of her head before he, too, fell asleep.

# CHAPTER 18

*May 16, 1990*

*Everybody's teasing me because I'm bringing a younger guy to my senior prom. They can't understand that I don't even notice other guys, and that if Jude couldn't come, I wouldn't be going. Ever since spring break, when we realized how it was between us, things have changed.*

*The only person I've really been able to tell is Caroline. She didn't blink an eye and accepted it as I would imagine she accepts that each day will become night. She asked me what had taken us so long to figure it out, since she's known for years, and that made me laugh. Caroline is so wise in so many ways. So quiet, but with eyes that see everything and with a heart that knows all. I hope I have a daughter just like her someday.*

*My mom helped me find the perfect dress. It's yellow, with small daisy appliqués and a sweetheart neckline. At first I thought the color made me look like a six-year-old, but when I tried it on I knew it was perfect. I imagined I could see myself in Jude's eyes, and I liked what I saw. I think my senior prom will be a special night I'll remember forever.*

*I made the mistake of saying that to Caroline, and her only comment was to make sure I brought condoms! I almost died. But then she told me she always carried them around in her purse just in case, and that shocked the hell out of me. She told me she's still a virgin and likely to remain that way for a long, long time, but that she always likes to be prepared just in case. She said that the first guy she slept with didn't necessarily have to be a guy she knew that well or even liked—just somebody with the right equipment who could teach her the mechanics of what's involved. That's so Caroline. For such a creative person, she's very methodical about most things. If I didn't think a career as an accountant or something would be a huge waste of her creative juices, I could imagine her being very successful as one. But then I wonder if her obsession with methods and order is her way of tying down a creative mind and joyful heart that would soar all day long without Caroline (and her mother) to rein it in.*

Caroline put her hands to her face for about the thousandth time that night, feeling the heat in her cheeks as she remembered the mortification of the previous day. She tried to focus on the embarrassment instead of the other emotions that seemed to bombard her every waking thought. Like the feelings caused by Drew holding her tightly in his arms. And the feeling of his warm breath on her neck and on the top of her head when he'd kissed her.

Most of all, she remembered the feeling of being under the water again, of the cold wetness against her skin like soft hands, and the power she felt as she pushed it aside to propel her body. In the moments before the chilly iciness had taken over her senses, she had almost forgotten why she'd given up swimming, why the self-punishment had been necessary, and how she could have once thought that the joy and rightness of her moving through water could ever be taken out of her life.

*I wish I could show you, when you are lonely or in darkness, the astonishing light of your own being.* She buried her face in the pillow again, remembering his words. How could he know just the right thing to say to her? The last time she'd seen Shelby, after Jude's funeral and before Shelby returned to college, she'd visited Caroline in the hospital and been witness to Caroline's battered body and soul, and to the hollow numbness that beat in her chest. And Shelby had said those same words to Caroline. Right before she'd told Caroline to get off her ass and stop feeling sorry for herself. Not in those exact words, but they had been just as effective.

She'd always meant to write or call Shelby after that, but by the time she was recovered enough to think about it, Shelby had gotten married. It had always seemed the ultimate betrayal to her, but now, years later, she couldn't help but wonder if there had been an underlying reason. After finally meeting Drew, she could almost understand. Almost.

Giving up on sleep completely, Caroline threw back the sheets and sat up to glare at the clock. One thirty in the morning was becoming way too familiar to her. Sliding on her slippers, she tried to look at the bright side of things. At least at this hour she could brew an entire pot of real coffee all for herself instead of that tepid stuff her mother was making her drink.

She put the coffeemaker in the laundry room so her mother wouldn't hear it, then wandered into the great room while waiting for the coffee to brew. Flipping on a lamp, she paused by the quilting table and gazed down at the scraps of fabrics, smelling the new cotton batting, her fingers itching to feel the tug of needle and thread. A stab of alarm hit her as she realized what little progress had been made. A few photographs had been silk-screened and attached to large squares of the blue fabric her mother had picked out, but everything else was scattered about the table in a haphazard mess with no sense of placement or continuity. Nothing had actually been attached to the backing piece at all.

Pulling the full carafe from the coffeemaker in the laundry room, she moved it to the folding table by her side and poured herself a cup. She had almost finished the entire cup before she decided to sit down and see if she could at least help get them started.

She spotted the yellow piece of satin and picked it up, smiling to herself as she remembered Shelby trying on for her the dress it came from. Somewhere in the boxes of photos, there was a prom picture of Shelby in the dress and Jude standing next to her. When she found it, she decided, she'd put it in a frame for Rainy. But right now she'd cut out a miniature yellow dress from the scrap and lay it down on the backing just to help them out.

When she first picked up the needle and began threading it with pale yellow, the old excitement gripped her and she could feel her brain working separately from what she was telling it to do. It was in those moments that she'd always thought of the most creative things. Jude had once told her that when he sat down at the piano to play, he felt the same way.

With a fabric pen, she drew an outline of the dress as she remembered it, then began to cut. In the silence of the sleeping house surrounded by the smell of coffee, she could almost believe that things were the way they had been when she was a girl, and she found comfort in it. But somewhere, in the back of her mind, she did know where she was—that her mother was sleeping alone in a bedroom nearby, that Drew and Jewel were in the house next door, and that an injured loon was being taken care of by a woman who had fought cancer and won—and that it wasn't such a bad place to be.

Jewel and her grandmother knocked on the Colliers' door at seven thirty a.m. Jewel didn't complain, because once she was on the swim team, she'd have to wake up even earlier on school days to practice or for meets. She hoped her dad had noticed how sprightly and alert she was when she'd stuck her head in his workroom to tell him where she'd be.

The door was opened by a bright-eyed and perky Caroline wearing a long sleep shirt and fuzzy slippers. Jewel almost looked past her shoulders to find out where this person standing in the doorway had hidden the real Caroline.

Grandma Rainy smiled, too, but it looked like the kind of smile you gave somebody who was wearing her shirt inside out. "Well, aren't you a breath of sunshine this morning." She moved inside the house as Caroline stepped back. "Is your mother up yet? I'm sorry to be here so early, but Jewel wanted to pick up the place mats you made before school."

Mrs. Collier made her appearance wearing an apple-green flowy dress thing with pants and matching house slippers with bows. Jewel had always thought that only people on TV commercials dressed that way.

"Good morning, everyone. I'll be dressed in just a moment—I just want to get the coffee started."

Caroline appeared not to have heard. She pointed to the craft table. "I actually have a bunch of place mats for you, Jewel. I can't seem to stop myself once I get started."

The bench that had been practically bare the previous week now held about fifteen multihued place mats. Jewel walked closer and picked one up. "Hey, they all have a bird outline stitched on them."

"It's a loon. I used to put them on all my quilts as a sort of signature. I hope it's all right."

"It's perfect—it makes them really stand out, I think." She held it higher to get a better look. "Wow, look at these tiny stitches. Did you use a machine for them?"

"Absolutely not. And I'd watch what I say if I were you. In some quilting circles, those can be considered fighting words."

Jewel laughed, then started picking up the place mats. She was startled to hear Mrs. Collier calling loudly from the kitchen.

"Caroline—why is the coffeepot in the laundry room?"

Caroline swore under her breath, using a word Jewel was pretty sure would send her to her room for a week.

"That's not regular coffee, is it?" Mrs. Collier marched into the room holding an almost empty coffeepot with the electrical cord dangling.

Caroline crossed her arms over her chest. "It might be."

Mrs. Collier let out a heavy sigh and put the pot down on a side table before approaching her daughter. "How do you feel?"

Her face brightened. "Really alert. Almost perky."

Mrs. Collier grabbed hold of one of Caroline's wrists, and Jewel watched her count beats as she looked at the clock on the wall.

"It's really fast. Have you checked your blood pressure this morning?"

"No, I haven't. And it was only caffeine—it's not like I OD'd on heroin or something." Caroline stumbled a bit and held her hand to her head. "Whoa. Just a little light-headed, that's all."

Pulling her daughter over to a sofa to sit, Mrs. Collier asked, "Did you drink any water?"

With her eyes closed and her head against the back of the sofa, Caroline shook her head. "I wasn't thirsty. I'd been drinking coffee all night and hardly felt the need for water."

Mrs. Collier turned to Jewel. "Could you please go get a glass of water from the kitchen and bring it here?"

Jewel nodded and raced to the kitchen. Even without watching the mother-daughter tug-of-war, she could still hear the battle being fought from the words that weren't spoken. But she noticed something else, too. Besides what was being said or not said, it was clear to anybody listening that both women were on the same side of the battlefield.

Jewel handed the glass to Caroline, then sat next to her on the sofa. "Why can't you have caffeine?"

"Good question. Why don't you ask the warden?" She indicated her mother with her elbow while taking a long drink of water.

Mrs. Collier crossed her arms over her chest the way Caroline had done when her mother first entered the room. It was so weird how much they looked alike. If Caroline ever got married, Jewel would have to tell her husband to look long and hard at Mrs. Collier because that's what he'd be married to in thirty years. Which, except for the fact that she was old, wouldn't be such a bad thing.

Caroline put the glass on the coffee table. Sitting beside her daughter, Mrs. Collier reached for the glass and handed it back. "You need to drink all of it. And when you're through, I want you to get more and drink all of that, too."

"Mom, really. I can take care of myself."

"Then why aren't you?"

Caroline sank back into the sofa without answering.

Mrs. Collier turned to Jewel. "In answer to your question, caffeine seems to have a negative effect on Caroline's blood pressure and heart rate—which isn't unusual with heart-transplant recipients. A little is okay every once in a while." She sent a pointed glare in Caroline's direction. "But too much can make her blood pressure soar and her heart beat at a much higher rate than it should—which is why we need to limit the caffeine. See, when a new heart is put in, a lot of the nerves are severed and the recipient loses a lot of feeling around the heart. A lot of times the recipient misses the signs of a heart attack because they simply can't feel the pain. Which is why we need to eliminate as many of the causes as we can."

"I didn't have that much."

Mrs. Collier narrowed her eyes. "How much? A pot?"

Caroline just stared at her mother and blinked.

"Oh, Lord, Caroline. Did you have two pots?"

Caroline gave her mom a little smile. "There's still a little left in the second pot."

Mrs. Collier sighed, then took the empty glass and stood. "Another thing with heart-transplant recipients is the danger of kidney failure. Caroline's antirejection drugs can also harm her kidneys. Which is why she needs to drink lots of water to keep them as healthy as possible." She turned and began striding toward the kitchen, her green floaty thing flying behind her like the cape of a superhero. "Of course, if one doesn't care about oneself, then one can just ignore all the medical advice and then do what one wants."

Her footsteps stopped abruptly, and both Jewel and Caroline leaned forward to see why she'd stopped.

Mrs. Collier stood next to Grandma Rainy by the craft table and they were both looking at the quilt that lay across the top. Jewel was about to turn away when she realized that her grandmother had tears slipping down her cheeks.

She moved to stand on the other side of her grandmother. "What's wrong?"

She didn't need an answer as she caught sight of the quilt. The top row of eight squares, each one ten inches wide, had been completed. Each one showed a part of her mother's babyhood, from the birth dates stitched on the first square to portions of baby blankets, clothing, and the actual shoelaces from her first pair of shoes. But the most special part of it was the tiny loon that had been stitched on each square. He seemed to be swimming from square to square, always seen in a different position, but sleek and beautiful and always pointing forward as if anticipating the next square.

Caroline joined them. "I would have done more, but I couldn't remember where all the scraps came from." She held up the yellow satin that had been cut into the shape of an evening gown. "I couldn't remember if this was from her junior or senior prom."

Jewel took the fabric. "Senior prom."

The three women looked at her in surprise.

"I, um, remember my mother telling me about this dress, that's all."

Mrs. Collier pulled out a neatly pressed linen handkerchief from her lounge pants and gently pressed it into Grandma Rainy's hand. "Take this before you make water spots on my table." Her voice sounded suspiciously thick, and there was no disguising her sniffle as she turned to Caroline.

Surprising everyone, she hugged her daughter. Caroline's hands lay at her sides as if she didn't know what to do with them. Grandma Rainy tugged on one hand and put it at Mrs. Collier's waist, and Caroline must have caught on, because she raised her other hand, too. They stood like that for a long time, and Caroline's fingers clutched at her mother's green robe as if hanging on to something precious she didn't want to let go.

Mrs. Collier pulled away first. "It's beautiful. I think it's the best one you've ever done." Her brows knitted together. "It reminds me a lot of the one you started for Jude. Remember that? I wonder whatever happened to it."

Caroline stepped away and began straightening the table that now resembled a dumping ground for retired quilters. "I don't know. It disappeared somehow after . . . when I was in the hospital. I have no idea what happened to it. I always thought that you had given it away with all of Jude's clothes."

"Oh, no. I would never have done that. It was so special. You'd spent so much time on it, remember? You had to sneak around Jude's room to find all the memorabilia you wanted to include on it without him getting suspicious. And I don't think he ever knew."

Caroline sank down in a chair as if the caffeine had already run through her body. "No, he didn't. And, actually, I never had it here anyway. I always kept it at Shelby's."

Both Caroline and her mother turned matching expressions to Rainy. "Did you find it in Shelby's things?"

Rainy slowly shook her head. "No, and I would have remembered seeing something like that. I'll ask Drew, since he has all of her things. Maybe he's had it all this time and didn't even know."

Jewel felt the pricklings of a headache sneak up on her from behind, and it promised to be a big one. She couldn't let her grandmother see it yet, though. She needed to run next door and look at the quilt in her mother's trunk one more time. She was pretty sure she knew now what it was, but she wanted to make sure that it was the stitched outline of a loon she'd spotted in the corner.

Jewel sat down and realized that all four of them were sitting at the table with the quilt stretched between them. "Hey, look. We're like an old-time quilting bee."

Grandma Rainy nodded. "You're absolutely right, Jewel. And I think that while Caroline's on a roll, we should stay here and keep working."

Jewel nodded enthusiastically. "I agree. And I think since this is sort of considered history and art rolled into one that I should be excused from school today so I can stay here and quilt. I could bring the place mats in after school today. They don't need them until then anyway."

The three of them stared at her with blank expressions, as if it had been too long since they remembered being in school and wanting to play hooky. After a moment the three of them said in unison, "Okay."

Then Caroline said, "Grab a needle. I'm going to have you sew this yellow dress on this blue square here. I'll let you pick whatever color thread you want to use. The point of these memory quilts is to use as much of your own style as you want to express the person being portrayed. Does that make sense?"

Jewel nodded, ignoring the pain inside her head, determined to learn as much about making memory quilts as she could. She wasn't sure where the idea had come from, but it was there. It was a need to finish telling a story in a quilt. She wasn't sure how it was going to end, but she knew she wouldn't be doing it on her own.

Rainy and Caroline picked up their own needles, holding them up like a surgeon held up his hands before surgery. Mrs. Collier smiled with barely suppressed excitement as if just now realizing that her goal to get Caroline quilting had finally come to fruition.

"Just give me a minute to go change."

Grandma Rainy lowered her bifocals to study her friend. "Margaret, how far did you have to chase the homeless woman to steal that outfit?"

"Oh, hush, Rainy. You're just jealous because I don't have to buy my clothes at the feed store." Mrs. Collier left the room in her usual graceful way, but Jewel couldn't help but notice that the woman almost skipped as she made her way across the room.

Grandma Rainy snorted as she turned back to the table and stared back at Jewel and Caroline. An odd look crossed her face for a moment, and Jewel thought that she'd detected her headache already. Instead she said, "If I didn't know better, I'd say you two were mother and daughter—there's something about the pair of you that's very much the same. I just can't figure out what it is."

Caroline grinned. "Oh, it's probably just our youthfulness. And the way our skin glows."

Grandma Rainy snorted again. "Or it's the bull you like to sprinkle in your conversation." She fixed her stare on Jewel. "Is your headache bad yet?"

Jewel concentrated on threading her needle and shook her head. "Uh-uh. I'm fine."

She felt her grandmother's stare on her as she knotted the thread, then picked up the bright yellow fabric and began to sew.

# CHAPTER 19

❧

CAROLINE PUSHED OPEN THE DOOR TO RAINY DAYS AND STEPPED inside. Rainy called out from the kitchen as Caroline maneuvered her way through the piles of handwoven rugs, homemade pottery, and stacks of place mats. She stopped short at the sight of the place mats and picked the top one off the pile to examine it. The little loon signature at the bottom told her it was definitely hers. Crumpling it in her hand, she marched into the kitchen.

Her words died in her throat as the door swung shut behind her. Rainy and Drew sat cross-legged on the floor, the loon, still with its wing in a white sling that strongly resembled a cloth diaper, waddling awkwardly between them.

"Oh, look—he's walking again!"

Rainy nodded. "Yep. Took the bandage off his leg this morning. Pretty soon he'll be ready to go swimming in the lake and then take the long flight to the coast. I think his mate has already gone. Jewel said she hasn't heard anything for a couple of weeks. We'll have to do it soon, though. Drew tells me the water in the lake is already pretty cold."

Caroline forgot the loon for a moment, but remembered to feel mortified in Drew's presence. She found she couldn't look at him, because if she did she knew she'd see the pity in his eyes. She didn't think she could take that. At least she had stopped herself from telling him the whole story. Because if she'd done that, he would be looking at her with pity and a measure of disgust thrown in.

She held the place mat out to Rainy. "Why is this in your store? I thought I was making them for the athletic club booth."

"Yes, well, in your enthusiasm, you seem to have made a lot more than they think will fit in the booth. And they keep coming.

You need to find another hobby, girl." She winked at Caroline as she adjusted the aqua headscarf on her head. "Your mother suggested selling the excess here—all profits go to the athletic fund, of course—and to advertise that the person who's making the place mats is auctioning off an entire quilt at the Harvest Moon festival."

"My mother did that? She didn't mention it to me."

Rainy shrugged before picking up the loon, which had waddled over to her knee and was starting to peck at it. "Yes, well, she knows how you hate to have people make a fuss over you, so she thought she'd just go ahead and do it."

"Why would she think something like that?" Caroline crossed her arms across her chest and tried not to notice how Drew was paying close attention.

"Well, I guess she's remembering when you used to go to swim meets and you'd tell her to stay home. You said that her being there and fussing over you just made you nervous."

She wanted to deny it, but she didn't want Rainy to call her on a lie, either. She *had* said that. But only because she wanted her mother to really want to come. If she had, certainly her mother would have overridden Caroline's objections and shown up at a swim meet. That kind of logic had made so much sense to a fourteen-year-old, but now only appeared like snowflakes on a mountain of misunderstandings.

Eager to change the subject, Caroline asked, "Have you sold any?"

Drew stood. "I sold twenty-three as of yesterday. At five bucks apiece, that's not too shabby. Jewel's working on a poster with a picture of her mother's quilt to advertise your auction. Who knows, maybe you alone will be able to fund a whole new stadium just from the proceeds."

Her gaze flickered up to meet his and then she just as quickly moved back to the place mat. "Oh. Wow. That's good news. I'll have to remember if I'm ever out of work, I'll have something to fall back on. It's a great boredom buster."

Even Caroline hated the way she sounded. But seeing Drew here only reminded her of all the things she'd said the day before, and she felt the need to put up walls again. They protected her from prying questions and helped her move on with her life as painlessly as possible.

Caroline sat down on the floor, attempting to get at eye level with the loon. That way she wouldn't have to look into the identical expressions of Rainy and Drew. *Damn.* When had she become so transparent that everybody could see right through her? She watched as the loon waddled toward her, its ungainliness reminding her of something.

She ignored Rainy and Drew and concentrated on the bird as it practiced walking, her mind churning. Was transparency actually a good thing and something you were entitled to as you grew older? For a brief moment she welcomed it, and even envisioned telling Rainy and Drew all of it. But Rainy's frail frame and scarf-covered head pulled her back. There was some pain that always needed to be held back, especially if it could only spread around the pain.

Rainy rested her hand against the top of Caroline's head, reminding Caroline of the old childhood game of Duck, Duck, Goose. "What should we do with him when he's better? We could keep him here all winter, you know."

Caroline shook her head, seeing things more clearly than she had in a very long time. "No, he needs to go back in the water as soon as he's able. I don't want him to forget the feel of it."

"No chance of that, I wouldn't think. He's born knowing the water; like a human baby knows its mother. Just like we always seem to be drawn back into the family fold, I imagine this ol' bird is drawn to the water." Rainy clucked her tongue. "Besides, he'd look silly being a land loon, don't you think? God knows He was definitely thinking about keeping this clumsy bird in the water when He made him. Boy, oh, boy, can those birds swim."

Caroline's throat had gone dry, which didn't matter because she didn't know what to say anyway.

Rainy saved her by speaking first. "I found a box of Shelby's clothes while I was looking for Jude's quilt in the attic. I think she put the box up there after college and I forgot about it. I'm going to give it to Jewel and let her go through it, but I thought I'd let you look first and see if there's anything you think we could use for the quilt." She bent to pick up the loon, which went into her arms without complaint. "And there's some bathing suits with the tags still on them that look about your size, and I remember your mom mentioning to me that you didn't pack any. They're yours if you want them. To swim in the pool, of course. Not the lake."

Caroline wanted to say no. But then she remembered the feel of the water again, and how she felt as she'd sluiced through it. *I've missed the water.* She gave a brief nod. "Sure. I'll look through it. Thanks."

"It's in the storeroom. Drew can help you load it into your car when you're ready to leave." Rainy reached into the pocket of her overalls and pulled out a tiny collar and leash.

Drew laughed. "Is that what I think it is?"

"Yep. How else do you think he'll get his exercise while he's recuperating? There's only so much bird poop I'm willing to clean up off this floor."

As if they'd done it many times before, Rainy attached the small collar around the bird's short neck, then placed him on the floor. Like a small, ungainly dog, he waddled toward the back door and waited for Rainy to open it.

Rainy put her hand on the knob before turning to face Caroline and Drew. "I'll be back in about an hour. Don't do anything I wouldn't do."

Caroline stood abruptly to protest but found herself staring at a closed door. Too late, she felt the blood rushing from her head and saw pinpricks of blind spots in her vision. Drew's arms were around her again, and she found herself sitting on his lap at the kitchen table, her head resting in what was becoming a very familiar place.

"Do you need some water?"

She shook her head. "No. I'll be all right in a minute. My medications make me a little woozy sometimes, especially when I stand up too suddenly."

"Oh. I thought it was the excitement from Rainy's suggestion."

With a weak hand, she slapped him on his chest.

"Hey, I thought you were supposed to be nice to me."

She sat up. "Did my mother tell you that?"

"Yes—accidentally. When I brought you home yesterday and you went into your room to change, she asked me how our day was. Since it would be hard to lie about you landing in the lake, seeing as how you carried your clothes in a wet bundle, I told her what happened. That's when she mentioned that you were trying to be nice to me."

Feeling completely recovered, Caroline extricated herself from his lap and sat down across the table from him. She smoothed the table runner so she wouldn't have to look in his face. "Did she mention why?"

He sat up, putting his elbows on the table. "Does there have to be an ulterior motive to be nice to me?"

She tried to hold back, but it was so hard where he was concerned. "Yes. There does."

He laughed and sat back in his chair. "So why would you be trying to be nice to me? And I'd give you a failing grade for yesterday, by the way."

She continued straightening the runner that was already without a single crease. *I wish I could show you, when you are lonely or in darkness, the astonishing light of your own being.* She tried to forget him saying those words, him holding her close, and his lips on her hair. She tried to find her walls again, but they seemed to have acquired large portholes that offered a clear view of the other side. Why was he so intent on destroying her defenses? It was time he learned that he wasn't the only one with an agenda.

"I'd like to know why you won't consider letting me try to sell your furniture ideas. It could be very lucrative—for both of us. I'm now the company's comptroller. If I brought in the kind of money I think your stuff will, I'd probably end up as CFO. And your name would be on every piece, so you'd still be recognized as the artist. Of course, these are just my preliminary ideas—I'd need to talk to my boss to work it out—but I'm sure a licensing agreement would certainly be the best thing for both of us."

Silently he watched her, and she tried not to squirm under his scrutiny. "And that's what you want? To be CFO?"

She nodded, feeling a small spark of hope.

"Are there any other goals that you want in life? Anything besides being CFO of Kobylt Brothers Furniture?"

She felt the same spark fizzle and die. Of course he wouldn't cooperate. Whatever had made her think that he would? Did she for one minute believe that his sympathy for her yesterday would translate to letting her have her way today? Of course not. And, on some level that she didn't really want to explore, she liked him for that.

She swallowed before answering, knowing it would be fruitless to lie. "No."

He just sat there, staring at her, his eyes unreadable. Finally he said, "Then I can't help you." He stood and carefully placed his chair under the table.

Caroline stood, too, trying to breathe out the anger through her nostrils as Dr. Northcutt had taught her. "Why? Why are you so opposed to a little success?"

He came to stand in front of her, their bodies almost touching. "Because there's more to life than success and money. So much more. I made a huge mistake with Shelby. For all intents and purposes I abandoned her and Jewel." He paused for a moment and swallowed. "Did you know that before Shelby died I had no idea what Jewel's favorite color was or that she didn't like macaroni and cheese? I didn't know the name of her best friend or her fifth-grade teacher. I didn't even know that she had to sleep with a night-light because she was afraid of the dark." He kept his voice steady and even, as if he'd had this same conversation with himself hundreds of times.

"I didn't know these things because I was busy pursuing the things my father had always taught me were more important than anything—success and money. And I always thought I had a good excuse for turning from my wife and daughter to pursue success. But in the end, excuses didn't matter." He turned away and walked to the refrigerator and jerked the door open, glass bottles shaking. He stared inside sightlessly. "Did you know that I wasn't with Shelby when she died? I stayed back in Charleston—catching up on paperwork, of all things. I don't think I could have saved her, but I could have saved Jewel from the trauma of being alone with her mother when it happened. Of almost drowning by trying to bring her mother's body in to shore." He let the door shut before briefly resting his forehead against the white metal.

Slowly he turned to face her. "She's afraid of the water, you know."

Caroline found her voice. "I know. She told me. She said Shelby had once said to her to find the one thing that she's most afraid of and do it. So she swims."

His cheek twitched into an almost-smile. "Yeah. That's exactly how Shelby lived her life." He moved back to the table and stood in front of her again. "What are you most afraid of, Caroline Collier?"

She felt the shallowness of her breathing and focused on filling her lungs slowly. She could tell he was noticing her efforts and it made her angry. "You go first. What about you? Are you afraid that you've given up everything that you loved to come here, and have found that it's not enough? Do you really want to run a little country store and make one-of-a-kind furniture pieces for the rest of your life? Will it make you happy?"

He drew back as if she'd struck him. "My daughter is my focus now. If I can make sure she grows up into a physically and emotionally secure woman, then everything will have been worth it."

Caroline didn't back away, and a fleeting thought reminded her that she'd learned it from him. "She's the one who fights her demons every morning by swimming in the lake. What have you done? And don't think for one minute that she's not aware that all of your sacrifices were about her—or that it hurts her to know that you haven't found what you're looking for."

His lips formed a grim, thin line. "Since when have you become such an expert on parenting and adolescent behavior? Besides the fact that you act like an adolescent most of the time."

It was her turn to draw back. "I think I've had enough for one morning. But do think about my business proposition. Something tells me that you miss using your brain as much as I do—assuming you have one." She wanted to stamp her foot or throw something, but settled for the more mature action of fisting her hands. "You can't let a past mistake rule your life. You need to move on—if not for your sake, then at least think of Jewel."

She turned to leave, then stopped in the middle of the floor, her own words thrumming through her head. Somehow she managed to move forward. Her hand was on the doorknob of the back door when he called her name.

Facing him, she realized that he had moved toward her and was once again close enough to touch. He reached up and tucked her loose hair behind her ear. "You can't let a past mistake rule your life. You need to move on. If not for your sake, then at least think of your mother."

She jerked back from him, her heels hitting the door. *You don't understand. It's different with me.* She wanted to say the words out loud but she couldn't. He might force her to make him understand, and she knew she couldn't.

Turning around to face the door again, she yanked it open and left, letting him close the door behind her.

*June 8, 1990*

*Jude and his family arrived yesterday. Caroline and Jude's school has been out for the summer since Memorial Day, but with all of our snow days, graduation has been pushed back to June 18. The senior prom is tonight. My yellow dress has been steamed and pronounced free of wrinkles by my mom and dad—and by Mrs. Collier, who came over and insisted on seeing the dress. She said she wanted to make sure that Jude had the right shade of yellow flowers in the wrist corsage he was bringing. I personally think she wanted to make sure that I would look good enough for Jude. Not that I blame her. Pretty much everybody pales in comparison when standing next to him.*

*Caroline came over, too, and tried not to be too interested in my dress, but I showed it to her anyway. She likes to pretend that she's not into the girl/boy thing and parties and dresses and other girly stuff, but I know different. She still hides herself in her own shell, and only those smart enough to look can see her incredible beauty. Obviously Atlanta must not have any smart high school juniors, because Caroline doesn't date. I joked with Mrs. Collier that when boys finally discover Caroline, she'll have to get a separate phone line for her daughter. Caroline just looked embarrassed and missed Mrs. Collier's hopeful expression. I don't think Mrs. Collier is desperate to see Caroline dating; I think she's just hopeful that someone else will soon see what we've been seeing all along.*

*Mr. and Mrs. Collier invited us all over to their house before we left for the prom, and we drank apple cider out on their back deck. The sun was just setting as a loon lifted up from a hidden nest on the shore and splashed over the water before rising into the sky. Jude, Caroline, and I watched it glide through the sun, crying out to the rising moon, before disappearing into the lake. Jude reached for my hand and held it tightly as if we suddenly didn't have all the time in the world. That's when my headache started and caused us to miss the first hour of the prom.*

*But through the pain of my headache, all I could see against my closed eyelids was the darkness under the lake where the loon cut through the water with strength and confidence, the orange-red sun lighting the surface above and drawing it back home.*

# CHAPTER 20

❧

CAROLINE KNOCKED ON JEWEL'S DOOR FOR THE SECOND TIME and wondered if she'd forgotten about her lesson this morning, but quickly dismissed the idea. Jewel was usually already on the dock tapping her foot impatiently while she waited for Caroline. If she were late this morning, then something had to be wrong.

She lifted her hand to knock again when the door opened. Jewel stood inside wearing her pajamas, but she had a large beach towel wrapped around her middle.

"Did you forget about our lesson this morning? I can wait while you change, if you're still up for it."

Jewel stuck her head out the door and looked both ways, as if checking to make sure her dad wasn't there watching, before opening the door wider to let Caroline in. "I can't have my lesson today."

"Why not? Are you sick?"

"Yes. No. Well, not really."

Caroline looked at her, trying to decipher Jewel's answer. The girl certainly didn't look ill. "Are you sick or not? I can go get my mom if you are. She's got a medicine cabinet that would make a hospital jealous. She's definitely the one you want to go to if you have an upset stomach or something. Just not if you have a scraped knee."

"No, it's nothing like that. I just . . . I can't wear a bathing suit. For about a week."

Caroline finally realized what was wrong. Gently she said, "Oh, I see. You got your period. Is it your first time?"

Jewel nodded, looking down at her bare feet and wiggling her toes.

"Do you need anything—pads or tampons?"

A small flush covered her cheeks as she shook her head. "No. My dad just went to the store for some stuff. He'll be right back."

"Your dad? Your dad went to the store to buy you sanitary products?" She tried to think of the Drew Reed she knew doing such a nonmacho thing, and found that it wasn't so difficult.

"Well. If you're comfortable with it, we could still go out to the lake—after your dad leaves, of course."

"I don't know. . . ."

"If you don't want to swim, we could still go down to the dock if you want. I've, um, borrowed a bathing suit, and I could show you a few things in the water while you watch—even if you don't get in."

Jewel's eyes widened. "You're going to actually get in the water?"

Caroline shrugged, trying to act casual about something that was scaring her to death.

"Cool. Then I'll definitely be there." She hitched the towel tighter around her middle. "Can I get you something while we wait? My dad just made a pot of coffee; I'll get you a cup if you'd like."

"Is it regular?"

Jewel nodded with a grin. "Yep. But I'm only going to let you have one cup, okay?"

Caroline rolled her eyes but couldn't help smiling. "All right. And I like it black—nothing that might interfere with the caffeine."

Jewel disappeared into the kitchen as she called out, "And I'll bring a glass of water, too."

Caroline just shook her head as she wandered into the dining room, noting that two more chairs had been made but not yet stained. She studied the table again, with the intricate inlays on the surface that resembled strokes of paint from a paintbrush. Flattening her hand against the table she once more felt the shock of awareness she remembered from the first time she'd done that. It was almost as if she could feel the passion and see the dreams of the person who had crafted it, almost as if it were a living thing.

She felt exhausted suddenly and sat down, resting her head in her hands. How long had it been since she had felt anything enough to transfer the feeling? To make her utterly exhausted yet exhilarated? She remembered the feeling when she used to race in swim meets, and she sometimes now caught glimpses of it when she played the piano or when she'd been working on Shelby's quilt. But now it always seemed to her to be something she denied herself. *For good reason,* she tried to tell herself, but the words weren't as convincing as they used to be.

Her gaze fell on one of the table legs she hadn't had the time to examine on her last visit. She remembered Jewel telling her that the room and its furnishings were dedicated to Shelby, and she thought about this as she knelt in front of the third leg.

This one had definite waves almost halfway up the table leg, each one a different shape and size, perfectly mimicking the waves in the ocean. She sat back on her heels, puzzled. Shelby had died in the ocean; why had Drew chosen to remember that here?

Placing her hands on the table leg, she slid them upward, feeling the smooth wood against her fingers, then stopped. She'd missed the sky part of the table leg—the empty expanse of wood rising above the water that held only a canoe and two people, both without oars. And above them, flying close to the bottom of the tabletop, was a flat-billed bird with a short neck and a long body soaring through the dark wood of night.

She brushed the tips of her fingers across the faces of the two people in the canoe and understood. She understood what Drew had meant when he'd carved this table leg. And she knew why there were only two people instead of three. *Jude and Shelby. Together forever in a place nobody else can go.* Rocking back on her heels, she fought the urge to cry, wishing that she didn't understand the depths of the man who'd carved them, and a little bit frightened that she did.

"Here's your coffee." Jewel stood behind her, clutching the towel with one hand and handing her a steaming cup of coffee in the other. "Do you like it?" she said, indicating the table leg with her chin.

Caroline stood and gratefully accepted the mug and took a scalding sip to knock down the lump that had formed in her throat. "Yes. Very much. Your dad is . . . an artist."

Jewel smiled. "Yeah. He's pretty talented. You'd think with two artistic parents I'd be able to draw more than stick figures." She shrugged. "Oh, well. At least I look like Mom. Otherwise I'd think I was adopted."

"No chance of that. It's uncanny how much you look like her."

They both turned at the sound of a slamming car door from outside, then simultaneously widened their eyes.

Jewel spoke first. "He can't know you're here—or he'll probably guess why, and I'm not ready to tell him." She grabbed Caroline's arm and started dragging her toward the front foyer. Caroline put her coffee cup on the unfinished tabletop and followed, wanting to tell Jewel that her dad already knew, and quickly dismissing the idea. It was between the two of them to work out, and she had no business getting in the middle of it.

Which was why she didn't protest too much when Jewel shoved her into the coat closet. She stood pressed against the door with plastic-covered winter coats against her back, nearly gagging on the heavy scent of mothballs. Muffled voices, a deep-pitched one and Jewel's lighter one, came through the door. The cadences were familiar to her as that of a parent and child, and the sound sent a stab of longing through her—a longing for the way things used to be when she'd been part of a family. *And the way things could still be.*

She pressed her forehead against the closed door and recalled her mother's words of hopefulness. *That didn't mean that there wasn't something else for us out there—something to help us make a new start. I still think there is.* Caroline shut her eyes, listening to Drew's rumble of laughter through the door. But wasn't it thirteen years too late?

Her eyes jerked open as she realized Drew's voice was getting louder. Before she could burrow deeper, the door opened and Drew thrust her coffee mug at her.

"I believe this is yours."

She took it and just stared at him, too surprised to find any words.

"Don't let her know that I know you're here. I'm going to leave now so you two can have your lesson."

He closed the door as quickly as he'd opened it, and Caroline couldn't help but smile. There was something sweet about a dad who would keep a daughter's secret until she was ready to reveal it.

Caroline sank to the floor and remained in the closet, sipping her coffee, until Jewel came to let her out.

Jewel sat in Caroline's chair on the dock, their positions reversed this morning. She watched as Caroline slid her sweat suit off, revealing very pale skin and slim, long limbs.

"Ever thought of being one of those underwear models who wear the wings?"

Caroline held the sweatshirt against her chest, fighting a smile. "You're so full of it. I'm flat as a board, and if I have three more heart surgeries people could play tic-tac-toe on my chest."

Jewel almost spit out her orange juice. "Please don't be funny while I'm drinking." She wiped at the drips of juice on her chin with her sleeve, shocked that Caroline would make a joke about her scar—and just as pleased. "Hey, can I be Xs?"

Caroline threw her sweatshirt at Jewel and hit her in the face. When she'd pushed them away so she could see, Caroline stood at the side of the dock, her toes over the edge, her black one-piece bathing suit making her look like a long, sleek bird.

"No diving." Jewel smiled at her own joke, but she sobered when she realized that Caroline wasn't paying any attention to her or to anything except for the dark water of the lake and something else that Jewel couldn't see.

Caroline moved her lips as if talking, and Jewel felt the telltale prickles of an oncoming headache at the back of her neck as she heard the silent words as if they'd been whispered in her ear. *Forgive me, Jude. Forgive me.* The lapping against the dock pilings seemed to have stopped, offering a gentle quietness like the kind found inside a confessional.

The sun pushed out behind clouds, shining light on the dock and their patch of water, and Jewel watched as Caroline stepped forward into the water, her entry hardly causing a splash. She popped up to the surface quickly, probably the same way Jewel had done in reaction to the cold. Caroline wiped her hair out of her face, then stood perfectly still, like a person who stepped onto a moving sidewalk and wasn't sure if they should stand or walk.

Then she leaned back in the water, letting herself float as she stared up into the bright sky, fanning her arms slowly to keep herself afloat. Jewel's head pounded louder now, making it hard to see, but she stood and walked to the edge of the dock so she could watch a miracle.

With long, sure strokes, Caroline began the back crawl, her movements at first choppy and unpracticed but quickly becoming stronger and more purposeful. She flipped after a while and swam back to the dock using her freestyle stroke, her body cutting through the water like a needle through fabric, soft waves in her wake.

Caroline stood up in front of the dock and looked at Jewel. "This water is freezing. How come you never told me it was this cold?"

Jewel shrugged. "I don't mind the cold. And I wanted to learn."

Caroline nodded. "You're doing a great job. I don't know if I've said that to you before."

"Nope. You don't have to—I can tell."

"Really? How?"

"Oh, I don't know—in the way you tell me to do it again, and the way that you start practically every sentence with, 'When you're on the swim team' like I'm a shoo-in or something." The headache was nearly blinding her now, but she wasn't finished. "And in the way you hug me when you're putting my towel around me at the end of my lesson." She smiled weakly, needing to see Caroline's reaction.

Caroline stood completely still in the water, watching Jewel with narrowed eyes. "But don't you need me to say 'good job' so that you know you're doing the right thing?"

Jewel shook her head. "No. My mom once told me that only your heart can tell you that you're doing something right. She said her aunt Margaret taught her that—I guess that would be your mother. She said that your mom thought that the trophies gave you the 'good job.' A parent's job was to let you know that she loved you whether you got the trophies or not."

Caroline continued to look at her, as if trying to translate a foreign language. Finally she dipped her head back into the water, turning her hair black. When she stood again, she said, "Did anyone ever tell you that you're a pretty smart kid?"

"All the time." She would have winked if the pain around her eyes hadn't been so intense.

Caroline seemed to notice. "Hey, are you all right?"

"Not really. I've got another one of those headaches—kinda hit me suddenly. Can you help get me inside and call Grandma Rainy?"

Without answering, Caroline pulled herself up on the dock and quickly dried herself off. Gently helping Jewel from her chair, she put her arm around Jewel's shoulders. "It's probably pressure from that big head of yours. Maybe I should ask Rainy to bring some humble pie along with her tea."

Jewel could see Caroline's worried expression despite her attempt at humor, and it warmed her. If only her dad could see Caroline as she and her mother saw her—as a warm, caring person—she was sure her dad would stop picking on her. As if testing out her theory, Jewel let her head fall against Caroline's shoulder and felt Caroline's arm tighten around her as they walked slowly up to the house.

Drew was just finishing hanging Jewel's poster advertising the quilt auction when Rainy came in after another quilting session at Margaret Collier's. She leaned against the closed front door and blew out a long breath.

Climbing down the ladder, Drew asked, "Rough night at the quilting bee?"

"You have no idea." Unbuttoning her thick cardigan, she added, "There's something about four women, all related somehow, sitting around a table and making a quilt for a dead woman whom they all knew. I always read in those parenting magazines to talk to your child about important things while you're driving a car or doing something else. It makes talking easier. I guess the same can be said about quilting. You'd think those women had taken a vow of silence for ten years and are now able to finally talk."

"Gee, sorry I missed it. Maybe next time you can invite me."

She raised an eyebrow. "Don't be so cocky. You know that saying about the hand that rocks the cradle? Same can be said about pulling a needle and thread. We'll have all the world's problems solved by the time we're through."

He laughed, then thought about a person with problems closer to home. "What about Caroline? Do you think you'll have her problems all solved by the time the quilt's finished?"

Rainy pushed away from the door. "I wish it could be that easy. There's a point where a person's hurts become a part of them, and to set them loose would be like losing a hand or a foot." She sighed rubbing her hands over her arms. "Not that Margaret and I and a whole heap of doctors haven't tried—we have, for thirteen years. I don't know what it will take. I sure was hoping that time spent up here with her mother would help. Caroline hasn't been back, you know—not since the accident."

Drew followed Rainy into the kitchen and sat down at the table while she put a teakettle on the stove. There was something about Rainy's kitchen table that seemed conducive to solving the world's problems. He should probably suggest she donate it to the United Nations. He smoothed his hands on the oak surface, remembering Caroline sitting here the day before, still feeling the sting of her words and hearing the hollowness in her voice.

"Caroline told me about the accident—how Jude died and why she needed a new heart."

Rainy set two mugs on the table, with tea bags hanging from them. "I can't say I'm surprised. She hasn't talked about it in thirteen years, but I figured you of all people would pry it out of her."

She sat down, her face looking drawn and tired. He placed a hand on her arm. "You stay seated. When the kettle boils I'll get it. You need to be taking it easy."

She grinned but it didn't hide the exhaustion on her face. "Look who you're talking to. I don't think after all these years of running this store that I know how to take it easy." She tapped her fingers against the tabletop. "No worry. It's a signed deal, and the store will be yours in a month. If you still want it, that is."

Drew looked at her in surprise. "Of course I want it. I wouldn't have signed the contract otherwise."

She just nodded, giving him the "I know better" look that she normally reserved for Caroline.

"When Caroline told me about Jude's car accident, I got the

feeling that she wasn't telling me the whole story—that she was de- liberately leaving something out."

Rainy regarded him silently, and he knew he'd guessed correctly. The kettle whistled and he got up to retrieve it, then poured the boiling water into the mugs, the steam rising into the air like kept secrets.

Rainy put her hands around the mug as if to warm them but kept her eyes on Drew. "Don't you be asking me to tell you more. It's not my place. If she thinks you should know, then she'll tell you. Otherwise, leave it be." She leaned forward to look in his face. "You don't know what she's been through, not really. Most people wouldn't have survived it at all."

"I know," he said, patting her hand. "I've learned that. Once you get through her prickly exterior, there's a great person hiding under- neath."

She turned her hand palm up and squeezed his. "I knew you'd see that. Just be patient."

He felt embarrassed all of a sudden, as if just now remembering he was talking to his mother-in-law. "It's not what you think, Rainy. It's just that Caroline . . . well, it's hard to miss her, you know what I mean? It's a small town, and everywhere I go it seems I bump into her and that huge chip on her shoulder. You know I've never been able to back down from a challenge."

She squeezed his hand again. "Don't be embarrassed. I under- stand."

He dunked his tea bag into the hot water one more time before pulling it out. He avoided looking into her eyes because he wasn't sure he wanted to see how much she really did understand.

"By the way, I had a picture of Shelby in my wallet, but it's not there anymore. I'm thinking it might have fallen out here in the store but I can't seem to find it. Have you seen it?"

Rainy shook her head. "No, but it's funny you should mention it. I had a small wallet-size photo of Shelby and Jewel when Jewel was born that I'd taken out of the frame to polish it, but when I went to go put it back in, the thing had just vanished. I hope it didn't get thrown away."

Drew nodded absently. "I'm sure they'll show up. If not, I'll go through Shelby's things back at the house and see if she kept negatives or duplicates."

The loon thrashed about in the straw bedding in his pen. Rainy stood and bent over to pet him. "He's getting restless. I think he senses the change of the season and is eager to be on his way." She stroked his back and spoke quietly to the bird. "Soon, little one. Soon you'll be strong enough to be out on your own, chasing down the moon."

Drew stood to join her, watching as the bird settled under Rainy's gentle touch, wishing that all problems could be as easily soothed, and imagining Caroline clinging to the wings of the bird, rising up into the night sky.

# CHAPTER 21

✒

*June 9, 1990*

*Caroline was right. Always carrying a condom in your purse is a good idea, because you never know when you're going to be needing it. I can't tell her, though. Jude is her brother, and even though they're so close, I just can't go there.*

*I didn't really plan for anything to happen, and I don't think Jude did, either. But after our ride dropped us off at our house, my parents didn't come out. I peeked inside and saw they'd fallen asleep in front of an old John Wayne movie on cable.*

*Jude took my hand and led me out to the path that goes around the lake. We walked holding hands for a long time and watched as clouds moved in and hid the moon. I remember smelling rain and Jude's cologne as he kissed me, then pulled me close so that my arms had nowhere to go except around his neck.*

*It was the most natural thing in the world to do. We took off our clothes and lay down together on the rich, dark earth that we know like our own beds. Jude had probably long ago realized that our coming together was something that was going to happen, but I didn't know it until that moment. I can't say if the earth moved, but I do know that the moon shifted on its course, taking us both with it, and when I looked up into his face it was like looking into my own. He is mine and I am his, along with the lake and the moon and the lonely loon that always evades capture no matter how much we try.*

Jewel closed the diary slowly, glad she'd read it, but a part of her wishing that she hadn't. More than ever she needed to keep it hidden from her dad. It wasn't like her mom had cheated on her dad; they hadn't even met yet when Jude took her mother to the senior prom. But as strong and confident as her dad appeared to be to everyone around him, she knew he would be hurt.

She stuck the diary beneath her mattress before going to the room where her mother's things were kept. The door was kept open now, but she was pretty sure her dad never came in here. Maybe he wasn't ready yet. Or maybe he just needed an invitation from her to go through everything together. The thought startled her. It was the first time she'd ever thought of her father as unsure or hesitant about anything, but the more she thought, the more she could see the truth in it. Her dad needed her to bring him into this room and deal with old memories he couldn't quite let go of.

Jewel opened the trunk, searching for the football jersey she'd seen before. She found it near the bottom, the number 02 emblazoned on the front in bright red. As she pulled it out, it unfolded and she saw the back for the first time. " 'Collier,' " she read out loud, holding it close to her chest, wanting to capture what her mother had felt, if only for a moment.

But in her hands it was cool and limp, an empty shirt that had once belonged to somebody she'd never met. She felt the absence, but that was all. Crumpling it into a ball beneath her shirt, she shut the lid of the trunk before returning to her room.

Caroline sat at the quilting table with Jewel and the two older women, and wondered how it had come about that she was sitting here doing something she had promised herself she'd never do again. She glanced up at her mother, who was squinting through her bifocals as she tried to thread a needle, and knew that his had been her mother's mission from the start. She just wasn't sure why.

Caroline reached over and took the needle and threaded it before handing it back. She warmed under her mother's appreciative glance and bent back to her own work, to the sewing and stitching of Shelby's quilt. She was aware of the four pairs of hands that held it,

one smaller and three larger, and how all of them had been part of the
life they were commemorating. They each added their own patterns,
their own thread, their own stitches, weaving them together to make
a whole. She supposed that was how Shelby's life had been: gently en-
riched by those she knew and those who knew her. It was a celebra-
tion, in a way, and Caroline wanted to thank her mother for bringing
her here to this table, with these women, but when she looked up to
speak, her mother stood, and the moment was over.

"Can I get anybody coffee or anything?"

"I'd like a beer."

Everybody turned to Rainy in surprise.

Margaret said, "It's only nine thirty in the morning, Rainy. You
can't have a beer."

"Who says? I'm sixty-nine years old. I've lost a husband and a
child and I'm recovering from cancer. I woke up this morning and
said, 'Damn—I've earned the right to drink whatever I want, whenever I want.' "

Caroline's mother stood looking at her best friend with her
hands on her hips. "That's ridiculous. You'll turn into an alcoholic if
you start drinking beer in the morning."

Rainy pushed her bifocals down her nose to stare up at her
friend. "I haven't had a beer since Bill died. I don't think having one
now will send me on the road to ruin." She put down the fabric she'd
been working on. "You have to learn how to relax, Margaret. Live a
little. I find that it's those times when I do something out of the ordinary that I learn something new. You should try it sometime."

Margaret pursed her lips. "Well, you can't have a beer."

Rainy frowned. "And why the hell not?"

"Because I don't have any. How about some orange juice?"

With a heavy sigh of resignation, Rainy said, "Why not? Guess
you don't have any vodka or anything around here to spice it up
with, huh?"

"Definitely not." Caroline's mother stalked off in a huff toward
the kitchen.

Caroline called out to her retreating back, "Can I have a cup of
coffee, please?"

When her mother returned, she placed a steaming mug of coffee in front of Caroline. "It's regular, so drink it slowly. You won't be getting another one."

Caroline rolled her eyes and kept sewing, concentrating on making a bird beak with light blue thread. "Thank you," she said, wishing briefly that she could be alone with her mother so that she might tell her thank you for other things.

But then her mother disappeared into the kitchen again and returned with a glass of water and a can of fiber supplement. "I've been meaning to ask if you're getting enough fiber. Just in case, I bought this at the grocery store on my last visit."

Caroline felt her cheeks flush and kept her head bent, feeling the glances of Jewel and Rainy. "I'm fine, Mom. Can we please change the subject now?" She wondered again at their changing relationship. She'd begun to consider it a symbiotic one that, like a vine growing on a tree, was one of support and mutual benefit. But sometimes, like now, she thought it was more like those of parasites and sharks.

"Oh, my gosh—look at this." Rainy had stopped sewing and had been going through a box of Shelby's papers she'd found in the attic. "It's that itinerary—remember? The one from when they were going to take that around-the-world trip."

Caroline stilled, almost feeling the sting on her rear end from the only belt whipping she'd ever received.

Margaret reached for the piece of paper. "Oh, yes—I remember that! Do you, Caroline?"

She nodded, focusing on the material in front of her, not able to face her mother. The whole memory still brought back the feelings of shame and powerlessness, as if the whole episode had happened yesterday. She'd been trying to assert her independence, and her mother had doused it like a bucket of water on a hot flame.

Her mother laughed softly. "When I saw my American Express bill I remember thinking, 'Wow, what a smart kid.' I think the thing that made me angry was that Caroline lied to me when I found the itinerary under her bed. That was the one thing I could never tolerate from either one of my children."

Caroline's hands stilled as she looked at her mother. She remembered the time she'd seen her crying on the back porch, seeing her as a grieving mother for the first time. She felt that way now, seeing not a stranger, but her mother as she'd always known her in her heart, but not in her eyes.

Her mother continued. "Even when I was yelling at you, and even afterward when I told your father about it, I remember being so proud to have a daughter smart enough to try to pull off something like that." She looked up at her daughter. "I couldn't let you know that, of course."

"Why not? It would have made all the difference to me. You were so mad I thought you were getting ready to send me to boarding school in Siberia."

Her mother chewed on her lower lip, an action Caroline couldn't remember ever seeing before. "I didn't want to undermine my authority by lessening your punishment." She sighed, her shoulders sinking. "I guess in hindsight I should have handled it differently. As a parent I could only do what I thought best. I figured that as long as you knew you were loved, you could handle any mistakes we made. That sort of became my parenting motto over the years. I made lots of mistakes where you and your brother were concerned. But I always loved you, and I could only hope that you knew it."

Caroline picked up her needle and thread and continued to sew, afraid to say anything or look at her mother, because if she did she knew she would start crying and never stop.

They were all silent for a long time until Rainy cleared her throat. "Well, gosh, Margaret, you're going to make us all cry and then we'll never get this thing done. Let's talk about something else now. Jewel—is everything ready for the Harvest Moon festival at school tomorrow?"

Jewel looked at Caroline and her mother as they both bent over their work, as if making sure they were finished speaking. "Yep—though Coach Dempsey wanted to know if there were any more place mats for our booth. He thinks we could sell them."

"Not unless Caroline has more here. We had ten sets of four at the store, and Drew said we've sold every last one of them. Real popular merchandise, those. Caroline, you'll have to talk with Drew about a marketing deal."

Caroline snorted. "Right. We'll do that right after we talk about a marketing deal for his furniture."

"What?" Jewel sat straight up in her chair. "Has he finally agreed to let you sell his stuff?"

"I wish. But he won't even consider it. What I'd really like to do is just send some photographs of a few of his pieces—like your dining room table—to my boss. Just to get a professional's opinion. But your dad won't even talk to me about it."

Jewel leaned forward. "I wish you'd try harder. He so needs to have something to occupy his mind—besides me and what I'm doing and where I'm going."

Rainy sent her a reproving look. "Now, Jewel . . ."

"I know, I know. I'm glad, really. It's been kinda nice spending more time with him. But the man is just sort of floundering, and it makes me feel guilty because I know he gave up so much for me."

Caroline and the two older women stared at her for a few moments before Rainy spoke. "Good Lord, Jewel. You sound more and more like your mother every day. Thirteen going on thirty. I won't ask where you got your brains, because it's obvious. But please try to act and talk like a child every once in a while, all right? You're my only grandchild and you're making me feel old."

Caroline's mother coughed and looked pointedly at Rainy. "You feel old because you are old, dear."

The phone rang and Margaret went to answer it. Caroline paused in her stitching, trying to listen. When her mother returned, she was halfway out of her seat. "Is it for me?"

"No. Just the bug man reminding me he'll be here tomorrow morning." She knitted her eyebrows. "Who were you expecting?"

"Not my boss, if that's what you're wondering. I was actually waiting for a call from Dad. I've left about three messages for him on his machine. I know you said he was out of town, but he should be back by now—or at least returning calls from wherever he is."

Her mother and Rainy exchanged glances. Rainy kept her head down as she said, "I wouldn't hold your breath."

Margaret sent her friend a piercing look. "Rainy, please don't start."

"Really, Margaret. You're way past the age of covering for him. Caroline's old enough to hear a few things now, don't you think?"

"No, I don't th—"

They had Caroline's full attention now. "What are you talking about?"

Margaret bent her head to her stitching but her hands didn't move.

Rainy said, "Just that your dad will call you when it suits him, and not before. That's pretty much how he's always been. If he doesn't feel like doing something, or there's a bit of unpleasantness to handle, he's gone so fast it's like lightning struck him in the butt."

Margaret had both hands on the table now and was staring at her friend furiously. "Stop it now, Rainy. This is neither the time nor the place." She nodded her head in Jewel's direction, indicating that there were young ears present.

"If you say so," Rainy said, her lips pursed as she began stitching again.

Caroline looked at her mother, but Margaret had already picked up her needle and was studying the corner of the quilt she'd been working on. Caroline stared at the top of her mother's head, willing her to look up. After several moments Caroline bent back to her own quilt corner, tucking the thought in the back of her mind to dig out whatever it was her mother didn't want to talk about.

They worked in silence for about a quarter of an hour until the old clock on the mantel chimed. Jewel looked up from where she'd been cutting out paintbrush shapes from an assortment of fabric scraps. It had been her idea to decorate the edges of the border with them, and the three women had thought it a brilliant idea—as long as they didn't have to cut out the intricate shapes. "What's tomorrow's date?"

Rainy's needle stilled as she looked over at Jewel. "September fourth." She nodded her head slowly. "It'll be three years since your mama passed."

"I know. I can't believe that I'm just realizing it now, though.

The first two years it was like December twenty-fifth to me, you know? And now it just sort of happens without my being aware of it." She looked at her grandmother. "Is that a good thing?"

Rainy reached over and took Jewel's hand. "It's a very good thing. Your mother was all about celebrating life. She'd be happy that you're living it, and doing such a good job at it, too."

Jewel looked up uncertainly. "Can we still go to the cemetery tomorrow? I'd like to bring her some mountain laurel blooms again. It's funny; I know we scattered her ashes far away, but I always feel like she's there in the cemetery under the stone with her name on it. And I think she likes it when I bring her flowers."

Rainy smiled, her eyes bright. "She does, sweetie. She does. But I'd like to go, too, so we'll make a plan for after school, all right?"

"I'll go, too," Caroline's mother said. "I haven't visited Jude since I've been back this time. I was thinking Caroline might like to come."

The old feelings of grief and guilt clutched at her heart, startling Caroline not only with their presence, but with their lack of intensity. It was almost as if the calm waters of the lake and the fresh air of the mountains had somehow built a cushion around her heart; buffers against painful memories and old heartaches.

"I don't think so. I—"

"You've never been, Caroline." Her mother's eyes were hurt but devoid of accusation. But the old anger evaded Caroline. In place of it, a feeling of shared grief and understanding inserted itself, amazing her with its rightness. It was as if she had suddenly raked away the dead pine straw in her mother's rose garden and discovered soft green stalks beneath.

She swallowed. "All right. I'll go. Just let me know the time."

If she didn't know her mother so well, she would have expected the woman with the exhilarated expression on her face to leap from her chair and pump her fists in the air. Instead Margaret Collier simply nodded her head and said, "Good. I'll let you know."

They all bent back to their work with the sound of the ticking clock accompanying the steady rhythm of needles pulling thread, like road maps of a short life long lived, taking each of the quilters to her own destination.

# CHAPTER 22

J EWEL SPOTTED CAROLINE ON THE DOCK SITTING IN THE OLD DI-
rector's chair with a pile of rectangular fabric pieces, about the size
of the place mats she'd been making, in a small stack beside her. As
Jewel approached, she studied Caroline's face, trying to figure out
exactly what had changed. It was softer, somehow, reminding her of
the steady glow of the night-light she had used ever since she was a
small girl.

Caroline looked up and actually smiled. Jewel smiled back and
held out her hand. "I brought you our phone, in case you needed to
use it."

Caroline's brow raised, but her smile didn't fade completely. "So
what do you want?"

"What makes you think I want anything?"

"Well, according to my observations and my chats with your
dad, you should be working a flea market stand. Bartering is your
middle name."

Jewel sat cross-legged on the dock in front of Caroline and
picked up a completed place mat. She smiled when she recognized the
picture stitched with needlepoint on the front of the water and
the canoe with two people and the loon in the sky. "Hey, I recognize
this."

"I would hope so. Your dad said he didn't mind me reproducing
it on a place mat. I actually made a bunch with the identical picture.
It's a lot easier to mass-produce that way, and your dad keeps asking
for more. He says he can't keep them on the shelves, they're selling
so fast. I'm making as many as I can, but ten per day is my limit."

She squinted up at Caroline. "That must make you feel great—
knowing that you're doing something other people appreciate."

Caroline stared at her for a moment. "Okay, Jewel. What is it that you want?"

Jewel pulled the Polaroids she'd taken that morning out of her sweatshirt pocket. "I took these pictures of some of my dad's furniture pieces. I was thinking that . . . well . . . maybe, if you wanted to, you could show them to your boss and . . . well, not sell anything, but just, well, see if he thinks my dad is as talented as you and I do."

Caroline's eyes widened in surprise. "Does your dad know you took these?"

"Of course not. Do you think he'd let me give them to you if he did?"

Caroline reached out for the pictures and began flipping through them. "He is unbelievable, you know."

Jewel grinned. "Yeah, that's for sure. He's also a great furniture maker."

Caroline's face turned pink as she continued to study the pictures. "That's what I meant, and you know it."

"Sure. I knew that." Jewel smirked, and Caroline swatted her lightly on top of the head.

"So. You want me to send these to my boss to see what he says. Won't your dad kill both of us if he finds out?"

"Well, there are laws that usually prevent that kind of behavior. I figured we could both handle his anger until he figures out how smart we were to do this."

Caroline stared out at the lake for a long moment, watching a waverunner on the opposite shore jump the waves caused by a passing motorboat. "I don't know, Jewel. Your dad was pretty adamant about not selling any of his furniture ideas. I don't thi—"

"He only said that because of me—and everybody knows it, including me. But if I'm the one telling him different, don't you think he'd listen? And I'm not saying we do anything behind his back. I'm just saying let's get the information together to help him decide. If he still says no, then we can let it drop."

Jewel knew she was getting through when Caroline looked down at her. "Why is this so important to you?"

It was her turn to study the lake and find the words to a question she had just learned to ask herself. "Because I love my dad. He did the most amazing thing for me—he changed his life and gave up something he really loved. And I do like spending more time with him. I've really learned a lot about who he is and what's important to him—and it's all stuff that makes me proud to call him my dad. But he's so . . . well, not himself. Sure, he gets to make furniture all day. But there's nothing else. I mean, we're talking about somebody who used to win arguments and beat confessions out of people without lifting a hand. He is *so* not wanting to run a little country store."

Caroline studied the top picture again—the one of her own swimming trophy cabinet. She looked at it for a long time before she spoke again. "You're right. Maybe we could just get the ball rolling a little bit and determine whether there really is any interest in his kind of furniture." She shrugged. "It could be that we're the only people in the world who think he's got something going on here."

Jewel pushed up from the ground and stood. "Right. Like that could happen. He's like Michelangelo except without the paintbrush. Your boss will love his stuff."

Caroline stacked the pictures and tucked them in her pile of place mats. "Well, I'm not promising anything, but I will get these in the mail tomorrow."

Jewel hugged Caroline, surprised to feel herself being hugged back. "Thanks. You won't regret it."

"I already am. But don't let that bother you. I can handle your dad."

Jewel waggled her eyebrows, making Caroline laugh. "That's for sure. Just be gentle with him."

She waved good-bye, and as she turned to go she felt a place mat hit her on her backside.

Caroline was still sitting on the dock three hours later when Rainy appeared, loon in tow on his leash.

"Thought I'd bring the bird to his home to start getting him used to it again. It won't be long until he's ready to fly." Rainy paused by her chair. "How are you feeling?"

"Fine. The doctor put me on antibiotics, but no serious effects from falling in the lake."

Rainy shortened the leash and picked up the loon, holding it like a baby cradled in her arms. "I wasn't talking about you falling in the lake. I'm talking about you jumping in the lake yesterday. On purpose."

"Oh. I suppose Jewel told you."

"Yep. She tells me everything—unless you swear her to secrecy, which you didn't."

Caroline nodded. "True. And no, I won't do anything as risky again as swimming in the lake. I promise to swim in a chlorinated pool from now on, so you don't need to mention it to my mother." She met Rainy's eyes. "I just had to do it. One more time."

"I understand. But you're going on thirteen years with that heart of yours, and you and I both know that's way beyond what's normal and expected. You need to be real careful."

Caroline rubbed the heels of her hands in her eyes. "I think about it every day. More so now."

Rainy sat down on the dock, the loon in her lap. "Why now?"

"I'm not sure." She shrugged, trying to find the words. There had been so much she hadn't told Rainy because of how frail the older woman had seemed from her illness. But now, with a bright green headscarf and pinkened cheeks, she looked more like the Rainy whose soft shoulders and warm arms had always given her rest.

Caroline took a deep breath. "I've been having this dream ever since I came here." She stopped and looked at Rainy.

"Go on. We're not going anywhere, so you might as well keep talking."

"Okay. Well, in this dream, I'm walking down a dark path where I can't see anything except for what's right in front of me. I'm not scared because I know there's somebody with me. And I'm pretty sure it's Jude, even though I can't see him." She felt the hot sting of tears and ground the heels of her hands into her eyes again to make it stop. "It's been the same every time—except for this last week. I still can't see Jude, but there's more light, showing the sides of the path with the trees and plants. And water. I can hear the sound of water now."

Rainy nodded, stroking the bird in her lap. "Have you told your mother?"

"Of course not."

Rainy nodded again. "I see. What do you think this dream means?"

"I don't know—I'm not a therapist. But I can't help but think that it means things are getting brighter." She smiled tentatively at Rainy. "I know that sounds obvious, but maybe I'm right. And I'm so damned proud of myself for seeing that, because three months ago I wouldn't have even realized that there was anything wrong."

"Brava." Rainy smiled and patted her leg. "Brava. You should tell your mother, you know."

Caroline looked away, fingering the unfinished place mat in her lap. "You know I can't. She'd think I was having delusions and send me to another shrink."

Rainy threw back her head and laughed. "In so many ways, you have your mother pegged, but in other ways your mind is shut tighter than a bear trap. Margaret is a lot stronger than you could ever imagine."

"I know my mom, Rainy. She goes off the handle when anything rocks her boat. I mean, Jude's death sent her around the bend, remember? She sent my dad away when I needed him the most. No matter how much clearer I see my mother now, I just can't get over that."

"What?" Rainy twisted in her direction so suddenly it made the loon squawk. "Do you really believe what you just said to me?"

"Yes, I do. Nothing's ever led me to believe differently. My mother certainly never pulled me aside and explained anything."

"Did you ever give her the chance?"

Caroline paused, thinking of all the times her mother had knocked on her bedroom door after the accident and Caroline hadn't answered. Or the many times since she'd become an adult and let her mother talk to her answering machine instead of picking up the phone.

Rainy's voice softened. "I know it isn't my place to interfere, but I have a feeling that if I don't it will be the next millennium before either one of you mentions this. So I'm going to tell you something your mother should have told you years ago, but didn't out of respect for you and your love for your father." She took a deep breath, holding it in her mouth before slowly letting it out. "When the accident happened and Jude died and you were so close to dying, your father fell apart. I know you won't remember any of this—most of the time you were in the hospital, and when you came home, your mother hid it from you as best as she could."

She stroked the long back of the loon thoughtfully. "He couldn't get out of bed. He stayed there day after day while your mother brought him food and something to drink. Then she'd go back to the hospital and stay by your side. Your father wasn't there when she asked that your brother's respirator be removed, and he wasn't there when she signed the papers for your surgery. She had lost a child and was about to lose another and she didn't crack. But your father did. He couldn't face what had happened to his perfect family. He made it to Jude's funeral only because your mother pulled him out of bed, bathed and dressed him, and then drove him. And afterward he took to his bed again and your mother went back to the hospital to be with you."

Caroline felt the hot tears slip down her face, but she didn't wipe them away.

"I'm not telling you this to shame you, Caroline. I love you too much for that. But you need to know. I'm afraid that you and your mother will never find each other until you understand the truth of how it was."

Caroline nodded, knocking some of her tears onto her hands and feeling them burn.

"Your mother lived like that for a whole year. Helping you through your recuperation and treating your dad like the invalid he had become. She was a mother and wife and she knew no other way to do it. So she did."

Rainy stood then, still cradling the bird and staring out toward the late-afternoon sun. "Your mother finally gave your dad an ultimatum, telling him that he could seek help or she wanted a divorce. She thought if she got serious, he would straighten up and at least try. Margaret had already taken him to so many doctors—with him dragging his feet, of course—but he always said he was simply griev- ing and saw no need to talk to strangers about it. Margaret truly thought that if she gave him an ultimatum, he would choose their marriage."

Caroline sniffed. "And he didn't."

"No, he didn't. He packed his bags the next day, arranged to sell his practice, and then moved to California. When life got tough, he got running. It didn't matter to him that he left a wife and daughter who loved him and needed him. It simply didn't matter."

Caroline closed her eyes, letting the tears flow freely now. She felt Rainy's kiss on the top of her head.

"I'm sorry I upset you. But you needed to hear it. I'm going to leave you now and let you stew on it a bit."

Caroline heard Rainy's footsteps and the waddle of the loon as they began to walk down the dock. They stopped and Rainy said, "We're going to the cemetery tomorrow afternoon when Jewel gets home from school. Are you still planning on coming with us?"

She nodded, unable to speak, and listened as the footsteps faded away. Finally she opened her eyes just as the sun began to set, sink- ing in lonely exile into the far shore of Lake Ophelia.

*November 16, 1990*

*I've been at USC for over a month and like it a lot. I am enjoying my classes and have made a lot of friends—but none of them is Jude. We call or write every day, but it's still not the same as being there. I miss him in the same way I suppose I'd miss my arm or my ability to see. But it can't be helped. We both agree that my education is important and this is something that we just have to get through. Besides, we'll see each other in a week for Thanksgiving break. The Colliers are coming to their lake house and I can hardly wait. I'm having such a hard time studying for my midterms because all I can think about is Jude, and the lake, and the secret places where we can go.*

*One of my best friends here at college is actually a guy. I met him on the first day of classes when I dropped my art history book on his foot and nearly broke his toe. I also dropped my coffee on the book when I reached for it, so that it was soaking wet. He was nice enough to share his for the entire class, which I thought was real sweet. His name is Drew Reed and he's from Charleston, although he doesn't like to talk about home or his family very much. He's a junior and a history major but he likes taking art courses for his electives. His dad doesn't know about this because Drew's dad has all these ideas about Drew being a lawyer in the firm where his dad's a partner. I don't think Drew shares the same plans, but goes along anyway. I wonder how many people out there are like him— living out somebody else's idea of what life should be like. I hope one day that he finds his true calling. He's such a great guy— nice and funny and smart. And I've seen girls drool when he walks by. I guess I'm immune because of Jude, but if I'd never met Jude, I could definitely say I'd have it bad for Drew Reed.*

# CHAPTER 23

D REW PULLED UP INSIDE THE SHADE OF A SCRUBBY PINE IN front of the old cemetery and turned off the ignition. Jewel hadn't said a word during the short ride and, as usual, he couldn't think why. For about the hundredth time he wished there were some sort of instruction manual for raising teenage girls. He drove her to school each day and picked her up afterward, and came and sat at the table with her when she did her homework, and he still could coax only the minimum number of words out of her lips. He had no idea what he was doing wrong, but had decided that if he just kept making himself available, she would eventually crack.

He studied her profile now, seeing again her mother's jaw and nose and gorgeous red, wavy hair. Instead of the familiar pull of grief, he felt only gratitude; gratitude for having been blessed with Shelby's presence in his life, even for such a short time, and for the gift of the beautiful girl sitting beside him.

"Are you ready?"

She nodded, bringing the bunch of mountain laurel blooms up to her nose. "It's getting better for you, too, isn't it? I mean, missing her."

She looked up at him and he nodded, but didn't say anything. He was too afraid that she'd stop talking.

"It's not that I don't think about her every day. It's just that I sometimes find that I've been working on something so hard that I wasn't thinking about how much I miss her."

He waited for a while to make sure she was finished speaking. "Yeah. I know what you mean. We'll carry a little pocket of sadness for your mother for the rest of our lives. And that's okay. But I think we're over the worst of it." He held out his hand to her and she took it.

"I think you're right. But why? Do you think it's just because it's been three years? Or has something else changed?"

He watched his little girl sniff the flowers again, marveling at how damned smart she was. "I would say a little of both. They say time is the great healer, and they're right. But I also believe that doing what we've been doing has helped, too—you with your quilting and me with my furniture. They've given us purpose and a reason to call ourselves something other than widower or motherless." He squeezed her hand. "And maybe you've found a good enough parent in me so that you haven't had to miss your mother so much."

Those beautiful eyes of hers—not Shelby's, and not his own, but distinctly Jewel's—looked back at him. "If I didn't know you any better, Dad, I'd say you were fishing for a compliment." And then, in a move that seemed to surprise her as much as it did him, she leaned over and kissed him on the cheek. "You're more than good enough. Now, can we go? Everybody will be waiting for us."

Drew pulled his key from the ignition, noticing that the small cross-stitched heart Shelby had given him when they were first married was missing from the key chain. Feeling an odd panic, he searched between the seats and on the floor, but the heart was gone. He looked up to see Jewel watching him.

"It'll show up, Dad. Come on, we're late."

They scrambled out of the truck, and after a backward glance at the floor mat he slammed the door shut.

Caroline stood at the edge of the cemetery watching Rainy and her mother approach a small dogwood tree near the stone wall that bordered the oldest section of the cemetery. She tried to move forward and join them, but something held her back. It was almost a feeling of not being wanted there; of waiting, and wanting, and fear of moving forward.

She turned at the sound of footsteps and spotted Drew and Jewel coming up the gravel path behind her. Jewel carried flowers in one hand and her father's hand in the other. The sight warmed Caroline, somehow made her feet move. Drew stopped in front of her, and Jewel continued on to where the two older women stood under the dogwood, the two markers lying beneath it.

"I'm glad you came." His voice reassured her, more than her

mother or Rainy had. Despite everything they knew and he didn't, the fact that he understood why this was so hard for her softened something inside of her and made her reach for his hand. He didn't look surprised when he took it, and when they moved to stand with the others he didn't let go.

Jewel knelt by the first marker and placed the beautiful purple flowers next to it. Then she kissed her fingers and touched her mother's name before standing and stepping back.

Caroline forced her eyes to move to the other marker set into the dark earth close by on the other side of the tree, shaded by its long branches, protected from strong winds and harsh sun the way a mother's arms had protected Jude and Shelby in life.

Her eyes blurred as she looked at her brother's grave for the first time and realized that the hand she now held was her mother's. They knelt together and Caroline leaned forward to read the inscription:

IF TEARS COULD BUILD A STAIRWAY
AND MEMORIES A LANE,
I'D WALK BACK UP TO HEAVEN
AND BRING YOU HOME AGAIN.

"I remember that," Caroline whispered, feeling her mother squeeze her hand. "We were in Saint Simons, in that old cemetery there, and Jude read it out loud to us. He said that's what he'd want on his tombstone."

Her mother kissed her fingers, then touched the name inscribed on the front. *Jude William Collier.* "I know. I'd forgotten all about it, but you remembered. You told me when you were still in the hospital that that was what needed to be written there. It's lovely. I'm glad you remembered."

Caroline only nodded, afraid to speak. She felt as if she were falling into the icy lake again, the brittle awareness of light and feeling. Of being alive. She could hardly breathe, and for a moment she fought for the surface, felt the pressure in her lungs as if they were starved of air. Her mother's arm went about her, and they were both kneeling in front of the marker, and suddenly Caroline could breathe again. It was as if her mother had reached her hand into the water and pulled her out into the bright sunshine.

Her mother brushed the hair off her face, her expression one of concern. For the first time Caroline wasn't annoyed by it. "Are you all right? Do you need some water?"

She shook her head. "No. I'm fine. Just . . . overwhelmed."

Her mother placed the back of her fingers to Caroline's forehead. "You feel warm. Maybe this wasn't such a good idea."

Caroline felt the old familiar flash of annoyance, and it comforted her somehow. It was like knowing things had changed, but not the old things that reminded you of who you were and where you'd been. "I'm fine, Mom. Really." She looked up at the concerned faces of Drew, Jewel, and Rainy and found a smile. "I'm just . . . thinking about Jude."

And she was. But now she wasn't thinking of how he'd died or how much she'd missed him for all these years. She was thinking about the person he'd been, and how he'd always made her smile. Then she remembered the last time she'd seen him, and what he had told her, and some of the joy left, leaving her confused and shaken.

She sat back on the grass that had started browning under the shortened days, following the cycle of the seasons. *Why, Jude? What did you mean?* Her question went unanswered as it had been for the last thirteen years, leaving her empty and wanting.

Her mother spoke softly, keeping her arm around Caroline and pulling her up. "I think we should go. This has been stressful for you, I can tell, and you need to get home and rest."

Caroline didn't resist. She allowed her mother to lead her from the cemetery and the two markers that slept side by side under the dogwood tree. She leaned into her mother, feeling the strength and comfort there that she had somehow thought she never needed, and wondering at the same time if it was too late to start needing it now.

The door to the spare bedroom was open, and Drew knew he'd find Jewel there. She'd been silent on the way home, and he hadn't intruded. She'd seemed preoccupied, and several times during the short trip from the cemetery he'd thought she was about to say something to him, but had remained quiet.

He found her standing by her mother's trunk, and she jumped when he called her name.

"I'm sorry. I didn't mean to startle you."

She brushed a strand of bright red hair off her forehead and smiled unevenly. "That's all right. I was just leaving."

Disappointed somehow, he stepped back to let her pass before remembering something Rainy had said. "By the way, Grandma Rainy is looking for a quilt your mom might have had in her things. It's a quilt Caroline was working on for her brother, Jude, before he died. Nobody's seen it, and we were thinking it might be in here with all of her things."

Jewel shook her head without even having to think. "Nope. Definitely not in here. And I've been through everything, so I'd know."

He took a step forward, not sure how to read her nervousness. "Are you sure?"

"Definitely. I've taken everything out of the boxes and put them back, so I definitely would know if I'd seen it."

"Oh." He thought back and counted how many times she'd used the word *definitely*. Curious now, he stepped into the room and sat at the edge of the bed. "Did you find anything interesting? I think your mother used to keep a diary when she was younger. I don't remember seeing it when your grandmother and I packed up her things before we moved."

Jewel shrugged. "If I do find it, I'll let you know."

"I was actually thinking you might like to read it. Sort of a way to get to know her better."

He thought for a minute she was going to cry.

She cleared her throat. "Well, if I find it, I'll let you know."

"Is there anything wrong?"

"No. I'm fine. I'm just . . . tired. Going to the cemetery today made me tired."

"Me, too. All those emotions, I think. They wear you out." He touched her arm. "How are you doing? Did the cemetery upset you?"

Shaking her head, she said, "No, it's not that. I guess I was just feeling sad for all the people she left behind. I sometimes think we have the rougher part of it. Same with Jude. His mother and sister don't seem to be able to move on. I don't think he would have wanted that any more than Mama would have."

He was silent for a long moment, wondering where he had been when his little girl had grown up. "We don't understand the circumstances, Jewel. It can be harder for some people. I think it just takes time—sometimes a lot of it."

She fiddled with her fingers for a moment, then came to join him on the edge of the bed. "Dad, there's something I need to tell you."

He could tell how uncomfortable she was and he wanted to make it easier for her. "Is it about the swim lessons?"

Her eyes widened. "You know about that?"

"Yeah—by accident. Caroline didn't tell me, if that's what you're thinking. I saw you one day and sort of figured it out. But what I can't figure out is why you didn't tell me."

She looked down at her hands. "Oh, no reason." She still didn't look at him.

He poked her in the arm. "Yeah, there is. And you can tell me. I promise I won't be mad or hurt."

She sighed and finally met his eyes. "It's just something I wanted to do on my own. I didn't . . . I didn't want you to interfere. Or embarrass me. I still haven't gotten over the time you jumped in the pool with me at the Y and yelled at my coach."

"I wish you'd stop reminding me and forget it."

"Like I could." She rolled her eyes. "I still have nightmares."

He put his arm around her shoulders. "I'm sorry. I was just so afraid for you. You were so scared of the water, and your coach needed to know that he couldn't leave you in the deep end by yourself."

"I'm over it now. Really. I mean, it's still not my favorite place to be, but Caroline's really helped me a lot. She went swimming herself this week, you know."

That surprised him. "She did? Did anybody push her?"

Laughing, she elbowed him. "No. She did it all on her own." Her face was serious again. "But it was the oddest thing. Before she jumped in I heard her say, 'Forgive me, Jude.' It was like she didn't think her brother wanted her to be swimming, but she was going to do it anyway. It didn't make any sense."

"Did you ask her?"

"No. I don't think she wanted me to hear."

He nodded and held her closer, staring at Shelby's trunk across the room. He was about to go over and open it when Jewel spoke again.

"I think you should start dating. And before you ask, yes, it will be weird, but I'll get over it. I don't think Mama would expect you to live alone."

"I've got you."

"You know what I mean. Like a girlfriend or wife."

He brought her closer and kissed her forehead. "I'm not going to have this conversation right now, all right?"

She nodded. "Fine. But you can be thinking about it, okay? Even if we're not going to have a conversation about it."

He stood and rumpled her hair like he used to do when she was small. "I'm going to go get changed. Maybe we can go for a walk after dinner."

"Sure. Sounds fun."

He walked past the trunk toward the door.

"Dad?"

Turning around, he faced her. "Yes?"

"I love you."

He smiled, his heart flip-flopping in his chest. He couldn't remember the last time he'd heard that. "I love you, too."

He walked out of the room feeling better than he had in a long, long time.

*May 16, 1991*

*I can't believe that my freshman year is over. It's gone by so fast. I've met so many new people, but I still feel that pull for Hart's Valley. I suppose it will always be home for me, regard-*

*less of wherever I find myself living. And I feel the same pull for Jude—always him. I've missed him. We see each other during every school break, but it's not enough. He says he's going to get a football scholarship to UNC so we can be together, but I told him he needed a better reason than me to come to school here. I tried to picture us both here, but I couldn't seem to focus the picture in my mind. I ended up with a blinding headache and had to miss my classes for an entire day. Drew came by with chicken soup and a bottle of aspirin to help me feel better. It did help—but not with the headache. It just made me feel loved and cared for and made me realize what a very special friend Drew is to me. I asked him to come visit me in Hart's Valley this summer, but he's going to be interning at his father's law practice. Besides, he said he didn't want to find himself competing with Jude for my attention. That made me laugh, but later I realized how very serious he was.*

*Last night I dreamed of home again, maybe because it's on my mind so much this week as I take my final exams and get packed up for the summer. In the dream Jude and I were out on the lake at night, in the canoe. We were both waiting for something, but I can't remember what it was. The moon was full and I could hear the loon crying somewhere out on the lake. And then I saw Caroline on the dock, sitting in her father's favorite chair. She was crying and waving for us to come get her, to not leave her behind. But no matter how hard Jude and I tried to paddle, our canoe stayed where it was, never getting closer to Caroline and the dock. When I woke up this morning, I remembered it so well that I could almost smell the lake water. And I could still hear Caroline crying for something she couldn't have, no matter how hard Jude and I tried to reach her.*

# CHAPTER 24

T HE SMELL OF FLOOR WAX AND OLD SWEAT ASSAULTED CAROLINE as she walked into the school gym, bringing back memories of Jude, and old friends, and of how young and full of dreams she had once been.

Her mother, wearing a brown tweed suit and heels, crossed her arms over her chest. "Well, it's been a long time since I've been to a Harvest Moon festival. I hardly know what to do." A small herd of children dressed as different-colored M&M's shuffled past, following a harried-looking mom.

Caroline indicated the gym with a sweep of her arm. "Mom, there's tons of booths inside and even more outside. Why don't you go over to the cakewalk and see if you can win a cake for us. I don't think there's any sugar-free ones, but I say live a little. And don't forget you had Jewel sign you up to work at the athletic association booth from seven until eight."

Her mother nodded. "Yes, I remember. I wonder how your place mats are selling. If they do as well here as they're doing at Rainy Days, I'd say you've made the right decision to get back to your sewing. I've always hated that you gave it up."

"Mom—now's really not the time or place. . . ."

"I know, I know. All right, then. I'm heading over to Jewel's booth. Want to come?"

Caroline shook her head. "No, I'd like to wander around a bit first. I'll catch up with you later."

"Are you sure?"

"Mom, I promise I won't get lost. And if I do, I'll find an adult to take me to you."

Her mother frowned, then, when she realized Caroline was joking, actually laughed. "All right. I deserved that. I'll see you later, then."

Caroline waved good-bye, then stood in the middle of the room looking around her, not really knowing what she was hoping to find. She smiled at a small brother and sister dressed as Winnie the Pooh and Piglet. The little boy was snapping the girl's pig snout so that it slapped her in the face, and the sister was retaliating by pulling on Winnie the Pooh's tail.

Somebody grabbed Caroline's hand, and she turned around in surprise to see Drew holding an enormous stuffed bear.

"Cute date," she said, smiling.

"She certainly is. I won her for Jewel at the pie-tossing contest. I hit Coach Dempsey three times in a row and I was quite proud of myself. But now Jewel's worried that she'll never make the swimming team. I was a bit worried myself, so I made sure he saw me put a big wad of bills in the donation jar."

Caroline frowned up at him. "She doesn't need any bribes to make the team. She's a damned good swimmer."

He studied her for a moment. "Do you think I don't know that? I took her to the Y last weekend and I was amazed. Her skills were always there—but you've helped her build up her confidence. Thank you."

She turned away, embarrassed. When had it become so easy to talk to him? Clearing her throat, she said, "You're welcome. I've really enjoyed spending time with her. She's so much like Shelby, it's amazing."

"Don't I know it." His gaze swung around the room until it rested on Jewel in the athletic association booth, who was waving at them. He waved back. "Are you staying for the bonfire tonight?"

Caroline shrugged. "I hadn't really thought about it. I don't think so. I came with my mom, and I don't think that's her kind of thing."

"How about I bring you home, then? That way your mom can leave early if she wants."

"Yeah, I guess. . . ."

"Great. It's all settled then. We'll find Margaret and tell her.

First, why don't we go do the water-balloon toss? I'd like to take my chances just so I can see you in a wet T-shirt again."

He was grinning, and she couldn't resist grinning back. She looked around the crowded gym at all the people dressed in costumes, talking and laughing. It sucked her in, as she supposed Drew had expected it to. She met his eyes. "I have to warn you: I have a great throwing arm, and I have every intention of staying dry."

"There you go again. You know I can't resist a challenge." He stuck out his hand. "After you. Loser has to carry the backpack on our hike tomorrow."

"Better get ready then, because it's not going to be me."

He laughed and followed her to the booth, where a plump vampire took their tickets and placed the large bear behind the counter.

"You two know how this works?" The vampire wore his fangs over braces, which made it difficult to understand him.

Caroline nodded. "Absolutely. We toss the water balloon to each other while we take a step back after every toss. And in the end he bursts the balloon and gets soaked."

The vampire laughed. "Yep. Something like that." He handed the balloon to Caroline and showed them both to the lines marked with masking tape. "You can start now."

Caroline smiled at Drew, trying to remember the last time she'd had this much fun. Or any fun. She thought of her own quilt again, thinking that there would be only two squares on the entire thing: one for work and one for sleep.

With a gentle underhand toss, she lobbed the balloon at Drew. He caught it carefully and then, with an evil grin, tossed it back to her. Each toss became more and more challenging, but both of them managed to catch the balloon without breaking it until they stood fifteen feet apart.

Drew had the balloon, and he smiled as he gingerly tossed it from one hand to the other. "So. What will you give me if I drop this here?"

"A pat on the back?" She looked innocently at him.

"I was thinking of something a little more intimate."

She blushed but didn't lose her composure. "A pat on the head, then."

He shook his head, then did a good imitation of a major-league pitcher doing his windup before a pitch, then released the balloon. It flew high overhead, and to Caroline it seemed to be moving in slow motion. She watched it sailing over her, and she had the sudden memory of Jude pelting her with water balloons when she'd made the swim team for the first time. It was the clearest memory she had of him: laughing and full of joy and as happy for her as she herself had been. *Yes, Jude. I see.* She placed her hands on top of her head and allowed the balloon to hit her hands, wet and stinging at the same time, the water cascading down her face like a blessing of holy water.

When she finally opened her eyes she spotted Drew in front of her, his face closed and concerned. "Are you all right? I threw it high enough so you could step out of the way."

She smiled and took his hand. "I know. I guess I wanted to get wet."

He looked down at her soaked T-shirt, and his mouth quirked. "Well, I got that part right." He pulled off his own sweater and held it out to her. "This is becoming a habit with us, isn't it? Here—put this on, unless you really do want to flash everybody here. I see a bunch of teenage boys over by the basket raffle and their eyes are about to fall out of their heads."

She quickly slid the sweater over her wet hair, enjoying the warmth and Drew's scent that clung to the soft cotton. Awkwardly she smiled up at him. "Sorry about getting your sweater wet."

"Trust me, Caroline, it's not a problem."

Caroline looked away and saw somebody waving from the athletic booth. "I think that's my mom—let's go see what she wants."

Drew took her hand and pulled her through the crowd. She was surprised to see her mother on her knees next to a seated Jewel and holding a wet paper towel to Jewel's forehead.

Drew squatted next to Caroline's mother. "Are you all right, hon?"

Jewel shrugged. "It just kinda hit me suddenly. And it's different this time, too. It's like more pressure than pain." Her eyes clenched and her hand went to her forehead.

"I'll take you home right now." He took the paper towel from Caroline's mother and gently pressed it against Jewel's cheek.

Caroline's mother stood. "Actually, they don't really need me here. I'd be happy to take her to her grandmother. Rainy's tea is the only thing that seems to help." Margaret still wore her tweed suit, but it now sported a rhinestone pumpkin pin.

Drew slowly shook his head. "I don't think so. She really seems to be in a lot of pain. I'd feel better if I were with her."

Jewel pulled her father's hand away from her face. "Dad, I'll be fine. Grandma Rainy always makes it better. Mrs. Collier has to drive by Rainy Days on her way home, so she might as well drop me off."

He still looked undecided. Jewel must have guessed this, because she said, "Really, Dad. Stay. I don't think your hovering over me is going to make me feel any better."

His eyes widened. "No, I don't suppose so."

"And Grandma Rainy gave you her cell phone so she can reach you if she needs you."

"True . . ."

She pressed her fingers against her forehead again. "Then it's all settled. Mrs. Collier will bring me to Grandma's and I'll just see you later."

"Are you sure?"

She nodded, her eyes closed. "Definitely. Just don't forget the blanket in the back of your truck for the bonfire."

Caroline studied Jewel's face for any hint of subterfuge, but the young girl really seemed to be in pain.

Drew stood. "Thanks for the reminder," he said, leaning over to kiss the top of her head. "I'll call Rainy so she'll have something ready for you when you get there."

While he was on the phone, Caroline turned to her mother. "How are place mat sales going?"

"You won't believe it—every single one of them. And look— Coach Dempsey blew up the picture Jewel took of her mother's quilt and posted it on this huge backboard. We've already sold over one hundred tickets for the auction." She indicated a six-by-six-foot whiteboard. Shelby's quilt appeared almost life-size, and Caroline had to step back to take it all in.

"We've done a pretty good job, haven't we?"

Her mother crossed her arms over her chest and nodded. "*You've* done a great job, Caroline. I've been telling everybody that you did the quilt and we just helped."

Warmth twisted inside of her as she faced her mother. "But that's not true."

"Sure it is. You're such an artist. I always wondered why you chose to be an accountant instead of something more creative. You're just so good."

A woman and her daughter came and stood by the whiteboard, and Caroline's mother moved toward them with a roll of raffle tickets. Caroline simply stood staring at her mother's back. Had she always believed those things? Or was this just the first time that Caroline had really paid attention long enough to listen?

Drew closed his cell phone and clipped it on his belt. "All right. Rainy's got the tea brewing already. I told her you would be there soon—and that I'll call a little later to see how you're doing."

He helped pull Jewel from her seat, and Caroline watched as the girl leaned into her father. His big hands went around her shoulders as her head rested on his chest. Margaret handed the roll of raffle tickets to a teenage helper in the booth and gently took Jewel from her father. She supported the girl in the same way Drew had, and Caroline wondered if that particular stance was something a person was born knowing or something you learned when you became a parent.

Drew tugged on her hand. "Come on. Let's put Mr. Bear in the truck and get the blanket. If we get there early enough, we can stake out the best spot for the bonfire."

Caroline nodded absently, feeling the now-familiar sense of going forward on a moving sidewalk, unsure of where she was heading but not quite ready to step off yet, either.

Drew watched Caroline from the corner of his eye as they headed out to his truck. There was something in the way she walked that seemed different to him. Her footsteps were surer and more solid, as if she had a good idea of where she was going now. He knew better than to mention it, though, sensing the old Caroline still close to the surface. But after seeing her face when he'd tossed that last water balloon, he knew that there was room now to hope.

He slung the blanket over his shoulder and led the way through the parking lot to behind the football stadium, where a farm pasture had been set up for the bonfire. Tall stacks of timber and kindling stood in a large triangle in the middle of a clearing where people had already begun to stake their claims on spots of ground with brightly covered blankets, creating the illusion of a large quilt.

"Over here," he said, leading Caroline to the edge of the pasture where small spruces marked the edge of the woods. "It will be easier to get to the truck this way and we won't be blasted by the heat."

She nodded, looking small and vulnerable swallowed in his sweater, and he found he couldn't stop watching her—this Caroline who seemed to be in the process of making peace with her past. She began to roll up the too-long sleeves of his sweater as she spoke. "We used to do this as kids—Jude and me. When we were real small our parents would come, too. My mom would pack a big cooler of food and drinks, and we'd stay here really late. Well, it was probably only ten o'clock or something, but when you're young it's way past your bedtime. We'd lie on our backs and look at the stars and pretend we were seeing the constellations our dad pointed out to us." She grabbed two corners of the blanket and helped him spread it on their patch of ground.

"Shelby would take Jewel to these kinds of things all the time. I can't say that I ever joined them." He felt the old stab of guilt, but this time it was tempered somewhat, as if the guilt didn't sit in front of him anymore, but had been left on the road somewhere far behind.

She sat down near the middle of the blanket and pulled her knees up. "It's going to be dark soon."

He sat next to her and put a small cooler on the blanket in front of them. "I come bearing gifts," he said as he opened it and handed her a beer. "Nonalcoholic for you. I hope you don't mind. Jewel and I were looking up heart transplants on the Internet the other day, and I saw that one of the things they suggest is for recipients to give up alcohol. I hope you don't mind."

He saw a flash of the old Caroline for a moment as she took the offered bottle. "Why on earth were you searching the Internet for that?"

He focused on opening her bottle, not meeting her eyes. "Jewel was curious about your donor. She was looking to see if there were any accounts of recipients having talents after the transplant that they didn't have before."

Despite the chilliness of the night, she held the frosty bottle to her cheek. "Did she find anything?"

"Not really. Several accounts of people with new talents, but most attribute it to their newfound energy and lease on life."

She looked up to where the light was just leaving the sky and the evening stars were beginning to shine. Turning toward him, she took a sip of her beer, then put it down. She deliberated over her words, and he waited until she was ready.

"You can tell her it's true. At least with me."

The bonfire exploded into light and flame behind them, creating a halo behind her head and a shadow where her face was. But when she turned her head, she glowed again as if the light that had fallen from the sky now filled her from the inside.

They watched the bonfire for a long moment before he spoke. "Did you know your donor?"

She nodded, her eyes meeting his. "It was Jude. They put Jude's heart into me."

She watched him closely, as if measuring his reaction. He wasn't sure what she was looking for, but all he could feel was the endless capacity of a heart to grieve and the even greater capacity to love.

He touched her face. "What an amazing gift."

She was looking at him oddly, her head tilted to the side as a person did when they couldn't hear clearly.

"What is it?"

She gave him a half smile. "Nothing. It's just . . . well, I've never told anybody before. I always thought their reaction would be . . . different."

He put his bottle in the grass and moved closer to take both of her hands in his. "I can't speak for anybody else, but I can honestly say that my first thought was that you have received the most incredible gift of love imaginable. From both Jude—and your mother. It was her decision, wasn't it?"

She didn't answer as hot tears splashed on his hands, and he lifted a finger to gently wipe her eyes.

"Maybe you haven't thought of it that way before?"

She shook her head. "I always thought it was my punishment— a reminder of my mistake."

He moved her into his lap, needing to put his arms around her, to somehow take the pain away. She affected him this way, and he didn't know why. *When did things change between us?* As he held her to him, he remembered holding her after she'd fallen into the lake. It had been then, he thought. When he'd seen the girl she had once been and become determined to find the woman she was supposed to be. And now, holding her in his arms, he found that he had.

Bending close to her ear, he whispered, "I wish I could show you, when you are lonely or in darkness, the astonishing light of your own being."

She looked up at him with a look of surprise, her eyes bright.

"If Jude had been given the chance to choose, where do you think he'd want his heart to be?"

She blinked in confusion, and he knew there was more she had to tell him. But it wasn't the time right now; now with the rising moon, the stars in the sky and the light of the bonfire making her glow as if from her own inner fire.

He bent his head to hers and kissed her, and one by one the stars went out, leaving only a burning glow behind his eyelids as she pulled him closer and began to kiss him back.

# CHAPTER 25

❧

*June 25, 1991*

*Jude and Caroline have been at their lake house all summer. When I'm old and gray, and I have to think back to a time when my life was perfect, I'll pick this summer. Caroline's been teaching swim lessons at the Y before she goes to swim camp next month, and Jude and I have been working at my grandmother's store. It's so wonderful to see him every day. I thought that maybe seeing him all the time might make me not miss him so much when I get back to UNC. But even at night when I know he's just next door, I miss him. This must be what an addict feels like—never having enough. I'm already wondering how I'm going to survive the weeks between when school starts and Thanksgiving break. He gave me his football jersey to sleep in, but it's a poor substitute for the real thing.*

*Drew sends a letter about once a week. He says he's actually enjoying working at his dad's law office but is looking forward to the start of school. He keeps his letters light and funny and impersonal, and I try to answer them in the same way, but I can tell that he's waiting for me to tell him that Jude and I are no longer together, but I know that will never happen. I miss Drew, but in the way that a girl would miss her favorite pair of shoes or her best bike when she's grown out of it. I wish that I could tell him this, but I think he already knows.*

*Last night, after everybody was asleep, Jude and I went swimming in the lake. We made love in the water and again on the shore, and more than ever I feel like there will only ever be the two of us. We just need to survive these separations, even*

*though it's killing both of us. As we lay on the dock with our
skin drying, and the full moon lighting the night like a giant
flashlight, we were waiting for the laughing call of the loon.
But he must have been sleeping, because all we heard was the
water lapping against the dock pilings, and the breeze blowing
our hair and chilling our skin.*

Caroline rose early the next morning, having slept soundly through
the night for the first time since she'd returned to Hart's Valley. She
felt lighter, as if a heavy burden she'd been used to carrying had suddenly shifted. It wasn't gone, but it was easier to carry. She looked at
her reflection in the bathroom and smiled, almost hearing Jude's
voice. *If I didn't know you better, Caroline, I'd say you were looking almost perky.* She had hated that word, which was why, of course, Jude
had always chosen to use it.

She dressed quickly in her hiking shorts and boots and hurried
out of her bedroom. She wanted to grab a cup of coffee and whip
out a few place mats on the sewing machine before her mother got
up and before Drew came to pick her up for their hiking trip. She
warmed at the thought of him, and allowed herself a little bit of
hope.

When she entered the great room, she found her mother fully
dressed in a lemon-yellow linen pantsuit, sitting at the quilting table,
her glasses perched on the end of her nose and quietly stitching on
a corner panel of Shelby's quilt. She looked up as Caroline entered,
and smiled.

"I didn't expect you to be up so early. I was up early myself
and I thought I might as well finish this square I was working on
yesterday."

Caroline waited for disappointment at the unexpected interruption of her solitude, but instead found herself looking forward to
being alone with her mother and working with her on the quilt. She
didn't analyze the feeling, wanting instead just to savor it before it
went away.

Caroline smiled back. "We're almost done with the quilt, and I guess at this point I just want to rush and get it finished. I apparently have three more quilts to make, thanks to the raffle—not including the one I already told Jewel I'd make for Coach Dempsey for the end-of-the-year party."

Her mother sat back in her chair. "Looks like you're going to be busy for a while. Are you planning on extending your leave or are you going to cart all the materials back to Atlanta?"

"Oh. I hadn't really thought about it. How long have I been here?"

"Almost two and a half months. I can't believe you haven't been keeping track."

Caroline walked slowly around the table examining the brightly colored squares. "I was—at first. And then . . . well, I guess I got kinda busy with the quilt and all those place mats."

She waited for her mother to say something, but instead Margaret put down the corner of the fabric she'd been working on and stood. "Speaking of which, have you seen your scrapbook? There's a great picture in there and a party invitation from Shelby's sixteenth birthday. I thought that would be a nice thing to put on the quilt." She began rummaging through the pile of pictures that were scattered over the cardboard table.

Caroline leaned against the table and stared at her mother. "What scrapbook? I never had a scrapbook."

Her mother didn't look up but continued rummaging. "Yes, you did. I gave it to you for your tenth birthday but you never put anything in it. So I borrowed it and have been keeping up with it ever since. As a matter of fact, a couple of weeks ago I took down all of your swimming pictures that I had in the bedroom and hallway and put them in your scrapbook. I figured when I gave it to you, you'd want them all together."

"You never mentioned it to me."

Her mother finally stopped what she was doing and gave Caroline a cursory glance. "Sure I did. Just about every time I called you back in Atlanta, whenever I didn't get your answering machine. I talked about it a lot, but you never asked to see it." She gave an elegant shrug. "But I kept working on it. I figured one day you'd be happy to have it." She tapped her painted fingernails absently on the tabletop. "Darn. I wish I could remember what I did with it. I could have sworn I left it right here."

She turned back to the piles of pictures while Caroline watched her, feeling like a person who'd just stepped though an elevator door to find only an empty shaft. She did vaguely recall her mother talking about a scrapbook. But she had blocked it out, like she usually blocked out her mother's telephone chatter, seeing it as just an unwelcome interruption in her orderly, predictable life.

Caroline picked up a needle with bright blue thread hanging from it and absently pricked her thumb with it, not enough to draw blood but enough to remind her of where she was and why she was here and that she was alone with her mother and they weren't fighting. She had so much to say but couldn't think of any word to start with.

The doorbell rang and they both looked at each other in surprise.

"It might be Jewel wanting to work on the quilt before school," her mother said as she walked toward the door.

Caroline craned her neck to see who it was and jerked out of her chair when she recognized the familiar face. She moved to stand next to her mother at the door.

"Ken—what on earth are you doing here?"

Her boss, and president of Kobylt Brothers Furniture, wore a golf shirt and pants and held a crumpled golf hat in his hand that he scrunched absently while he stood facing them. His black Mercedes sat in the driveway, covered in dust.

He gave her a sheepish smile. "Well, Helen has been after me for about a year to come up for a week to our house in Highlands. And when I got those pictures from you, it was just an added incentive."

Caroline looked past his shoulder to the car. "Is Helen here?"

"Oh, no. I dropped her off at the house—it's only about a half hour away. I told her I was going to go check out the golf course." He winked. "She hates it when I bring business on vacation."

"Business?" Caroline's mother asked, her eyes narrowed in suspicion. "Have we met?"

Caroline pushed the door open wider and ushered him inside.

"Oh, I'm sorry. Mom, this is my boss, Ken Kobylt. Ken, this is my mother, Margaret Collier."

"Nice to meet you, ma'am." They shook hands, but Margaret's demeanor remained cool.

"What business?" her mother asked again.

"Mom, could you get us some coffee? I'd like to talk with Ken alone for a few minutes and then I'll explain."

Her mother's lips thinned with disapproval before she nodded. "All right. But you're getting decaf."

Ken raised an eyebrow.

"Don't let her bother you—she's just worried about me." Caroline wanted to smile at her own words. Had she ever acknowledged that her mother worried about her? Had she even ever realized it herself?

They moved into the great room and Ken immediately went to the trophy cabinet. "This is the one in the picture, isn't it?" He ran his hands down the smooth side of the cabinet, in the same way Caroline had when she'd first seen it.

At her nod, he continued. "I need to meet this guy. I'd like to talk through some ideas I have. I want to mass-produce some of his pieces, but in a very limited way. That way we can keep it exclusive—with a predetermined number to be made. This piece alone I know we could retail for ten grand."

Caroline sat down, feeling exhilarated and deflated at the same time. This was certainly good news for her. But she couldn't even begin to think about how Drew was going to react. "What's wrong? You don't look as excited as I thought you'd be." Ken sat on the opposite sofa and steepled his fingers.

"It's not that I'm not excited—don't get me wrong. I know Drew's stuff is amazing, and it's gratifying to know my hunch was right. But we have a little problem." She could see his eyes lighten. Problems were his forte.

She continued. "I know I mentioned this in my letter I sent with the photos. It's just . . . well . . . Drew Reed, the furniture maker, is, um, well, reluctant. He doesn't want to be a commercial success. He makes furniture for his own pleasure." She watched as Ken smiled dismissively, and she realized that three months ago she would have had the same reaction. She had been an astute businesswoman, seeing things and making decisions in clear black-and-white. But now, somehow, her black-and-white world was suddenly tinged with yellow. And blue and red and orange, it seemed—all the colors she had used on Shelby's quilt. Nothing seemed clear at all.

"Not a problem. If you could arrange a meeting while I'm here, I'm sure I can persuade him to change his mind."

"I don't think you understand, Ken. Drew isn't motivated by money. The most important things to him are his daughter, his artistry, and his time. He's found in his past that those three things and making money seem to be mutually exclusive."

Ken's smile didn't even slip a notch. "Oh, one of those. I see. Well, that will help me narrow my approach, anyway." He slapped his hands on his knees. "So can you tell me where I can find Mr. Reed?"

Caroline was starting to get annoyed—a completely unfamiliar feeling where her boss was concerned. They had worked together for almost eight years, sharing the same goals and methods for success. Her reluctance to join him in his enthusiasm startled her while at the same time reassuring her. Maybe she did have Jude's heart, after all.

She stood just as her mother entered the room carrying a tray with coffee and pound cake slices. "Look, Ken. I need to talk with Drew first. And then if he wants to talk further, I'll let him know that you're staying in Highlands and we can arrange—"

The doorbell rang again, and the three of them turned to stare at the closed door.

"I'll get it," Caroline and her mother said in unison.

Caroline put her hand on her mother's arm. "Mom, please. It's Drew. He's picking me up for our hike. Let me talk with him first, okay? I'll get everything straightened out."

Her mother shook her head, but glided past her with the coffee tray and a bright smile for Ken.

Drew waited on the doorstep when Caroline opened the door. He was looking curiously at the car in the driveway, and Caroline responded by stepping outside with him and closing the door behind her.

"You've got company."

"Yes. We do." She wanted to talk about the night before, and about the pictures she'd sent and about the man inside. But more than anything she wanted to stand there with him in the silence and just be.

He waited for her to continue, but when she didn't he said, "I wanted to tell you in person that I'm going to have to miss our hike today. Jewel's headache has gotten worse and nothing seems to be helping it. She's staying home from school, and I'd like to hang around to keep an eye on her."

"That's fine. I'll stop by later to see how she's doing. Is there anything you need?"

"No, I think we're covered—"

He was interrupted by the sound of the door opening behind them. Ken stuck his hand out toward Drew just as Caroline's mother appeared in the doorway behind him with a look of annoyance on her face. "Mr. Kobylt, I think this is a private conversation."

"I understand you're Drew Reed." He pumped Drew's hand up and down.

"Yes, I am. And you would be . . .?"

"Ken Kobylt, president of Kobylt Brothers Furniture. I'm a great fan of your work."

"Excuse me?" Drew darted a look at Caroline.

"I work with Caroline, and she sent me a few pictures of some of your furniture pieces. Most impressive, if I might say. You are a true talent."

Drew went completely still, the look in his eyes almost predatory. Caroline could see why he was once considered a formidable court opponent. That one look made her feel as if she were on a witness stand and he was about to wring her dry. She swallowed and faced him, knowing that this was what she and Jewel had been fearing all along, just not so soon.

"I don't remember giving her permission to take pictures of anything, much less send them to you."

Ken nodded, making an effort to appear compassionate. "Oh, I'm aware of that. She told me up front that you weren't keen on the idea. But after seeing what you can do, I'm prepared to work with you. Make a mutually beneficial offer."

"I'm not interested."

Drew stepped off the porch and began striding toward his house. His back door opened and Jewel moved slowly toward him, a white washcloth pressed to her head with one hand. She stopped before she reached him, and Caroline could see that she was swaying on her feet. Caroline began to run.

She reached Jewel at the same time Drew did.

"It's bad, Daddy. It's never been this bad before. I can't see right. My eyes are funny."

Her knees buckled and Drew caught her, lifting her in his arms. His face was cold when he turned to Caroline. "Call Rainy. Tell her I'm taking Jewel to the emergency room at Highlands Medical. Ask her to meet us there."

Margaret appeared, her high heels held in one hand as if she'd taken them off to run. "I'll call Rainy—you two just go. Let Caroline drive. You'll want your hands free for Jewel."

Caroline could see he wanted to argue, but then he looked down at Jewel, to where her skin had gone a pasty white, and all he did was nod.

Margaret touched Caroline on the arm. "Take the Cadillac—it's got a big engine. I'll meet you at the car with your purse and keys." Her mother took off at a run again, but Caroline spared only a couple of seconds to watch.

Drew called out to Margaret just as she reached her back porch and had practically pushed Mr. Kobylt out of the way to jerk open the door. "And could you please bring one of Caroline's shirts for Jewel—she just threw up."

With a quick nod, Margaret disappeared into the house.

Caroline touched Drew briefly on the arm. "I'll bring the car out to the driveway so you don't have to carry her down the hill."

He nodded his head stiffly, sending her a brief look that was somewhere between anger and terror. She recognized the expression. It was one that had once greeted her every morning in the mirror, and it made her heart ache.

She raised her fingers to his cheek. "It's going to be all right." She had no reason to believe it, only that she felt it in her heart and knew how much he needed to hear it.

Jewel moaned, and Caroline began moving quickly toward the garage, but was intercepted by Ken Kobylt dangling car keys in front of her. "No, here. Take my car. It's real fast and will get you there quicker than any Cadillac."

"Thanks," she said, taking the keys and sliding into the black Mercedes to start the engine. Margaret had come out of the house and handed Caroline a shirt for Jewel and then two large bath towels to Drew in the backseat.

"Drive carefully," she said to Caroline as she began pulling out of the driveway. "I'm going to call Rainy right now, and I've already called Highlands Medical to let them know you're on your way."

"Thanks, Mom," she said, then watched in surprise as her mother sent her the thumbs-up sign. Torn between wanting to laugh and needing to cry, she carefully backed her way out of the long driveway, then pushed the gas pedal down as far as it could safely go.

# CHAPTER 26

WHEN CAROLINE FINALLY RETURNED HOME LATER THAT evening, the porch light was turned on, but her mother, Ken Kobylt, and her mother's Cadillac were gone. She leaned wearily against the closed door for a long moment, wanting to fall down where she stood and sleep for days.

Instead she found herself moving toward the piano. She remembered how Jude had liked to play when he was feeling bad—after arguing with a friend or playing badly on the football field. She understood it now, and didn't fight her own desire to find peace and solitude somewhere within the black and white keys.

Her fingers were surer now, drawing from some inner resource Caroline had never realized she had, or, if she had, had never allowed out. She used both hands, finding the melody with the right hand and the accompaniment with the left. It was a piece she recognized from when she used to lie under the piano when Jude played, unformed and unpracticed, but unmistakably beautiful. The act of moving her fingers on the keys and creating music relaxed her, restored her, and somehow fulfilled her in the same way her swimming once had and the way her quilting still did.

She was smiling to herself when her mother returned, surprising Caroline by appearing by the piano, having walked in the front door without being heard. Caroline abruptly stopped playing.

"That was beautiful, Caroline. You never told me you could play."

Caroline absently plucked at a note. "I didn't know I could—not until I came here and saw this piano and just started playing."

Her mother nodded. "You always had musical talent, you know. When you were really little, you used to climb up on the piano bench and make up your own songs or repeat something I'd played."

"I did? Why did I stop?"

"I'm not sure. Maybe it was when Jude started playing—which was about the same time he learned to walk. He'd do the same thing you did—just pluck out notes or replay favorite tunes. I think at some point you decided he was better at it than you were, so you stopped and became Jude's audience."

Caroline's forefinger continued to hit middle C as she considered her mother's words, vaguely remembering a feeling—or was it a scrap of music floating in the air?—of when she was very, very small. She jerked her head up suddenly, remembering Mr. Kobylt. "Where's Ken? I still have his car."

"I took him home. He's really a sweet man, but I didn't want him here when you got back, and I think he wanted to get back to his wife. I told him we'd bring his car to him tomorrow. How is Jewel?"

The pain and worry she'd been trying to forget hit her anew, and she dropped both hands into her lap. "I stayed for the first CT. It's a cerebral aneurysm—just like Shelby had. And it's weird because she had a scan a month ago and there was nothing." She shrugged. "The doctors said it was just a random event. The good news is that it's not bleeding—not yet. We got her to the hospital in time, it seems."

Her mother placed her hands over her heart. "Thank God. So where is she now?"

"They're doing what they can to release the pressure now, but they're airlifting her to Children's Hospital in Atlanta tonight. She'll need to have surgery tomorrow to block the blood flow through the aneurysm so that it doesn't rupture. Rainy's with Drew, and he asked if I'd come home and pick up a few things for Jewel and drive to Atlanta tomorrow."

"I'm going with you."

"There's no need, Mom. I can manage fine."

"It's a long drive and you're tired. You should have somebody go with you. I'll go pack my overnight case now."

The exhaustion and worry over Jewel pushed at Caroline, making her want to push back. She looked at her mother, her hands in open supplication. "Why do you do that?"

"Do what?"

"Treat me like a little child."

"Because I'm your mother and you're my daughter. Somewhere, in that unwritten book that's given to every mother at childbirth, it's in there."

"What—that you should fuss over your children whether they want it or not?"

"No, that you should love your children whether they want it or not."

Caroline left the piano bench and stood, hugging her arms over her chest. She came to a stop in front of Jude's picture. "You never cared when I was little. Why have you decided that now that I'm thirty years old, you're going to start trying to be my mother?"

Margaret sat down inelegantly on the vacated piano bench, as if all the air had flown out of her. "Oh, God, Caroline. No. Oh, God, no." Her mother took a deep breath before continuing. "Perhaps I made a mistake when you were growing up that made you think that. But when you pushed me away in your desire to be independent, I let you go, no matter how much it hurt me." She sighed, and Caroline pictured her mother's slim shoulders rising and falling inside the lemon-yellow jacket.

"I thought it was what you needed. And then Jude came along, and he was so completely different from you. Not that I loved you any less; it's just that he always needed me more."

The old memories of her childhood and her mother clashed with recently made ones, creating enough confusion and anger to push aside the grief and worry. She welcomed these feelings; they were familiar to her in a way that forgiveness never had been. She turned to her mother, still hugging herself tightly.

"And then he was gone, and you didn't have anybody else to need you anymore. I guess I was second choice, but I was there."

Her mother's eyes were damp. "Oh, no, Caroline. You were never second choice. You were my firstborn. We had tried for so many years for a baby, and then you came along. I never thought I could love somebody so much. Even after Jude was born, there was always a special place in my heart just for you. And you grew so fast and so independent—and I was so proud of you even though it meant you had no real use for me."

She sniffed and reached into the pocket of her jacket for a perfectly folded linen handkerchief. During her entire lifetime, Caroline had never known her mother not to be prepared with a fresh handkerchief.

"When I learned that you needed to take a few months off work, my first reaction was sheer joy. I finally saw the chance to mother you. Since you were a toddler, you've never allowed me. I'm sorry if it seems like I'm smothering you."

Caroline wiped her own tears with the sleeve of her shirt. "Oh, Mom. I have known all my life that Jude was your favorite child. And I don't blame you for that. Everybody loved Jude—including me. But please—not now. Don't try to pretend that you haven't spent the last thirteen years wishing that Jude hadn't been the one to die that night."

Her mother marched over to her, and for a moment Caroline was afraid of what she saw in Margaret's eyes. She shook when she spoke. "No, Caroline. Not for one minute. Not for one second. Have you really believed that all these years?" She raised fisted hands and pressed them against her chest. "When the doctors told me that your heart was damaged beyond repair, I told them to take mine. You were my little girl. And even now, after all these misunderstandings between us over the years, don't you know that you're the daughter I've always wanted? Don't you? If there were a store where I had to go pick out a daughter and there were rows and rows of baby girls, I'd still pick you. You're mine. Whether you had a brother or not, you're mine. And I never wanted it any other way."

Caroline turned her back to her mother again, unwilling to comprehend. Too many years had passed, and she found herself aching for the simple existence of only three months before; days when she got by on presumptions and independence, and never thought about the hidden wells of feelings she'd neatly tucked away around her heart.

She stared out the window, at the dying light of day, fighting the voices that seemed to be warring in her head. "If you really loved me, then you'd let it all go. It's too late to rehash the past. Whether you wanted to or not, you taught me how to live on my own, not to need anybody. I'm happy that way. Why can't you just let it all alone?"

She sensed her mother's presence behind her and then her voice, soft but strong. "Because you've been crying for the moon for over thirteen years—and you can never, ever have it. Jude is still dead, and you can't change it. Is this how you think he would have wanted you to live? A part of me inside dies each time I see you alone and hurting—and unwilling to meet me halfway. I've tried, Caroline. I've really tried to get through to you—to let you know how much I love you. I want you to live that life that was promised to you when you were born. The life that Jude's heart was meant to live. And I don't know what else I can say or do to make you listen and believe. I've always loved you and I've always wanted what's best for you. I've tried to show you, but somehow I've failed."

Her voice was thick with tears, and Caroline heard the sounds of her mother blowing her nose softly into the linen handkerchief. "I won't give up, Caroline." The feathery touch of her mother's hand brushed her on her shoulder, like a tentative butterfly touching down only briefly on unsure terrain. She wanted to feel her mother's touch again, but didn't know how to ask. Margaret took a deep, shuddering breath before speaking again. "But I don't know what else to do."

Caroline hugged herself tighter, wanting so badly to hug her mother instead but unsure of the steps involved. She wiped her eyes and nose with the sleeve of her shirt again. "I can't talk about this now. I need to worry about Jewel and Drew. And nothing else. It's too much."

They each stood their ground, as they had done for so many years, the small space between them no wider than an arm's breadth, but deeper than the ocean and just as treacherous.

Her mother was the first to speak. "I'm tired. I'm going to bed. But I will drive with you in the morning."

Caroline turned her head slightly and nodded once, then listened as her mother's footsteps slowly faded into the back of the house. She wasn't sure how long she stood there staring out the window and listening to the grandfather clock tick away the minutes. It marked the hour with a chime once, and when it started to chime the second time, Caroline picked up her purse and left the house, shutting the door quietly behind her.

She used the key Drew had given her to let herself into the house next door. The house was dark and quiet, as if filled with the ghosts that were now filling her head. She moved swiftly through the downstairs rooms, flipping on all the light switches. She paused in front of the dining room table as she'd done the last time she'd been there, recalling that she'd never seen what Drew had carved into the fourth leg.

Slowly she approached it and squatted down to get a better look. Her gaze slid down the length of it, then back to the top where the leg met the table, wondering if she'd missed something. Both hands rubbed either side of the leg, but met with only smooth, bare wood. *What are you saying, Drew?* She somehow knew that the leg was the way it was meant to be, and that the dining room table masterpiece was complete. She stood and stared down at the plain wood of the table leg. *What does it mean?*

Leaving the room, she moved toward the stairs, remembering where Drew had told her Jewel's room was. The bedroom door was partially closed, and when she pushed it open Caroline saw that a reading lamp by the bed had been left on and the bedspread was rumpled where it looked like Jewel had been lying on top. A journal lay open in the middle next to an old teddy bear, the pages covered in a flowing, rounded handwriting.

She stepped toward the bed, intent on closing the journal and bringing it with Jewel's things in case she wanted it. But when she bent to pick it up, the date on the top entry caught her attention. *November 15, 1991.* Six days before Jude died. She moved closer and caught the word *Jude. Shelby's diary,* she thought as she picked it up. She looked at the pages for a long moment, not reading, but not able to close it either. Her hands shook with indecision. But here, in her hands by some miracle, lay a piece of her life that she had thought gone forever. But there it was, an account of the days before her life had irrevocably changed.

Slowly she sat down on the edge of the bed and began to read.

*November 15, 1991*

> *Thanksgiving break is finally here. Jude and I survived not seeing each other for almost three months, but now we both feel as if we need to make up for lost time. I'm sure there are no doubts for our parents concerning the depth of our relationship, but I know neither one would agree to our sharing a room, so we haven't bothered to ask.*
>
> *It's cold outside, but we've found that leaves make a great insulator. Yesterday we went to our secret lake and made a huge pile of leaves. We were so tired from our efforts that we fell asleep on the pile. When we woke up we made love, and it didn't occur to me until this morning that we didn't use any protection. I counted the days in my cycle and figure I should be okay. Not that I don't think that one day we will have a child together. But not now, when we're so young, with so much of life ahead of us.*
>
> *Caroline's here on Thanksgiving break from the University of Georgia and has been working on Jude's quilt. She hopes to have it ready for Christmas. She's only got three rows done, and I have no idea where she's going to find the time to finish it by then, but she swears it will be. It's hard because she has to leave it here, since there's no room in her dorm for all the stuff she needs for it. I hope she finishes it before I have to go back to school. It's so gorgeous—even though it only shows the first seventeen years of Jude's life. She says she's going to give it to him with lots of empty space at the bottom and that when he does something special, she'll add it.*
>
> *The only black spot on my school break is that I have to drive everywhere. Jude's mom took away his driving privileges because he just got his second speeding ticket in three months. He keeps begging me to let him drive, but there's no way I'm going against Mrs. Collier on this. Jude begs and begs me, and I don't know how much longer I can say no. I know he's been*

*asking Caroline, too, but so far we've both stood firm. Caroline says Jude needs to learn his lesson and stick to his punishment. Jude's like water on rock, though. I wonder which one of us will finally give in.*

Caroline's hands were shaking so badly she almost dropped the journal. She should stop reading. It wasn't hers and it was never intended to be read by her. But she felt as if she were driving by an accident in slow motion, and she couldn't stop herself from looking. She turned the page, realizing that there had been a huge gap in time when Shelby hadn't written in her journal, and began reading again.

*January 1, 1992*

*Today is the first of a New Year. A time for resolutions and new beginnings. I suppose that's why I've chosen today for my wedding day. My dress is hanging in my parents' bedroom, waiting for me to put it on, and Drew and his parents are staying at the Colliers'. Caroline isn't coming to the wedding. She's still too weak from the surgery, but even if she were well she wouldn't come. I can't blame her. She sees my marrying Drew as a betrayal of Jude. And in some ways she's right. I only wish I could tell her everything.*

*The baby is due in August, so Drew and I thought it would be best to get married sooner instead of later. His parents and my parents have both said that we don't have to get married just because I'm pregnant. But we love this baby so much already that I can't imagine not giving it two parents who are committed to each other. And Drew is so excited about being a father—he says it's the best thing that's ever happened to him, with the exception of meeting me. I wonder if he'd feel the same if he only knew.*

*I can't tell Drew the truth now. How could I break his heart like that after everything he's done for me since Jude died? I was an empty shell, and Drew filled me up with his love. I owe him my affection and my gratitude—and this child. In my grief, I sought his love selfishly, giving my body to him because it helped heal my wounds, if only temporarily. I didn't realize then how much of his heart and soul he'd given to me. But this baby and this marriage will join us together, and maybe one day erase the pain I feel each and every day. And my secret is mine to keep. Telling even my mother would be like a betrayal of Drew. For whatever wrongs I've done to him, that is one thing I could never do.*

Caroline looked up from the journal, dry-eyed. *Oh, Shelby, what did you do?* And then she thought of her mother, being a grandmother all these years and not knowing it, and of Drew. *Drew!* What would this do to him?

Caroline closed the journal and stood. She'd bring it with all of Jewel's things, not willing to leave the journal there where anybody could find it.

As if in slow motion, she moved to the dresser and took out a few changes of clothes and stacked them on top of the journal. Then she moved to the closet to pull out a clean pair of jeans. When she tugged on the closet door it stuck, and she realized something had been shoved on the floor of the closet and was now caught between the bottom of the door and the carpet. After a lot of pulling and cursing, Caroline finally got the door open.

She glanced at the bottom of the closet to determine what it had been and felt the breath leave her lungs in a loud whoosh when she spotted the quilt. Kneeling, she picked it up, recognizing the red-and-blue border even after all this time. She sank both hands into the soft cotton, holding on to it as if she'd finally found her long-lost brother. With a wary heart, she brought it over to the bed to get a better look at it.

She saw the first three rows that she'd done, the ones with his baby blanket, a football jersey with the number 02 on the back, and a brown cutout of a football that read HPHS 1992 on it. But now there were more rows completed, nearly filling the entire quilt except for two rows on the bottom. Looking closer, she recognized one of her swimming photos silk-screened onto a square, and a picture of her at Shelby's sixteenth-birthday party. *Where did these come from?* She sat back, trying to recall a conversation she'd had recently about Shelby's birthday party photo. She stared hard at the quilt, seeing one of the place mats she'd made in the last few weeks and an appliqué of one of her swimming trophies made from a bathing suit.

*Jewel.* Caroline suddenly recalled the snippets of conversations she'd had with Drew, her mother, and Rainy about little things that had suddenly been misplaced. And here, on Jude's quilt, were most of the missing items. *But why?*

She picked it up again and buried her face into her brother's quilt, with her own stitches intermingling with Jewel's, somehow connecting her brother's life with her own in one flawless transition. She studied her brother's portion, at all the things he loved and held dear—and then moved her gaze to the unfinished section symbolizing her own life unlived.

*Jewel,* she thought again, feeling an urgency to see her, to work out all the confusion from the journal and the quilt that were fighting for space in her brain. *And Drew.* What was she going to tell Drew?

Quickly she wrapped up Jewel's clothes and Shelby's journal inside the quilt, throwing the teddy bear on top as an afterthought, and let herself out of the house. She'd take the second car and leave the Cadillac in case Margaret decided to come on her own in the morning. First she needed to write her mother a note to let her know where she had gone, and then she was driving to the hospital in Atlanta as fast as she could go.

# CHAPTER 27

SHE REACHED THE HOSPITAL SHORTLY AFTER MIDNIGHT, BUT THE bright lights and activity inside gave no nod to the late hour. Parking as close to the bustling entrance as she could and leaving everything in the trunk of her mother's car, she ran inside, worry and panic pushing her forward to the reception desk. She focused on Jewel instead of the hated hospital green and the sound of her footsteps on the linoleum and the smells of the hospital that always reminded her of her long stay there thirteen years before. She fought her fears and her memories all the way up to the third level and the waiting room where she found Drew.

She walked into his open arms without a word, giving as much comfort with her own arms as she was getting from his. Laying her head on his chest, she asked, "Where's Rainy?"

"She was exhausted and Jewel's stabilized, so I sent her to a hotel to get some sleep. I think she's more worried about Jewel than she was about her own cancer."

"Sounds like Rainy."

They both smiled as Drew led her to a bright orange vinyl couch next to a coffee table littered with parenting magazines and children's books with missing covers.

"How is she, Drew? How is Jewel?" His hair stood up in front as if he'd spent several hours pressing his hands against his forehead.

"The doctors say she should be fine. Brain surgery is never easy, but she's young and healthy and they don't anticipate any problems. She's scheduled for seven o'clock in the morning."

She squeezed his hand. "I'm glad I came tonight, then. I'm not going to leave until it's over—if you'll let me."

He nodded and she squeezed his hand tighter.

He swallowed, then said, "I told Jewel that I had asked you to go get a few of her things from her room and bring them. She got real agitated when I told her that, but wouldn't tell me why. But she insisted on talking to you before her surgery."

"Oh." It was her turn to swallow. "Will we have time?"

"Not likely. But one of her nurses just came in and told me Jewel was fighting sleep until she could speak with you. She said if you arrived before it was time to prep her for surgery, that she would let you talk to her." He looked at her closely. "Do you have any idea what is so important that she needs to tell you?"

Caroline nodded. "I do. But it's between Jewel and me, okay?"

"Is it about the furniture? She already told me that it was her idea to take the pictures and send them."

She gave an unexpected laugh. *If only it were that simple.* "No. I'm sure it's not."

He closed his eyes for a second, and when he opened them again she saw the determined lawyer with all emotions stored away someplace safe.

He held out his hand. "Come on, then. Let me take you to the nurses' station and they can bring you to Jewel's room."

She could tell how much this was hurting him, and she wanted to offer him some assurance. They stood and she took his offered hand. "She loves you very much, you know."

His jaw clenched; then he nodded once before leading her to the nurses' station.

The nurse pushed open the door to Jewel's room and put her finger to her lips as she indicated the closed drapery partition in the middle of the room hiding Jewel's sleeping roommate.

Jewel's eyelids were heavy but her eyes remained open and focused on Caroline as she approached the hospital bed. The nurse had pulled up a chair and Caroline took it, reaching for Jewel's hand.

The nurse held her hand up. "Five minutes," she whispered before leaving, closing the door softly behind her.

Caroline leaned forward. "How are you feeling?"

"Better. My head still hurts—just not as much."

"Good." She waited for Jewel to speak again, listening to the silence filled with hums and whirs of the machines that measured and dosed, and haunted the far reaches of her own memories.

"Did you read the journal?"

Caroline hesitated for only a moment before nodding. "Yes."

"Good. I was hoping you did. Did you hide it?"

"Well, I brought it with me, in case you wanted it."

"Don't . . . don't tell my dad, okay?" Jewel's hand curled into her own, pressing the closely clipped nails into her palm.

"He needs to know, Jewel. He needs to know the truth."

"I know. But I want to tell him myself." She closed her eyes briefly, and Caroline watched as a tear made its way down the young girl's cheek. "Promise me that if something happens tomorrow, I want you to tell him something. I want you to tell him that no matter what, he's my dad. That knowing the truth hasn't changed anything for me. And tell him . . . tell him I love him."

Caroline felt the door open behind her and she stood. Leaning over Jewel and avoiding the IV line, she kissed her on the forehead. "You're going to be fine, Jewel. You can tell him yourself, okay?" A tear fell on Jewel's cheek and she realized it was her own.

Caroline straightened but Jewel pulled her back. "Did you see the quilt?"

"Yes." She smiled weakly. "You've been busy."

"Yeah—it was hard keeping it from everybody."

"But why, Jewel? Why did you think you needed to finish it? And why not tell anybody?"

"Miss? You need to leave now." The nurse had the door open wide.

Caroline held up her hand, then turned back to Jewel. "Why?"

She looked up at Caroline with those eyes that had always seemed so out of place in such a young face. "I found the quilt in her trunk a few months ago, and when I heard you talking with your mom about it, I knew what it was and I figured my mom took it after Jude died for some reason. And she wanted me to finish it. It's weird . . . but sometimes I feel her with me and I can hear her talking to me as if she were really there. I think that's how I figured out about . . . Jude's heart."

She looked up at Caroline to gauge her reaction, but Caroline just nodded. Jewel continued. "I think she wanted to show you something and you wouldn't understand it until I was finished with the quilt. Does that make sense?"

Caroline shook her head and straightened. "I'm not sure."

"Miss, you really need to leave now."

"Okay, I'm coming." She brushed Jewel's hair off her forehead and forced a smile. "Get some sleep now. I'll see you tomorrow, all right?"

Jewel gave her a thumbs-up and Caroline answered with her own, then left the room with the impatient nurse close on her heels.

She found Drew sitting on the same vinyl couch, his head in his hands. He looked up when she entered and she made herself smile. "She's fine. Just needed to get a few things off her chest, that's all. She'll talk to you about it soon." She looked into his eyes and knew that whatever Jewel told him, it would all be okay. Whatever wrongs had been done were in the past and they had been done in the name of love. They would survive. All of them.

He nodded, and she noticed how the cheek stubble and messy hair only added to his appeal. It was just one of the things that drew her to him, including how he made her laugh and how he loved his daughter.

"When you packed her things, did you get her teddy bear? It was one of the things she asked about."

"Yes—I left it in the car with her clothes. Do you want me to go get it?"

"No, I don't want you going out there again in the dark."

"Drew, they might need you for Jewel. Don't worry—I parked near the entrance under a light. I'll be fine."

His mouth formed a thin line. "Thanks. But be careful. And if you're out there too long, I'm calling out a search party."

"Yes, Mom. I'll hurry." She kissed him on the cheek. "I threw a couple of pillows in, too, just in case. I'll get them and maybe we can get a little sleep."

He raised an eyebrow. "Are you suggesting that we sleep together, Caroline? What would your mother say?"

Surprised, she asked, "How can you joke at a time like this?"

He didn't flinch. "How could I not? And who says I was joking?"

She rolled her eyes and shook her head, somewhat glad to be back on familiar ground with him, then left the room.

The nearly deserted parking lot made it easy for Caroline to find her car. She'd parked under a light so she could see and easily slipped the car key into the trunk lock. When she'd left the house, she'd been in such a hurry that she'd just thrown everything inside. Now she stood in the bright light of the street lamp with the trunk lid open and stared inside at the mess she'd made.

The light illuminated the red border and Caroline reached for it, her fingers clutching the cotton of the quilt as she pulled it out of the trunk. *Oh, Jude,* she thought, bringing the quilt to her face, smelling the fabric and the night air. With her eyes closed, she could still see the bright colors, the football jersey and the swimming trophy, all of it connected by the hand stitches of a young girl. All during the drive down to Atlanta the question as to why Jewel had done it had gone through Caroline's mind over and over. And now, as she stood in the dark holding her brother's quilt, she remembered what Drew had told her that night at the bonfire. *You have received the most incredible gift of love imaginable. From both Jude—and your mother.*

She stumbled against the edge of the car, the heaviness of understanding loosening her joints and making it hard to stand. She hugged the quilt as she if were hugging all the people she loved in her inadequate arms, all the people who were a part of the quilt—including Drew. The tears surprised her as she looked up in search of the moon. She no longer cried for it. Instead, she counted her tears as one would count blessings, suddenly aware of how many she'd been given and how much gratitude was long overdue to the woman who had given her all of them.

Slowly she began gathering the scattered clothes and the diary, wrapping everything up inside the quilt, feeling the weight of it all as if she held the moon in her arms as she made her way back through the darkness.

When Drew awoke, it was to find that somebody had slipped a pillow under his head and that a warm body was curled up next to him. He opened his eyes and saw Caroline, her eyes bright and open and staring at him. She held Jewel's teddy bear in her hand, her index finger nervously plucking at the bear's nose.

He sat up quickly. "Is everything all right?"

Her hand felt warm on his shoulder. "Everything's fine. Jewel's surgery is still an hour away. I just called Rainy and she's on her way."

He stretched, feeling as if his neck would never sit straight on his shoulders again. "Thanks for the pillow—I guess I was a lot more tired than I thought."

"You're welcome." She smiled at him—a different kind of smile than he was used to from her. It was a warm smile, and he couldn't help but wonder if she'd been rehearsing it so she could use it when it was time to talk about her boss and the pictures of his furniture.

"What?"

"What?"

"I don't know. You're smiling. And it's making me nervous."

"I'm just smiling. Really. I'm worried about Jewel, and I know we still have to have our little talk about how the pictures ended up on my boss's desk, but I feel like smiling."

"Good. Keep doing it. Because I'm worried sick, and seeing you smile is helping."

"Okay. I can do that." She grabbed his hands with both of hers and held tight.

They both looked up in surprise as Margaret entered the waiting room. She was fully dressed but her eye makeup was smeared and there was a small pink curler still lodged on the top of her silver-blond hair.

"Sorry I'm late. I got Caroline's note when I got up in the middle of the night for a glass of water. I came as fast as I could—I even put on my makeup and did my hair while I was driving." She patted her hair self-consciously, narrowly missing the curler. "I'm sure I'm a wreck, but I needed to be here." Her gaze dropped to the bank of chairs where Caroline had spread a large dark-blue-and-red quilt while he'd slept. Noticing it for the first time, he stood and moved closer to examine it.

Margaret lifted her hand and touched the first square, a baby-blue blanket with JWC monogrammed on it. Lightly she brushed her fingers over the line of squares, from Little League, to a football jersey, and then the picture of him with Shelby in a yellow dress. Her fingers paused, as if wanting the story to stop there. But then they moved on to what appeared to be Caroline's life: swimming trophies, bathing suits, and quilted place mats. He recognized the cross-stitched heart that had been missing from his key chain, and smiled to himself at the resourcefulness of his amazing daughter.

Margaret spoke, her voice uneven. "This is Jude's quilt, isn't it?"

Caroline moved to stand beside him and spoke, her voice hesitant. "Yes, but Jewel's picked up where I stopped. See?" She pointed to the square where Jude's life intersected with Caroline's—the square where Jewel had place the cross-stitched heart.

Drew touched the quilt, feeling Shelby's presence so strongly he thought that if he turned around he'd see her out of the corner of his eye. He studied the colorful squares, trying to understand the story they told, and marveling again at the daughter who had made it, and the remarkable woman who had given her life. Caroline touched him on the shoulder and he turned to face her.

"Jewel told me that . . . that she felt her mother wanted her to do this for me; to help me understand."

He embraced her, welcoming her warm presence against his chest.

She lifted her head. "See, when I saw the quilt, I finally understood." She placed her hands flat on his chest, and he felt his heart stretch and swell. "I finally know what Jude was trying to tell me." She laid her head between her hands. "Right after the accident, when the car had finally come to a stop and the horrible pain in my chest was gone, I saw Jude. I knew he was dead, even though he didn't look hurt. He was sitting on the ground next to me, talking. We were holding hands, and I knew we were about to go away together. I was warm, and comfortable, and so happy that the pain had stopped and I was ready to go wherever he led. But then he let go of my hand and told me that I needed to stay."

Drew's arms held her closer as Margaret held out a fresh linen handkerchief. It was so absurd, and so much Margaret, that Caroline laughed through her tears. After wiping her eyes, she continued. "I wanted to go run after him, and make him take me with him but he said I couldn't. And all these years, I've been thinking that I was supposed to stay here as my punishment, and that's how I've lived my life."

Drew cupped her face and made her look at him. "And now?"

"Now I've seen Jude's quilt, with his life and my life intertwined, and I realize it isn't the story of our lives, but the story of his heart. And how much I've cheated both of us by letting those last rows remain empty."

He kissed the top of her head and squeezed her before releasing her. Caroline faced her mother, and Drew was struck again at how similar they were, especially now with their matching expressions of atonement mixed with surprise.

"In all these years, I've never thanked you—not once. So thank you, Mom. For everything. For everything you did after the accident. For the choices you had to make so I would live. And for everything before then and since then that I never thanked you for."

Mrs. Collier blinked back tears as her hands fluttered in the air before coming to rest on Caroline's arms. "You don't need to thank me, Caroline. I just . . . I just want to be your mother. If you'll let me."

They came together with a laugh and a sob, their arms reaching around the other easily as if each had been practicing in dreams for a very long time.

A nurse entered the waiting room, holding a clipboard.

"Mr. Reed?"

"Yes."

"Your daughter is being prepped for surgery. She wants to see you, and you've got some final paperwork to fill out and sign. Can you come with me?"

He nodded, feeling sick all over again, the way he'd felt when he'd found out that Shelby was dead. How could he cope if something happened to Jewel? He'd always known how much he loved her. Maybe it was the human condition that made people not realize how much somebody meant to them until they were faced with their loss.

Caroline put a hand on his arm. "I'll be right here, all right? Everything's going to be okay."

He nodded, somehow feeling that she was right. As he left with the nurse, Rainy arrived.

"Am I too late?"

He lowered his head to kiss her on the cheek. "No, she's about to go in. Do you want to come talk to her again?"

She shook her head. "No. I said what I needed to say last night. Right now should be just the two of you. Tell her I'm here and I'll be waiting for her until they're done and she's in recovery."

"Okay, I'll tell her."

He hugged her, then left, turning around long enough to see Margaret and Caroline still hugging and sharing the lacy white handkerchief.

By the time he'd signed all the paperwork and spoken briefly with the surgeon, Jewel was already on the gurney. She looked bald under her hospital cap, and he hardly recognized her except for the eyes. He took her hand, feeling the long, slim fingers. No longer the little-girl hand he remembered.

"How are you doing?"

She rolled her eyes, and he was somewhat comforted by the familiar act. "Except for the needles and tubes running out of me, I'm fine."

"Yeah. Sorry." He took a deep breath, thinking about all the things he'd rehearsed to make her feel better and wondering why he couldn't remember a single one. He took a long shot. "From now on, I want you to do whatever makes you happy. If you want to try out for the swim team, then I'm not going to stop you. You're old enough to make your own decisions."

She smiled and rolled her eyes again. "You should too, Dad."

"What? Try out for the swim team?"

"No. Do what makes you happy. If you want to go commercial with your furniture, then do it. We'll make it work."

He just nodded, not sure what he should say.

"Dad?"

"Yes, sweetie."

"I found Mama's journal. I've been reading it and I want you to read it, too. Tell Caroline—she has it and she'll give it to you."

"Okay. Anything in particular you want me to read?"

"All of it."

"All right."

"And Dad?"

"Yes?"

"I never wanted any other dad, no matter what. Nothing will ever change that."

He looked at her oddly, wondering if the anesthesia was beginning to take effect. "I know, sweetie. I'm yours and you're mine, remember? We used to say that a lot, didn't we?" He watched as nurses wearing surgical caps and masks came forward to begin wheeling the gurney into the operating room. "Everything's going to be okay. I'll see you in recovery." He kissed her forehead. "I love you."

"I love you, too, Daddy."

He stood and watched as they wheeled her away, feeling as if his heart had been taken from him and tucked into the smooth, pale hand of his daughter, who wasn't too old to call him Daddy, after all. He turned and found his way back to the waiting room with the orange vinyl chairs and fluorescent lighting and the one person in this world who knew more about pain and grief than anybody had a right to, and was still strong enough to let a bereft father lay his head on her shoulder.

# CHAPTER 28

*August 29, 1992*

Yesterday I gave birth to the most beautiful baby girl in the world. It's hard to see what color her eyes are going to be, but her hair is definitely red. And, judging by the way she screamed as she was forced out into the world, she's a redhead through and through.

Drew and I had been discussing names all month, and I thought we'd decided on one of each. But this morning, when he held our daughter right after I'd fed her, he said he'd changed his mind about the girl name we'd picked out. He wanted to call her Jewel, because, next to me, she was the most precious thing in his life. It made me cry, and I became even more convinced that I did the right thing eight months ago. I know Drew would love this baby even if it wasn't his. He went through the entire pregnancy with me, and read all the parenting books I bought. At night he would sit for hours with his hand on my belly, waiting for the baby to move, and sharing all of his dreams for our future. She's his as much as she is mine. And that's why I won't tell him. There is nothing to be gained from it, and when I see her small head cradled in his large hands, I want to weep with how blessed I am. I lost Jude, but in return I have gained a family, and for that I can't be sorry.

My mother once told me that our paths in life are usually hidden except in hindsight. I understand that now. Loss and grief do that to a person, I guess. I tried to tell Caroline when I called her about the baby, but I knew she wasn't listening. She's having a rough time since the accident, and I sometimes *wonder if she'll ever get over it. I know she took it hard when I told her I was getting married. I was so tempted to tell her the whole truth. Maybe one day I will be able to tell her and her mother that there is a part of Jude still on this earth so that they can discover with me the parts of him that are within Jewel.*

*I still have Jude's quilt, and I'm glad I didn't give it back. I have a strong feeling that one day Caroline's going to need it. I've had headaches lately where I have visions of a girl with long red hair working on the quilt. But the quilt wasn't showing the story of one life; it was showing the journey of a heart too strong to stop beating.*

*I have to go now. The baby's fussing (again), and while I know that Drew will take the stairs two at a time to get to her, I'm the only one who can nurse her. Drew has made me the most wonderful rocking chair where I sit when I'm feeding Jewel. It's the most beautiful thing I've ever seen. I hope he continues to make things—he's so good at it, and it makes him shine from the inside. When I'm sitting in his chair and nursing our baby, I know the feeling of true contentment. I can only look forward to the future the three of us will share together and know that should something ever happen to me, my husband and daughter will have each other and never lack for love.*

Drew found Jewel sitting in Caroline's chair out on the dock. She'd been home from the hospital less than a week, and she was still pale and tired, but already he could see color in her cheeks and sense her impatience at having her movements restricted. She was eager to swim again and spent a lot of time on the dock, watching the water. A bandanna covered her shorn head, but when she looked at him as he approached she beamed a smile, and he was quite sure he'd never seen anybody look so beautiful.

He stopped and stood next to her. "How are you feeling?"

She shrugged. "Better than yesterday. Probably not as good as I will tomorrow, but I'm getting there." She poked a finger under her bandanna to scratch her scalp. "My head's getting itchy where the hair's growing in, and it's driving me crazy."

Smiling, he touched her cloth-covered head, then handed her Shelby's journal. She looked at him with surprise as he sat down on the dock, his legs stretched in front of him.

"Did you read all of it?"

He nodded.

"All the way to the end?"

He nodded again. "I did." He touched her lightly on the leg. "And I'm sorry you had to find out . . . about Jude that way."

"It's all right. It was sort of like Mama telling me herself, you know? I think she meant for me to find her diary."

He felt himself grin. "Yeah, that sounds like your mother."

He leaned his head against the arm of her chair and she touched him lightly on the forehead. "Yeah—and you sound like my father."

His eyes met hers. "What do you mean?"

"Well, just that I know what you sound like when you're happy, or you want to share something with me or teach me something. I know your laugh, and I know what you expect from me, and I know how to beg until you give me what I want. I know when you're angry and when I shouldn't push you anymore. And when I was a little girl I remember how I couldn't go to sleep unless you sang to me."

He looked up into the face of this smart, beautiful, wonderful girl and knew she would always be the daughter of his heart. He looked away, out toward the lake, afraid he might cry and really make a mess of things. "Do you wish . . . do you think you would have had a happier life if Jude had been here to be your father?"

The chair creaked as she leaned toward him. "That's kind of like asking if you'd be happier if Caroline hadn't sent in those pictures. Or if Mama didn't die. Like we have a choice or something about things we can't control." She looked out across the lake, her eyes reflecting the light from the water. "Mama always told me that life would never be a straight line. It's the people who expect their lives to follow a straight path who kind of get bogged down in the sudden curves." She grinned at him, her Shelby grin. "And now, thanks to me and Caroline, you have this new great career." A bird flew across the water, its cry echoing in the still air, and he watched her grin fade softly. "And I couldn't imagine having a better dad. Ever." She turned her head away from him to hide her tears, and he let her.

He reached for her hand and held it, feeling the need to touch her when he told her. "I loved your mother, you know. More than I thought was possible for me. When I married her, I had the best intentions. I knew how much she had loved Jude, and I think I must have suspected about her pregnancy, too. That's why when I read the diary I wasn't that surprised. It all made sense—Shelby trying to take care of both of us so we wouldn't be hurt. And all the while her heart was breaking. But at the time it didn't matter to me why she agreed to marry me. I had a chance to make Shelby a part of my life and I jumped at it. I figured I could love enough for both of us."

He looked up into the face of Ophelia, imagining he could detect a softening in her stone expression. "She loved me, too, in a way. Just not the way she had loved Jude, and not the way I loved her. So I turned to my work. I wanted to somehow fill that . . . emptiness, not really realizing until it was too late that it was pulling me away from her—and you. I want you to know that. It wasn't that I loved you or your mother any less. I just needed to work—for me. I enjoyed it, and that gave me the excuse to throw myself into it."

Drew stopped for a moment, listening to the silence on the lake and feeling the slow, steady rhythm of his heart, and his daughter's hand in his. Finally he said, "Right before your mother died, I had decided to do something about it. I was going to cut my hours at the office; make more vacation plans. Of course, by then it was too late."

Jewel squeezed his hand. She understood; he'd known she would. "Yeah, well, and now we're here. And, as Mama would say, we're where we're supposed to be."

Drew stood and gently pulled Jewel from her chair, feeling the truth of her words. "Smart girl."

"I get it from my parents."

He gave her a quizzical glance.

She rolled her eyes, bringing them both back to common ground. "You and my mom, Dad. Of course."

He put his arm around her shoulders and squeezed. "Yeah, of

course." He began to lead her back to the house. "Let's go find Caroline. She's been busy preparing all these documents for me to sign, and I've think I've made her sweat enough with my stalling."

Jewel snorted. "Yeah, and I can't wait to hear her choice of words she'll give you for making her wait so long."

"Yep. It's bound to be good." He could even feel the anticipation.

"So are you two dating now?"

Drew shrugged, not sure if this was a conversation he wanted to be having with his daughter. "Sort of, I guess. Just getting to know each other right now and taking it slowly."

Jewel sent him her beautiful smile again and he smiled back. They walked along in silence for another moment before he said, "Did I ever tell you that I couldn't imagine having a better daughter?"

"Yep," she said softly, her voice sifted through the air and over the still lake. Holding her mother's journal against her chest, she put her head on his shoulder as they walked the rest of the way to the house.

Caroline sat at Rainy's kitchen table watching as Rainy checked her itinerary again to make sure she hadn't left anything out. Jewel sat on the opposite side, her feet propped up on another chair, wearing a pink bandanna that matched the one Rainy wore. In the three weeks since her surgery, Caroline had helped Jewel accumulate a large collection of colorful bandannas, one to match every outfit. In the hospital Jewel had told the nurses to shave off all of her hair so she and Rainy could be twins, and the memory of it made Caroline smile. It was something Jude would have done.

"I'm so glad your mother has decided to come with me on my European trip, Caroline. She's promised me that she won't bring more than three suitcases and that she won't attempt to teach the British how they should be holding their silverware."

Caroline reached across the table and picked up a stack of brochures. "I'm just happy that you're doing this, Rainy. Even if it's not actually a retirement trip."

Rainy shrugged. "Yeah, well. I never really wanted to retire, anyway. I was kinda glad when Drew asked me to reconsider. I knew it
was only a matter of time after I heard about the marketing deal
your boss was offering him. I was wondering what on earth would I
do when I returned from Europe. I couldn't even imagine not getting to come here every day." She smiled across the table at Caroline.
"And now with you staying on to manage my new quilting section
and furniture catalog, I'm all pumped up for something new and exciting. I just couldn't picture Drew being thrilled about cotton batting or homemade honey, you know?"

Jewel adjusted the knot on her bandanna. "Amen. He is *so* much
easier to live with these days. He only called Caroline's cell phone
once on the trip over here to make sure I wasn't overtired or anything." She rolled her eyes. "I guess some things will never change."

Caroline stood to get the whistling teakettle on the stove. "No,
they won't. Better just accept it now—it'll make things a lot easier
for you as you get older."

Rainy let out a hoot. "Well, girl. I'd say you just gave away for
free what it took you thirty years to learn. Can't say I ever thought
I'd live to see the day."

The back door opened as Caroline put the mugs of tea on the
table, and everyone turned around to see Caroline's mother standing
in the doorway carrying a shopping bag from Neiman Marcus.

"Good Lord, Margaret. What have you done?"

Caroline gaped at her mother. She wore mismatched pajamas
and high heels, and her hair, still rolled in pink curlers, was covered
with a green silk scarf. "Mom?"

Margaret entered the kitchen and dumped the shopping bag on
the table. "I brought beer. Got a can opener, Rainy?"

Rainy snorted and yanked a beer can out of the bag. "You don't
need a can opener for beer, Margaret. Now, what on earth are you
doing?"

Margaret lifted her shoulders and let them fall, an elegant shrug
even under the flannel pajama shirt. "Well, Caroline shouldn't be the
only one to change. She's always telling me to lighten up, so"—she
swept her hands in front of her body—"here I am. I'm out of my

house, my hair isn't done, my clothes don't match, and I'm about to drink a beer at eleven o'clock on a Saturday morning."

Rainy threw back her head and laughed, then tossed her arm over her friend's shoulder. Margaret was biting her lower lip to keep from smiling. "You are one crazy lady, and I guess that's why I love you so much. Just promise me that you'll leave this outfit behind when you pack for our trip."

Margaret's mouth widened into a grin. "Only if you promise me you'll leave your overalls behind."

Rainy bumped her with her hip. "You just wish you could look this good in overalls."

Jewel was laughing too, and Caroline was happy to see spots of color on the girl's pale cheeks. "Grandma Collier, do you have any of those pink curlers left? I could Velcro them to my scalp so everybody would think I had more hair under my scarf."

Caroline's mother walked around the table to give Jewel a kiss on the cheek. "You can have these, sweetheart. And by the way, have I mentioned how much I just love to hear you call me that?"

"Only about a hundred times. But you're welcome."

A brief tapping sounded on the back door before Drew walked in, his eyes quickly taking in Caroline's mother and the beer on the table. "I'm afraid to ask."

"Grandma Collier's just learning how to chill, Dad. Caroline and I are teaching her."

He closed the door slowly. "I see. And who's the beer for?"

Rainy reached into the bag and handed him one. "Whoever wants one." She looked inside the bag again. "Here's a couple of nonalcoholic ones. I assume those are for Caroline, Margaret?"

Caroline rolled her eyes as she stood. "Maybe later." She walked over to Drew and kissed him on the lips. "Are you ready?"

Margaret looked up in surprise. "Ready for what?"

Drew casually looped his arm around Caroline's shoulders. "We're going to set the loon free. You're all welcome to come."

Margaret picked up the shopping bag. "We'll all go. I'll bring the beer so we can make a toast."

Rainy moved toward the pen in the corner of the room. "I'll get the bird. I'm going to miss the little fella, but I can't say I'm going to miss cleaning up after him."

Drew helped Jewel out of her chair and they all made their way outside to the dock. Rainy bent to unhook the leash and collar, then picked up the bird. "Caroline, I think you should do the honors, since you were the one who found him."

Caroline stepped forward and took the bird, her hands strong and confident around his body. As if by agreement, everyone except Caroline and Drew stayed in the grass to watch. Moving toward the edge of the dock, she knelt and felt Drew kneel beside her.

He turned to her, his blue eyes clear and matching the color of the morning sky. "Are you ready to let it go?"

She bent her head so their foreheads touched. "Yes," she said softly. Then, pulling back and looking into his eyes, she said, "Thank you."

"For what?"

"For being there for me. For understanding me."

In answer, he leaned forward and kissed her on the lips, soliciting a soft whoop from Rainy.

Gently Caroline turned toward the water and dropped the bird onto the surface.

He landed with a splash and seemed surprised for a moment, as if he were wondering where he was and what he should do. Then with steady determination, he began to paddle hard in the water, propelling himself forward as he gained speed. His webbed feet seemed to be skipping on top of the water until, with a burst of sound and spray, he lifted into the air, soaring through the blue ceiling of sky and then disappearing into the woods surrounding Hart's Peak.

It seemed to Caroline that the stone face of Ophelia watched the scene with a softening around her eyes, as if the legend were true and she really did have a human heart. As was her old habit, Caroline's fingers found the crest of scar tissue beneath her T-shirt, then patted the site of the old incision. Since the accident the scar had felt like an open window to what lay inside: all the pain, guilt, and loss that had flooded her and obliterated everything else.

But now all she felt was a reminder of the brother she had loved and lost, and of all the beautiful things she still had in her life, finally noticed when she had taken the trouble to see.

Drew helped her stand and pressed a can into her hand. He pulled her close against his side and she allowed herself to lean into him. At Rainy's signal they all raised their cans to the sky and to the absent loon, soaring somewhere beyond their vision. The flight of the loon reminded Caroline of the hand stitches on her quilts: holding together the past with the future, each stitch stopping and starting and meandering through row after row, moving forward from one lifetime to the next.

She looked up into the empty sky and spotted the pale white shade of the moon fading into the morning light. Smiling, she took Drew's hand, and together they turned to walk down the dock toward the others, leaving the loon, the moon, and the dark water of the lake behind them.

**Karen White** is the author of five previous books. She lives with her family near Atlanta, Georgia. Visit her Web site at www.karen-white.com.

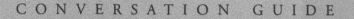

# PIECES

## *of the*

# HEART

KAREN WHITE

This conversation guide is intended to enrich the
individual reading experience, as well as encourage us
to explore these topics together—because books,
and life, are meant for sharing.

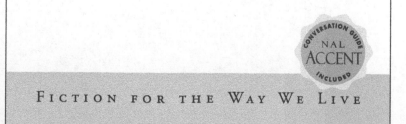

# A CONVERSATION WITH KAREN WHITE

*Q. How many books have you written? Did this novel pose any special or unforeseen difficulties?*

A. I have written seven books, and all but one have been published or are slated to be published.

I wouldn't call this book more "difficult" to write than the others, but it was certainly different. I write what has been called "grit lit"—Southern family dramas. I've always included lots of family angst, a bit of laughter, sometimes a mystery, and of course a great love story. Although I've always had lots of different relationships involving my books' characters, the main relationship was usually a romantic one. In *Pieces of the Heart*, however, the main relationship actually involves the protagonist, Caroline, and her mother. There is a love story in this book, but it definitely takes a backseat to the mother-daughter relationship.

*Q. How did you come up with the idea for* Pieces of the Heart? *What inspired this story?*

A. I remember reading or hearing on the news several years ago the story of two siblings injured in a car accident and one of the siblings became the organ donor for the other. The drama of the situation stayed with me for years until I found a book in which I could use it. Since I'm one of four children (and the only girl) and I'm also the mother of two children twenty-one months apart, the whole situation was especially poignant for me. As any mother or sibling can tell you, sibling rivalry plays a vital part in sibling relationships—including vying for the love and attention of parents. I thought that coupling this with a family tragedy would be a strong platform on which to build a story about exploring family relationships and finding forgiveness.

*Q. You describe the North Carolina mountains with as much beauty and mystery as the South Carolina low country, in your last novel. Have you spent much time in the mountains? Is it a place you know well? Do you prefer one or the other?*

A. The low country has a very special place in my heart, and I will definitely be revisiting it in future novels. However, Caroline's story needed to be told in a different environment, which is why I chose a quiet mountain lake house. I have been a frequent visitor to the North Carolina mountains and have enjoyed the warmth of the people, the stunning beauty of the fall foliage, and the quiet solitude. I thought this to be the perfect place for a woman with a wounded heart to start asking questions about her life and to perhaps find the right answers.

*Q. Loons play a prominent role in the story—they are in the water, on quilts, and in Rainy Days, being nursed back to health. What does the loon mean in the context of the story? Why is it important?*

A. While I was researching this book and trying to find native wildlife to use in the book, I came across the Indian legend of the loon and I was hooked on this amazing and unusual bird. I thought it serendipity when I discovered that loons are found in the northern United States and Canada and migrate south, through North Carolina, for the winter. To have a loon stop in North Carolina and decide to stay instead of flying farther south would make such a wonderful statement in the novel. I like to think that the loon symbolizes the beloved Jude, still present in the lives of those who loved him. The loon is also necessary to remind Caroline about what she used to be as a champion swimmer, and how much she misses the water. The call of the loon brings her back to the past, to happy memories of Jude and the good parts of her childhood, and is a catalyst for her change. Symbolically, the loon is set free at the end of the novel, just as Caroline is freed from her past.

Q. *Every character in this story has his or her own way of dealing with grief—Caroline closes off from others; Margaret fusses about; Drew changes his entire way of life. Which coping mechanism do you most identify with?*

A. I think I identify a little with all three, but I find myself acting more like Caroline in dealing with grief. Like Caroline, I can make myself believe—at least for a little while—that if I don't talk about it or acknowledge the "bad thing," then it doesn't exist. I think it's a survival mechanism, perhaps, shielding those who need to be shielded until the psyche is ready to deal with the pain.

Q. *Do you quilt? Are you involved in a quilting group?*

A. My friends and family find it amusing that my protagonists always have wonderful skills like gardening, cooking, sewing, or—in this case—quilting. Unfortunately, I'm woefully ignorant of all the above. However, I have two friends who make memory quilts, the kind of quilts Caroline makes in *Pieces of the Heart*. The first one that I saw was to be a gift from a mother to her daughter who was graduating from high school. It was so beautiful and so moving and I knew it was only a matter of time before I had to have one appear in a novel. I was so pleased to be able to use the whole memory quilt idea and process as a major part of this book.

# CONVERSATION GUIDE

*Q. What's the message of this book, to you? Did you have this message in mind when you began to write the book, or did it emerge over the writing of the book?*

A. As I see my parents get older, and as I raise my own children, I find myself looking back at my childhood more and more. I examine my old hurts as a child would pick at a Band-Aid, not always sure I want to see what lies beneath. We often ask ourselves why certain things still sting, even after the passage of so many years. I found it very cathartic, as an author, to write about a parent and adult child bringing the old hurts to the surface to face the light of day, exposing them in new and unexpected ways. I suppose the message of the book would be that it's never too late to ask for forgiveness—of others or of oneself. Subconsciously, I probably had this in mind when I started the book, and I allowed Caroline and Margaret to take over and say it for me.

*Q. Caroline and Margaret's relationship is one of the most fraught in the book. What is it about the mother-daughter dynamic that makes it so difficult for people?*

A. When people ask me to tell them about this book, I always tell them this is the perfect book for any woman who's ever had a mother. It's pretty universal. As a daughter, and as the mother of a daughter, I think I have a unique perspective about this relationship—it seems we're always trying to emphasize how different we are from our mothers, but how much our daughters are like us. It's like we're trying to correct the errors of the generation that came before us while passing on only good to the one that comes after us. And we don't understand why our daughters don't agree! In *Pieces of the Heart,* Margaret and Caroline are so much alike in so many good ways, but they don't recognize it until they must face another crisis together.

# CONVERSATION GUIDE

*Q. What are you working on now?*

A. My next book, tentatively titled *Learning to Breathe,* is set in rural Louisiana and focuses on the youngest of five grown sisters, Brenna O'Bryan. Brenna lives on the surface of her life, never delving too deeply into it for fear of being disappointed. She collects unopened war letters, liking the way they feel, as if she is holding in her hand possibilities of what might be. When she discovers an entire mailbag filled with old letters from a WWII soldier who still lives in her town, she uncovers an ill-fated love story and unravels a secret from her own past. This sets in motion a chain of events that forces her to examine the assumptions that underpin her life.

# QUESTIONS FOR DISCUSSION

1. In this story, water emerges as a motif and plays different roles throughout. Describe those roles. To whom is water important? Why?

2. How does quilting help these characters? What is it about quilting that opens up their lines of communication?

3. At certain points in the novel a character will observe to him- or herself how alike Caroline and her mother are. In what ways is this true? How are they different?

4. Drew is having second thoughts about taking control of Rainy Days. He seems to miss working in a courtroom. How does he resolve his doubts?

5. Caregivers assert that there are five stages of grief—denial, anger, bargaining, depression, acceptance. What stage of grief is each of the main characters in? Give proof to support your ideas.

6. Jude was the favorite son—a golden boy. When he dies, Caroline quits the one thing she is better at than Jude, and stops swimming. Why does she quit? What finally leads her back to the water?

7. We get to know Shelby through Jewel's eyes as she reads her mother's diary. What kind of woman was Shelby? What kind of mother?

8. Why does Drew pursue Caroline, even when she makes it clear that she has no interest in his attention?

9. Why does Jewel keep Jude's quilt a secret?

10. Caroline and Drew find an injured loon and nurse it back to health at Rainy's shop. What does the bird symbolize to them?

11. Why does Caroline resent her mother so much? What does she learn over the course of her stay at home that makes her change her mind, and how do they resolve their differences?

12. In what ways does Drew feel he's failed as a father and a husband? How does he try to make up for these past failures?